Amanda Stevens is an a̶ [barcode obscures text] fifty novels, including th̶ [barcode obscures text] Graveyard Queen. Her bo̶ [barcode obscures text] as eerie and atmospheric and 'a new take on the classic ghost story.' Born and raised in the rural South, she now resides in Houston, Texas, where she enjoys binge-watching, bike riding and the occasional margarita.

USA Today bestselling author **Kacy Cross** writes romance novels starring swoonworthy heroes and smart heroines. She lives in Texas, where she's seen bobcats and beavers near her house but sadly not one cowboy. She's raising two mini-ninjas alongside the love of her life, who cooks while she writes, which is her definition of a true hero. Come for the romance, stay for the happily-ever-after. She promises her books 'will make you laugh, cry and swoon—cross my heart.'

Discover more at millsandboon.co.uk

THE DISAPPEARANCE

AMANDA STEVENS

COLTON'S WILDERNESS RESCUE

KACY CROSS

MILLS & BOON

First Published in Great Britain 2025
by Mills & Boon, an imprint of HarperCollins*Publishers* Ltd
1 London Bridge Street, London, SE1 9GF

www.harpercollins.co.uk

HarperCollins*Publishers*
Macken House, 39/40 Mayor Street Upper,
Dublin 1, D01 C9W8, Ireland

Special thanks and acknowledgment are given to Kacy Cross for her contribution to *The Coltons of Dark Canyon* series.

ISBN: 978-0-263-42017-3

0126

THE DISAPPEARANCE

AMANDA STEVENS

Chapter One

Day One

Claire Tinsley clung to the edge of her seat as the plane touched down in the middle of a thunderstorm. Within moments, they were taxiing across the wet tarmac toward the gate. Closing her eyes, she took a relieved breath and relaxed her grip. She wasn't afraid of flying—travel had become a passion—but she was absolutely terrified of what she might find at the end of her journey.

Almost there. Soon she would know.

The trip had been interminable. From Rome to Amsterdam to Austin. Now she faced a ninety-minute drive to San Miguel, a quaint, eccentric town tucked deep in the Texas Hill Country. She would have preferred flying into San Antonio. She could have shaved time off her drive and avoided a city that held a lot of bad memories for her. Austin would always remind her of the grief and fear of her early childhood and the loneliness and isolation of her teen years. However, after a cryptic text from her brother, she'd wasted no time in booking the first available flight that got her into the vicinity.

She fished out her phone and glanced at the screen, hoping against hope that a new message would pop up now that they were on the ground. No such luck. Connor's last text seemed more ominous than ever: I need you. 1136 River-bend Road. Hurry!

The message had been sent nearly twenty-four hours ago while Claire had been vacationing in Europe with two of her closest friends. Since then, nothing but dead silence on Connor's end. No explanation. No follow-up. No anything. Her twin brother had gone completely incommunicado, and her frantic calls had gone straight to voicemail.

In between packing and making hasty travel arrangements, she'd contacted area hospitals to make sure he hadn't been admitted. Her imagination had conjured all sorts of accidents and illnesses. Then she'd reached out to some of his friends and former colleagues in Austin to see if anyone from his old life had heard from him. She'd played it cool, not allowing herself to panic even when she discovered that no one had seen or heard from him since his move. He'd cut himself off from the people he'd known for years, and that didn't sound like Connor at all. Finally in desperation, she'd called the San Miguel Police Department in the hope they'd send someone to the address to check on him. The dispatcher hadn't been helpful. Apparently, an unanswered text message wasn't a high priority.

Even knowing her brother the way she did, she still tried to convince herself he was just being dramatic, but the explanation rang hollow. Connor wasn't prone to overreaction. If anything, he downplayed turmoil because he didn't want to worry her. Which was probably why he hadn't told her about the move to San Miguel until he knew she couldn't talk him out of it.

No matter how many times she reminded herself that the move was his decision alone, his relocation had caught her completely off guard. One day he'd been living a seemingly happy and productive life in Austin, and then the next thing she knew, he'd quit his teaching job at a prestigious private school, sold his small townhome along with all the furnishings and cashed out his retirement plan. What disturbed her more than his impetuous move, however, was his evasiveness. Whenever she suggested a visit, he'd put her off, claiming he still needed to get settled first.

In hindsight, something had obviously been going on with her brother for quite some time, but Claire had been too preoccupied to investigate. She'd been too caught up in her own career and personal life for far too long, and now she regretted some of her choices. Actually, she regretted a lot of things, but this was hardly the time to wallow.

The storm clouds had dispersed by the time she left the airport and the sun had come out. Luggage stowed in the cargo space of her rental SUV, she set out in a southwesterly direction through rolling hills, lush grasslands and dizzying canyons. The proliferation of mesquite and cacti along the roadside reminded her that despite the emerald vistas, she was still in Texas, and the Chihuahuan Desert was only half a day's drive away.

Off the beaten track, San Miguel nestled atop the banks of the picturesque Medina River, once known as the Rio Mariano. The cowboy capital of the world was just down the road, but Bandera and San Miguel were culturally and visually worlds apart. The former was still known for its dude ranches and cattle-drive heritage while the latter had retained the Spanish influences of walled courtyards and red-tile roofs. In recent years, San Miguel had become something of a haven for creatives and eccentrics looking to escape the high cost of urban living. The Hill Country version of Marfa, some said. Claire supposed that was why her brother had been attracted to the place. The lower cost of living would allow him to paint more and teach less.

She and Connor had grown up in Austin, but back then Claire's familiarity with the Hill Country had mostly been relegated to the outlet malls in San Marcos, which she and her great-aunt had visited every summer before school started. Their aunt had been a lovely, generous guardian, and neither child had wanted for anything, including affection. But Annabel Tinsley had also been overprotective and at times, a bit smothering. Not her fault. Considering how their living arrangements had come about, she'd had every right to be cautious.

Claire lowered her window, hoping the fresh air would help revive her after such a long trip. The scenery along the Medina River was breathtakingly beautiful, and she berated herself for not having explored the area more thoroughly when she had the opportunity. As an adult, she'd tried to make up for her insular upbringing by traveling abroad as much as time and her finances would allow. Those trips and her career as a criminal analyst in Washington, DC, had widened her horizons, but they'd also taken her away from her brother. The separation hadn't been entirely her doing, at least not of late.

Once inside the town proper, she stopped at a small grocery store for a bottle of water and ibuprofen. The dull throb of a tension headache had been manageable for most of the trip, but fatigue and an empty stomach compounded the pain and she couldn't take it any longer. She parked, got out and once again checked her phone as she hurried toward the entrance. The glass door opened suddenly and she collided with a body before she had time to glance up. The man stumbled back, dropping his bag as he used his cane to grapple for balance.

Claire's hand shot out to steady him as the items in the bag scattered. He appeared to be around her age or a bit older—probably in his mid-thirties—and thankfully able to regain his equilibrium without crashing to the pavement.

She said in horror, "I'm so sorry! It was entirely my fault. Are you okay?"

He had a good grip on the cane now and offered a quick, unassuming smile as he adjusted his footing. "No harm done except to my ego. And to my oranges." He nodded to the rolling produce.

"Here, let me." Claire scrambled to scoop up the fruit. Only a few had escaped, but they seemed to have a mind of their own. She chased them down and used her own tote to collect them. "I hope they're not too bruised. I'll be happy to replace them. It's the least I can do."

"No worries. They'll be fine. Easier to juice this way." His voice was a rich baritone with a slight drawl. The low cadence sent an unexpected shiver up Claire's spine.

"That's kind of you to say," she replied, somewhat taken aback by her reaction.

"Lots of things to worry about these days. Bruised citrus isn't one of them." He bent with some difficulty to retrieve the other items.

"Oh, please let me." Their fingers brushed as she reached for a pack of batteries. She snatched her hand away as their gazes collided for only a split second. Then they both straightened and stood awkwardly for a moment. Claire surreptitiously studied his features as she transferred the oranges to his bag. He was tall with a slim but muscular build. Despite the cane, he must work out, she decided as she took note of his biceps and the broad shoulders beneath his T-shirt. Then she wondered how he'd been injured. *Not your business. Not why you're here. Get your headache medicine and go find your brother.*

He looked slightly bemused by the encounter. "New in town? Sorry. I couldn't help noticing the out-of-state plate on your vehicle."

"It's a rental. You never know where those cars have been. As for me, I just drove in from Austin."

He nodded. "I thought so. I'm good with faces, and I'm pretty sure I would have remembered yours." He adjusted his cane as he gave her another smile, this one slower and anything but unassuming.

She felt that same tremor up her backbone. His eyes were nearly black and shaded with a thick fringe of lashes. A lock of brown hair had fallen across his forehead, and he balanced his cane and the grocery bag in the same hand as he swiped it back. He was an attractive man, no question, with his chiseled jawline and smoldering gaze. Almost too good-looking, Claire decided, as she mentally took stock of her own bedraggled appearance.

Brushing her hand down her rumpled travel pants, she said briskly, "Again, I apologize. I'll watch where I'm going from now on."

"Always a good idea." His tone shifted enigmatically as he gave a brief nod toward the deepening shadows across the street. "You take care out there."

"I...will." She gave him a puzzled glance as she brushed past him to the door, forcing herself not to look back until she was safely inside the store. Then she peered through the plate-glass window as she pretended to peruse the shelves.

Bag in one hand, cane in the other, he limped toward a late model SUV not unlike her rental. The sun was just sliding beneath the treetops. The light spangled through the leaves, dappling the parking lot. But she could see him clearly through the windshield of his vehicle. He sat behind the wheel staring back at her. Embarrassed, she glanced away and grabbed something off the shelf. When she looked outside again, he was gone. *Just as well.* She wasn't there on a social visit, and she certainly wasn't looking for a romantic adventure.

Still...

She couldn't tell if she was relieved, disappointed or indifferent. Maybe just curious, she decided. With an inward shrug, she returned her focus to shopping. She located the pain medication, but by then, hunger pangs called her attention to the food section. She'd been too stressed to eat at any of the airports along her journey, hence the headache. Moving back to the front of the store, she grabbed a small basket and tossed in some fruit, along with a few less healthy choices as she prowled the aisles. Then while waiting to check out, she read back over the flurry of messages she'd sent to her brother from the various airports, each sounding more desperate than the last.

She thumbed a new text: I'm in San Miguel. Where are you?

"Miss? Are you ready?"

She glanced up. The customer in front of her had disappeared, and the clerk behind the counter gave her a patient if somewhat strained smile.

"I'm sorry. Lost in thought," Claire muttered as she stepped up to the register to check out.

"Find everything you need?"

"Yes, thank you." She placed the basket on the counter with a grimace. "I guess there's a reason they say never to food shop on an empty stomach."

"Happens to the best of us."

The clerk chatted in a friendly manner as she rang up the purchases, but her glances seemed wary. Claire had no idea why she would have aroused the woman's suspicion, although she probably did look a bit sketchy with her drooping ponytail and rumpled clothing. Not to mention the dark circles under her eyes and the worry lines across her brow.

She smiled to reassure the woman as she tapped her credit card on the screen.

The clerk gave her an answering smile. "Art or antiques?"

"I beg your pardon?"

"Most people find their way to San Miguel for the art festivals or the antique shops." She slid the receipt across the counter. "Or the river if you're the outdoorsy type." She gave Claire a doubtful once-over.

"None of the above. I'm just here for a brief visit. Actually, maybe you can help me. I'm looking for an address on Riverbend Road. My GPS seems to have trouble pinpointing the location. Can you at least tell me if I'm headed in the right direction?"

"Riverbend Road, you say?" The woman's tone noticeably cooled.

"Yes. Am I getting close?"

"A little too close for my liking."

Claire felt a prickle of apprehension at the back of her neck. "What do you mean?"

The clerk glanced through the plate-glass window where Claire had parked her rental. "Cop or reporter?"

She frowned. "What makes you think I'm either?"

Another shrug, another wary glance. "I've never seen you in the store before and here you are asking about Riverbend Road. What am I supposed to think?"

Claire stared at her in confusion. "I don't understand."

The woman reached for a paper bag underneath the counter. "Ever since it happened, they've been swarming in here like a plague of locusts. First the cops, then the reporters. We even had a couple of Feds sniffing around the other day. When you mentioned Riverbend Road, I assumed you were one of them."

The woman's ominous tone deepened Claire's chill. "I'm sorry, when what happened?"

The clerk lifted a brow. "You really don't know?"

Claire shook her head slowly.

"There was a murder on Riverbend Road. A bad one. More like a slaughter from what I hear."

Pulse accelerating, Claire managed to suppress a shudder as dark visions strobed through her head. *Don't go there.* Just because Connor hadn't answered her texts or calls… just because their father had been brutally murdered twenty-five years ago…

Don't think the worst. History doesn't have to repeat…

She swallowed hard. "Who was murdered?"

The clerk still seemed guarded though she answered without hesitation. "A local painter by the name of India Cortez. She used to be a big deal in the art world. You didn't hear about her death on the news?"

The art world. Her brother's world.

Claire ignored the obvious connection as she drew a quick breath. She felt sorry for the dead woman's family, but she couldn't prevent the enormous wave of relief that washed over her. Connor wasn't the victim. Whatever else might be wrong, he was alive. She had no reason to believe otherwise, and nothing else mattered at that moment.

"I've been out of the country," she explained. "I just got back today. You said it was more like a slaughter. That's a strong statement." She remembered the stranger's shift in tone, and his warning to take care out there. What on earth was going on in this town?

The clerk looked instantly regretful. "I shouldn't have said that. No point in ruining your trip with the gory details. Besides, we aren't supposed to talk about it."

"Why not?" Claire pressed her.

She took a moment to answer. "I guess the powers that be want to control the rumor mill. Murder is bad for business, especially in a place like this where much of our economy relies on tourists and day-trippers."

"But you said the murder had already been reported on the news."

"That's true. I did say that."

"So why can't you talk about it?"

The clerk busied herself bagging the groceries. "Like I said, no reason to burden you with the details. Trust me, you don't want those images in your head."

"I'd rather know than not know," Claire insisted.

Her gaze lifted. "You say that now. You might not think so if you find yourself alone in the dead of night."

They fell silent as the clerk finished her task and Claire continued to fret. Her trip to San Miguel was getting stranger and more disturbing by the minute. Something was obviously very wrong in this town. First Connor's cryptic message and then his silence. A perfect stranger's warning to take care and now the store clerk's revelation of a murder—a slaughter—that no one was supposed to talk about. Maybe she should let the matter drop, Claire thought. Just walk out the door and be on her way. The sooner she found her brother, the sooner she could rest easy.

But already those memories of her father's violent death were taking her down a dark path. She'd spent a lifetime trying to suppress images that suddenly came rushing back. Crawling out of bed and stealing to the top of the stairs as loud voices echoed up from the kitchen. Her father shouting for her and Connor to run. Then crawling out a bedroom window, climbing up to the rooftop, fleeing across slippery shingles in a rainstorm. Huddling behind the chimney, hands clapped over their mouths to stifle their screams.

They'd only been seven years old at the time. Seven years old when their father had been savagely murdered in their home. Seven years old and already running for their lives. Running from a criminal past that had caught up with their father one balmy summer night deep in the bayou country of southern Louisiana.

Claire tried to shut down the memories. The past was over and done with. The possibility of a link between Connor's ominous text and a woman's brutal demise was remote, but until she spoke with her brother face-to-face, she couldn't dismiss any possibility.

Tucking her hair behind her ears, she assumed what she hoped was a sympathetic facade. "When did it happen?"

"Six days ago, and it still seems surreal."

"Did you know the victim personally?"

"I only knew her when I saw her, which wasn't often. She was a bit of a recluse."

Claire gave a knowing nod. "Even so, it must be distressing, a murder happening in a place like this."

The clerk let out a heavy sigh as if relieved someone, even a stranger, understood and empathized with her fear. "You have no idea. The town has changed over the years. People moving in and out, businesses coming and going. But I never thought I'd be afraid at work or even worse, in my own home. To think that one of us could be capable of that kind of cruelty…what is the world coming to?"

"You think she was killed by someone local?"

A shadow passed over her features. "I don't know. I hope not, but I can't say that stranger danger would make me feel a good deal better. It's just as scary to think about a predator coming into town, roaming our streets, preying on women who live alone." She shot another glance toward the door, then lowered her voice as if afraid of being overheard even though they were the only two people in the store. "Are you sure you want to hear this?"

Claire nodded. "I'm bound to sooner or later, so it may as well come from you."

"I guess that's true." She paused. "India was found stabbed

to death in her art studio. Dozens of wounds all over her body. Torture, is what I'd call it. My friend's cousin works for the county coroner's office. He was called to the scene to help move her. He said he'd never seen so much blood in his whole life." She leaned forward, her voice still hushed. "But that's not even the worst part."

Claire felt that same prickle of apprehension at the back of her neck. Torture wasn't the worst part?

"The killer used a rope and pulley to hoist her up to the ceiling where a pair of giant wings had been mounted for an upcoming exhibit. My friend's cousin said she was still alive at that point. They could tell by the blood patterns or something. He said the killer probably stood there and watched her bleed out. If she screamed, no one heard her."

Claire's stomach roiled at the graphic description. "Do the police have any suspects?"

"All I know is that there haven't been any arrests. That's why we're all so on edge. Whoever did it is still out there. He could be watching us through the window at this very moment."

Claire resisted the urge to glance over her shoulder. "No witnesses, I take it."

"None that I've heard about." The clerk paused again, then said in that same quiet voice, "A lot of people have access to the Compound. They've been renovating for weeks now. Workers in and out all day long, not all of them from around here. The killer could have used a truck to haul in the pulley and no one would have even noticed."

"What's the Compound?"

"The Creative Collective." The woman air quoted the name. "It's called the Compound because of the walls."

A walled compound. A murder without witnesses or suspects, the victim stabbed and tortured and her body put on display like an art exhibit. Stranger and stranger, Claire thought. "What's inside?"

"Of the Compound? India's private home and studio. A communal studio space and cabins for students and artists in residence. The whole place sits atop a bluff with amazing views of the river. Prime real estate these days. The land alone would be worth a fortune on today's market."

"Could that have been a motive?" Claire wondered aloud.

"It's possible. Everyone around here knew India would never sell. That place was her pride and joy. She built it years ago when she first moved back to the area. Artists came from all over the country to study and work with her. Like I said, she used to be a big deal."

India Cortez. Claire ran the name around in her head as a faint memory stirred. Did she know the name? Had Connor mentioned the artist in passing?

"You said the Feds have been sniffing around. Why would the FBI get involved?"

"Apparently, they blew into town to examine a symbol the killer drew on the wall. They think it might have been left by a member of a well-known drug cartel. Someone they've been after for a long time. That doesn't make any sense to me, though. How would India Cortez become the target of a—what are they called?—sicario when she barely ever left the compound?"

Claire's mind raced. Among other areas that demanded her expertise, it was her job to study patterns, commonalities and anomalies in order to pinpoint and sometimes predict criminal trends in certain areas. She wasn't an expert in cartel symbolism, but she knew someone who could put her in touch with one. "What did the symbol look like?"

The clerk's wariness returned. "You sure ask a lot of questions. Just like the reporters who come through here."

"I'm not a reporter, I promise. I'm just in town to see my

brother," Claire explained. "But I can't help being curious. As you said, murder is rare in a place like this. And the way the body was displayed—exhibited—it almost seems like mockery."

"Or just plain evil."

Yes, that, too, Claire thought. Maybe the killer wanted the notoriety. Or maybe he or she was sending a message. "As for the symbol, have you ever heard of deliberate misdirection? Maybe the killer used that symbol to try and throw the police off track."

The clerk latched on to the possibility. "That makes more sense than India being involved in drug trafficking."

"It's just a thought." Claire put away her credit card and grabbed her bags. Time to make her exit. "Thanks for the information."

"I probably said too much. I never seem to know when to keep my mouth shut. It's just that India's murder is all any of us can think about."

"I understand. And I'm glad you told me. I wanted to know."

The woman gave her a worried look. "A piece of advice? Darkness falls quickly around here once the sun goes down. Get where you're going while it's still daylight. You don't want to be caught out alone after dark."

Claire thanked her again, then headed for the door.

"Miss?"

She glanced over her shoulder.

"You're closer than you think."

Claire scowled. "I'm sorry?"

She nodded toward the street. "Riverbend Road. Take a left at the first traffic light."

Chapter Two

Claire was tempted to research India Cortez's murder as soon as she got back to the car. She took out her phone, but changed her mind and thumbed another text to Connor instead. Where are you? Why won't you answer me? I'm driving to the address you gave me right this minute. 1136 Riverbend Road. Please be there!

She put away her phone, telling herself yet again that his mysterious text following on the heels of a gruesome homicide was just a coincidence. As was the fact that the victim had been a renowned artist. San Miguel was known for its vibrant art community, which was undoubtedly the main reason Connor had been attracted to the place. Chances were good that he'd crossed paths with the dead woman at some point, but that didn't mean he was in any way connected to her murder or that he might be in danger.

On and on Claire's mind raced as she made excuses in order to calm her fears. But a little voice at the back of her mind kept prodding her. Why had he sent such an urgent, opaque message when he knew she was out of the country? When he knew she would worry herself sick until she heard back from him? If he was really okay, why hadn't he answered her?

Visions from their past swirled in her head once more.

Shaking herself, she opened a bottle of water and gulped the pain medication before heading out. She could see the clerk inside the store. The woman had left her post behind the register and now stood at the plate-glass window peering out. Claire waved as she put the car in reverse and eased back. The clerk didn't return her wave. Instead, she lifted a cell phone to her ear as she watched Claire maneuver out of the parking space.

Nothing unusual about making a phone call, Claire told herself, but she couldn't help noticing that the woman seemed extremely tense. Which was understandable, considering the circumstances. The murder of a prominent citizen in such a grisly fashion was bound to have an effect on the whole town, especially those who worked and lived alone. No wonder the woman was jittery.

Apparently, the store clerk wasn't the only person in town who remained apprehensive. Claire noted the same guarded expression on the weathered countenance of an elderly man pumping gas and again on a young woman's furrowed brow as she jogged along the sidewalk. No friendly waves or even a tentative nod as Claire drove slowly down the street. Nothing but sidelong glances from pedestrians and long stares from shopkeepers hovering in doorways. San Miguel was a picturesque town of shady boulevards and pastel buildings, but the long shadows of late afternoon suddenly seemed ominous.

Pulling to a stop at the first traffic light, Claire ran a hand up and down her arm where goose bumps had popped. Working herself into a state did no one any good, least of all Connor. His urgent message was cause for concern, but no need yet to panic. Maybe he'd lost his phone after he texted. Or he'd turned it off as he sometimes did when he painted. *Just find his place and figure out where to go from there.* If Claire had learned anything from her job as a criminal analyst, it was to refrain from forming conclusions without all the pertinent data.

A horn bleated behind her. She glanced in the rearview mirror, startled to see a patrol car behind her. Then she realized the light had turned green and the officer was giving her a gentle prod. She made the turn and nosed into the nearest parking lot to allow the police car to go around her. Holding her breath, she almost expected the officer to pull in behind her, but instead he accelerated and was soon lost from sight.

She sat shivering in the balmy heat as the clerk's graphic description came back to her: *My friend's cousin said she was still alive at that point. They could tell by the blood patterns on the floor or something. He said the killer probably stood there and watched her bleed out. If she screamed, no one heard her.*

Gripping the steering wheel, Claire eased out of the parking lot and drove along the street, checking for house numbers. By this time, the sun had dropped well below the tree line and the sky had softened. *Darkness falls quickly around here once the sun goes down. Get where you're going while it's still daylight. The last thing you want is to be caught out alone after dark.*

The commercial area of strip centers and gas stations soon gave way to a more diverse mix of shops and residential dwellings. Despite her misgivings, Claire couldn't help but appreciate the eclectic flair of the neighborhood. A myriad of open-air eateries, antique shops and art galleries lined a walkable boulevard. The homes grew exponentially larger and farther apart as she drove along, some of them hidden behind limestone walls draped in bougainvillea.

Finally, she located the address from Connor's text message. 1136 Riverbend Road. The house sat back from the street on a wooded lot also protected by a wall, but the gates were open and she drove straight through. She pulled around the circular drive, parked in front of the house and sat gaping at the property.

The stucco facade glowed a soft apricot in the sunset. An outdoor staircase curved gently up to a covered gallery where hanging baskets of ferns stirred in the breeze. The house looked a little worse for wear, but the gardens were beautiful with an abundance of fruit trees, fountains and flowering shrubs bursting with color.

Claire sat amazed. Could this really be Connor's home? How on earth could he afford such a place, especially now that he'd quit his teaching position? She hoped he hadn't run through his savings already, but then she reminded herself that she and her brother were thirty-two years old. His finances were none of her business. People who knew them would occasionally and gently remark that she had a tendency to be too practical, too buttoned-up. A taste of her brother's impulsiveness might do her some good. Still, she couldn't help stressing. The house was just another piece of a puzzle that was becoming more complex by the minute.

She cut the engine and got out of the car, gazing in first one direction and then the other as she headed up the flagstone path to the front door. Connor's car was nowhere to be seen. Maybe he'd parked in the back or given her the wrong address. Reminding herself once again not to jump to any conclusions, she rang the bell, waited a beat, then knocked.

Somewhere above her, a door opened and closed. She heard footsteps on the gallery and then a woman called down. "Can I help you?" Her voice was throaty with a heavy drawl. Claire wondered immediately who she was and what, if any, connection she had to Connor. She retreated back to the walkway as she tilted her head toward the gallery.

A middle-aged blonde peered down at her. She was striking on first glance, with curls piled haphazardly atop her head and ruby lipstick glistening on full lips. The vivid floral kimono she wore gaped open to reveal a lacy bra, faded jean cutoffs and a pair of white western boots. Her choice of attire was interesting to say the least.

Despite the softness of her round face, Claire detected the hard glitter of suspicion in the woman's cornflower blue eyes. She was quickly becoming accustomed to that look.

"You better not be here trying to sell me something," the woman warned as she pulled the robe around her and fastened the belt. "There's a sign on the front gate as plain as the nose on your face. No soliciting." She stopped for a breath. "How'd you get in here anyway?"

"I'm not selling anything," Claire assured her. "And the gate was open."

The woman muttered something under her breath.

"I'm looking for Connor Tinsley," Claire quickly explained. "He asked me to meet him at this address." A note of doubt crept into her voice. "Does he live here, by chance?"

The blue gaze narrowed. "Depends on who's asking."

"I'm his sister. Claire Tinsley."

"His sister?" She lifted a perfectly sculpted brow. "He never mentioned anything about a sister. In fact, I was under the impression he didn't have any family at all."

What had Connor said to make her think he was an orphan? And why did it matter? "I can show you my ID," Claire offered.

"Not necessary. Not *yet*," the woman added, still with a note of wariness. "I can see a resemblance. Same nose. Same eyes." She bent to place her forearms on the wrought-iron railing as she gave Claire a critical perusal. "I just find it a little strange that he never mentioned you."

"My brother is a private person," Claire said. "He doesn't like to talk about himself."

"He's a quiet one, all right. I'm Marion Palmer, by the way. I own this place."

Claire decided to try flattery to soften the woman's brusque manner. "It's a beautiful property. The grounds are especially lovely. So quiet and peaceful. Must be a lot of work, keeping it so well-groomed."

"The day I can't handle a few weeds is the day I pack it in." But she looked pleased by Claire's observation and added begrudgingly, "The house is divided into two apartments. Your brother rents the ground floor and I'm up here. Just the two of us right now, but there's a guesthouse out back if you're interested."

"I won't be in town that long. I'm only here to see Connor."

"Well, if you were hoping to catch him by surprise, looks like you're out of luck. His car isn't in its usual space." She nodded toward the circular driveway. "You say he was expecting you?"

"He asked me to come, but we never set a specific time." Claire glanced around. "How long has he lived here?"

"A couple of months. He came along after my previous tenant left unexpectedly. Just up and took off in the middle of the night owing me two months back rent."

"That's too bad," Claire murmured.

Marion shrugged away her misfortune. "Happens more often than you think. People have a tendency to come and go in this town. Some just disappear and you never hear from them again."

Or they get murdered. Claire tried to keep her tone neutral without giving away her deep concern. "Have you seen Connor today?"

"No. I've been in San Antonio for a few days. I just got back a little while ago."

"His car was gone when you arrived?"

"Yes, but that's not unusual. He comes and goes as he pleases. I don't ask questions." She straightened and sauntered toward the staircase, the silky fabric billowing behind her as she started down the steps. Pausing halfway down, she hiked up the robe before she sat down. She was a little older than Claire had originally guessed. Probably a year or two shy of fifty, judging by the deepening lines around her eyes and mouth. But she was still attractive, with a slim figure and toned legs.

Leaning back against her elbows, she kept her gaze fixed on Claire. "Have you tried calling him?"

"Yes, of course. I've called. I've texted. I even sent emails. I haven't heard back from him in over twenty-four hours. I'm starting to get a little worried."

"I doubt there's cause for alarm. He's probably working and lost track of time. He does that, you know. Gets on a roll and no one sees him for days." Her tone and manner seemed to have warmed a bit. "Maybe you should drive out to the Compound. I'm betting that's where you'll find him. He's likely got a million things to do before that place reopens."

Claire's heart skipped a beat. "He works at the Compound?"

"He didn't tell you?"

"We haven't talked much since he moved to San Miguel."

"Apparently, not." She watched Claire intently. "Honey, he doesn't just work at the Compound. India put him in charge. He oversees the renovations, the gallery exhibits, the classes. Everything. That's a lot of responsibility for someone who only arrived in town a short time ago. But India was always impulsive, not to mention susceptible to a pretty face. I wouldn't be surprised if she included him in her will."

Shock rolled over Claire. What on earth had Connor been up to in San Miguel? Marion Palmer might have been talking about a stranger or someone Claire had only met in passing rather than her twin brother. Why hadn't he told her about his new job? About the murder of his employer? What else was he keeping from her?

I need you. 1136 Riverbend Road. Hurry!

Her mind continued to race as Marion studied her with avid curiosity. "If you haven't spoken to Connor, then you don't know what happened out there, do you?"

She swallowed past the bitter taste of fear in her throat. "I know about the murder. I heard about it when I first drove into town."

"But do you know about the *way* she was murdered?"

"Yes, I think so."

"Strung up like a piece of meat," Marion said with an exaggerated shudder. "The worker who found her thought he'd stumbled upon some kind of bizarre art installation. Can you imagine? I've given her death a lot of thought these past few days. About who around here would be capable of such a thing."

"And?" Claire asked with genuine curiosity.

Unlike the clerk at the grocery store, Marion Palmer seemed to have no qualms about discussing the murder. In fact, Claire could have sworn the woman enjoyed the lurid conversation.

"I don't believe it was a stranger passing through town as some would like to believe," she said. "I guess it makes them rest easier thinking the culprit is long gone by now. But that kill was personal. I'd bet good money on it. Someone had it in for dear old India."

A grudge killing? "You may be right," Claire said. "In any case, I can only imagine how upsetting it must be. Something like that happening in your own backyard. The police haven't yet made an arrest, have they? The whole community must be on edge."

Something indefinable gleamed in Marion's eyes. "Just

because they haven't made an arrest doesn't mean they don't have suspects. The deeper they dig, the more motives they'll likely turn up. Ivy was never the innocent she pretended to be."

Claire gave her a puzzled look. "I'm sorry, who's Ivy?"

"Oops, sorry. Even after all this time, I still sometimes slip up." She gave a careless shrug. "India-Ivy…same person, same secrets, same bad habits."

"You knew her personally?"

"About a hundred years ago. We grew up in the same small town. Back then, she was just plain old Ivy Cotter. Then she won a scholarship to a fancy art school back East and she couldn't shed her old friends fast enough. She was always a little ashamed of where she came from, so she changed her name to something more exotic and came up with a more compelling backstory. She found herself a rich husband and benefactor, and for a while, our little Ivy was queen of the art world."

"What happened?"

"Long story short, her husband divorced her like he did his first wife, and her talent eventually burned out. She moved back out here to the Hill Country where she could invent yet another persona, that of a rich, mysterious patron of the arts. People around here ate it up with a spoon. They were only too happy to play along with her delusions because she brought a certain cachet to an already eccentric community."

"But not you? You didn't buy the new persona?"

She flashed Claire another look. "No matter what she called herself, I could always see right through her." The blue eyes glittered with something unpleasant. Jealousy? Resentment? An old grudge? "She was still the same heartless person I knew in high school. A woman who saw what she wanted and took it. Be it someone else's husband, someone else's property, someone else's talent. Your brother would know a little something about that."

"What do you mean?"

She got up and dusted off her cutoffs. "Ask him when you see him." She turned and started up the steps.

Claire called after her. "Wait!"

Marion glanced over her shoulder.

"Can you let me into his apartment? I'd like to take a look around. Maybe he left a note."

"I don't invade my tenant's privacy unless it's an emergency." She gave Claire a pointed look. "Is it an emergency?"

"I don't know. I hope not."

"Let me know when you decide." She turned back to the stairs. "In the meantime, if you were to come across a spare key under the doormat or a flowerpot, I wouldn't be able to stop you from entering the apartment. Oh, and if you don't find him at the Compound, try the Crooked Ferret. The artsy types like to slum there from time to time. The place is a dump, but I guess it appeals to their bohemian senses." She gave a nod in the general direction. "Just down the street. Follow the music. You can't miss it."

"Thanks."

Claire waited until she heard the upstairs door close before she walked back over to the entrance. The conversation left her uneasy, not because Marion Palmer was outspoken with an undisguised edge of bitterness, but because her revelations about Connor had exposed just how far apart the two of them had drifted.

She was still trying to digest those revelations as she searched for a spare key. Not only had Connor's path crossed with the dead woman, he'd worked for her. In just two short months, a wealthy divorcée had put him in charge of her business and finances. She may even have put him in her will. None of that made the slightest bit of sense to Claire, nor did such a position sound like something her brother would ever want. Connor was the least mercenary person she knew, and he also happened to be the kindest and most generous. If he'd ingratiated himself into India Cortez's life so quickly, he must have had a damn good reason for doing so. What that reason could be, Claire had no idea, but she intended to find out. Just as soon as she located her brother.

She looked under the mat then tipped flowerpots until she finally located the spare key. Letting herself in the front door, she paused in the foyer as her eyes adjusted to the dim interior. Floor-to-ceiling windows covered the back wall of the living area, but the room before her lay in deep shadows. For a moment, she could have sworn someone stood on the other side of the glass peering in at her.

An image of the man she'd collided with at the grocery store leaped to mind, though why he would be at Connor's apartment, she couldn't imagine. The silhouette vanished as she entered the room, and Claire told herself the fading light had fooled her vision. No one was there, least of all the man with the cane.

She called out her brother's name, softly at first and then louder as she held her breath, hoping against hope that he would appear at the end of the corridor, her sometimes moody, sometimes goofy brother who, at the tender age of seven, had saved her from a monster.

What if it was her turn to save him?

For the second time that day, Ben Dornan lost his footing as he stumbled back from the window. He muttered an oath as he reached for the cane he'd left behind in his vehicle. Flattening his hand against the wall to steady himself, he realized two things. He was becoming too reliant on the damn thing and a recent mishap with a ladder had set back his recovery more than he would have hoped.

He took a moment to catch his breath and consider how he was going to get back to the street without being seen. He didn't think the person on the other side of the glass had spotted him. Despite two surgeries on his left knee—the latest just six weeks ago—he was still able to move quickly enough to avoid detection.

However, in the split second before he'd darted from view, he was certain he recognized her. She was the woman who had bumped into him at the corner store, spilling his oranges and very nearly knocking him off his feet. He hadn't seen her around town before their collision and never with Connor Tinsley, so what was she doing in his apartment?

The answer came to him at once and he swore again. She must be the sister. Claire Tinsley. Wasn't she supposed to be out of the country? Or back in DC where she lived and worked? Connor had assured him she wouldn't be a problem, yet here she was.

At least now Ben understood the niggling sense of recognition that had plagued him since their encounter. He knew her name now, but he still couldn't explain her presence. Best case scenario, she'd popped in for a surprise visit, but he had a bad feeling she was at her brother's apartment for the same reason as he. Connor wasn't answering his phone or his messages. Ben hadn't been able to get in touch with him since returning late last night from a round of medical appointments in Houston.

He told himself that wasn't necessarily a bad thing. Before he left two days ago, he and Connor had agreed it might be a good idea to lay low for a while. Connor's professional relationship with India Cortez made him a person of interest, not only with the police, but also with the media. The town was crawling with reporters. The last thing either of them needed was someone poking around in the past, dredging up names that had long since been buried. It was imperative that Connor's birth name remain hidden. Ben's, too, for that matter. Dornan was his mother's maiden name and the alias he used back when he worked undercover. Resurrecting an old persona had seemed like a good idea at the time, but without the Bureau having his back, a fabricated history might not hold up under intense scrutiny.

At the moment, however, the more pressing issue was what to do about the sister. If she started asking too many questions, she might well put a target on her own back.

He risked another glance through the window. She remained in the foyer as she called out to her brother a second time. She sounded worried. Not panicked, but definitely concerned. Ben could work with that. Someone who kept her head under pressure wasn't likely to go off half-cocked. Her cool composure just might buy him enough time to head her off before she did or said something that could put all their lives in danger.

Leaning back against the wall, he closed his eyes. The burning pain in his knee was so intense, he felt a little nauseous and his physical therapist's latest warning came back to mock him. *What did I tell you about taking care of yourself? The more unnecessary stress and strain you put on that knee, the longer your recuperation. Which means a longer waiting period before you can be reinstated to active duty. If you can return to the field at all, and right now, that's a big if. Do your exercises, stay off ladders and we'll see.*

In other words, there were no guarantees he'd ever be able to return to his old life. A shattered knee was a lot to come back from even at his age. The FBI required field agents to pass an annual fitness test to remain active. The sit-ups and push-ups he could handle, but the pulmonary fitness test also included a three hundred-meter sprint and a timed mile and half run. Neither of which he would be doing anytime soon.

So here *he* was, caught between a rock and a hard place.

Physical limitations aside, he should have known better than to risk the remnants of his career by working an off-the-book investigation. But he'd been bored and more than a little angry at his circumstances when he received the text from Connor: I think I've found him.

Those five simple words had thrown Ben for a loop, and he'd responded with a slightly acerbic text. Really? You think you've found him? After all this time?

After a quarter of a century and a trail that had gone cold when they were children? In San Miguel, Texas, of all places? A town little more than an hour's drive from the city where Ethan and Emily Cross had gone to disappear. The proximity had seemed too much of a coincidence, but Connor had been insistent, offering proof via texts, phone calls and finally an email that had hooked Ben despite his misgivings:

I'm sending you a photo of a painting I took at a gallery in Austin. Notice the medallion around the woman's neck. The embossed emblem is unusual. One of a kind. I'd know it anywhere. My father wore that medallion until the day he died. It was a gift from my mother. It disappeared the night he was murdered. Only one person could have taken it—the man who killed him. How it ended up around India Cortez's neck in a self-portrait, I have no idea. But I know this. Stroud is close, Ben. I can almost feel his presence in this little town.

Ben had needed something to focus on apart from his recovery and the bleak prospects of his future, so he'd rented a place in San Miguel, partly to help Connor search and partly to keep an eye on him. The problem was, neither had ever seen James Stroud. After twenty-five years, his appearance would have changed anyway, perhaps subtly with age and drastically with plastic surgery. He'd never been arrested so there were no fingerprints or DNA in any of the databases to help identify him. James Stroud could be any one of any number of people in San Miguel.

But Ben would have plenty of time to obsess about Stroud once he got himself out of his current predicament. The sister would probably be preoccupied for the next few minutes familiarizing herself with the apartment. That left Marion Palmer. Her connection to the dead woman might be an avenue worth exploring, but right now Ben was more concerned about the view from her upstairs windows. He couldn't sprint down the driveway, relying on speed and agility to make a clean getaway as he once would have done. At the moment, he probably couldn't make it halfway to the street before collapsing in agony.

His only option was to wait. Dusk would fall soon and the acute pain in his knee would eventually subside. Once his dexterity returned, he could make his way slowly to the street using shadows and the lush landscaping as cover. The other means of escape—going over the back wall—was out of the question under any circumstances. For a split second, he pictured himself vaulting effortlessly over the six-foot barrier as he once had been able to do. Then he shook off the gloom and focused on his new reality.

While he waited, he carefully maneuvered back to the window so that he could glimpse inside. Claire Tinsley had turned away from the windows, but he had no trouble putting features to her slender silhouette. Light brown hair with golden highlights and the same amber eyes as her brother. The same tentative smile and innate wariness. Considering their past, a cautious nature was understandable.

She couldn't know it, of course, but her path had crossed with Ben's long before she'd crashed into him at the grocery store half an hour ago. Had she felt even a sliver of recognition? Had the same sense of familiarity nagged at her after they parted? Probably not. Too many years had passed since that fateful night, and she'd had far graver things on her mind than the awkward nine-year-old kid who'd been summoned to keep her and her brother company.

Some of Ben's memories of that night had waned over the years, but certain details still came back to him with absolute clarity. Terrified twins turning up at his house in the middle of the night was an event he wasn't likely to ever forget.

His dad had ushered the frightened pair into the den where they'd sat clutching hands and trembling beneath the warm blankets he'd wrapped around their shoulders. He'd sent Ben downstairs to sit with them, hoping a kid close to their own age might help reassure them. But he hadn't been any good at comfort. He remembered asking if they wanted to play video games. Stupid question, in hindsight, after what they'd been through. When they remained wide-eyed and unresponsive, he turned on the TV to distract them while he slipped into the kitchen to eavesdrop on his parents' hushed conversation. Parts of the discussion had been lost with time, but he still remembered enough to fill in the gaps. When he'd thought about that night over the years, he always pictured his parents at the kitchen table as though they were in a scene from a movie, one that he'd watched so many times, he could recite the dialogue by heart.

"This can't be happening." His mother's voice had been little more than a harsh whisper as she sat pale and wide-eyed across from Ben's dad. She drew her robe around her as if she could somehow protect herself from the evil that had invaded their home. "What were you thinking, bringing them here?"

"I know what I'm doing," his dad had insisted.

"Do you?" Her voice rose. "This can't be legal, and God knows it isn't safe."

"Keep your voice down. They'll hear you."

"That's the least of our worries. I know they've been through a terrifying ordeal. I'm not without sympathy. No child should ever have to witness the murder of a parent. But our son's safety has to come first."

His father reached for his mother's hand. "Ben will be fine. We'll all be fine. Stroud is long gone. He won't linger in any place for too long. Not after tonight. If he's smart, he'll be halfway to the border by now."

"That's what you claimed about his threats." His mother pulled her hand away. "They're just bluster, you said. Nothing to worry about, you said. Now he's killed a man in cold blood. Tortured him in his own kitchen. What if he comes here next?"

"He won't."

"You don't know that. If he thinks those children can identify him—"

"They can't. They never saw his face."

"But he can't know that for sure, and a man like James Stroud doesn't take chances."

"Deb, relax. They'll only be here for the night. A day or two at the most. We've located their dead mother's aunt in Texas. She's eager to take them in. There are people who can push through the adoption, and then they'll have her last name. Ethan and Erin Cross will be gone forever."

But as it turned out, his mother had been right to worry. Months after the orphaned twins had been relocated to Austin, Texas, the monster who had murdered their father had come back for Ben's dad.

The hell of it was, everything had seemed back to normal by then. His parents were getting along, school was out for the summer and all was right in Ben's world. His mind had been on baseball that day. His suburban neighborhood had seemed calm and peaceful as he rode his bike home from practice, the long summer break stretching before him.

He could still remember the heat of the sun beating down on his back and the smell of honeysuckle and hot asphalt in his nostrils. He could even remember the sound of kids' laughter in the distance the day Special Agent Raymond Navarro had been gunned down in his own driveway, the only witness the nine-year-old son who had adored him.

Chapter Three

Claire made a quick tour of the apartment. While she hurried from room to room, she called Connor's number and listened for a ringtone. Nothing but silence. No sign of an accident or struggle. No evidence that he'd left in a hurry. She tried to take comfort in the tidy state of his living quarters and the fact that his phone was at least still ringing before going to voicemail as opposed to being turned off or otherwise disabled. However, at this point, nothing short of her brother walking through the door would ease her mind.

She went back to the foyer and stood as she had when she first entered the apartment, letting her gaze wander from floor to ceiling, from corner to corner. Again, nothing seemed out of the ordinary and yet she couldn't dismiss that fleeting shadow she'd glimpsed earlier. She strode over to the wall of windows and stared out into the garden. She could just make out the roofline of the guesthouse through a canopy of low-hanging branches. She might have wondered if she'd caught sight of another tenant on their way home, but according to Marion Palmer, the guesthouse was empty at the moment.

Claire peered through the trees for several more minutes, acquainting herself with the back of the property. Beyond the guesthouse, a brick wall encased the wooded grounds and garden. Nothing moved except for the gentle sway of branches in a steady breeze, which might account for the earlier movement at the window. Trying to shake off her unease, she checked the locks on the French doors then turned her back to the windows.

Satisfied that no one else was about except for Marion Palmer in the upstairs apartment, she took the time to thoroughly study Connor's accommodations, noting the wear and tear on the furnishings and appliances, which she'd missed earlier. The house wasn't quite as luxurious as she'd first thought, but the living, dining and kitchen combination was spacious, as was the primary bedroom and bathroom. During her initial search, Claire had discovered a second, smaller bedroom and a guest bathroom down a narrow hallway off the kitchen. She could bunk there while she waited for Connor to make contact. If Marion Palmer objected, well, Claire would cross that bridge when she came to it.

In a corner of the living room near the windows, her brother had carved out studio space. Art supplies had been neatly stacked atop a wooden desk and an easel had been positioned to capture the morning light. Claire walked over to the desk and thumbed through a sketchbook. Her brother had been busy. Dozens of faces peered up at her. She recognized one of the subjects immediately. He'd made no attempt to disguise the hard gleam in his landlady's eyes nor the slightly brittle quality of her smile. Instead, he'd subtly captured with pencil and paper something that Claire had intuited earlier. Marion Palmer was not a very nice person.

Claire continued to peruse the pages, feeling unsettled. Flipping through the sketchbook was a little too much like invading her brother's private space, but she justified her action by reminding herself of the mission. She needed to find her brother no matter what she had to do. If his work provided an insight into his whereabouts or even his frame of mind, then she would search every page.

She paused on another female subject, this one unfamiliar to her. Bobbed hair framed a narrow face with sharp cheekbones and dark, piercing eyes. The eyes were so penetrating, in fact, it almost seemed to Claire that the woman could peer from the page straight into her soul. She'd never met India Cortez, wasn't even sure she'd heard the artist's name before today, yet she instinctively knew she was staring at the artist's visage.

The dead woman had been no great beauty, not in the traditional sense, but her hooded eyes and enigmatic smile were deeply compelling, like a modern-day Mona Lisa. Despite her aura of mystery, she seemed almost birdlike and fragile, which made the circumstances of her demise seem even more tragic.

Claire kept turning pages, riveted by her brother's talent. Mixed in with the portraits were sketches of the river and the historic buildings downtown. The sheer volume of his work astounded her. It seemed as though Connor had been captivated to the point of obsession with his new surroundings. Why she found that notion disturbing, she couldn't say. San Miguel was a beautiful little town worthy of an artist's admiration and attention. Yet, the proliferation of sketches seemed discordant with inspiration. The drawings seemed more like a visual record than an homage to his adopted hometown. And the detail in the portraits... Claire had the strange notion that her brother had been looking for something in all those faces.

She kept going until she came across the final portrait in the sketchbook. Here, Connor had drawn an older gentleman seated at a table with a shot glass and a half-empty whiskey bottle in front of him. The man's face was haggard, his eyes haunted. Bearded and grizzled, he looked as if he carried the weight of the world on his shoulders. He was dressed entirely in black except for a flash of white beneath his dark shirt that might have been a Roman collar.

A shiver crawled up her backbone though she had no idea why. She was certain she'd never seen the man before, but Connor had evidently captured something that touched a chord. She closed the book, her pulse racing inexplicably.

She thumbed through some loose sketches on his desk before turning her attention to the easel. A drop cloth hid Connor's work in progress. Again, she hesitated, wanting to respect his privacy, but knowing she couldn't afford to leave any stone unturned.

The cloth fell to the floor with a gentle tug, revealing the unfinished portrait of a young woman with long, glossy hair and dark, soulful eyes. Connor had painted her in profile, emphasizing the intensity with which she stared into the distance, as if focused on something—or someone—that only she could see. Her chin rested on her hand, her fingers entwining a silver chain from which a tiny cross dangled. Her expression was inscrutable. A hint of worry mingling with bewilderment. The emotions touched a different kind of chord with Claire. She experienced something bordering on kinship with the subject. Claire had no idea of the woman's identity, but she could well understand Connor's fascination. She was stunningly beautiful even in profile, with none of the hard edges and unpleasant truths revealed in the black-and-white sketches.

Claire took out her phone and snapped a photo of the painting, then carefully returned the cover to the canvas before moving away from Connor's workspace. She'd always known he was a talented artist. When they were kids, he would spend hour upon hour with his sketch pads. Once, on a rare occasion when he'd been allowed to stay overnight with a friend, Claire had crept into his room and gone through his drawings. The images of hooded killers and dripping knives had been so upsetting that she'd scrambled out of the closet and never dared to look again. There was a quality in his current work that gave her the same sense of disquiet, as if he were revealing a part of himself—a glimpse into his hidden world—that she could never hope to understand.

Taking a deep breath, she returned her attention to the apartment. Now that she knew Connor wasn't lying unconscious or on his deathbed somewhere, she decided to make a more leisurely search of his rooms, looking for clues. Plus, it wouldn't hurt to familiarize herself with all the nooks and crannies in case she needed a place to hide or make a hasty escape. That she would even entertain such a concern was a testament to her deepening unease.

Connor, where are you? Please, please be all right.

Her brother was the only family she had left in the world and at that moment, Claire had never felt lonelier or more helpless. Somewhere in the apartment, among her brother's belongings, had to be some sign or signal that would explain his absence. She just needed to keep looking until she found it.

She returned to his bedroom and checked the closet and dresser drawers where his clothing was still neatly put away. His empty suitcases were stored underneath the bed. His toothbrush, razor and toiletries were tucked away in the bathroom.

If nothing else, the search gave her a sense of purpose. She was finally doing something concrete to locate her brother, but too many dark images still rolled around inside her head. If he was in trouble, why hadn't he been more specific? Was his absence connected to India Cortez's murder?

Claire was absolutely certain her twin would never harm another living soul, but what if he'd seen or heard something incriminating? What if he'd gone into hiding because the killer was now looking for him? The thought of her brother being hunted by a cold-blooded murderer terrified Claire, even though she wasn't sure she bought the explanation. Connor would never knowingly put her in danger. He wouldn't have asked her to come if he thought she was at risk…unless he was just that desperate. Unless he had nowhere else to turn.

Just stop. He's fine. Until you know otherwise, stop thinking the worst.

But that was easier said than done. Returning to the kitchen, she opened the refrigerator door and peered inside. Not a lot of food, but the milk was still fresh.

She followed the narrow hallway back to the spare bedroom. The closet was empty except for a plastic storage bin filled with paint-stained T-shirts and rags. She spent a minute rifling through the contents before giving up. The dresser drawers were empty as was the bathroom medicine cabinet and vanity. Evidently, no one had been staying with him.

The bed was made up and looked all too inviting. Claire realized she hadn't slept in over thirty-six hours, and exhaustion was a slow creep. Napping on the plane had been impossible. If she could just close her eyes for a few minutes, the brief respite might do wonders for her morale. But she was too afraid to succumb because once she drifted off, she might not wake up until the next day. With each passing moment, she was starting to worry that time might be of the essence.

She settled for a quick shower and change of clothing. The hot water helped revive her and the fresh jeans and crisp cotton shirt made her feel more presentable. Twisting her damp hair into a bun at the back of her head, she grabbed her bag and left the apartment.

Seated behind the wheel of her rental with the engine idling, she took the time to look up the address of the Compound—the Creative Collective—and then to glance through driving directions in case her GPS failed her again. She didn't want to wander off from the apartment not knowing where she was going or how to get back. It would be dark soon, and she had every intention of heeding the store clerk's warning.

A curtain stirred in one of the second-floor windows. She wondered if Marion Palmer was up there staring down at her. After those first few hostile moments, the woman had been relatively helpful, but she hadn't been able to disguise her cagy nature. Not from Claire and apparently, not from Connor.

She ignored the tingle of apprehension as she pulled around the driveway and headed out. The road grew progressively hillier and more winding. For a while, she managed to put her worry for Connor out of her mind as she concentrated on the drive. A few miles from the apartment, Siri alerted her that the destination was just ahead on the left.

Slowing, she spotted the limestone wall overhung with branches and flowering vines. Pulling up to the gate, she pressed the intercom button and waited. When no one answered, she killed the engine and got out to peer through the wrought-iron bars. Despite the stunning surroundings, the place seemed desolate and lonely, almost as though it was now haunted by India Cortez's ghost. Claire couldn't help but remember the clerk's reluctant description of how the body had been hoisted to the ceiling to bleed out. According to her account, the victim had been stabbed multiple times, with cuts all over her body. Had the killer wanted something from her? Was that why he'd drawn out her death? Or was inflicting agony his sole purpose for killing?

The breeze had picked up with the waning light. Moments earlier, the place had seemed almost preternaturally silent, but already nocturnal sounds had started to intrude.

An owl hooted from a treetop, warning her that twilight was only a hair's breadth away. Inside the wooded compound, it seemed as though darkness had already fallen.

She pressed Connor's number and for a split second, could have sworn she heard a ringtone in the distance. Then she realized with a sinking heart that the sound had been nothing more than wishful thinking. She had the strongest urge to call out to her brother, to scream his name at the top of her lungs to make her presence known in case he needed her. But that wasn't a good idea under the circumstances. A few days ago, a killer had viciously made his presence known in this very spot. What if he still lurked? What if he'd returned to the scene of the crime?

The longer she stood there peering through the gate, the wilder her imagination. She turned to leave just as the sound of a car engine broke the silence. She thought at first the vehicle was approaching from within the compound, perhaps summoned by the intercom. A second later, however, a black SUV turned off the street and pulled in behind her car, blocking her in. Her heart started to pound in trepidation before she noticed the light bar across the roof and the police department decal on the driver's-side door. A patrol officer. Relief washed over her as she waited.

The vehicle idled for a moment or two before the engine was cut. The door finally opened and a man climbed out. He stared at her from a distance as if assessing his risk before he ambled toward her. He was tall and lanky with a catlike gait that seemed both indolent and predatory. Even in the pre-dusk gloom, she could tell that he was older, perhaps late fifties or early sixties with a weathered complexion and sandy hair that had receded to a sharp widow's peak. He wore a khaki uniform with a badge clipped to the breast pocket of his shirt and a leather holster riding at his hip.

He looked vaguely familiar, and Claire wondered if she'd

glimpsed his portrait in Connor's sketchbook. Then she decided it might just be the uniform. As she observed his approach, she assumed what she hoped was a nonconfrontational demeanor. She gave him a nod, her glance dropping to his name tag, but she couldn't make out the lettering.

He returned her nod. "Evening, ma'am."

"Good evening, Officer."

"It's 'Chief,'" he quickly informed her. "Gil Bennett, San Miguel Police Department. You do realize you're trespassing on private property, don't you?" His manner was unhurried, but his gaze was sharp and unblinking. "Mind telling me what you're doing out here?"

Claire cleared her throat, wondering what *he* was doing there. Was it just a coincidence that he'd happened along at the same time as she? Or had someone alerted him to a possible intruder? Someone inside the Compound, perhaps? She felt almost compelled to turn and peer through the gate, but she resisted the impulse. "I'm looking for my brother," she told him. "I understand he works here."

"Not at the moment, he doesn't. No one does. Everyone is gone. This place is closed until further notice."

"Because of the murder?" She instantly regretted the blurted question. He'd seemed mildly curious before, but now she noted a stiffening in his posture as his gaze narrowed.

"What do you know about the murder?" he demanded.

"Nothing," she replied quickly. "Just what I heard in town."

"People like to talk. You can't believe everything you hear."

"I'm sure that's true." She hoped the details of India Cortez's murder had been greatly exaggerated by the store clerk, but Marion Palmer had pretty much corroborated the woman's version. *Strung up like a piece of meat.*

The police chief seemed to relax a bit as he glanced past her to the gate. "We've had a problem with trespassers. Reporters, looters, gawkers, you name it. You'll have to pardon my suspicion."

"I understand. I'm not here to cause any trouble. I'm just looking for my brother." Claire's palms were sweating by this time, but she resisted the urge to wipe them on her jeans for fear of appearing guilty. She'd done nothing wrong and Chief Gil Bennett had been nothing but personable and professional, yet a sense of foreboding had been building ever since he arrived. There was something about his voice... about the way he carried himself...

"I'll need to see some ID," he added in an amiable tone.

"Of course." She angled her head toward her rental. "It's in the car."

He moved back a step and waved her toward the vehicle. "Take your time."

She brushed past him and opened the car door, digging inside her bag until she found her wallet, all the while trying to keep him in her periphery without being obvious about it. Police chief or not, she had no intention of turning her back on him. They were alone on a country road in the middle of nowhere with darkness approaching. Her great-aunt had instilled in her and Connor at a very young age the need for caution, to always be alert and aware of their surroundings. To always locate the exits. The advice had seemed stifling during Claire's teenage years, but had served her well living alone in a dangerous city.

Straightening, she turned and handed him her license.

He used the flashlight on his phone to examine the information. "This is your current address?"

"Yes, sir."

"You're a long way from home."

"I'm a long way from my current address, but I grew up

in Austin. My brother just recently moved to San Miguel. I'm in town for a quick visit." Despite her misgivings, she briefly entertained the notion of telling him about Connor's worrisome text message and his subsequent silence. The man was a cop, after all. Who better to help her sort things out than the local police chief? But in the next instant, a little voice reminded her to be more circumspect. She had no idea where Connor was or why he hadn't made contact again. What she did know was that the woman he worked for— the woman who had put him in charge of everything—had been savagely murdered, perhaps even tortured. Maybe it was best not to call attention to her brother's absence until she knew more about his situation.

All this ran through her mind in the blink of an eye as she surreptitiously studied the police chief.

As if sensing her scrutiny, he glanced up from the license. "Your name's Tinsley."

She nodded. "Claire Tinsley."

"Your brother is Connor Tinsley?"

"Yes." She tried not to outwardly react to the mention of his name. Did the chief know something she didn't?

He paused for a long, tense moment. "Why did you come out here looking for him tonight? Didn't he tell you the place is closed?"

"I haven't spoken to him. I just drove into town a little while ago," she said. "He wasn't home when I arrived. I talked to his landlady, and she suggested I might find him out here." The thought crossed Claire's mind that Marion Palmer had deliberately sent her on a wild-goose chase. Why she would do such a thing, Claire had no idea, but ever since arriving in San Miguel, she felt as though she were walking through a minefield. She freely admitted that some of the explosives had been planted by her own imagination and suspicious nature. She found herself questioning everyone's motives, including the poor frightened clerk at the corner grocery store. Not to mention the local police chief. *Keep it together*, she warned herself.

He handed her back the license. "When you find him, tell him Chief Bennett would like a word."

Claire cleared her throat. "May I ask what about?"

A part of her hoped he would ignore the question. She wasn't sure she was ready to hear his explanation. Instead of brushing her off, however, he seemed to consider his answer before he shrugged and said, "Just a couple of follow-up questions after his initial interview. We're talking to everyone who lived or worked at the Compound. Turns out, your brother may be one of the last people to see the victim alive."

Claire managed to keep her voice even though her stomach was suddenly in knots. "Do you have a card I can pass along?"

"He knows where to find me." He glanced back toward the street. "If I were you, I'd get a move on. This road can be treacherous after dark. Lots of hills, lots of curves. Sometimes a deer will come out of nowhere."

"Thank you for the warning. I was just leaving when you pulled up."

"I'll let you be on your way then."

He gave a curt nod to end the conversation, then headed back to his vehicle. Claire climbed into her rental and locked the doors. She watched his progress in the rearview mirror. The SUV's headlights came on as he started the engine. Enough daylight remained to blunt the impact of the high beams, but she squinted just the same. He sat with engine idling for a moment before switching to low beams and backing out of the drive onto the street. Claire waited, allowing him to put some distance between them.

As the sound of his engine faded, she started her own vehicle. The headlights came on automatically and for a moment, she could have sworn she saw someone standing on the drive just beyond the gate. Her heart thudded as she watched the shadow dart into the woods.

A deer or coyote, she told herself. Not a person. Not her brother. Not the killer.

Chapter Four

As it turned out, Claire didn't go straight back to the apartment. Dusk rolled in as she headed toward town, and the glow of lights from bars and restaurants beckoned. Hunger pangs reminded her of how long she'd gone without a warm meal. As she drove along peering at signs, a purple neon ferret with a flickering tail caught her attention. The Crooked Ferret, the sign read. One of Connor's hangouts, according to Marion Palmer.

Impulsively, Claire pulled into the parking lot, her tires crunching on gravel as she parked beneath the gnarly branches of an oak tree. Far from a trendy establishment, the building was reminiscent of yesteryear watering holes—license plates and beer signs hammered into weathered plank siding, picnic tables scattered beneath the trees and classic southern rock playing in the background. A smaller neon ferret hung over the entrance as the vintage string lights on the patio glowed a welcome. It was still early on a weekday evening. Only a few pickup trucks and SUVs were scattered about the parking lot.

Claire got out of the car, locked the doors and scanned the area to see if she could spot Connor's vehicle before she climbed the wooden steps to the porch. She paused in the vestibule to peer through the glass door. A handful of patrons sat hunched over wooden tables or at the bar with drinks in front of them.

She searched from one side of the room to the other. Connor was nowhere to be seen, but she didn't have a complete view of the space and some of the customers had their backs to her. She opened the door and stepped inside, her gaze immediately colliding with the dark-haired subject from her brother's painting. Claire almost gasped. The young woman must surely have a connection to Connor.

She was busy behind the bar. She gave Claire a friendly smile, then returned to her task of putting away a tray of clean glasses. She seemed oblivious to Claire's shocked expression as she called over her shoulder, "Be with you in a sec!"

Claire nodded as she stared after the young woman. Her hair was pulled back in a ponytail, highlighting her flawless complexion and exquisite bone structure. She was just as lovely in person as in Connor's painting. Her casual work attire of jeans and a logo T-shirt complemented her soft curves and slender physique. No wonder Connor had wanted to paint her, Claire thought. She could hardly imagine a more inspiring subject.

Another bartender stood at the opposite end of the bar with an open laptop before him. He also glanced up when Claire entered, his gaze behind wire-rimmed glasses mildly curious, but he made no move to wait on her while the younger bartender busied herself with the glasses. Instead, he bent back to the computer screen without a second glance.

Claire took another scan of the room, her disappointment at Connor's absence intensified by worry and exhaustion. Even though it had seemed a long shot to find him inside, a part of her had been hoping he would be the one to look up with a smile when she came through the door. With the exception of a few glances, no one paid her the slightest attention. She took a seat at the bar and waited.

The young woman quickly finished her task, then wiped her hands on a towel as she came over to Claire. "Sorry for the wait."

"Not a problem," Claire said. "I'm in no hurry."

The woman gave her another smile, this one a little more tentative as she searched Claire's face. "You look familiar. Have you been in before?"

"This is my first time."

She gave Claire a bemused perusal as if she were still trying to place her. "Welcome to the Crooked Ferret. I'm Mia. What can I get for you?"

"Information, I hope." Claire could almost feel a physical recoil from the other side of the bar as she took out her phone and swiped to a recent photo of Connor. Undaunted by the woman's inexplicable reticence, she slid the phone across the bar. "Have you seen this man? I understand he comes in here sometimes."

The young woman studied the image for only a split second before glancing up with a shrug. But she couldn't quite hide the flare of emotion in her dark eyes, followed by the same wary look with which Claire was becoming all too familiar. "Sorry. A lot of people come through that door, especially in the summer. We get all kinds. After a while, faces start to blend together."

You're lying, Claire thought. Connor's photo had garnered a reaction, so why was she pretending she didn't know him? *What are you hiding?*

Take it easy, Claire warned herself. She drew a breath as she tamped down a rush of anger. Losing her temper and creating a scene wouldn't get her the information she so desperately wanted. Besides, the woman obviously knew Connor or at least had seen him. Her unwitting response to his photo was the closest thing Claire had had to a clue since arriving in San Miguel.

She tapped her finger on the screen. "Please look again. I was told he comes in here with friends from the Compound. Please. It's important that I find him."

"I already said I don't know him. I don't know what else I can tell you." She frowned, her tone becoming increasingly hostile. "Why are you looking for him anyway? Is he in some kind of trouble?"

"I hope not."

The dark eyes narrowed. "Are you a cop?"

"I'm not a cop," Claire said with a sigh. "And before you ask, I'm not a reporter, either. I'm his sister. My name is Claire Tinsley."

Surprise flashed across the woman's features, followed by something that might have been relief. Or fear. "His *sister*?"

Claire leaned forward, letting her voice drop with urgency. "You know him, don't you? Please, Mia, if you know where I can find him—"

"I don't," she said with finality, but the use of her first name seemed to break through her defenses. She shot a glance toward the other bartender, then said in a hushed voice, "I've seen him in here. Sometimes he comes in with friends, sometimes alone."

"When was the last time you saw him?" Claire asked.

She mopped at an invisible spot on the bar with her towel. "I don't remember exactly. A few days ago, I guess, but that doesn't mean he hasn't been in since. I've been away dealing with a family emergency. My cousin—" She seemed to catch herself. "Never mind about that. Why are you looking for him? Can't you just call him?"

"I've tried. He isn't answering."

"Does he know you're looking for him?"

Claire hesitated, unsure how much she wanted to reveal.

She felt a sort of kinship with the woman because of her portrait in Connor's apartment, but that connection was tenuous at best. "It's…complicated," she said. "I just got into town a little while ago. His landlady thought I might find him here or at the Compound."

The dark eyes widened as her hand slipped to her throat where the tiny silver cross from the painting nestled in the hollow. "You didn't go out there, did you?"

"Yes. As a matter of fact, I just came from there."

"You went alone?" She looked stricken as her gaze darted about the restaurant. "Did no one tell you what happened out there?"

A shiver went through Claire as much from the woman's reaction as from her memory of the dark energy of the place, of the rush of a shadow behind the wrought-iron gate. "I know about the murder and, yes, I found the place a little unsettling. But I went anyway because Marion—his landlady—thought he might be working there. He wasn't. Everyone was gone."

"You mean Marion Palmer?" She caressed the smooth metal of her necklace between her thumb and forefinger.

Claire nodded. "Do you know her?"

"I know who she is. I've seen her in here before." She leaned in. "A piece of advice? I would be very careful about what I say around her. She likes to talk."

"To gossip, you mean. I imagine there's been plenty of talk since the murder."

She flashed another glance toward the end of the bar. "I would be careful what I say about that, too."

"Why? It's common knowledge, isn't it?"

Her hand fell away from the cross, and she tucked a strand of hair behind her ear. She kept her voice low, but now Claire detected a note she couldn't quite define. "Did you know your brother worked for India Cortez? The dead woman," she added, in case there was any confusion.

"Marion mentioned something about it."

"Did she tell you that it was more than just business between the two of them? They were close."

Claire tensed. "How close?"

"It's not what you're thinking," the woman was quick to clarify, and Claire could have sworn she blushed. "Their relationship wasn't romantic or anything like that. Besides the age difference, Connor is—"

"Connor is what?"

She looked uncomfortable. "What I'm trying to say is that given their relationship, it might not look so good for your brother if the police know you're looking for him. They might start to think he's skipped town."

Claire had had a similar thought earlier with Gil Bennett, but to hear someone else echo her concerns was a shock to her senses. Her response was automatic. "My brother would never hurt anyone."

"I wasn't trying to imply that he's guilty. From everything I've seen, he's a good man. He's always been kind to me."

For some reason, Claire felt the sting of hot tears behind her lids. Connor *was* kind. For as far back as she could remember, he'd always gone out of his way to help anyone in need whether he knew the person or not. How he'd become entangled in something so sinister as India Cortez's murder, she couldn't imagine. But she intended to keep digging until she found Connor, the truth, or both.

She blinked away the tears and kept her voice even. "Go back to what you just said about Connor and India. About the closeness of their relationship. If it wasn't romantic, then what was it?"

"To use your word, it was complicated."

"How?"

"A while back, India had an exhibit at a prominent gallery in Austin. It was the first showing she'd had in over a decade, and it generated a lot of media attention. That's where she and Connor met, I think. He attended the exhibit and they hit it off. Anyway, people started clamoring for her paintings. Galleries all over the country wanted to host her work. I guess the pressure was too much for her and she couldn't deal. After Connor went to work at the Compound, she started passing off some of his art as her own."

Claire said in astonishment, "And he knew about this?"

"It was part of their arrangement."

She digested the information for a moment. "You seem to know a lot about my brother's business. How is it you know so much about his arrangement with India?"

"People talk and a good bartender listens." But the flicker of deception in her eyes gave her away.

"I think it's more than that. You know him, don't you? Outside this place, I mean."

She tried to recover. "You're reading too much into what I said. That's my fault. I shouldn't repeat gossip."

Claire leaned in. "Answer me this. If my brother is nothing more than a customer to you, then why did you lie for him? Why are you so protective of him? And why does he have an unfinished portrait of you in his apartment? Did you pose for him?"

Her blush deepened but she said nothing.

Claire steadied her tone. "Please. I'm not trying to pry into your personal life. I just want to find my brother."

She sighed and nodded. "Okay, yes, we are friends. And, yes, I am protective of him. After everything that's happened, why wouldn't I be? Sooner or later, the cops are going to need to pin that murder on someone. The pressure is building for an arrest. We're all just trying to look out for each other as best we can. But I swear I don't know where he is. I haven't heard from him, either."

"I believe you." Claire took out a pen and paper from her bag and wrote down her number. "If you do hear from him, please call me. And if you need to see me in person for whatever reason, I'll be staying at his apartment, at least until Marion Palmer kicks me out." She slid the paper across the bar. "In the meantime, is there anyone you can think of who might know where he is? A friend or acquaintance I can talk to?"

Mia folded the paper and slipped it in her pocket. "No one like that, but I may know someone who can help you. Someone who has a knack for finding things."

"You mean like a private detective?"

"Not exactly," she hedged. "He used to be a cop. He's here tonight, but I won't point him out or tell you his name. I respect his privacy. If you're interested, I can give him your number. He'll call you."

"That all sounds very clandestine." Not to mention, suspicious. Claire wanted to trust Mia—*someone* in San Miguel—but she'd spent too many years studying crime statistics and before that, building her defenses. Nothing had seemed right about this situation since she received Connor's message over twenty-four hours ago.

Mia didn't seem at all offended by her reluctance nor did she press the issue. Instead, she nodded in understanding. "You're right to be careful. A lot of people in this town aren't who they seem."

Before Claire could ask for an elaboration, the woman's attention shifted to the door where someone had just entered. Without missing a beat, she put her hand over Claire's cell phone screen and slid it back across the counter.

Claire glanced over her shoulder. The man who had introduced himself to her earlier as the chief of police stood just inside the door, feet slightly apart as he surveyed the room. Her first thought was that he had followed her to the Crooked Ferret, but then she remembered he'd left the Compound before her. She'd even waited until his lights had disappeared before heading back to town. Of course, he could have pulled off somewhere and waited for her to pass.

You're being paranoid.

But was she?

His gaze met hers, and he nodded in recognition before heading into the establishment. He spoke to the man with the laptop as he passed. The bartender looked up from the computer screen, said something in response, then closed the lid.

Claire watched the chief make his way through the room. Maybe it was her imagination, but his nod had been more than just an acknowledgment of their previous meeting. The look he gave her had seemed knowing, secretive.

He stopped to converse with another customer, his back still to Claire. He bent over the table, placing both hands on the surface. She couldn't see his face or hear any of the conversation, but from his body language, she deduced the confrontation was anything but pleasant. When Gil shifted his position, Claire had full view of the man who sat opposite him. Her heart jumped at the familiarity of his care-worn features. She hadn't noticed him earlier. She supposed she'd been too singularly focused on searching for Connor, but she recognized him now from his sketch, the one that had elicited such a strong reaction from her. The Crooked Ferret was turning out to be a who's who of faces from her brother's artwork.

He waved a careless hand as if to shoo away the chief. When he reached for his drink, Gil Bennett put a hand over the glass. Their exchange seemed quite heated until the seated man got up from the table and staggered toward the back of the establishment, presumably where the restrooms were located. Gil Bennett took a seat two tables over as if he meant to keep an eye on the inebriated man.

Claire had been riveted by the brief clash. Now she turned back to the bar to ask Mia his name, but her coworker had finally left his position at the laptop and strode toward them. She could sense Mia's tension as he approached.

He said at her side, "The chief's had a rough day by the sound of it. Take him over his usual and tell him it's on the house. Let's see if that improves his mood. And, Mia? Keep an eye on the padre while you're at it. He started early tonight and that never ends well."

Mia flashed Claire a cautionary look before she hurried off to complete the tasks. The man behind the bar gave her a tight smile as he went through the motions of wiping down the counter in front of her. He looked to be about the same age as Gil Bennett—probably late fifties or early sixties, but where the chief was trim with sinewy muscles, this man had a stockier build. Not heavy by any means, but his jawline had softened, and his middle had widened with age. His freckled complexion gave him a youthful appearance on first glance that belied his receding hairline and the fan of wrinkles around light blue eyes peering at her through wire-rimmed glasses.

"Did Mia take your order?"

"We were just getting around to that." Claire collected her phone from the counter. "I'll have a beer. Whatever you have on tap is fine."

"Coming right up." He returned a few minutes later with a frosty mug topped with a thin layer of foam. "Would you like to see a menu?"

Her stomach growled a warning and she nodded. "A menu sounds like a good idea. Or I can just order from the board." She nodded toward the handwritten menu over the counter.

"Suit yourself. I'll be back in a minute to take your order."

"I already know what I want. A burger medium well with the works."

He jotted down the order and said without glancing up, "We're casual around here. You can eat at the bar or pick any table you like."

"The patio okay?"

"Sure thing." He looked up then with a hint of a smile. "We'll find you."

"Can I ask you a question?" she said before he turned away.

The faint smile flashed again. "You can always ask."

He had a pleasant voice. Smooth and well-modulated like a newscaster. So smooth as to almost be slippery, but again, she was creating her own explosives in that imaginary minefield. She slid the phone back across the counter. "Do you know this man? I understand he's a regular here."

His gaze dropped to the phone where Connor's image smiled up at him. "I've seen him around. I wouldn't exactly call him a regular, but he comes in from time to time. Nice guy. He usually sits in the back if he's with his friends." He pointed to a corner table. "If he's by himself, he sits out on the patio with a sketch pad. The kid's talented. I'll give him that."

"Do you remember the last time you saw him?"

"No, but I don't come in every night. I'm only here tonight to pitch in where needed. We're shorthanded since Mia's cousin disappeared."

Claire glanced at him in alarm. "What do you mean, disappeared?"

"Vamoosed. Split. In the wind. Translation, he had a hankering to see his girlfriend and decided to head south without out notice."

"But he's okay?"

"As far as I know." He picked up Claire's phone and handed it back to her. "What's this about anyway? Is this guy in some kind of trouble?"

"No, nothing like that. I just got into town and I—we seem to keep missing each other." She hoped her shrug and casual tone convinced him. She didn't want to call any more attention to Connor's absence than she already had, but how was she going to find him if she didn't ask questions?

"I'm sure you'll catch up with him sooner or later. San Miguel isn't that big. In the meantime, enjoy your evening."

"Thanks." She picked up the mug and carried it out to the patio. The night was still warm, but the breeze blowing in from the river felt refreshing. She'd lost count of how long she'd been up. By this time, she was so tired she could barely stand without swaying. Food first, then sleep. Then she would start her search anew for Connor.

The patio was nearly empty. A couple sat near the railing murmuring across the table to one another. A larger party had congregated at one of the picnic tables. The man she'd plowed into at the grocery store sat facing the entrance. Claire stopped short, shocked yet again by a familiar face. He appeared absorbed in his phone and didn't notice her. Before she could decide whether or not to acknowledge his presence, his head came up and their gazes met for the second time that day.

Claire felt color flood her face as she nodded, then turned away quickly and hurried toward a vacant table. Her phone pinged as she sat down. She checked the screen anxiously, hoping the incoming text was from Connor. No such luck. One of the friends she'd left behind in Italy messaged to see if everything was all right. Claire thumbed a brief summary and then they texted back and forth for a moment before signing off. She placed her phone on the table and glanced up.

The man with the cane loomed over her table. She felt the flutter of an unwanted attraction in the pit of her stomach as he smiled down at her.

Chapter Five

"Hello again. Remember me?"

Her smile seemed nervous as she glanced up at him. She cleared her throat before she spoke. "Yes, of course I remember you. Hard to forget the man I practically knocked off his feet."

"Yet here I am still in one piece." Ben tried to appear relaxed, hoping to put her at ease, but her presence in San Miguel had created a complicated situation. Her brother had been adamant about not involving her in their plans, but he was nowhere to be found at the moment. In his absence, it was up to Ben to figure out what to do. Striking the right balance was tricky. If he revealed too much too soon, she might panic and run straight to the police. The last thing Ben needed was Gil Bennett nosing around, especially considering the police chief's sketchy background. On the other hand, if he held back, she would continue to ask questions, thus putting a spotlight on her brother's absence and perhaps a target on her back. Either way, it was imperative he gain her trust as quickly as possible.

He smiled down at her. "I figured as long as we're going to keep running into each other like this, we may as well introduce ourselves. I'm Ben Dornan."

"Claire Tinsley." She extended her hand and they shook.

"Tinsley." He pretended to mull the name over for a moment. "You wouldn't be related to Connor Tinsley, would you?"

"You know my brother?"

"We've met."

"When? How?"

She looked guileless, gazing up at him with widened eyes and slightly parted lips. Guilt prickled at his deception, but then he reminded himself that lives were at stake, including hers. She couldn't know the truth until he was certain of her reaction.

In the split second before he answered, he studied her features. Her light brown hair was pulled back in a loose bun, highlighting the dark circles under her eyes and the strain in her face. All that visible tension made her seem vulnerable, though Ben suspected she was anything but helpless. She and Connor had been raised with the knowledge that danger potentially lurked around every corner and that death could come swiftly and unexpectedly. He understood the wariness in her eyes only too well.

He nodded toward the vacant chair opposite her. "May I?"

"Yes, please." She waved a hand toward the chair, then waited patiently while he accommodated his knee and leaned his cane against the table. "How do you know my brother?" she asked anxiously.

"We both come in here for dinner fairly often. I'm not much of a cook and apparently, neither is he. Despite appearances, the food here is good and the beer is always cold."

She seemed immune to his lighthearted banter. She slid her hand across the table, as if imploring him to tell her what she wanted to hear. "When did you last see him?"

Her eyes were like golden orbs beneath the string lights. For a moment, he found himself mesmerized by her earnest gaze, and he lost track of the conversation as his mind darted back to the night they first met. That terrified little girl had grown up to be an incredibly attractive woman, which could pose a whole new set of problems if he let it.

He shook himself. "I'm sorry, what?"

If possible, her gaze grew even more intense. "When was the last time you saw Connor in here? Or anywhere, for that matter."

He pretended to think back. "Must have been over the weekend. I've been away for a couple of days. I just got back from Houston last night so I can't say for certain when he was last here." Her muttered oath caught him by surprise. "Did I say something wrong?"

She scowled across the table at him. "I just find it a little strange that everybody in town seems to know my brother, but no one can remember the last time they saw him. Apparently, you all picked the same time to go away. It's almost as if someone handed you a script."

Her sarcasm was biting. He said defensively, "I don't know what you mean."

She angled her head toward the bar. "Mia claims she had a family emergency and the older bartender says he doesn't work here every night. Connor's landlady just got back from San Antonio so she can't say when she last saw him, either. And now you. You have to admit, it's quite a coincidence."

Ben tried to keep his tone light, but in her shoes, he'd probably be a little skeptical, too. "You think we're all lying to you? That would be kind of a bizarre conspiracy, wouldn't it?"

"I honestly don't know what to think. This place…" She looked as if she wanted to say something more, then shrugged. "Maybe it's just me. I'm tired and frustrated. It's possible I'm reading too much into things. Jet lag will do that." She closed her eyes briefly. "I apologize for the over-reaction."

"No apologies necessary," Ben said. "But just so you know—I was in Houston for two days of back-to-back doctors' appointments. I can show you the receipts if you like."

She looked embarrassed. "I'll take your word for it."

"To further clear the air, the older bartender you referred to is Lyle Fincher. He owns this place, along with several other businesses in town. So he wasn't lying, either. He usually only comes in a couple nights a week. As for Mia Soto—"

She put up a hand to stop him. "You've made your point."

"I wasn't trying to make a point. I want to put your mind at ease. There's no conspiracy."

The conversation had taken a downward turn, but at least she hadn't sent him away. He winced as he rubbed his knee. "Believe me, I would rather have been here than where I was. The physical therapist I see has a sadistic side."

Her expression softened as she glanced at the cane. "What happened? That is, if you don't mind my asking."

"Nothing exciting. Just an old-fashioned car crash. I won't bore you with the details."

"I hope I didn't cause any further damage when I plowed into you earlier. I'm not usually so careless."

He grinned to reassure her. "You can make it up to me by allowing me to buy you a drink."

She smiled back, but only faintly. "I'm still working on my first one, but thanks."

"Would it be all right if I join you?"

He sensed an infinitesimal hesitation before she shrugged. "Sure."

He motioned for the waitress and ordered a beer for himself. When he turned back to the table, she looked a little more relaxed. The brief intermission seemed to have put her at ease.

She gazed at him across the table. "Can I ask you a question?"

He sat back in his chair and stretched his knee. "Shoot."

"Do you know who that man is seated alone at the table just to the left of the bar? He and Gil Bennett were talking a few minutes ago. Their conversation seemed a bit animated."

Her use of the police chief's name threw Ben for a loop, though he tried to hide his shock behind a teasing question. "How do you know Bennett? Don't tell me you've already had a run-in with our local law enforcement."

Her smile turned wry. "As a matter of fact, I have. I drove out to the Compound earlier looking for Connor. Chief Bennett pulled in behind me and gave me a warning about trespassing on private property."

"Did you tell him you were looking for Connor?"

"In passing. I had to give him a reason for my being at the Compound. Otherwise, he might have ticketed me. Or worse, arrested me." She gave him a curious scrutiny. "Why does it matter what I told him?"

Ben leaned in. "Can I be frank?"

She looked startled and more than a little dubious. "Of course."

"Gil Bennett isn't a man I'd put my trust in."

"Why? What's he done?"

"Nothing to me. But I've heard talk. Just be careful," he warned.

She looked a little shell-shocked by his candor. "I have to say, San Miguel isn't at all what I expected. I always thought of this town as an artists' refuge. A quiet, quaint place where creatives come when they tire of the big city."

"It is, but you have to remember, we're only a few hours' drive from the border. Lots of people moving in and out or just passing through. It's a good place to disappear if you don't want anyone to find you."

Her gaze turned guarded. "Is that why you're here?"

"Hardly. A buddy offered me the use of his cabin. Seemed as good a place as any to recuperate." He paused as the waitress brought out his beer and placed the glass mug on the table. He nodded his thanks before she turned and disappeared back inside. "I didn't mean to highjack the conversation. You were asking about someone inside the bar?"

She looked as if she wished she'd never brought up the subject. "It's not important."

"You asked about him so it must be important to you. Do you want me to go inside and take a look?"

"No, please don't bother."

"It wouldn't be a bother." He took a sip of his beer, holding her gaze over the rim of his mug. "Can you at least describe him?"

She reluctantly relented. "Older and tallish with a slim build. Salt-and-pepper hair and beard. He looks as if he carries the weight of the world on his shoulders if you know what I mean. Lyle called him 'padre.'"

"Ah." Ben nodded as he tried to reclaim a more casual demeanor. "That's Sean Greggory. He lives in the apartment above the bar so he's a regular. Interesting fellow. From what I gather, he used to be a priest."

She lifted a brow. "He must have a story."

"A good one, if you can believe the rumors. He supposedly had a torrid affair with a married woman back in the day. Their relationship created a huge scandal in his parish. As the story goes, her family was prominent. They had enough money and clout to get him kicked out of the priesthood. *If* you can believe the rumors."

"What does he do now?"

"He claims to be writing a book about the old missions in the San Antonio area. I believe he asked Connor to do some sketches for him. From what I can tell, though, he mostly sits in the bar and drinks."

"That's sad."

"He does appear to be one of those tragic figures," Ben agreed. He watched her for a moment in silence. "If you don't mind my asking, why are you so interested in Sean Greggory?"

She looked uneasy. "It's…nothing."

"Doesn't sound like nothing."

"Just me letting my imagination get the better of me."

"Tell me." His voice came out sharper than he meant, but she didn't seem to notice.

"Earlier, I saw a sketch of him in Connor's apartment. I had a rather negative reaction to his portrait."

"Did you recognize him?"

"No, I'm certain I've never seen him before. Which is why I can't explain my reaction."

"Sometimes no explanation is needed," he said. "You just have to trust your gut."

"True, but I'm not exactly in a normal state of mind at the moment."

Ben nodded sympathetically. "You're worried about your brother. When was the last time you heard from him?"

She glanced down at her phone without answering.

The tension at the table had returned along with her defenses. "Sorry. I didn't mean to pry. You just seem so concerned. I thought I might be of help."

"I am concerned," she admitted. "And to answer your question, I received a text from him late yesterday afternoon. That's why I'm here in San Miguel."

"Yesterday? So you've had recent contact." Ben had been trying to reach Connor ever since he returned from Houston the night before. If Connor could text his sister, why hadn't he been in touch with Ben?

"I was on vacation in Italy with a couple of friends," she continued. "We'd gone out for an early dinner. The text came over dessert. He…suggested I come to San Miguel."

"And just like that you dropped everything?" That didn't sound right. Not after Connor had been so resolute about protecting his sister.

"I'd been wanting to come ever since he moved. We've both been so busy lately." She paused as if to collect her thoughts. "Anyway, here I am."

She was holding something back. He could tell by her hesitancy. By the way she lowered her eyes to keep from meeting his watchful gaze. "You traveled all the way from Italy because of a text message. Now that's sisterly devotion."

She pretended to sip her beer, though the liquid barely grazed her lips. "Connor and I have always been close. We've always had each other's back no matter what. He asked me to come and so I came."

"But here you are tonight without him," Ben said. "Seems a little strange that you flew all that way only to be left alone on your first night in town. I can't help but feel I'm missing a piece of the story."

"As you said earlier, I won't bore you with the details."

He wasn't bored. Far from it. "Are you ready for another drink? That beer must be getting warm by now."

She glanced at her half-finished mug. "If I drink another drop, I'll be out like a light."

"Jet lag can be a killer," he commiserated.

"You have no idea."

He slipped in another question while she seemed distracted. "So you haven't heard from Connor since that text?"

She shook her head.

"Can I see the text?"

She placed her hand over her phone as if protecting the stored contents from his prying eyes. "That's a private communication between my brother and me. I'm sorry I ever brought it up. If I didn't know better..." Her voice turned accusing as her gaze narrowed. "You seem a little too invested in my brother's whereabouts. Are you a cop?"

"In another life," he said.

That stopped her. "What do you mean?"

He absently rubbed his knee. "I was in law enforcement for nearly fifteen years before the car crash. Now I'm sidelined for the foreseeable future. I have no official standing at the moment. Anything you and I say here tonight is off the record. It goes no further than this table."

"And I'm supposed to take your word for that?" she challenged.

"I hope you will. I'd like to help if I can. You came here looking for your brother. It's obvious you're worried about him. I may be a little rusty, but I'm still pretty good at tracking people down."

She said in surprise, "So *you're* the guy."

"I'm the guy?"

"Mia told me about you." She folded her arms on the table. "She didn't mention a name, but she offered to give my number to an ex-cop who's good at finding things. Those were her words. She was talking about you, wasn't she?"

"Sounds like me. Is she going to give me your number?"

"I asked her not to. No offense, but I don't know you. For all I know, you could be trying to scam me."

"I assure you, I'm not."

"But you'd say that regardless, wouldn't you? This is my problem," she insisted. "I'll figure out what to do. Besides, it's very possible my brother has secluded himself somewhere while he works. He'll get in touch when he's ready."

Lost her again, Ben thought. He'd pushed too hard and now her defenses were up, maybe for good this time. But no matter what she said to the contrary, she didn't really believe Connor had gone off somewhere to work. Her distress was too obvious. She also had no intention of asking for Ben's help. That, too, was obvious. He felt compelled to blurt out the truth, but that would be a mistake. She might panic, create a fuss and then he really would lose control of the situation. Their whole mission depended on stealth and anonymity. Flying under the radar. Right now, he just needed to keep her from going to the police until he could locate Connor. He rubbed his knee as he tried to think of a way to get himself back in her good graces.

"Are you in pain?"

The question caught him by surprise, but he wasn't above courting sympathy to soften her up. "A little," he admitted.

"How did the crash happen?"

"Like I said, nothing too exciting. I was T-boned at a stoplight on a Sunday morning. Not a cloud in the sky and no traffic to speak of. A delivery truck came out of nowhere. Shattered my kneecap and broke five ribs. Recovery is taking a lot longer than I anticipated." He didn't much like talking about the accident, but he'd learned a long time ago that when working undercover, the truth was always easier to push than a lie. If he opened up a little, maybe she'd do the same.

"That must have been awful," she said.

"It's been a long haul," he admitted. "The first surgery had complications so we ended up doing it all over again a few months later. Believe me when I tell you, I know about frustration."

She seemed to appreciate his honesty. They were still a long way from full trust, but at least it was a start.

"You were a cop here in San Miguel?" she asked.

"No, not here." He hated to get too specific. He had a cover to protect, after all. Connor was the only other person in town who knew that Ben was a federal agent on medical

leave, and they'd both agreed on the importance of conceal-
ment. "I was based in Houston for several years. Before that,
I was in New Orleans."

She was silent for a moment as she took in his revelations.
"I thought I detected a hint of New Orleans in your speech."

"And here I thought I'd lost that accent years ago."

She shrugged. "I have an ear for accents. With you, it's
all in the vowel pronunciation."

"When was the last time you were in New Orleans?"

"It's been a while."

He'd wondered if she would admit to having spent her
early childhood in southern Louisiana, but no. She was too
well trained for that. For all intents and purposes, Austin,
Texas, was her hometown just as Claire Tinsley was her
name.

"What about you?" he asked. "What do you do for a living?"

"I work for a company that compiles data for the Department of Homeland Security."

"What kind of data?"

"In general, we study and analyze networks, supply chains
and suspicious activities associated with criminal organizations and multinational companies that could pose a threat
to national security."

He noticed she was careful not to elaborate, but instead
gave him a general job description.

"Sounds like we're in the same line of work," he said.

"Yes, but instead of wearing a badge and carrying a gun,
I sit in a cubicle and stare at a computer screen all day."

"Necessary work," he said.

"I like to think so."

The conversation lulled while the waitress brought out
her food order. Ben took that as his cue to leave. They were
ending on a positive note, but it was best not to press his

luck. If he hadn't heard from Connor by this time tomorrow, he'd take the next step.

He scooted back his chair. "I'm glad we ran into each other tonight. Let me give you my number before I leave. If you change your mind or just need to talk, call day or night. No matter the time, no matter the situation. I mean that." He scribbled his number on a paper napkin and slid it across the table. "Keep it close, just in case."

Their fingers brushed briefly as she reached for the napkin. She drew back with a visible shiver.

"Did I say something wrong?" he asked.

"No, I…" She trailed away, looking unsettled. "I had one of those odd moments of déjà vu, but we've never met before today. Have we?" She sounded uncertain.

He smiled. "Not in this life."

A FEW MINUTES LATER, Ben paid his tab and left. Mia Soto caught his eye as he walked by the bar. She nodded almost imperceptibly toward the door and then held up a finger, asking him to wait for her outside as her gaze darted to Lyle Fincher. He appeared to be in a one-sided argument with Sean Greggory. Apparently, Sean wanted another drink and Lyle had cut him off. Sean swayed toward the bar as if he intended to instigate a physical confrontation, but it was obviously an idle threat. The man could barely stand on his own, let alone throw a punch. Lyle merely folded his arms and held his ground until Gil Bennett interceded. He put an arm around Sean's shoulders and led him back to his table.

Ben took in the scene, remembering what Claire had told him about her strange reaction to the sketch in Connor's apartment. She was certain she'd never seen Sean Greggory before, but what if she had? What if that sketch had triggered a long-lost memory? Not just her memory, but Connor's as well. Maybe that was why he'd felt compelled to draw Sean Greggory in the first place.

He was still mulling over the possibility when he walked outside into the fresh, night air. The evening was warm with a mild breeze whispering through the trees. He rounded the corner of the building and waited in the dark with a shoulder against the wall. The music was muffled where he stood and night sounds intruded. He could hear crickets chirping in the ditches and a bullfrog down by the water. Closing his eyes, he cleared his mind of all thoughts of the car crash that may have ended his career. He put aside Connor Tinsley's disappearance and the reason he'd lured Ben to San Miguel in the first place. For a few moments only, he felt at peace.

He heard the side door open and the tranquility of the evening drifted away even before he turned. He gave a low whistle, then waited as Mia hurried toward the sound.

"Ben?"

"Over here."

Her voice sounded anxious in the dark as she approached. "Thank you for waiting for me. I had a hard time getting away. Lyle keeps reminding me that we're shorthanded because of my cousin. It's like he blames me for Hector's absence."

"Still no word?"

"No, and my aunt is worried sick about him. So am I." She paused, her face pale and tense in the dark as she gazed up at him. "Ben, he left Matamoras two days ago. It's only a five-hour drive to San Miguel."

"Are you sure he was coming straight home? What about his girlfriend? Maybe he took a detour to see her."

She shook her head. "I checked. She hasn't seen him, either. No one has seen or heard from him since he left my aunt's house. You said to let you know if you could do anything to help." She bit her lip. "This is me letting you know. Can you help us?"

"I'll do what I can. When was the last time you talked to him?"

"Just before he left for Matamoras. He said he would be back in a couple of days to take care of some unfinished business."

"Did he say what that business was?"

She sighed. "He just kept telling me the less I knew the better."

That sounded ominous. "Was there a reason he left town when he did?"

He could sense her mounting tension. "It wasn't to avoid the police if that's what you're thinking."

"I wasn't thinking anything. I'm just asking questions."

"Sorry. I'm a bit defensive when it comes to Hector. He's been in some trouble before, but that was a long time ago." She leaned back against the wall. "My aunt is recovering from a major illness. She and Hector have always been close. He tries to spend as much time with her as he can, but it's difficult. He has to work. Like everyone else, he has bills and obligations…" She trailed off. "My poor aunt has enough to worry about without all this added stress. She's certain something has happened to him. She gets these premonitions, these visions…" Another pause. "I don't expect you to believe me, but I'm very afraid she's right. Something bad has happened to my cousin."

Ben tried to keep her calm. "Visions aside, let's not jump to any conclusions. Didn't you tell me once that Hector often takes off on a whim?"

"This time is different. I can feel it." She hugged her arms around her middle. "My calls go straight to voicemail. I think his phone has been turned off or disabled."

"That'll make GPS tracking more difficult," Ben mused.

"What I can do is ask someone I know to triangulate cell tower signals to pinpoint where he made his last call or sent his last text."

"Won't you need his phone records?"

"Let me worry about that. First things first. We need to make sure he wasn't picked up and detained on either side of the border. That would explain why you haven't heard from him. We can also check the date and time his passport was scanned by Customs and Border Protection if and when he reentered the country. That'll give us a timeline."

She looked a little stunned. "I don't know how to do any of that."

"I do," Ben assured her. "Just try and relax. Think back. Did he say or do anything to give you a clue as to the unfinished business he mentioned?"

She took a long moment to answer.

"What it is?" Ben prompted.

She glanced up at him. "I think it may have something to do with a piece of jewelry he found a while back. A medallion on a silver chain. Very substantial and very unusual."

Ben's attention sharpened. Could she possibly mean *the* medallion? The one that had led Connor to San Miguel? The one that had persuaded Ben to abandon his recovery and join him here?

His heart was suddenly thudding, but he kept his voice neutral as he queried her. "What's unusual about it?"

"It has some kind of strange emblem on the front and an inscription on the back."

"Do you remember the inscription?"

She shrugged and shook her head.

"What about the emblem? Can you describe it?" It was all Ben could do not to grab her shoulders and demand answers. Instead, he repositioned the cane and waited.

"I only had a brief glimpse. Hector showed it to me at

work one night and I told him to put it away. I was too afraid someone else might see it."

"Why would that matter?"

She didn't answer.

"You think he stole the piece?"

Another pause. "I don't want to believe it, but how often do you *find* a one-of-a-kind necklace that appears to be pure silver?"

"This is important," Ben said. "Did he give you any hint as to where he came across the piece? Stolen or otherwise," he added.

"No. But it could have been anywhere. His job at the bar is a side hustle. He also has a handyman business. He's worked for most everyone in town at one time or another, including the police chief."

Strange how Gil Bennett's name kept cropping up. "What did he do for Bennett?"

"I don't know. I never asked. But he did complain after the job was finished that the chief refused to pay him. He kept putting Hector off every time he would ask for the balance."

"Do you think Hector took the necklace as compensation?"

"I guess it's possible, but a silver medallion with a fancy emblem doesn't seem like Chief Bennett's style."

Maybe, maybe not. Ben had learned a long time ago that looks could be deceiving. "Did the two of them have a confrontation over the payment?"

"Like a physical confrontation?" She shook her head. "Hector is too smart for that. He knows to be careful with someone like Bennett."

Good for him. "Let me ask you this. What do you know about the chief's background?"

She said in a hushed voice, "Do you really think he had something to do with Hector's disappearance?"

"I'm just asking questions," Ben said.

She said reluctantly, "There have always been rumors about him being on the take, but no one seems to know him personally. His background, his family…it's all a mystery. I remember hearing once that he was hired sight unseen as the chief of police."

"Who hired him?"

"The town council, the mayor. Who knows? It was a long time ago. I was just a kid when he first came to town, so I don't remember any of the details. But I do know this. Having a shady background isn't all that unusual in San Miguel. People without pasts show up here all the time. But not me. Not my cousin. We were both born and raised in this town. My aunt moved back to Matamoras a few years ago to be near her *amá*, but Hector stayed on. This is his home. If anything has happened to him—"

"Try and stay focused," Ben advised her. "Think back. Did he show you the necklace before or after Connor came to town?"

Her eyes widened in surprise. "What does Connor have to do with this?"

Everything, Ben thought. "I'm still working on a timeline," he said.

She gave him a skeptical look, as if she didn't really buy his explanation. "It was before."

"You're sure?"

She nodded. "Ben, what's going on? Why are you so interested in that necklace?"

"It's the only clue we have at the moment," he hedged.

"Can I say something before we go any farther?"

He braced himself for a barrage of questions that would be difficult to answer without fudging the truth. "What is it?"

"Regardless of how Hector came by that jewelry, he's a

good person," she insisted. "He would never even hurt a fly if he could help it."

"I sense a 'but,'" Ben said.

She sighed. "He can also be impulsive, and he likes to impress important people like India Cortez."

"He knew India?"

"He did odd jobs around the Compound for years. She was always good to him. She wasn't kind to too many people, but I think she appreciated Hector's loyalty. In a strange way, I think she wanted to protect him."

"Do you think he gave her the necklace?"

"I know he showed it to her. He told me that she had a passion for unusual jewelry. She collected pieces from all over the world. He said she was so taken with the piece that she sketched the emblem on the medallion and then later she painted herself wearing the necklace in a self-portrait."

Ben was all too familiar with that painting. India Cortez's self-portrait was why both he and Connor Tinsley had ended up in San Miguel. The medallion that had been taken by a killer in New Iberia, Louisiana, had turned up twenty-five years later around the neck of a reclusive artist in San Miguel, Texas. What were the chances that Connor Tinsley, of all people, would have attended the art exhibit in Austin that featured India's self-portrait? That he would have recognized the painted emblem a quarter of a century after his father's murder? That he would have reached out to Ben with his suspicions? *I think I've found him.*

Ben shook himself out of his reverie. "You think Hector still had the medallion when India was murdered?"

"I asked him that very question. I was afraid the police might find it in India's possession and somehow trace it back to Hector. He admitted he still had it, but he said he wished he'd never found it. He said the medallion was cursed. It had brought him nothing but bad luck. All he wanted to do was return it to where he found it."

"And you think that's why he was coming back to San Miguel?"

"Yes, and I'm beginning to think he was right. That medallion *is* cursed," she said with a shiver. "Think about it. Hector and Connor both worked for India Cortez. The three of them were connected. Now she's dead and both of them are missing."

Hector's possession of the medallion was a major development. Ben wondered if Connor had made the same discovery. "It's possible Hector and Connor are both lying low until the heat dies down. As you said, they both worked for India Cortez and were likely among the last to see her alive."

She said in a worried tone, "Surely you don't think either of them had anything to do with the murder."

"No, but keeping a low profile is exactly what I would do if I were a person of interest in a homicide investigation."

"You men and your secrets," she said with an edge of disdain. "I may not have my aunt's gift of premonitions and visions, but I have instincts and common sense. You're all hiding something. First Hector, then Connor and now you. Why can't you trust me with the truth?"

"It's not a matter of trust," Ben said. "The truth could be dangerous."

He could sense her mounting fear. "You think India was killed because of that necklace, don't you?"

"I don't know."

"What about Hector?" she asked. "Is my cousin dead, too? Is that what you're keeping from me?"

"I've no reason to believe any such thing. Give me some time to look into things," Ben said. "I'll find him."

"I really want to believe you."

"Then trust me. Trust your instincts. You came to me for a reason."

"Will you help Connor's sister?"

The question caught him off guard. He tried to keep his voice carefully neutral. "She doesn't appear to want my help."

"Maybe not yet. But if she comes to you, don't hold out on her. She has a right to know everything."

"It's not my place to tell her anything," Ben said. "But if Connor doesn't surface in the next twenty-four hours, I'll have no choice. I can't have her running all over town asking questions and drawing attention. Until I can find out what's really going on, we all need to act as though nothing has happened. You can start by going back inside before Lyle comes looking for you."

She straightened and shot a glance toward the side door. "Talk about a man and his secrets," she muttered. "Lyle has been acting very strange lately."

"Strange how?"

"For one thing, he comes in a lot more often than he used to. He says it's because we're shorthanded, but I think he has an ulterior motive. He watches the staff like a hawk. Especially me."

"All the more reason not to arouse his suspicion," Ben said. "Keep your head down and your eyes and ears open. Let me handle the rest. And Mia? Whatever you do, don't mention that medallion to anyone else. Pretend you never even heard of it."

Chapter Six

After his conversation with Mia, Ben told himself to go home, ice and elevate his knee and get some rest. Sleep had been a little hard to come by these past few weeks, especially since he'd weaned himself off the painkillers. The temptation was still there, especially on a night like this when the burning throb was a constant torment, but he knew better than to become too dependent on that floating numbness. *Just walk it off.*

Not great advice considering the trail down to the river was dark, rugged and overgrown with roots and vines that could be tripping hazards even for the uninjured. The cane could only help so much. He took his time, lulled by the sound of lapping water. By day, the river was a clear bottle green, shaded by a thick trellis of maple leaves and the lacy fronds of the bald cypresses that lined the banks. By moonlight, the water darkened and took on a mysterious sheen.

He found a spot at the river's edge where he could lean a shoulder against a tree and rest his knee. For a moment, he was tempted to take off his shoes and wade out into the cool water the way he would have as a kid. The sparkle of moonlight on the surface and the fecund scent of the woods reminded him of the night fishing trips he'd taken as a boy with his dad. He didn't think about his dad much these days. It was getting harder to remember what he looked like. Twenty-five years was a long time. But the one thing he would never let himself forget was the fact that Raymond Navarro had been one of the good guys. A rare breed in law enforcement who had been both protective and fearless. A devoted family man and a dedicated federal agent. A true white hat whose death to this day had yet to be vindicated.

We may have found him, Dad. After all this time, can you believe it? We think he's here in San Miguel, hiding in plain sight. Actually, it was Connor Tinsley who picked up the trail. Remember him? The kid you knew as Ethan Cross? He had a twin sister named Emily. She goes by Claire now and she's...

A sound intruded into his fantasy conversation. He was so lost in thought he almost missed the soft pad of footsteps on the trail. He thought at first Mia had followed him down to the river, but he knew better than to assume. He held his silence and melted back into the darkness as he waited.

Seconds later, Gil Bennett emerged from the trees. He drew up short, his gaze scanning the immediate area before he seemed to vector in on the spot where Ben hid in the shadows. He held his breath, certain for a moment that the police chief had pinpointed his hiding place. Then Gil turned and cocked his head as if trying to track an infinitesimal sound. He strode back toward the path and drew his Glock semi-automatic. "Who's there?"

"It's me, you idiot. Put that thing away." Lyle Fincher came down the path, apparently oblivious to the noise he made as he approached the bank.

Ben remained frozen, his gaze darting to Gil, who stood ramrod straight, his back to the water. The police chief tilted his head yet again. "Shh. Listen."

"What?" Moonlight glinted off Lyle's glasses as he glanced over his shoulder. He remained still for a moment, then brushed what might have been a cobweb from his hair and swore. "I hate these woods. We couldn't meet inside like normal people?"

"Too many eyes and ears in the bar tonight." Gil peered down the path behind Lyle. "Are you sure you weren't followed?"

"Who the hell would follow me? No one else knew we were meeting, and you're already here. Now put that gun away and let's get down to business."

Gil reluctantly holstered his weapon, but he continued to scour their surroundings as if he had intuited an unwanted presence. Ben leaned heavily against the tree trunk and closed his eyes. He'd stood in one place for too long and now the white-hot agony in his knee had become nearly unbearable. He didn't dare shift his position to accommodate the pain. He was concealed by the heavy shadows along the water's edge, but even the slightest movement could give him away, and Gil Bennett seemed to have an itchy trigger finger. Not a good idea to make himself a target. Ben sucked in his breath and waited.

"Let's hear it," Gil said. "What's the complaint this time?"

"You know damn well my complaint. The situation has gone from bad to worse while you're out there playing detective. I thought you said you'd handle things."

"And I will," Gil said. "All in good time."

"What the hell does that mean?"

"It means I have other responsibilities. I'm not going to drop everything just because you find yourself in a bind. And for the record, I'm not *playing* detective. My department is in the middle of a real homicide investigation."

"And that, in a nutshell, is the problem," Lyle said. "Stop dragging your feet and make an arrest. The sooner you put someone behind bars, the sooner every Tom, Dick and Harry with a badge goes home. That damn cartel symbol is still bringing them out of the woodwork. FBI, DEA, ATF and every other three-letter agency you can think of. Everybody wants to be a hero."

"Feds." Gil's tone hardened with contempt. "They always think they're smarter than the locals."

"And they usually are. You've certainly been doing nothing to disabuse them of the notion." Lyle continued to pick at something in his hair. By now, the movement seemed almost compulsive. As if catching himself, he dropped his hand to his glasses. He removed the wire frames and started polishing the lenses will equal vigor. "The killer couldn't have manipulated the situation any better. I'll give him that. Obfuscate the crime scene with symbolism. Disguise motivation with torture. Taint forensics by staging the body. The more grotesque the details, the greater the confusion. Think about it." He put the glasses back on and adjusted the earpieces. "He's got you people running around town like a bunch of headless chickens. Take away all that noise and it's just murder."

"I'm not so sure it is just murder," Gil said. "Have you considered the possibility that the cartel symbol was left by, you know, the cartel? Maybe they're sending you a message."

Lyle was silent for a moment. "I'm sure you meant sending *us* a message. And whose fault would that be if they are? They're not exactly known for patience. As long as the Feds keep sniffing around, we're dead in the water. Do you have any idea how much money we stand to lose every damn day we remain inoperable? Get off your duff and make something happen. You've got a viable suspect. What the hell are you waiting for?"

"An arrest may not be as easy as you seem to think," Gil said. "Connor Tinsley has apparently gone to ground."

Ben silently swore. Connor wasn't just a person of interest. By the sounds of it, Gil Bennett and Lyle Fincher intended to railroad him for India's murder. All the more reason why Ben needed to find him before they did.

"It can't be that hard to flush him out in a place like this," Lyle said. "A manhunt just makes him look all the more guilty. His sister is having dinner on the patio even as we speak. Put a tail on her, if you have to. Just tie up all your loose ends so we can get back to work."

"And if the kid's innocent?"

Lyle scoffed. "Nobody's truly innocent. Connor Tinsley had means, motive and opportunity. Rumor has it, India even put him in her will. That *kid* stands to inherit a fortune. What more do you need?"

Gil shrugged. "We're looking at other suspects. Connor Tinsley isn't the only one with a motive."

"That's hardly surprising, considering India Cortez was a coldhearted—"

"Don't talk about her that way." Gil's harsh tone startled Ben. The shift seemed to come out of the blue.

"Why the hell not?" Lyle demanded.

"Some lines you just don't cross."

"Oh really? You could have fooled me."

"Maybe you don't know me as well as you think you do," Gil said. "And maybe I know you a little better than you think."

"What's that supposed to mean?"

"You once mentioned that you've been collecting India's paintings for years. You probably don't even remember telling me that, do you? Just a harmless little boast after a few drinks. But I remember. And now I'm starting to wonder if you decided all that artwork would be worth a lot more money if the artist was dead."

Lyle's laugh was anything but good-humored. "You think I killed India Cortez to make a buck or two off her paintings?"

"You tell me."

"Two can play at that game, my friend. I saw the way you looked at her when you thought no one else was around. They say unrequited love is the cruelest love of all," Lyle said with a chuckle. "It eventually turns to resentment and then to rage. You don't strike me as the kind of man who handles rejection all that well."

"And you don't know what the hell you're talking about," Gil said in a dangerously calm voice.

"I know this. Either you do your damn job or I'll find someone who will. Nobody's innocent and everybody's expendable. You best remember that."

Gil's hand shot out and wrapped around Lyle's throat. "You still don't know who you're dealing with, do you?"

Lyle muttered something unintelligible. He tried to pry Gil's hand away, but the police chief's fingers closed like a vise around his neck.

"Let's get one thing straight," Gil said through gritted teeth. "I don't work for you. You pay me to do a job and once that job is done, we're done. Understood?"

Lyle managed to nod.

"And as long as we're handing out free advice, here's something *you* best remember." He shoved Lyle up against a tree trunk. "The last person who started thinking of me as expendable lived just long enough to regret it."

CLAIRE WENT STRAIGHT home from the Crooked Ferret. She'd been hoping to find Connor's vehicle in the drive and a light on in the apartment, but no such luck. Even the upstairs apartment was dark. She half-expected the landlady to appear on the second-floor gallery and demand that Claire vacate the premises at once. Luckily, all remained silent.

She let herself in the front door, turned the dead bolt and then went back to the guest bathroom where she brushed her teeth and washed her face. Slipping into pajamas, she crawled between the sheets and folded her arms behind her head. She was almost too exhausted to sleep. Her mind kept racing with possibilities. What if Connor was lying hurt somewhere? What if he couldn't get to his phone to call for help?

On and on her thoughts raced until she finally focused them on Ben Dornan. He'd offered his expertise, but she knew nothing about him. Something told her there was more to his story than he let on. Why would an ex-cop seclude himself in a place where people came to disappear? What or who was he hiding from?

Still, his offer was tempting. She dealt in data and statistics. Searching for a missing person—much less her own brother—was out of her realm of expertise. An ex-cop would know the right questions to ask, the right places to search. He might pick up on clues that she would miss.

She mulled over the possibility until she finally grew drowsy. Ben was still floating around in her head, along with all those questions he'd asked about Connor. *Why do I get the feeling he knows more about my brother than he's saying?*

She turned on her side and fluffed her pillow. *And why am I so drawn to him even though I don't trust him?*

Suspicion and attraction made for a dangerous combination in her book.

And that was her last conscious thought until she woke up a little while later, her heart pounding. She hadn't been afraid of the dark for a very long time and yet she resisted opening her eyes, terrified of what she might find in the room with her.

No one was there, of course. Stress and worry had brought back the old nightmare. She'd been dreaming about the night their dad was murdered. The scenario was always the same. A noise awakened her. At seven years old, she was more curious than afraid. She crawled out of bed and padded to the top of the stairs where a strange voice halted her. Then recognizing her dad's voice a moment later, she crept down the stairs, across the foyer and into the dining room where she could peek into the kitchen. Her dad was sitting in a chair with his hands tied behind his back. Blood dripped from the side of his face and from the knife a man held to his throat.

The stranger loomed over him. "Where is it?" he demanded. "Where *is* it?" He repeated the question over and over like an automaton. *Where is it? Where is it? Where is it?*

Claire wanted to cover her ears to block the awful singsong. She wanted to close her eyes to all that blood and torture. Instinct and her dad's warnings kept her silent. She mustn't cry. She mustn't make a sound or let the stranger see her. She backed away from the door and retraced her steps to the foyer. Her brother met her on the stairs. They sat clutching hands until their dad's scream boomed through the dark house. *"Run!"*

Up the stairs, down the hallway, into her brother's room. *Lock the door. Hurry!*

Her brother knew what to do. They both did. Grab the phone their dad had hidden underneath the nightstand. Go out the window, climb up to the roof. *Hide, hide, hide.* Call the favorited number. Ask for Agent Ray. *He's in the house. He hurt my dad. Can you help us?*

Stay together. Stay hidden. Don't come out no matter what you hear.

As the remnants of the nightmare faded, Claire reached for her phone on the nightstand and glanced at the time. Not even midnight. She'd slept for only a couple of hours, and it was still the first day of her search for her brother.

Rolling onto her back, she stared at the ceiling. Hardly any sleep in over thirty-six hours had left her muddled and anxious. Little wonder the nightmare had returned. She closed her eyes and practiced the breathing technique a therapist had taught her years ago. No good. Her mind was once again strobing as the events of the past two days came back to her. Suddenly, she felt wide awake and her pulse quickened inexplicably. She lay still, listening to the house. All was silent. Not so much as the creak of a floorboard came to her, and yet she had the strangest feeling she was no longer alone.

Just nerves and exhaustion.

But she couldn't shake the notion of an intruder no matter how hard she squeezed her eyes closed or how tightly she gripped the covers. Swinging her legs over the side of the bed, she rose and hurried across the room to open the door a crack and peer down the hallway. Nothing moved. No sound came to her.

She eased down the hallway, through the kitchen and into the living area, her gaze sweeping the unfamiliar area as she stood shivering in her pajamas. When nothing jumped out at her, she drew a relieved breath and told herself to calm down. She was in a strange place and her brother was still missing. Her imagination was bound to go a little wild.

Moonlight streamed in through the wall of windows so that she could see straight out into the garden. She went over and checked the locks on the French doors. Everything was still secured. *Go back to bed and get some sleep.*

Instead, she hugged herself tightly as she stared out into the night, heart flailing against her rib cage. And then she saw him. The manifestation of her nightmare.

He stood at the edge of the garden, nearly invisible among the shadows. For a moment, she thought she might still be dreaming. But no. He was there. He was real.

Not her brother. She hoped not the killer. She was almost certain the man watching the apartment was Ben Dornan.

Chapter Seven

Day Two

When Claire awakened again, sunlight streamed in through a slit in the window blinds. A chirping bird in the tree outside the bedroom gave her a fleeting sense of peace. She threw an arm over her face and allowed herself a moment to drift before picking up her phone from the nightstand to check the time. After nine. Normally, she was up by seven and now she had a panicky feeling that something important may have happened while she slept in.

Throwing off the covers, she scrambled out of bed to shower, brush her teeth and dress in a clean pair of jeans from her suitcase. During her exploration of the apartment the day before, she'd taken note of a small laundry room next to the guest bathroom. Gathering up an armload of dirty clothes from her travels, she stuffed them in the washing machine without much regard to sorting. She tossed in a detergent pod, set the controls and went out to the kitchen to scrounge for breakfast. Blueberries from her purchases at the corner store, milk from the fridge and cereal from the pantry. Everything went into a bowl, which she carried over to the French doors to stare out at the garden while she ate.

No sign of a trespasser on this bright, summer morning. With sunlight spangling down through the mesh of oak and maple leaves, she could almost believe the figure she'd glimpsed last night had been nothing more than a relic from an old nightmare.

She didn't really believe that, of course. She'd been wide awake when she spotted the figure and so certain of his identity that she'd almost opened the door to confront him. Almost. No matter how many years passed without incident, she was still a product of her upbringing. Caution came naturally. So she'd watched and waited and the moment her attention wavered, he'd disappeared. Vanished like a ghost in the night, leaving her to wonder just what in the world Ben Dornan was up to.

Turning her back to the windows, she went into the kitchen to rinse her bowl and tidy up while she waited for the wash cycle to finish. At loose ends, she finally wandered over to Connor's desk and flipped through the pages of his sketch pad until she landed on the careworn countenance of Sean Greggory, the ex-priest with a questionable past. *Had* she seen him somewhere before? She was almost certain the man was a complete stranger, yet as she stared down at his likeness, she felt an odd sinking in the pit of her stomach followed by a tingle of alarm at the back of her neck. *Sometimes no explanation is needed. You just have to trust your gut.*

And what exactly did her gut tell her about Ben Dornan? She wanted to believe he was exactly who he said he was. A former law enforcement officer willing to help find her brother. It would be so comforting to have someone on her side, someone who knew the lay of the land, so to speak. San Miguel was a strange place. She needed someone watching her back but she wasn't at all sure she trusted Ben Dornan to do that.

A loud ding signaled the end of the spin cycle. Closing the sketchbook, she returned to the laundry room to transfer the wet clothing to the dryer. Afterward, she went out to the garden to look for footprints, following the flagstone path to the back of the property where she'd spotted the watcher by the wall. Kneeling, she examined the ground and surrounding vegetation. No footprints, no indentation from a cane. No broken twigs or trampled plants.

Once again, she considered the possibility that she'd dreamed the episode or maybe her imagination had played a trick on her in the moonlight. She'd been dead tired, after all. Either scenario seemed more likely than Ben Dornan watching the apartment, but then, how could she be sure of anything? By his own admission, people came to San Miguel to disappear. For all she knew, he could be hiding out from his own dark past.

She considered running a background check on him, but anything other than a cursory screen would be difficult. Her security clearance limited her access to the kind of government databases needed to request a deep dive on a particular individual.

Pondering how many favors she would need to call in to get the full picture, she took the flagstone path to the guest cottage. The structure echoed the architecture of the main house. Same stucco facade, same red-tile roof and French doors that opened out into the garden. She cupped her hands and peered through one of the panes. A face stared back at her.

Startled, she jumped back and lost her footing on a loose stone. She hit the ground hard, but immediately leaped to her feet, ready to fight or flee. The door opened and Marion Palmer stood gaping at her on the threshold.

Today Connor's landlady wore white jeans with flip-flops and a pink T-shirt that matched her lipstick. Her hair was pulled up into a high bun with blond tendrils exploding in every direction.

Blue eyes narrowing suspiciously, she leaned a shoulder against the doorframe and folded her arms. "What the hell, girl? You scared me half to death."

Claire was instantly contrite. "I'm sorry. I thought the guesthouse was empty."

"So you thought you'd just mosey on back here and have a snoop?"

"No. I mean…" She sighed and gave up the denial. "Actually, that's exactly what I did. Again, I apologize."

Marion shrugged. "At least you're honest." She glanced briefly over her shoulder into the dim interior. "Does this mean you've changed your mind about a short-term rental? The place is spic-and-span if you're interested."

"My plans are up in the air at the moment," Claire said. "I thought I'd stay in Connor's apartment until I hear from him. If that's okay with you," she added.

"I take it you found the spare key." She didn't wait for a response. "As long as Connor's fine with the arrangement, it's cool with me." She added a caveat. "So long as you don't throw any wild parties and the rent's paid on time."

Claire smiled. "No wild parties planned. And thank you." She tucked a strand of hair behind her ear. "Can I ask you a question? Were you home last night around midnight? I'm not trying to be nosy," she quickly assured her. "I happened to be looking out the window and I thought I saw someone out here."

"In the guesthouse?"

"In the garden. You didn't see or hear anything unusual, did you?"

"Slept like a log all night. Male or female?"

"Male, I think."

"You didn't recognize him?"

Claire hesitated. "It was dark, and he was over there by the wall. I didn't have a good view of him."

"Are you sure it wasn't Connor?"

"Definitely not," she said. "I would recognize him even in the dark. Besides, why wouldn't he have come into the apartment?"

"You tell me."

Her sly tone caught Claire off guard, and she found herself hesitant to continue the conversation. "Like I said, it could have been my imagination."

"Never hurts to keep an eye out. This town used to be a safe haven, but not so much anymore. Bad people are always passing through. Some of them decide to stay, unfortunately." Marion eyed her for a long moment. "*Still* no word from Connor? That's odd. You two didn't have a falling-out, did you?"

Claire frowned. "What makes you ask that?"

"It's just strange he hasn't been in touch. Or that he didn't come home last night. Seems like he might be trying to avoid you."

Claire felt defensive all of a sudden. "We didn't have a falling-out. Connor and I have always been close."

"Yet he never mentioned you to me. Or to anyone else in town that I know of. Like I said. Odd."

Okay, Claire thought. *You've made your point.*

"Did you check the Compound like I suggested?"

"I drove out there after we talked," Claire said. "The gate was locked and no one answered the intercom. The place looked deserted. Everyone was gone."

Marion's tone turned cryptic. "Just because no one answered the intercom doesn't mean no one was there. And anyway, if I had a missing brother, I wouldn't let a locked gate stop me from searching."

Claire was beginning to feel manipulated, as if Marion wanted to goad her into going back out to the Compound. For what reason, she couldn't imagine. "It doesn't make sense that he would be there," she said. "Even if he has things to take care of before the Compound reopens, wouldn't he come back to the apartment to sleep? At the very least, he would have answered my calls."

"Assuming he wanted to speak to you." Marion examined her nails. "If it makes you feel any better, cell coverage can be spotty out that way. That's why the creatives like it so much. It's quiet. It's secluded. Just nature and their art. And now with classes and everything else shut down, your brother would have the whole place to himself. He could hole up in one of the cabins and shut himself off from the world indefinitely if he wanted to."

Why was she being so insistent that Connor could still be at the Compound? Claire thought about her run-in with Gil Bennett outside the entrance and wondered again if his arrival had been the result of someone's tip. It almost seemed as if Marion wanted her to get caught trespassing, but why on earth would she care one way or the other?

Claire decided to keep her plans vague just in case. "Maybe I'll make another run out there later."

"You do that." Marion turned to lock the door. "In the meantime, I'll try to think of any other places you might look. Connor mentioned something about sketching the old missions in the San Antonio area. The closest one to us is Mission San Miguel. It's not on the trail. Too far away. You don't read much about it in the tourist brochures because it's mostly just piles of rock and a few crumbling walls. Lots of rattlesnakes, though."

"Someone told me he was sketching the missions for Sean Greggory's book," Claire said.

"That old drunk?" Marion scoffed as she pocketed the key. "He's been working on that book for the past decade—or so he claims—yet no one has ever read a word."

"You don't believe he's actually writing a book?"

Marion's expression turned derisive. "Who knows what he's up to? He's one of those people who just seemed to turn up in town one day. No family, no friends, no visible means of support. He's just…there. No one knows any more about him now than they did ten years ago."

"He's an ex-priest, isn't he?"

Marion gave her a sidelong glance. "Who told you that?"

Claire shrugged. "I heard it from someone."

"You can hear a lot of things around here. Gossip is a way of life. We'd all be bored out of our minds if we didn't indulge in a few spicy rumors now and then. Doesn't make any of them true. At least, not altogether true."

"I get that," Claire said. "But I'd still like to talk to him about Connor. He lives above the bar, doesn't he?"

"Last I heard, but I don't recommend a drop-in. He's not always sociable, especially if you catch him in a mood. Most days he's harmless. Just drinks and keeps to himself. But on a bad day, he can get pretty obnoxious. You never know when you might say something that will set him off. No, I don't recommend a visit." Her tone was adamant. "In fact, you'd do well to steer clear. Put it this way. You don't get kicked out of the priesthood for being a Boy Scout."

"Assuming the rumors are true," Claire said.

"True or not, that old buzzard creeps me out."

Yeah, me, too, Claire thought. Still, a brief conversation couldn't hurt. If her brother had agreed to sketch the missions, that could account for his absence.

She wanted to go back to the apartment and decide how to spend the rest of her day. Maybe a trip to Austin to visit some of Connor's friends might be in order. Or she could download a map and follow along the San Antonio Missions Trail—*El Camino de San Antonio Missions*. The less productive alternative was to wander around San Miguel in the hopes she might spot her brother. She had no intention of returning to the Compound. At least not yet. She couldn't shake the notion that Marion was trying to herd her back out there for some reason.

"This morning, I thought I might drive around for a bit and take in the sights," she said. "Any recommendations?"

"There's always the river if you like communing with nature. Rent yourself a tube and float away your troubles. At least that's what the sign says. Just don't forget your sunscreen," Marion advised. "Out on the water, the sun can be deceptive. If something cultural is more your speed, you can take in the big summer art festival in town. Starts today and runs all weekend. Lots of local arts and crafts, food trucks, live music. People come from all over."

"Sounds interesting."

"Deadly boring in my opinion, but this one has possibilities. The Arts Commission has decided to dedicate the event to dear old India. There's even talk about renaming the park in her honor." She twisted up a loose curl and tucked it underneath the rubber band. "Relatives of the current namesake might have something to say about that. Could create a few sparks if they make the announcement at the festival."

"Will some of her pieces be on display?" Claire was keen to see if she could detect Connor's hand in some of India's artwork.

"Oh, no doubt. You might even see some of Connor's work as well. The Compound will be well represented. In fact, I wouldn't be surprised if that's why you haven't heard from him. He's probably been out there getting ready for the festival."

Claire desperately wanted to believe that was true even as a little voice cautioned her about false hope. "What time does it start?"

"Runs from noon until sundown, but they'll be setting up early if you want a sneak peek."

"Thank you for telling me about it."

Marion shrugged. "No skin off my teeth. Maybe I'll see you there. The art doesn't do it for me—I've seen my fill of bluebonnet fields and barbed wire fences—but the people watching can be fun. You see all kinds."

"I'm looking forward to it." Claire turned to go back to the apartment, but Marion stopped her.

"Not so fast. My turn to ask you a question."

Claire was instantly on guard. "Okay."

"Who's your new friend?"

"I'm sorry?"

Marion gave her a knowing look. "Come on, now. Don't be coy. I saw you together at the Crooked Ferret last night. You two looked pretty chummy from where I was sitting. He's got a name, doesn't he?"

Claire sidestepped the question. "You were at the Crooked Ferret? I didn't see you."

Marion smirked. "I'm not surprised. You were otherwise occupied. Quite the eyeful, that one. I thought about stopping by to say hello, but you seemed deep in conversation. I didn't want to disturb you."

"You misunderstood the situation," Claire said. "I wasn't *with* him. I don't even know him. He invited himself over to my table."

"Is that so?" The woman's taunting manner vanished and she scrutinized Claire. "For real? You really don't know him?"

"I never saw him before yesterday," Claire said.

Marion seemed genuinely relieved. Her expression relaxed and her tone softened. "That makes what I have to say a little easier."

Claire stared back in confusion. "What do you mean?"

"The guy you *weren't* with. I've seen him before."

"I'm sure you have," Claire said with a shrug. "He says he has dinner at the Crooked Ferret several nights a week."

Marion's voice dipped. "That's not where I saw him. He was here, with Connor."

Claire tried not to show her unease, but all of a sudden her heart had started to thud and her mouth had gone dry. "You saw him in Connor's apartment?"

"In this very garden." Marion kept her voice low and conspiratorial. "They were having a pretty intense conversation. Just like the two of you were last night. Which is why I was sure you must know him. I thought he might be a family friend or something."

"He's not," Claire assured her. She took a moment to settle her pulse. "When did this meeting taking place?"

"I don't recall the exact day, but it was late in the afternoon. I remember all the long shadows across the garden. If I had to guess, I'd say it was a week or so before the murder. The weather was mild for June. Still cool enough that time of day to have the windows open. I heard voices coming from the garden. I looked out and saw them down here. I don't think they realized my windows were open or how easily their voices carried. It seemed to be a pretty heated discussion."

"Are you sure it was the same man?"

She put a hand on her hip and gave Claire another look. "Honey, you don't forget a face like that. It was him all right."

Claire nodded absently, her mind racing. "Could you tell what they were arguing about?"

"I only picked up a word here and there. Something about a necklace. A medallion, Connor called it."

"They were arguing about a necklace?" That made no sense to Claire. A *necklace?*

"That's what I heard."

"I don't doubt you. I just find it hard to imagine my brother caring enough about a piece of jewelry to argue over it. He's not into that kind of thing at all. He's never even owned a watch."

"Well, I don't think they were arguing about *his* necklace."

Her enigmatic tone caused Claire's heart to skip another beat. "No, I guess not."

Marion paused for a split second, then said, "You know who did have an interest in unusual jewelry? A passion, you might even say."

Claire shook her head slowly, her stomach knotted with dread.

"India Cortez, that's who. Our little Ivy." Marion looked quite pleased with herself. "She had an extensive collection. So large, in fact, you never saw her wear the same piece twice. The really expensive pieces came from her husband before the divorce. The result of a guilty conscience, I always figured. I'm sure he cheated on her. India was no prize, let me tell you. Cold as ice and never much of a looker." Her bitterness toward the dead woman crept back in. "Still, she did have a way with men. I'll give her that."

Claire ignored the cattiness. "Why would they argue over a piece of India Cortez's jewelry?"

"That's what I kept asking myself."

"And?"

"I can only guess, of course, but I'm pretty good at reading body language. Connor seemed to be holding his own, but the other man was definitely the aggressor. I got a very strong sense that your Mr. Cool was trying to get your brother to do something he didn't want to do. You know what a five-finger discount is, don't you?"

"He wanted Connor to steal a piece of India's jewelry?"

"You said it, I didn't."

Connor, what have you gotten yourself mixed up in?

There had to be a rational explanation. Connor would never be party to anything criminal. Never in a million years would he follow in their father's footsteps. Not when they'd both been eye witnesses to how that particular story had ended.

Claire tried to remain calm, but her stomach roiled in distress. She took several breaths and tried to shake off a terrible sense of foreboding. "Did you tell the police about the argument?"

"I never gave it another thought until I saw you with that guy last night. Mr. Cool. Even then, it took me a while to place him, but I knew I'd seen him somewhere before."

"His name is Ben Dornan," Claire said. "Does that ring a bell?"

"No, but who even knows if that's his real name? It's not unusual for a con man to have several aliases."

"A con man?"

"San Miguel may still look peaceful and picturesque, but there's something dark about this town." Marion paused, her eyes glittering like sapphires in the morning light. "You can tell me to buzz off if I'm getting too personal, but you seem a bit naïve so I'm going to give you another piece of advice. Be careful with that guy."

Claire didn't think of herself as naïve. Far from it. She felt as if she'd been on guard her whole life. But maybe that was the problem. Maybe she'd fooled herself into thinking she was immune from deceit.

Even from her own brother.

A LITTLE WHILE LATER, Claire returned to the apartment and tried to distract herself by finishing her laundry and making the bed. Connor had always been a bit of a neat freak so there wasn't much else to do in the apartment but brood.

She kept going back to the sketchbook and memorizing the faces. Only after she made a few passes through the book did she realize that one of the pages was missing. The slice was so precise she hadn't even noticed it the day before. Or had someone come into the apartment while she was gone and cut out one of the sketches? Or worse, while she slept. The same someone she'd spotted in the garden watching the apartment. The same person, according to Marion Palmer, who had argued with Connor about a necklace days before India Cortez had been murdered.

Once again, she had to wonder about Ben's motive. He'd seemed sincere in his offer to help and she could have sworn his concern for Connor was genuine. But a con artist knew how to manipulate. She had to make sure her attraction didn't cloud her judgement.

The mystery of Connor's absence was getting more twisted by the hour. Was he deliberately avoiding her as Marion had suggested? But why? Why send an urgent message asking her to come to San Miguel, only to vanish upon her arrival?

She couldn't even go to the police for fear they'd misconstrue her brother's disappearance as proof he'd fled town after the murder. Ben had warned her about trusting Gil Bennett, but what if he had his own reasons for avoiding the authorities?

Try as she might, she couldn't stop the whirlwind of images and dire possibilities raging inside her head. She had to get out of the apartment. Into the sunshine. Into the fresh air. Her brother's apartment had suddenly become as claustrophobic as a cave.

Dropping the sketch pad into her tote, she changed from sandals to sneakers and left the apartment with every intention of checking out the art festival in town. However, at the end of the driveway, she wavered, then turned right instead of left, which would have taken her downtown. Heading out into the countryside, she lowered her window, letting the warm wind whip through her hair as she pressed the accelerator.

She told herself she just wanted to drive and clear her head. The scenery was beautiful in the morning light, the fields and ditches aglow with vervain, primrose and purple coneflowers. The heady sweetness of honeysuckle drifted through the open window, followed by the fainter, violet notes of the huisache trees.

Before she knew it, she found herself driving past the Compound again. The gates were still closed and presumably locked. She had no real intention of finding a way inside, but Marion's suggestion that Connor might be sequestered somewhere on the premises had triggered another glimmer of hope, along with mounting anxiety. She could no longer pretend everything was okay, that her brother would turn up with his charming smile and a reasonable explanation at a time and place of his choosing. Connor would never deliberately put her through needless worry. He was her rock just as she had always tried to be his. They were linked in a way that was even stronger than their twin connection. The experiences of their early childhood had forged a bond that had held strong even during long periods of physical separation. Until recently. Now Claire had to admit to herself that her brother had been keeping things from her. Important things. Maybe even dark things.

She found a place to turn around and drove past the Compound entrance a second time. There was hardly any traffic at that time of morning. She didn't have to worry about blocking the road as she slowed and crept past the gate. About a hundred yards from the entrance, she found another place to turn around, and pulled onto a narrow dirt road that was nearly hidden by a thicket of Texas mountain laurels. In spring, the blossoms would perfume the air with the scent of grape soda. Now the glossy leaves and twisted branches provided cover for her vehicle from the main road.

She inched as far along the dirt ruts as she dared, killed the engine and got out. Now she truly was trespassing on private property, but she ignored her reservations as she hiked back to the main road. Crossing to the other side, she made her way along the shoulder until she came to the corner of the limestone wall that surrounded the Compound. She paused, glancing around uneasily as she gathered her nerve. What if Marion really had manipulated her into coming out here? She could be walking into some kind of ambush or trap for all she knew. But if there was even a small chance that Connor was inside, then she had to take that chance. He needed her help. Nothing else mattered at the moment.

Once again, she lamented her lack of field experience. She didn't even own a weapon, though she knew how to use one. Crime analysis wasn't very useful in scaling a limestone wall. Instead, she used her common sense.

The wall was too high to climb, but a nearby live oak with thick branches drooping over the top caught her eye. She hadn't climbed a tree since she was a kid, but desperate times called for desperate measures. Securing her bag across her body, she reached for the lowest branch and hoisted herself up. She wouldn't go too high, just far enough to crawl along one of the gnarled limbs and jump down on the other side.

Easier said than done. A jagged twig snagged her tote, another her jeans. Finally, she was over the wall. Lowering herself from the branch, she dropped down onto a cushion of grass and wildflowers. Pausing yet again to get her bearings, she swept her gaze over the wooded landscape until she glimpsed a roofline rising through the treetops. She set off in that direction, dead leaves crackling beneath her feet.

Bees buzzed around the trumpet-shaped flowers of the desert willows, and overhead, a red-tailed hawk floated on air currents. On any other day, she would have enjoyed her trek through the woods. The scents and scenery were mesmerizing. But all she could think about on that fragrant summer morning was her brother. *Please, please let him be all right.*

Located on the banks of the Medina River, the Creative Collective, i.e. the Compound, consisted of six cabins—presumably where guests and students stayed—separated from the main house by a common building divided into individual studio spaces. India's private studio was a grander affair. Like her home, the rustic structure was constructed of limestone, cedar and long windows that looked out over the river and into the woods beyond.

The private studio was where her body had been found suspended from the ceiling.

Claire put up a hand to shade her eyes. Sunlight bouncing off the glass walls dazzled her vision, and for a moment, she could almost believe that India Cortez stood inside, staring at her through the windows.

Shaking off the illusion, Claire decided to search the cabins first. She wasn't quite ready to tackle India's home and certainly not that private studio. She'd have to work up her nerve for that.

Knocking on a cabin door, she kept a watchful eye on the immediate vicinity as she waited for an answer. Nothing. She called Connor's cell and put an ear to the door to listen. Silence. She circled the structure, peering in the windows before moving on to the rest of the cabins. The initial search took her about thirty minutes. Afterward, there was nothing left to do but check out India's home and studio.

She climbed the porch steps and knocked loudly on the heavy, carved door. She even called out to her brother. "Connor? Are you in there?" Nothing came back to her but the eerie echo of her own voice. *Are you in there...in there... in there?*

Circling around to the back, she did the same thing at the rear entrance before turning her attention to the breezeway that connected the main house to the studio. Her gaze lifted to the sloped roof that accommodated two large skylights and a vaulted ceiling.

She could see through the nearest window all the way to the other end of the studio. All was quiet inside. Still, she hesitated, paralyzed by visions of the murder and that ever-deepening dread. She was almost relieved to find police tape crisscrossing the entrance.

See? You can't go inside. The door is still barricaded. No visitors allowed.

She might have turned around then and there if not for the memory of Marion's goading voice: *If I had a missing brother, I wouldn't let a locked gate stop me from searching.*

A light breeze carried the intoxicating fragrance from the magnolia blossoms that nestled in glossy leaves over-head. The perfume hung heavy on the morning heat, rich and cloying. Above the slanted roof, the blue sky was cloud-less. A more idyllic setting Claire could hardly imagine and yet just days ago, something dark and evil had invaded this heavenly space.

The moments ticked by while she bolstered her courage. No one else was about. She was all alone in this deserted place, and common sense told her not to linger. If Connor was here, he would have come out by now.

She turned in a slow circle to scan the immediate area. Nothing. Then she moved quickly down the breezeway to the studio entrance before she could change her mind. The yellow crime scene tape warned her not to enter. She cer-tainly wasn't prepared to break in, but when she gave the door a gentle push, it opened with barely a creak. Glancing over her shoulder, she bent to ease through the tape.

Other than looking for her brother, she had no clear motivation. No idea what she expected to find or even what she hoped to accomplish. The studio beckoned, and if she were honest, a morbid curiosity responded.

The interior was far more utilitarian than the exterior suggested. The floors were concrete, stained with an intricate mosaic of paint dribbles. Light streamed in unfiltered through the tall windows and overhead, heavy cedar beams supported the two-story vaulted ceiling. The furnishings were rustic and practical—wooden worktables, stools on steel casters, easels in various sizes, large cabinets of long, flat drawers to accommodate art paper and canvases.

Claire took it all in from the doorway, then stepped inside and closed the door before she lost her nerve. As she moved deeper into the studio, her gaze lifted and froze on the massive wings suspended from one of the beams. The store clerk's description of the murder scene came rushing back to her: *The killer used a rope and pulley to hoist her up to the ceiling where a pair of giant wings had been mounted for an upcoming exhibit. My friend's cousin said she was still alive at that point. They could tell by the blood patterns or something. He said the killer probably stood there and watched her bleed out. If she screamed, no one heard her.*

Someone had been in to clean up the studio, but she could see deep stains on the concrete floor. She could also smell fresh paint. It seemed odd to her that a crime scene would have been so quickly and thoroughly scrubbed, but the police had undoubtedly been in immediately to gather trace and forensic evidence.

The snowy wings simultaneously fascinated and repelled her. The tips had been dipped in red paint, almost as if India had had a premonition of her own demise. Claire shivered, though the space was warm, almost sticky. And so very quiet. No sound came to her from the deep recesses of the building, nothing so much as the hum of an AC unit or the drum of her own heartbeat. But as she stood gazing up at those blood-tipped wings, she could almost imagine the heat of a phantom breath on the back of her neck.

Goose bumps popped along her bare arms despite the common sense that told her no ghost was afoot. No human, either. She was alone in the space where India Cortez had drawn her last breath. That alone was a chilling thought.

Shifting her gaze from the wings, she walked around the space, examining the projects that had been abandoned on the worktables and easels, and a few scattered canvases that were propped against the walls. Maybe it was her imagination or the power of suggestion, but she could have sworn she detected her brother's hand in some of the pieces.

Captivated by the artwork and ever cognizant of those hovering wings, Claire failed to recognize the stealthy signals that would have alerted her she was no longer alone. The swish of the door. A draft of air. Soft footfalls against the concrete floor.

The hairs at the back of her neck lifted a split second before a hand fell lightly on her shoulder and she whirled with a gasp.

Chapter Eight

Claire's eyes widened as her hand flew to her heart. Ben put a finger to his lips to silence the scream that seemed to tremble on her lips. He pointed to the windows that looked out on a wide parking area beneath the trees. Reluctantly, her gaze slipped from his face to the view. A black SUV with a light bar across the top and an insignia on the door had pulled up outside the studio. A moment later, the door opened and the police chief exited the vehicle.

Ben's mind flashed back to the meeting he'd witnessed at the river the night before. Gil Bennett and Lyle Fincher were obviously engaged in a criminal enterprise—drug trafficking, most likely—that had been compromised by India Cortez's murder and the subsequent influx of federal agents. Ben wasn't particularly concerned about their extracurricular activities at the moment. His current situation notwithstanding, he could always plant a bug in the right ear and then stand back while the appropriate authorities handled the matter without his involvement. No need to blow his cover.

However, Lyle's insistence on a speedy arrest did worry him, though he had to admit railroading Connor Tinsley made a certain amount of sense from their perspective. If they could drum up enough proof that India had been murdered by an employee—even better, one who stood to inherit a portion of her estate—the investigation then became the local police's jurisdiction. No cartel connection, no Feds. Ben wondered if Connor had somehow gotten wind that he was about to be picked up. That would explain why he'd gone off the grid so suddenly. Anyone on the run these days knew enough to ditch a cell phone. Plus, his silence gave Claire plausible deniability if questioned by the police. If she didn't know where he was, she couldn't incriminate herself or inadvertently lead the cops to his hiding place.

All this went through Ben's mind in the space of a heartbeat as Claire's gaze darted back to him. He pulled her down behind a worktable, out of view from the windows.

She lifted a questioning brow. "What now?"

He angled his head in the direction of the rear door as he said in a hushed voice, "Back exit. Stay low."

Using the worktables and easels for cover, they made their way to the back of the building only to find that the glass door wouldn't budge. The dead bolt could only be turned with a key, which was missing from the lock.

Ben made a quick assessment. They were sitting ducks inside the studio. Any minute now, Bennett would come through the main entrance and spot them. What excuse could either of them offer for being inside India Cortez's private space, let alone slipping through a police barricade? That was assuming they would even be given the opportunity to explain.

He whirled and pointed to a wooden door across the room that he hoped was a side exit. The last thing they needed was a confrontation with Gil Bennett. An arrest would lead to too many questions and quite possibly a background check. And if things got physical, he wasn't altogether certain he could handle Bennett in his current state, even if he had the age advantage. What he lacked in agility he could make up for with training and experience. But a bad knee was a bad knee. Bennett was wiry, ruthless and armed, a man not to be underestimated no matter his age.

By this time, they were on the other side of the studio. Ben opened the door and peered inside. The narrow space beyond was windowless and smelled faintly of turpentine. A storage closet of some sort. Not ideal. They would be trapped inside if Bennett decided to explore. At the moment, however, he didn't see an alternative. The only option was to hide and bide their time.

He took quick note of the shelves of supplies and solvents that could be used as a weapon or a diversion. Then he stepped back to allow Claire to enter. He came in behind her and left the door cracked so that he could track Bennett's movements if and when he entered the studio.

The space was dark except for a sliver of light from the doorway. They were standing so close Ben could feel the warmth radiating from her body. He closed his eyes briefly and regrouped. The close quarters and the shock of finding her in the studio had momentarily thrown him off his game.

Earlier, when he first came into the studio, he'd been so stunned to find her gazing at the wings that he almost convinced himself she was a mirage or an apparition. Her attention had been rapt, almost dreamlike. The light shining down through the skylights had sparked off the gold highlights in her hair and shimmered on her suntanned skin. She looked unearthly standing beneath those wings. Ben had paused inside the door for the longest moment to observe her, mesmerized by her stillness.

And now here they were, scrunched together in a storage closet. He didn't dare move a muscle for fear of inadvertently deepening the contact. As if sensing his dilemma, she glanced up at him. He felt her tremble before she turned back to face the studio.

A few moments later, the breezeway door opened and Gil

Bennett stepped through. He paused just inside the entrance to examine the space. "Anybody here?" His tone was gruff and all business.

Ben could sense Claire's tension, but he kept his attention on Bennett. He didn't dare look away because a quick response might be the only thing that could save them.

The police chief sauntered into the room, his boots click-clacking on the concrete floor. "Anybody here?" he called a second time, but his tone had changed. Gone were the sharp edges of a police chief on the hunt for a suspect. His voice took on an almost taunting quality. "Come out, come out, wherever you are."

Claire glanced up at Ben. He lifted a shoulder and shook his head. He had no idea what the man was up to. Was it possible Bennett had seen one or both of them enter the studio? Or had he driven out here looking for Connor? If he was on official business, why had he come alone? And why the mocking tone? If he knew they were hiding in the storage room, why not force their hand?

He strolled about the studio as if he had all the time in the world, sliding a hand along the edge of a worktable here, adjusting the position of a rolling stool there. Then, his back to the storage closet, he tipped his head to the ceiling. Like Claire, he stood motionless for the longest time, apparently captivated by the spectacle of those giant, red-tipped wings. Or did a memory hold him enthralled?

The blood splatters had already been cleaned up, the windows washed and the walls freshly painted. But the concrete floor beneath the wings had been indelibly stained. Bennett had positioned himself in the center of the darkest stain. The very spot where India had bled out. The old adage about killers returning to the scene of their crimes flicked through Ben's head. Sometimes they really did.

Claire touched his sleeve. He acknowledged her unspoken question with a slight shake of his head. *Your guess is as good as mine.*

Bennett remained under that strange spell for several minutes before he suddenly whirled, as if startled from his reverie by an imperceptible disturbance. Ben heard nothing. Neither he nor Claire had made a sound, but something had obviously spooked the man. His hyperawareness reminded Ben of that moment at the river when the police chief had vectored in on the spot where he was hidden. Apparently, Gil Bennett had a keen intuition. Or maybe Ben just had a knack for being in the wrong place at the wrong time.

He shifted slightly, taking pressure off his injured knee. By this time, Bennett had started to circle the studio, not so casually this time. He opened drawers in worktables and cabinets, becoming visibly agitated the longer he rifled through the contents. The more exasperated he became, the more frenzied his search. He swore repeatedly as he jerked open drawer after drawer, the string of four-letter words culminating in a frustrated explosion. "Damn it, where the hell is it?"

Beside him, Claire gasped. Ben gave her a warning tap. She nodded and clapped a hand to her mouth.

Bennett swung around, his eyes narrowing as he seemed to notice the storage closet for the first time. He took a few steps in their direction, his hand resting on the grip of his Glock.

Claire clutched Ben's arm, her fingers digging into his flesh. Another second and the police chief would be at the door. Adrenaline started to pump as Ben braced himself. Surprise would be their best chance. All in, all at once. Take him down before he had time to get off a shot.

Bennett paused, cocking his head as if trying to decide whether or not he'd actually heard a noise. His hesitation worked to their advantage. A staticky call on the radio clipped to his belt claimed his attention. He used his shoulder mic to respond and then with one last glance around the room, he strode from the studio.

Ben waited a beat, then cautiously pushed open the door and they both stepped out. He went over to the window, pressing himself against the wall as he stared out. A thin cloud of dust trailed behind the SUV as Gil Bennett headed down the driveway.

"He's gone." He glanced back at Claire with a grimace. "That was close."

She looked pale and tense as she nodded. "Too close. For a minute there, I was certain he'd open the storage room door and find us."

"You and me both," Ben said. "I'm not sure how we would have talked our way out of that one."

She shuddered. "Assuming he would have waited for an explanation."

"Good point. He strikes me as the shoot first and ask questions later type." Ben leaned a shoulder against the window frame as his gaze swept the grounds. He thought again of that discussion he'd overheard at the river. Gil Bennett was not a man to be taken lightly. He was armed, dangerous and if last night was any indication, up to his neck in illegal activities.

So what had he been looking for in India Cortez's studio? And why now? The murder had happened nearly a week ago. As chief of police, he would have had any number of opportunities to go through her things.

Ben glanced over his shoulder, his gaze zeroing in on the stained concrete beneath the wings. The fact that the area had already been cleaned and the walls painted was a little surprising, but not suspicious. Every homicide investigation was different, and sometimes a scene could be released in a matter of hours. Standard procedure would have had the forensics team at the studio immediately. The investigators would have spent hours combing through every inch of the space, collecting evidence before and after the body was removed. A hasty cleanup would only be suspect if it occurred before the scene had been processed or if the original DNA samples were deliberately destroyed or contaminated or if the chain of custody was compromised.

He went back to his original question. Since the police had already released the scene, what had the chief been looking for?

Ben had a rule about jumping to conclusions, but he couldn't ignore that overheard conversation or the fact that Bennett's behavior was strange. The taunting quality of his voice…his mesmerized focus on those wings…just plain odd. Lyle Fincher had accused him of being secretly in love with India. Had he been thinking about that unrequited love as he stared up at those wings? Had he been lamenting on what might have been…or reliving a revenge kill?

So much for not jumping to conclusions, Ben thought morosely. But he was only human, and Bennett's frantic search had raised a lot of questions. One thing seemed obvious. His visit to India Cortez's studio had little to do with his position as chief of police. He'd been on a personal mission. Whatever he'd been looking for was important enough to make him desperate. That brought up a question of timing. The contents of the studio would have been thoroughly examined during reconstruction. Anything suspicious would have been bagged, labeled and logged into evidence. Either the elusive item could only be identified as incriminating by Bennett or he had reason to believe someone had hidden something in the studio after the scene had been released.

Ben's mind went immediately to Mia's cousin. Hector Zavala sometimes worked at the Compound as a handyman. Over the years, he and India had become friends. It stood to reason that she would give him a key to the front gate and possibly to the studio. According to Mia, Hector had grown superstitious of the silver medallion. If he truly believed the piece to be cursed, maybe he decided to get rid of it before he left town, hiding it in the one place where the police had already searched. If Gil Bennett had been looking for the medallion, then that meant—

"What do you see out there?" Claire asked anxiously.

"What?" Ben shook himself out of his deep reverie and glanced back at her. "Nothing at the moment. Just keeping watch to make sure he's gone."

She looked alarmed. "Do you think he's coming back?"

"Probably not immediately, but we should think about getting out of here," he said. "We'll give it another minute or two just to make sure he's really gone. Meanwhile, stay away from the windows."

The dust had already settled along the driveway, but Ben knew better than to relax prematurely. If Gil Bennett knew, or even suspected, that they were hiding in the storage closet, his abrupt departure could have been a ruse to draw them out. He could easily double back on foot and catch them unprepared. Why he would do so, Ben could only guess. Maybe he thought they could lead him to either the medallion or to Connor or to both.

"What do you think he was looking for?" Claire asked.

"Your guess is as good as mine. Somehow, I don't think he was here on official business."

"His behavior was bizarre, wasn't it? It wasn't just my imagination."

"No, he was definitely acting strange," Ben agreed.

She ran a hand up and down her arm. "This is new for me. I'm not used to hiding in closets from trigger-happy police chiefs. I find it all a bit nerve-wracking."

"Just a bit?" He smiled before turning back to the window, probing the wooded area beyond the cabins where the trees could provide cover for an interloper.

Behind him, she said in a strained voice, "I just realized something. You're not using a cane today. You're barely even walking with a limp. It's like you made a miraculous recovery overnight."

He shrugged as he glanced back at her. "Hardly miraculous. I have good and bad days. Today is a good one. Yesterday, not so much."

"If you say so."

He frowned at her tone but decided to let it go. "What are you doing out here anyway? And how did you get here? I didn't see your vehicle outside."

She lifted her chin, her gaze direct. It seemed that her earlier nerves had vanished. Now, she seemed to have a bone to pick, but he had no idea what he'd done to upset her. He could have sworn they'd ended last night's conversation on good terms.

"I hid my car down the road in a laurel thicket. Then I climbed over the wall."

"That was resourceful."

"Not really. Just common sense. I assumed the front gate was still locked, so I knew I had to find another way in. And I didn't want to get caught trespassing. Getting thrown in jail isn't exactly on my bucket list, especially after what we just witnessed. As to your first question…" She paused. "I could ask you the same thing. Why are *you* here?"

"You first."

She looked as if she might dig in her heels, but then she shrugged. "Isn't it obvious? I was hoping to find Connor. Or at least, some kind of clue. He didn't come back to the apartment last night. I thought he might be here working."

"You haven't heard from him at all?"

She shook her head. "It's been well over thirty-six hours

since his last text. Not one word from him in the whole time I've been in San Miguel. That's not like him. He would never purposely worry me this way. I know it's not helpful, but I just keep picturing him unconscious in a ditch somewhere."

"Not at all helpful," Ben agreed. "That kind of thinking does no one any good. And anyway, thirty-six hours really isn't that long. There could be any number of reasons why he hasn't been in touch."

"Such as?"

"I don't know. Maybe he got tired of answering endless questions about the murder. Maybe he just needs a little space."

She seemed to consider the possibility for a moment. "But why wouldn't he just tell me?"

"You'll have to ask him. I'm as much in the dark as you are."

"Are you, though?"

"Of course, I am. If I knew where he was, I'd tell you."

She looked as if she wanted to challenge his assertion, but then she sighed. "I could barely sleep a wink last night. I was so hoping to find him here this morning. His landlady seemed confident that he would be holed up in one of the cabins working on an exhibit for the art fair in town."

"His landlady? You mean Marion Palmer?"

"You know her?"

"Only by reputation. Apparently, she's a known busybody."

"She doesn't think too highly of you, either," Claire muttered.

"That's funny because I've never even met the woman."

"Yet you had no problem forming an opinion of her based solely on hearsay."

"You're right," he conceded. "I should know better."

"Although you probably weren't far from the truth," Claire allowed.

"What exactly did she have to say about me?"

"She saw us talking at the Crooked Ferret last night. Apparently, she thinks I'm a bit naïve. She warned me about trusting the wrong people. And I have to say, she has a point. I'm beginning to wonder if there's anyone in this town I can trust."

"You trust Connor, don't you? And, despite Marion Palmer's warning, you can trust me, too."

"I'd like to believe you," she said.

"Then trust me when I say, we really need to get out of here."

She stubbornly resisted his suggestion. "I'm not leaving until I've had a chance to search the place myself. It'll go faster if you help." She shuffled through a stack of papers on one of the worktables.

He decided to confront her attitude head-on. "Do you have a beef with me this morning?"

She avoided his gaze. "What do you mean?"

"You seem different. Distant. Have I said something to offend or upset you?"

She lifted her gaze to the wings. "This place disturbs me. We're standing in the room where a woman was brutally murdered barely a week ago. Not just murdered, but tortured. Something would have to be terribly wrong with a person if they weren't affected by what happened here."

He tried not to read anything into *that* observation. "Are you sure that's all it is?"

"What else could it be?"

"I don't know," he said. "I'm hoping you'll tell me."

She frowned. "Why do you care so much? You barely know me."

"That's true. But I feel like we have a connection." He softened his voice. "Am I wrong?"

She glanced away, but not before he saw something spark in her eyes. "I don't know what we have... Ben."

The hesitation and the slight emphasis she put on his name drew a warning prickle across his scalp. She knew something. Whether someone had been whispering in her ear or she'd found out something on her own, he had no idea. But her alarms bells had definitely been triggered.

He tried to play off her concern with a shrug. "You're right. I'm here for the same reason as you. I'm looking for clues, signs, evidence—anything that might hint at Connor's whereabouts. He couldn't have just vanished into thin air."

"That's another thing," she said. "Why do you care so much about my brother? The two of you are just acquaintances, right? You only know him casually from the bar."

"I can't be concerned about an acquaintance? You're obviously worried about him. I'd like to help if I can. I feel like we'd make a good team. We both bring a certain set of skills to the table."

She paused yet again as if considering the possibility. "I appreciate the offer, but there's a reason I told Mia not to give you my number. This is personal for me. I can find my brother on my own."

"Just think about it."

Connor had told him once that Claire worked for a government contractor with deep contacts in the Department of Homeland Security. Maybe she'd had someone run a background check on him. That would explain her attitude. His name wouldn't have generated any hits from a casual search, and the files pertaining to his undercover work would still be classified. The dearth of information on one Ben Dornan would have raised serious doubts. The former law enforcement officer that he claimed to be would have left a very visible cyber trail. Citations, citizen complaints, internal affairs reports, performance reviews, disciplinary board findings—all a matter of public record. He had to figure out what she'd discovered and what assumptions she'd drawn before he slipped and said too much.

But he'd have to give something in order to get something in return. "As it happens, I'm looking into another missing person incident. The two searches could overlap, so don't think I'm going against your wishes. San Miguel is a small town. We're bound to run into one another again at some point."

"Wait." Her tone turned anxious. "Someone else is missing? Someone connected to my brother?"

"Maybe," Ben hedged. "It's a long shot, but I'm not ruling out the possibility."

"Who is it?"

"I probably shouldn't say too much without permission from the family."

She rounded the table and leaned against the edge as she folded her arms, looking defensive and aggressive at the same time. "Is he Mia Soto's cousin?"

Ben stared at her in surprise. "How do you know about Hector?"

"Lyle Fincher mentioned last night that the bar was short-handed since Mia's cousin disappeared. And Mia is the one who told me about you so I just assumed—"

"What else did Fincher say?"

His sharpness seemed to take her aback, but she answered without hesitation. "He figured Hector had gone off to visit his girlfriend."

"He didn't. Mia has already talked to her."

"Well, then…" She trailed off. "How long has he been missing?"

"He left his mother's house in Matamoras two days ago on his way back to San Miguel. No one has seen or heard from him since."

"That sounds ominous." Her shield dropped, and for a moment, he saw the flicker of cold fear in her eyes. "And you think his disappearance is somehow connected to Connor?"

"I said it's possible."

"Did they know each other?"

"They both worked for India Cortez, so chances are good they at least met a few times."

"They both *worked* for her?" Her gaze turned incredulous. "That doesn't sound like a long shot to me. Why would you wait until now to tell me this?"

Ben was careful how he answered. "I only met you last night and you made it pretty clear—then and now—that you aren't interested in my help."

"Yet here you are anyway." Her temper flared. "You should have told me. Now I'm beginning to wonder what else you're keeping from me."

"What do you think I'm keeping from you? I already told you. I don't know where Connor is. That's the truth."

She glared at him. "If you really care about the truth, you'll admit that he's more than an acquaintance."

"As I said last night, I see him in the bar on occasion—"

"Just *stop.*" Her tone turned accusatory. "I know you know him."

Now they were finally getting somewhere. It seemed she'd reached the end of her patience, and now all Ben had to do was wait for the reveal. He kept his expression neutral as he watched her.

His silence seemed to provoke her. "Don't just stand there. Admit it."

He lifted a shoulder. "Admit what?"

Her cheeks flushed with anger. "You were at Connor's apartment a week before India's murder. The two of you argued in the garden. Apparently, you were trying to get him to do something he didn't want to do. Like steal an expensive necklace from India Cortez. A medallion of some sort."

Ben tried not to react to the accusation, but her revelation jolted him. She knew a lot more than he'd anticipated. Somehow, she'd found out about the medallion, probably from Connor's landlady. Marion Palmer was one of those people who lived for gossip, which was why Ben normally avoided her at all costs. That day in the garden had been an exception. He'd been on his way out of town and had only stopped by for a quick update. Connor had had his opinion of how best to proceed with their plan and Ben had his. With no significant movement in weeks, Connor was losing patience. He wanted to shake things up to try and flush James Stroud out into the open. Ben had been adamant that they hold the line. One wrong move and not only would their lives be at risk, Stroud could disappear for another twenty-five years.

There had been no argument, no falling-out, no coercion on either side, but Ben understood how the discussion could have been interpreted the wrong way. And Claire was hearing everything through the filter of a third party. Marion Palmer had undoubtedly put her own spin on the confrontation. Now that Claire's suspicions had been heightened, she was looking at everything in a new light. She'd probably gone back over their previous conversation and was now asking herself a different set of questions. Sooner or later, she'd start connecting the dots and then Ben would have a real situation on his hands. Either he'd have to break his word to Connor and bring her into the plan, or he'd have to find a way to convince her that her presence in San Miguel would do more harm than good. Either scenario would take a great deal of finesse.

"Well?" she demanded. "Aren't you going to deny it?"

"It's not what you think."

She sighed. "It never is with people like you."

"People like me?"

"Liars."

Her assessment stung more than it should have under the circumstances. "You don't know anything about me," he said quietly.

Her eyes glittered. "I know you're hiding something. I know you tried to get my brother to do something he didn't want to do. How dare you do that to him? Our father was a criminal. Did he tell you that? He was murdered in cold blood because of something he'd done before Connor and I were born. And now you're trying to get my brother to follow in his footsteps."

"Your father was murdered?"

Too late, she realized she'd spilled too much. She looked instantly regretful, but she tried to cover the slip with a meaningless platitude. "What's past is past. We're talking about Connor."

Ben decided to let her off the hook. Instead of pressing her for details, he merely nodded. They were heading into very dangerous territory, and he had no idea how she'd respond or who she'd run to for help if she found out the man who murdered her father—and his—might be lurking around the next corner. It still sounded farfetched even to Ben.

She folded her arms and waited to debunk any explanation he offered. He chose his words carefully.

"If you think coercing your brother is even remotely possible, then you don't know him as well as you think you do. Connor is one of the most moral people I've ever met. And one of the most stubborn. No one can talk him into doing anything he doesn't want to do, let alone something criminal."

"I know that." She looked a little flustered by his steadfast defense of her brother. "That doesn't mean you wouldn't try."

"I didn't."

The anger seemed to drain out of her. She looked per-plexed and forlorn, and for a moment, Ben just wanted to make that look go away, no matter what he had to tell her.

"What were you arguing about?" she asked. "Please, just tell me."

"I'm sorry. I can't."

"Why?"

He closed the distance between them. He thought she might retreat, but she held her ground. "You deserve an ex-planation, but not here, not now and not by me. You need to talk to Connor."

"He's not here," she said in frustration. "That's the whole point of this conversation."

"And that's why I'm asking you to be patient for a little while longer. This isn't the time or place. Claire—" he placed his hands lightly on her shoulders "—do you really want to help your brother?"

"You know I do."

"Then go home. Go back to DC and wait to hear from him. It's what he wants."

"Then why did he ask me to come here?"

Ben was still trying to figure that one out.

"He said he needed me. He texted me the address of his apartment and told me to hurry. Does that sound like he wants me to go home?" She pulled her phone out of her bag and scrolled to the message, then held up the screen for Ben to read for himself: I need you. 1136 Riverbend Road. Hurry!

Terse and cryptic, the message didn't sound like Connor. Not in tone, not in content. He would never deliberately drag his sister into a dangerous situation. The opposite, in fact. He wanted her far away from San Miguel while they tried to unravel James Stroud's assumed identity. If Connor hadn't sent that message, who had? And why?

Obviously, something had gone very wrong while Ben had

been in Houston. Connor had run into trouble. Either he'd somehow been strong-armed into sending his sister a message or—perhaps more likely—someone had sent the text from his phone to entice her to San Miguel. If Connor really had gone to ground, then Claire could be used to lure him out. If he'd been taken, well...that was a whole new worry. Ben needed time to think before he reacted.

"Not to sound like a broken record, but we need to get out of here."

She gazed up at him, her eyes like liquid amber in the light. "So you keep saying, but I'm not budging until you tell me what's really going on."

He lifted a hand to rub the back of his neck. "I wish I knew. It seems I know even less today than I knew yesterday."

"What does that mean?"

"Things happened while I was away. Unexpected things."

"Like Connor's disappearance?"

"Yes, among other things." He searched her face, her perfume suddenly filling his nostrils. She smelled like the woods, a clean, sunshiny fragrance with hints of wildflower. A fragrance that was totally incongruent with the somber nature of their conversation. He could easily be distracted by that intoxicating scent if he let down his guard, but he wouldn't do that. Right now, focus was everything. "I need time to figure things out. And I need you to trust me."

Anger flickered again, but she still didn't pull away. "You haven't given me one good reason why I should."

"I can give you the best reason of all," he said. "Your brother trusts me."

That seemed to take her aback for a moment. Then she sighed. "So you say. Maybe I'd be more inclined to trust you if I knew what you're keeping from me—" She broke off, looking distressed. "Wait. He isn't—"

"As far as I know he's fine," Ben quickly assured her. "Let's keep it that way. I meant what I said. The best way to help Connor is to go home."

She gave him a resentful look. "What happened to teaming up with me?"

"It's better this way. Stop asking questions, stop calling attention to his absence. Go home and let me handle this." He took a chance and brushed a tendril of hair from her face. "I'm not the bad guy, Claire."

"But you'd say that regardless, wouldn't you?"

"Probably."

His candor seemed to melt her resentment. "Just tell me one thing." She put her hand over his. Instead of pushing him away, her fingers clung to his for a moment. "Someone was watching Connor's apartment last night. Was it you?"

"A lot of strange things have been happening around here lately. I wanted to make sure you got home safely."

"I still don't understand why you care so much."

His gaze burned into hers. "Yes, you do. Deep down, you do. Maybe you just don't want to admit it."

She didn't pretend to misunderstand. "I can't do this right now. Finding Connor is all that can matter."

"I know that." He squeezed her fingers before he released her. "If you won't go home, then at least let me help you. Let's look for him together."

"I'll think about it," she finally conceded.

"Which part?"

She closed her eyes on a tremulous breath. "One thing at a time, okay?"

CLAIRE WAS STILL fretting when she left the Compound. She went out the front gate rather than trekking back through the woods. In her current state, she didn't much care who saw her. If Gil Bennett returned and decided to arrest her for trespassing, so be it. Maybe she could get some answers from *him*.

Of course, an arrest was the last thing she wanted. She needed to be free to search for her brother and, freedom aside, she wasn't about to put her faith in local law enforcement. If the police chief turned out to be dirty, maybe his subordinates weren't to be trusted, either. Connor was out there somewhere and he needed her. Through no circumstances of his own—she was certain—he'd become embroiled in something very dangerous. Murder, missing persons and possibly theft…she could only guess at the rest. Her brother had summoned her to San Miguel for a reason. He knew she was the one person he could always count on. She wanted to believe he could count on Ben, too, but she couldn't afford to misjudge or make a wrong move.

The sun beat down on the back of her neck as she trudged along the shoulder of the road. Ben had parked closer to the Compound and had offered her a ride back to her vehicle, but she needed time to think.

And as much as she hated to admit it, there was another, more intimate reason why she wanted to keep him at arm's length. He was right. There was a connection. She'd only just met him and despite her suspicious nature, she was drawn to him in a way she couldn't explain.

Mr. Cool, indeed. The man was a walking red flag. He knew she was worried sick about her brother, and he still wouldn't give her a straight answer. His caginess was maddening. Maybe he didn't know where Connor was at that exact moment, but he knew something. Why else would he try and persuade her to leave town?

And yet…

Her mind drifted back to the studio. His light touch on her shoulders, the way he'd said her name, the way their fingers had entwined. That warm note in his voice and the earnest gleam in his eyes when he insisted that he wasn't the bad guy—

She came to a dead stop as she drew even with the oak tree that she'd climbed earlier to scale the wall. It wasn't so much a sound or a peripheral movement that had startled her. More of an instinct, a gnawing fear that someone had tailed her from the Compound and was now lurking behind the wall, listening for her as she listened for him.

A flock of blackbirds took flight from the treetops and power lines, spooked from their perches by a sudden threat. They were so thick against the sky that for a moment, the sun was momentarily blocked. In that premature gloaming, Claire heard the telltale crunch of a twig or pinecone where the watcher had misstepped.

She wanted to believe that Ben had decided to follow her and make sure she made it safely back to her car. But when they parted at the front gate, he'd gone off in the opposite direction, supposedly headed back to his own vehicle. And anyway, why would he conceal himself behind the wall? Why wouldn't he call out to her?

Why didn't she call out to him?

Because she knew Ben Dornan wasn't the one skulking behind that wall. Claire had the terrifying notion that India Cortez's killer was already stalking his next victim.

Chapter Nine

Claire remained motionless. Other than the drumming of her heart, the countryside had gone silent now that the blackbirds had resettled. No flapping wings, no chattering from the trees. Even the bumblebees seemed to have vanished.

She peered through the oak canopy, almost expecting to see a dark-clad figure creeping along one of the gnarled branches. A killer who stalked and tortured his victims and strung them up from the ceiling to bleed out. The image was chilling, and she chided herself for allowing her imagination to go that far.

Quickly crossing to the other side of the road, she set out in a jog toward her vehicle. By the time she reached the hidden lane, she was sweating profusely. The shade from the mountain laurels had provided little protection from the heat. The leather seats in the SUV were almost too hot to touch. She slid in, wincing as she locked the doors and started the engine.

Instead of fleeing back to civilization as any rational person would do after such a fright, Claire forced herself to drive slowly along the wall, scouring the surrounding landscape for anything untoward. She pulled into the drive and sat with engine idling as she peered through the wrought-iron gates. Nothing moved. No one prowled the shadows that she could discern. Even Ben was long gone, either headed back to his cabin or on another mission. The Compound appeared deserted, shaded and sheltered by live oaks that wove an impenetrable canopy over the curving drive. Still, Claire waited. She needed to prove to herself that nothing more than her imagination had spooked her.

But she wasn't so sure about that. Even safely inside her locked vehicle, dark images descended, and she found herself shivering in the scorching heat. When she was a kid, she would sometimes awaken in the middle of the night with the same overpowering dread. A lingering terror that her dad's killer might be lurking somewhere nearby, waiting for the opportunity to slip into her room and slit her throat.

It was the old fear that finally triggered her flight. She backed out of the drive, then pressed down on the accelerator, putting as much distance between her and the Compound as quickly as she dared. By the time she reached the town limits, the oppressive dread had dissipated into a ubiquitous unease. San Miguel held too many secrets. The place was starting to wear on her nerves. She summoned her great-aunt's wise advice. *Stay vigilant and cautious, but never panic. A clear head can save your life.*

Claire added her own note to that warning: *Don't let Ben Dornan get under your skin.*

In hindsight, antagonizing the one person in this town who seemed to have the strongest connection to her brother might not be the best idea. He was evasive and downright deceptive, but like it or not, she needed to stay close to him. That decision alone made her feel less passive, and her mood improved as she approached the downtown area.

Driving back into downtown San Miguel, Claire found a place to park a few blocks from the town square. Slipping her sunglasses on, she got out of her car and followed a trail of revelers back to the outdoor venue. Colorful tents and booths had spilled onto the surrounding park, and food trucks lined the cordoned-off streets. Strands of music drifted down the sidewalk as a live band conducted a sound check. At any other time, she would have soaked up the celebratory atmosphere. She would have enjoyed strolling through the exhibits or finding a place in the shade to people watch. Not so today. She was there for one purpose only. She found an unoccupied bench with a view of the square and sat down. Twisting her hair off her neck, she scanned the growing crowd. No Connor. No Ben. Not a single face she recognized.

She watched and waited, sweat trickling down her temples and beading on her forehead. She mopped it away with a tissue she found in her bag. Her phone pinged an incoming text message. She glanced at the screen, startled to recognize Ben's number:

Hey. I hope I didn't come on too strong earlier. I don't want to scare you away.

She thought about her response, keeping in mind her earlier resolution to stay close to him: I don't scare easily.

Good. I meant what I said. If you won't go home, I think we should look for Connor together. It's safer that way.

She replied: You're persistent. I'll give you that.

Is that a yes?

I said I'll think about it.

Fair enough. I'll call you when I get back.

Where are you going?

We'll talk soon.

Still evasive, she thought as she put away her phone.

More and more people had crowded into the square and her view became obscured. After a while, she got up and worked her way around the area, taking a moment to admire the arts and crafts. People seemed friendlier today. More relaxed. Maybe because the murder had become old news by now. Or maybe because among the tourists and out-of-towners that had poured into San Miguel for the weekend festivities, Claire no longer stood out as a stranger.

The booth that housed the India Cortez exhibit had been given a place of honor near the gazebo. The display consisted of a dozen or more framed pieces, most of which were self-portraits. As before, Claire searched for Connor's signature technique in the brushstrokes and composition. She was no expert by any means, but she knew her brother's work. She couldn't imagine why he would have agreed to such an arrangement. His art had always been very personal to him, but he must have had his reason for allowing India to leech off his talent. Maybe that was a bit too harsh, Claire decided. She should refrain from jumping to conclusions until she heard the whole story from Connor.

"That poor woman," a male voice lamented behind her. "Struck down just as her work was enjoying a renaissance."

Claire assumed the person was addressing a companion, but she glanced over her shoulder anyway. The man who stared back at her was none other than Sean Greggory, the ex-communicated priest, and he appeared to be alone.

"I'm sorry, were you talking to me?" she asked.

"Just musing aloud." He gave her an enigmatic smile as

their gazes met through their respective sunglasses. Gone was the intoxicated and belligerent man from the previous evening. Today, he looked almost dapper with his salt-and-pepper beard neatly trimmed and an old straw Panama hat shading his face. She glanced at his neck, automatically searching for the Roman collar in Connor's sketch. Instead, he wore a threadbare linen shirt with the throat unbuttoned and the cuffs rolled to his forearms. She glimpsed the sparkle of a silver chain peeking from beneath the fabric.

Trepidation cooled her answering smile though she wasn't physically afraid of him, surrounded as she was by throngs of people. She'd even noticed a few uniformed cops in the crowd. What threat could he pose in broad daylight? Besides, if he'd commissioned sketches from her brother for his book, he might know something that could prove useful.

He didn't seem at all put off by Claire's reticence. He moved boldly alongside her. "Forgive me if I'm intruding..."

"You're not. It's a free country." She stepped aside to make room in front of the display. She could feel his gaze on her, but she kept her focus on the paintings.

"Lovely, aren't they?"

"They're interesting." And a bit narcissistic in Claire's opinion, but she was defensive of her brother and, therefore, biased. Pushing her sunglasses to the top of her head, she pretended to give the exhibit her undivided attention while acutely aware of the man beside her.

After a moment, he said, "You're Connor Tinsley's sister." It was a statement, not a question.

She turned in surprise. "How did you know?"

"Word travels fast in a place like this. I heard you were in town, and of course I can see the resemblance up close. Same mouth, same chin." He cocked his head as he observed her through his dark glasses. "Ah, yes. Those same golden eyes. The color is unusual and really quite striking."

She murmured her thanks, but the compliment discomforted her. She didn't think he was trying to hit on her. His regard seemed almost grandfatherly, which, in a way, was even more unsettling since she'd never set eyes on him before last night. She thought of Connor's sketchbook in her bag and wondered what had prompted him to draw the man in the first place. And then she wondered again about the missing page from the same sketchbook as she gave Sean Greggory a sidelong glance. *Who are you and what do you know about my brother's whereabouts?*

"When was the last time you spoke with Connor?" she asked in what she hoped was a conversational tone. She slipped her sunglasses back on so that he wouldn't be able to read too much into her scrutiny.

"Just a few days ago. He dropped some sketches by my apartment and we had a nice chat. As a matter of fact, your name came up. He said you were on an extended trip through Italy. I take it your plans changed."

"He told you about my trip?" The revelation caught her off guard. Everyone else in town had seemed surprised to learn that Connor even had a sister. They were both naturally reserved, so it seemed out of character for him to reveal her travel plans to a virtual stranger.

"He mentioned it only in passing," Sean explained. "I could tell by the way he spoke about you that you two are close. You look so much alike. There can't be that much difference in your ages."

"Not much, no." Claire purposefully kept her answer vague. The question seemed odd and a bit too probing. Sean Greggory didn't need to know that she and Connor were twins. He didn't need to know anything about her. She was suddenly glad that her eyes were hidden behind the sunglasses.

"He's an interesting young man, your brother. I've thoroughly enjoyed our brief conversations."

"He's one of the good ones," she said.

"That's certainly been my impression."

The note of formality in his speech and demeanor seemed incongruent with their rustic surroundings. Everything about Sean Greggory seemed a little off, as if he'd donned faded clothing and an old-world facade to disguise his true nature.

Claire searched his camouflaged features. "Where did you meet him?"

"Connor?" His expression turned thoughtful. "I believe our first meeting was at a local watering hole not too far from here. I have a little apartment over the bar. We got to talking one night after the place cleared out, but I already knew who he was before he told me his name. His reputation preceded him."

She frowned at that. "What do you mean, his reputation?"

He waved a hand over the crowd. "Haven't you noticed? San Miguel is a community that celebrates the creative spirit, and your brother is a talented artist in his own right. I'd heard about his work before I actually met him."

"It's nice to know his talent is appreciated," Claire murmured.

His tone shifted as a note of mystery crept in. "I can tell you for certain that no one appreciated his gift more than India Cortez. She seemed to have a knack for finding and nurturing raw talent."

"Isn't that a good thing?"

His shrug seemed anything but casual. "You would have to ask your brother how their collaboration worked out for him."

What was he getting at? Claire wondered. Was he not so subtly casting suspicion on Connor by insinuating his arrangement with India Cortez gave him motive?

She fought the urge to distance herself from the man. She might not be physically afraid of him in the middle of a crowd in broad daylight, but she still didn't trust him. The longer they conversed, the more his speech patterns niggled. His pitch shifts and word stress were subtle but distinct. Southern for sure. Deep South, maybe. The thought crossed her mind that he might be using a more formal way of speaking to disguise a regional accent.

Curiosity got the better of her. "This may sound strange, but you seem so familiar to me. Is it possible we've met?"

"Have you spent much time in San Miguel?"

"No. This is my first visit."

"Likely not, then. I've been here for far longer than I care to remember. Before that, I traveled. Mostly to places south of the border that you've probably never heard of."

"How long were you there?"

"In Mexico? Off and on for a number of years. I call it my wanderlust period."

"And before that?"

He turned back to the exhibit. "Before that is a very long story."

She wondered if that long story included an illicit affair and an excommunication. Or was his background as a disgraced priest as fake as his demeanor? "Why did you decide to settle in San Miguel?"

"The people, the scenery. Sometimes the weather, though today isn't one of those times." He mopped the back of his neck with a linen handkerchief. "The architecture reminds me of the parts of Mexico I fell in love with."

"Why did you leave?"

"The simple answer?" His smile turned ironic. "I grew old. I missed home. There came a time when the nomadic lifestyle was no longer suitable. And I always felt as if I'd left things…unfinished." His sigh seemed more nostalgic than regretful. "I decided to come back to the States and get serious about writing my book."

Yes, that book that no one had been able to sample. Claire tried to appear only mildly curious. "Earlier, when you said no one was more appreciative of my brother's talent than India... I had a feeling you wanted to say more."

"You're very perceptive." He glanced over his shoulder before answering. "India had a way of latching on to talent that wasn't always to the benefit of her protégé. Don't get me wrong. She was a fine woman in many respects, and she brought a lot of prestige to the community when she moved here. But she wasn't above using those closest to her—even her most loyal supporters—to get what she wanted. People were stunned by the horrifying details of the murder, but deep down, not many were all that surprised."

"She had enemies?"

Another enigmatic smile. "Don't we all?"

"Did she pass other people's work off as her own?" Claire asked bluntly.

He brushed off the possibility with a shrug. "Even if she did, does it really matter now? She's gone, and I'm a bit superstitious when it comes to speaking ill of the dead. And I've always been of the belief that some questions are better left unanswered."

"I don't share that belief," Claire said. "I prefer everything out in the open."

"Everything?"

She could have sworn there was a subtle taunt in his tone. Had Connor let something slip about their past? She couldn't imagine he would be so careless. Surely he'd picked up on Sean Greggory's discordant vibes. Surely he shared the same misgivings as she. The fact that he had apparently befriended the man was a puzzle to Claire, but the portrait in his sketchbook was brutally honest. Nothing flattering about the haggard features, the haunted eyes, or the half-empty whiskey bottle Connor had added to his drawing.

As if intuiting her unease, Sean turned to peruse the crowd. "Do you know if your brother has a booth here today?" he asked in a matter-of-fact tone. "I was looking forward to seeing more of his original art."

"He isn't here," Claire said. "I thought he might have taken the day to work on some sketches for your book."

The suggestion seemed to surprise him. "He told you about our little project?"

"No, not Connor. Someone else must have mentioned it."

"I see. Well, in any case, I don't think my book would keep him away from the festival. He's not on deadline. To be candid, I'm not in a position to offer much in the way of compensation. Your brother has been very generous with his time and talent, but now that India is gone and the future of the Compound uncertain, I wonder how much longer we'll be able to keep him in San Miguel."

"I was under the impression that he would stay on and run the Compound. If not permanently, then at least to tie up loose ends. I imagine he'll be busier than ever over the next few months."

"You could be right. Selfishly, I hope he makes time for his art. And I don't just mean my sketches."

He sounded genuinely fond of her brother. Rather than softening Claire's attitude, his regard unsettled her. *Who the hell are you?*

She watched him from her periphery. Her reaction to meeting him in person was so different from the dark emotions that Connor's drawing had initially evoked. His subtle charm and quaint manner made it easy to think of him as harmless. Claire had to remind herself that it could all be an act. Like so many people in this town, he seemed to be hiding something. Sean Greggory might not even be his real name. He could have invented a persona with a sordid history to keep people at arm's length. To keep the curious from asking too many pointed questions about his past. Whatever his backstory, he was an intriguing man to say the least.

"India certainly favored self-portraits," Claire murmured, refocusing her attention on the exhibit. "The pieces all look basically the same to me except for her clothing and accessories."

"No, no, look at the eyes. That's where you'll find the real India. I've always thought her self-portraits were a means of self-reflection."

Claire gave him another sidelong glance. "That's an interesting observation. You sound as if you knew her personally."

"We were friendly for a time after I first moved to San Miguel. For whatever reason, she took a liking to me and would invite me out to the Compound every so often for drinks and conversation. She was fascinated by my travels through Mexico and never seemed to tire of my stories. But as she grew older, she became more guarded, sometimes to the point of paranoia. For whatever reason, I fell out of her favor, and over time, we both became cloistered in our own way. She closed herself up in the Compound and I lost myself to the bottle."

Claire could almost feel sympathy for him despite her qualms. Whatever else he might have done, Sean Greggory sounded as though he'd experienced loneliness, the acute kind that had settled so deep in his bones, it had become a part of him.

Claire knew that loneliness, a longing so powerful it would sometimes take her breath away. Growing old alone and guarded wasn't how she wanted to picture the rest of her life, but the circumstances before and after her father's murder continued to subtly shape her every thought and move. It wasn't easy to open herself up to close relationships when her very existence had once depended on secrecy. Connor was the only living soul who knew the truth about their childhood, but they didn't talk about the past. They'd been told a long time ago that Emily and Ethan Cross could be nothing more to them than distant memories.

Claire had allowed herself to wander too far down the rabbit hole, and now forced her attention back to Sean Gregory. "I would love to hear more about your book sometime. The San Antonio missions have always intrigued me," she lied. "Do you suppose I could have a look at my brother's sketches?"

"Yes, of course," he replied a little too enthusiastically. "A tour might even be in order. You must have Connor set something up for us."

Not exactly what she had in mind. A tour was pushing things, especially considering her visceral reaction to the man's portrait. She'd been angling for something more immediate and started to press him, but he suddenly seemed distracted. She turned to glance in the same direction, but nothing stood out to her.

"Is everything okay?"

He looked anxious and sickly all of a sudden as he gave her a hasty apology. "You'll have to excuse me. I'm sorry to cut our conversation short, but I'm feeling claustrophobic in this crowd, and the heat has become a little too much for me." He mopped again at his now mottled complexion.

"Would you like to sit in the shade for a few minutes? Can I get you something cold to drink?"

"That's kind of you to offer." He wrapped the handkerchief around his neck. "No, I think it's time I head back to my apartment."

Claire couldn't help but be concerned. The man didn't

look well, and the spell seemed to come on out of the blue. "Are you sure you're okay?"

He put a hand to his heart. "It'll pass in a bit. It's been a pleasure speaking with you—Claire, is it? Lovely name. Perhaps we'll see each other again soon. In the meantime, enjoy the rest of your day."

And just like that he was gone. Claire stared after him for a moment, wondering why he'd approached her in the first place. Sure, it was a small town, but had word really spread that quickly about her arrival? Or had Sean Greggory gone out of his way to make contact?

As she skimmed the crowd, her attention was caught by a man standing near one of the food trucks. His facial features and the color of his hair were partially obscured by a baseball cap and sunglasses. His height and build were similar to Connor's, and he was outfitted in much the same way she'd seen her brother dress countless times over the years— faded jeans, sneakers and a red T-shirt. From a distance, the yellow graphics on the front of his shirt appeared to be the lion mascot from the private school in Austin where Connor had taught before uprooting his life to move to San Miguel.

The man stood with one shoulder against a lamppost as his head slowly swiveled from side to side, taking in the crowd. He turned in her direction and straightened, his attention seemingly locked on her. She removed her sunglasses, hoping he would do the same. He didn't. Instead, he gave her a nod, the gesture so brief as to be almost imperceptible. Then he turned and walked quickly away, lost within moments behind the long lines that had formed at the food trucks.

He wasn't Connor. Claire knew that. But she couldn't be one hundred percent certain. He dressed like her brother. He'd even nodded in the same vague way as Connor when he became distracted.

She got out her phone and called his number. He was too far away and the music too loud to distinguish a ringtone. And anyway, her call went straight to voicemail.

Dropping the phone in her bag, she hurried through the crowd, bumping against shoulders and brushing against arms. "Pardon me. I'm so sorry. Please, excuse me…" She muttered apologies all the way across the square and onto the sidewalk. The lines at the food trucks parted for her, and she caught sight of a red shirt in the distance. Then the man turned a corner and disappeared. Claire hesitated for only a split second before she set off after him.

A minute or two later, she rounded the same corner and glimpsed him again. This time he stopped, turned and for a moment, she thought he meant to wait for her. His gaze lingered before he abruptly stepped off the sidewalk and vanished down a side street.

Claire stopped for breath, wondering why on earth someone would pretend to be Connor. Maybe that was reaching. Maybe the guy just happened to own a shirt from her brother's former school and maybe all this was just a strange coincidence.

Or maybe he really was Connor and he needed to speak to her away from prying eyes.

As anxious as she was to catch up with the man, she knew enough to be cautious. What if she was being lured away from the crowd for some dark purpose?

With that in mind, she approached the alley with more than a little apprehension. Strands of music from the festival floated after her. A group of passersby chatted and laughed among themselves as they headed to the park, and she could hear traffic from the next street over. Normal sounds. Safe sounds. Still, she hesitated, her senses on full alert.

Buildings crowded the one-way access, filtering the sunlight, but she could still see the guy in the red shirt up ahead.

She paced her pursuit, keeping him in sight but with enough distance for safety. But was she safe? Or was she being extraordinarily foolish? What if she threw caution to the wind for the first time in her life and ended up assaulted—or dead—in some gloomy alley in San Miguel, Texas?

She could list any number of reasons why she should turn and head back to the safety of the festival, but instead she kept going, glancing over her shoulder now and then to make sure no one was following her.

The buildings on either side of the alleyway were hardly skyscrapers. Only a handful were even three stories, but she felt boxed in. The rear service doors that opened into the alley were undoubtedly locked. No place to hide should she run into trouble. She kept going, ignoring the warning prickle at the back of her neck as she vectored in on that red shirt. He came to the end of the alley and paused. She cupped her hands around her mouth and called out to him to see how he would react. "Connor!"

His name bounced off the brick walls and echoed back to her.

He didn't so much as glance over his shoulder, and she wondered if he'd even heard her. Or more likely, the name meant nothing to him.

She called again, and this time he turned, lifting his palm in her direction as if to silence her or keep her at bay. Then he whirled and exited the alley.

The message had been received loud and clear. She wasn't to follow him. But Claire was more confused than ever. If he wasn't Connor, why was he even trying to communicate with her?

She could almost hear her great-aunt's voice in her ear. *Claire. Don't do anything rash. What have I always taught you and your brother? Impulses are dangerous. Think long and hard before you act.*

They had also been taught to look after one another no matter what, and Claire had never felt more strongly that Connor needed her. This was not the time to be timid.

By the time she reached the street, the man in the red shirt was nowhere to be seen. She walked down to the intersection in both directions. She even crossed the street and peered down another alleyway. She wanted to stand on the corner and shout her brother's name until he came out of hiding, but the same trepidation that had gripped her outside the Compound wall kept her silent now as she retraced her steps across the street.

What now? She had no idea how the man had vanished so quickly. Had he gone into one of the shops? Maybe he was inside at that very moment watching her through a plate-glass window. She stood indecisively, searching windows and doorways. No sign of him anywhere.

Maybe it was for the best. Following a stranger down an alley wasn't exactly the responsible thing to do. And he was a stranger. She knew he wasn't Connor. She *knew* it. But she'd become so desperate for answers that she'd gone against everything she'd been taught and willingly put herself in harm's way.

Had she really been at risk, though? The man had done nothing threatening. In fact, the opposite. He'd tried to discourage her from following him. The notion that *she* might have actually frightened *him* seemed a bit comical in hindsight. She would probably be able to laugh at the situation later when she knew her brother was safe.

A pedestrian passed by while Claire stood vacillating. She didn't know him, but his gray hair and beard reminded her of Sean Greggory. Her amusement vanished as wariness seeped back in, and she wondered again about his motive for approaching her at the festival. She didn't think their meeting was happenstance. Now that she reflected back on the anxious way he'd glanced around the crowd, she couldn't help wondering if he'd been searching for the man in the red shirt. Had he helped set her up? For what purpose, though?

They'd spent most of their time talking about India Cortez, but somehow Claire didn't think the dead woman had been the real focus for either of them. She had a feeling she wasn't the only one who had been fishing for information.

But…time enough to worry about Sean Greggory later. She couldn't stand on the street dithering forever. She had to go back the way she came to get to her vehicle. She could avoid the alley and take the long way around, but why should she? From where she stood, she could see all the way to the other end. No one was in front of her or behind her. No shadows lurked atop buildings. The man in the red shirt was long gone, and who even knew where Sean Greggory was at that moment?

A few feet in, however, Claire started to regret her decision. Her uneasiness was so overpowering that she whirled and started to backtrack to the street.

You're imagining things. No one is there. You're fine!

But another voice was already whispering in her ear. *Someone is watching you.*

Somewhere nearby, a rustling sound caused her to start. A rat mostly likely. Or an alley cat. She glanced over her shoulder. Nothing. She sped up, stumbling over a crack in the asphalt. She righted herself, but in the split second her attention had been diverted, a door swung open behind her. Before she could turn, let alone brace for impact, a hard body slammed her into the wall, knocking the breath from her lungs. A hand clapped over her mouth and an arm tightened around her waist, dragging her across the alley.

Gasping for air, Claire tried to fend off the attack, but her captor was strong and he'd caught her off guard. She kicked, she pounded, she sank her teeth into his palm, but he only swore and tightened his grip. He hauled her through a doorway into a pitch-black space that smelled of sawdust and fresh paint. Then he brought her up against him and said in her ear, "Hello…sis."

Chapter Ten

Claire went completely still with shock. Definitely not Connor. Her brother had never once called her by that nickname and besides, she knew his voice. This man's accent was deep West Texas.

He lowered his hand from her mouth. "Just be cool, okay? No one can hear you in here anyway."

Claire gulped in air. "What do you want? Money? I only have a few dollars in my bag."

"You wouldn't lie about that, would you?" He curled his fingers around the strap of her tote and jerked it off her shoulder as he simultaneously pushed her away.

Stumbling over a board, she fell to her knees, crying out as her flesh connected with a nail. The sharp prick was nothing compared to her terror in that moment. She was certain he meant to shoot her and leave her for dead in that dark, dank room.

"Who are you? Why are you pretending to be my brother? Where's Connor?"

No answer.

"Where did you get that shirt?"

"You ask too many questions. That'll get you in trouble around here."

"Who *are* you?"

"Go home…sis. Go home before you find yourself in a boatload of trouble."

"I'm not your sister."

She heard a low chuckle a split second before the door closed behind him as he fled back into the alley.

The windowless room was completely dark now. Claire scrambled to her feet and stood for a moment getting her bearings before she limped across the room, running her hands over the metal door until her fingers closed around the knob. It turned easily, but the door wouldn't budge. She put her shoulder to it and then her whole body. The exit had been blocked from the outside.

Without a phone, she couldn't call for help or even see her way around the dark room. Arms outstretched, she moved slowly about the space, stumbling over obstacles until she located the interior door. It, too, was locked from the other side. She pounded on the door and called out for help. This was a commercial area. Surely someone must be working inside the building. But in the next instant, she realized the boards and nails scattered about the floor and the smell of sawdust and fresh paint likely meant the place was closed for renovations.

She beat on the door for another few minutes, then made her way back to the alley exit where she pounded until her knuckles hurt. She was just about to give up and search for a crowbar when the door opened a crack, letting in a stream of filtered light.

"Hello?" a female voice called softly through the opening.

Claire felt a rush of relief as she called out, "I'm here! I got locked inside—"

The door opened wider. "Claire?"

"Mia?" She felt a rush of relief at the familiar face peeking in through the doorway. "Oh, thank God." She stepped quickly outside, glancing both ways to make certain they were alone in the alley.

Mia touched Claire's arm in concern. "What happened? Is that blood on your jeans? Are you hurt?"

"A man grabbed me and locked me inside that room."

Mia's eyes widened. "Just now?"

"Did you see anyone in the alley?"

She shook her head. "No one."

Claire took a quick breath. Her heart was still racing. "Who knows how long I would have been stuck in there if you hadn't come along."

Mia's eyes darted past Claire to the open doorway. "What did he want?"

"He stole my bag and took off."

"This bag?" She held up Claire's tote. "I found it just down there. He probably grabbed your wallet and tossed the bag when he ran off."

Claire took the tote from Mia and rummaged inside.

"Is anything missing?"

"My wallet is still here. So is my phone." Her fingers closed briefly around her good luck charm. The amethyst crystal meant the world to her. The keepsake was the only material possession she had left of her previous life.

Removing her wallet, she glanced inside. "My driver's license and credit cards are here. He didn't even take the cash."

"Then what did he want?"

"That's a good question." Claire bent to examine her knee.

"That's a lot of blood," Mia said. "What happened?"

"I fell on a nail. At least, I think it was a nail. It was so dark inside, I couldn't see anything."

"We need to get you to a doctor. There's a clinic a couple of blocks over."

"I'll get it tended to later." Claire straightened. "Right now, I want to know how you found me."

"I saw you leave the festival. I tried to catch up to say hi."

She was still anxiously eyeing the doorway. "You didn't recognize him? Are you sure? Sometimes things come back to you after the trauma is over."

"My back was to him until he pulled me through the doorway, and it was pitch-black inside. But I'm certain he was the man I saw at the festival pretending to be Connor. Mia, how did you get the door open? It wouldn't budge from the other side."

"It wasn't locked. He shoved a board underneath the knob. But wait a minute. You said there was a man at the festival pretending to be Connor?"

"He had on a shirt from Connor's old school. He even mimicked some of Connor's mannerisms. But he wore sunglasses, and a cap pulled down over his face, so I never really got a good look at him."

Mia looked stunned. "Why would someone pretend to be Connor?"

"Probably to lure me away from the festival. And it worked." Claire was still going through her tote. She felt the color drain from her face. "Oh no! Connor's sketchbook is missing. I put it in my bag before I left the apartment this morning. Now it's gone."

Mia glanced around the alleyway. "Maybe it fell out when he tossed the bag. We can look for it on our way back. Let's just get out of here. Are you sure you can walk?"

"Yes, I'm fine. I want to go back to the festival. Maybe I can spot him in the crowd."

But she wasn't really fine. Not physically, not mentally. With every passing moment, she could feel something dark closing in on her.

AT MIA'S INSISTENCE, they stopped by the clinic on the way back to the festival. A nurse practitioner cleaned and stitched Claire's wound and then gave her a tetanus booster to be safe.

The local anesthetic deadened the pain, but her knee felt stiff as they walked back to the square. She was grateful when Mia pointed to a bench in the shade. The Connor imposter was probably long gone, but just in case he'd decided to linger, two pairs of eyes were better than one. Once Claire was settled, Mia hurried off to find something cold to drink, returning a few moments later with two icy bottles of water.

"Thank you." Claire held the bottle to her heated face before twisting off the cap. "You're a lifesaver. In more ways than one."

Mia shrugged, cradling the water bottle between her legs while she pinned up her hair. "It's just water. And if you're referring to what happened in the alley, that board was barely shoved up under the knob. You would have freed yourself in another few minutes."

"Or I could have been trapped for hours or even overnight. I'm just glad you found me when you did," Claire said.

Mia grimaced. "I almost didn't. Even from a distance, I could tell you were preoccupied, and I didn't want to bother you. But something prodded me to follow you. I had this overwhelming feeling that you were in danger..." She trailed off, her gaze shifting back to the crowd. "It's hard to explain without sounding all woo-woo."

"There's nothing mystical about intuition," Claire said. "Well, maybe there is, but we all have it. We just don't always listen to it."

Mia nodded. "I think you're right. Anyway, I walked several blocks looking for you before I realized I must have somehow missed you. I backtracked and decided to check the alley. I found your bag and then I heard shouting and banging. I had no idea what was going on until I opened that door."

"I'm still trying to make sense of it myself," Claire muttered.

"Maybe it would help to go back over what happened," Mia suggested. "That is, if you don't mind talking about it."

"I don't mind, but I'm not sure I can add much more to what I already told you. I noticed this man near the food trucks. He seemed to be watching the crowd. When he saw me, he did a little head dip that reminded me of Connor. He was about my brother's size and height, and he wore a red T-shirt with what looked to be the mascot from his former school. I knew he wasn't my brother, but I wasn't completely sure. And I had to be sure."

"So *you* followed *him.*"

Claire gave her a wry smile. "It seemed like a good idea at the time."

"I would have done the same. Go on. You followed him into the alley…"

"By the time I got to the other end, he'd disappeared. I figured he'd ducked into one of the shops or restaurants to evade me, but now I think he must have gone through to the back of the building and waited at the rear door for me."

"How could he know that you'd go back the same way you came?"

"A calculated risk, I guess."

"And you'd never seen him before?"

"I don't think so."

Mia fell silent as she watched the crowd. "I looked up the address of the building while I waited in line for the water. Most of the buildings on that block are owned by Riverview Properties. That's Lyle Fincher's company."

"Lyle Fincher." Claire repeated the name in surprise. "What reason would he have to be involved?"

"All I know is that he's been buying up properties and businesses around town for years. Most of the buildings on that block are in various stages of renovation. The guy who attacked you could be someone who's done work on the project and still has access." Mia set the water bottle aside and drew up her knees, wrapping her arms around her legs as she grew pensive. She looked young and earnest, and Claire wondered again about her relationship with Connor. Somehow, she didn't think their connection was the casual friendship Mia had made it out to be. At least not on her end.

Claire studied the woman's profile. "How long have you worked for Lyle?"

"I've been at the Crooked Ferret for over a year. In all that time, he only comes into the bar maybe once or twice a week at the most. Now, all of a sudden, he's there every night."

"He told me he was helping out because the bar is short-handed," Claire said.

Mia rolled her eyes. "We're always shorthanded. He's just using that as an excuse."

"Why do you think he's coming in so much?"

"I don't know, but he's been on edge lately. He's always watching the door like he's waiting for someone. And he watches the staff like he thinks we're stealing from him. Especially me."

"Why you?"

She glanced at Claire. "Maybe it has something to do with my cousin."

"The one who's missing?"

She said in surprise, "How do you know about Hector?"

"Actually, it was Lyle who mentioned him first. Then Ben Dornan told me how worried you are about him."

She closed her eyes briefly. "I am worried about him, and my poor aunt is beside herself. But I don't want to talk about Hector right now. We need to figure out who insti-gated your attack."

"This isn't your problem, Mia. I appreciate your help, but I don't want you getting involved."

"Maybe I want to get involved."

"Why?" Claire asked.

She shrugged. "Maybe I need the distraction."

"Because of your cousin?"

"Because I'm tired of feeling helpless."

Claire knew that feeling only too well, but the last thing she wanted was to put someone else in danger. "We can talk about what happened. We can share information and try to figure things out, but I don't want you doing anything risky on my account."

Mia cut her a glance. "Like following a stranger down a deserted alleyway?"

"Exactly like that. Agreed?"

"Agreed." But her slight hesitation made Claire nervous.

"Let's take it step by step," she said. "Why would someone assault me in broad daylight just to steal a sketchbook?"

"Maybe he heard me coming and panicked," Mia said. "He grabbed the first thing he could find in your bag."

"It would have been just as easy to grab my wallet. The only reason I had the sketchbook on me is because I noticed earlier this morning that one or more pages had been sliced out. Maybe by Connor, maybe by someone else."

Mia looked intrigued. "What do you think was on those pages?"

"No idea. Connor drew a lot of portraits. I remember thinking when I first thumbed through that sketchbook how prolific he's been since moving to San Miguel. But something about his work bothered me. I had a strange feeling that he was looking for something in all those faces he drew. Maybe someone thought there was something incriminating in that sketchbook."

"But how would anyone know it was in your bag?" Mia mused.

"That's a good point," Claire said. "And maybe you're right. Maybe you spooked him and he grabbed the sketchbook as an afterthought. Maybe his real motive was just to scare me into leaving town. He said I ask too many questions. He said that could get me in trouble around here."

Mia rested her chin on her knees as she continued to scour the crowd. "Do you think we should go to the police?"

"I'm not going to the police," Claire said flatly. "Aren't you the one who warned me about drawing too much attention to Connor's absence? And you were right. I don't want the cops thinking my brother has split town. And, anyway, how would all this sound to them? I willingly followed a stranger down a deserted alleyway because he looked like my brother, and the only thing taken from my bag was Connor's sketchbook. Those two things alone would send up red flags all over the place. Besides, I don't trust Gil Bennett. And if you can't trust the chief of police, how can you trust the officers under his command?"

Mia turned. "Why don't you trust Gil Bennett? Has something happened?"

Claire gave her a quick rundown of Bennett's odd behavior in India Cortez's studio that morning. "He was obviously looking for something."

"Do you think he had something to do with India's murder?"

"Nothing would surprise me at this point," Claire said. "For Connor's sake, I think we need to keep what happened in that alley between the two of us."

"What about Ben?"

A shiver traced down Claire's spine at the mention of his name. She fiddled with the water bottle, pretending indifference. "What about him?"

"He used to be a cop. Maybe he can help us figure things out. Besides…" She gave Claire a sidelong look.

"What?"

"You two seemed to hit it off last night."

"We were just talking."

"Okay."

"We *were*."

"I believe you. But I've been a bartender long enough to recognize the difference between a casual flirtation and a meaningful connection. The way he looked at you—"

"You're imagining things," Claire insisted. "*Besides*...how well do you even know him? Or maybe the better question is, how much do you trust him?"

Mia said without hesitation, "I trust him. If I didn't, I wouldn't have asked him to find my cousin. Connor trusts him, too."

"He told you that?"

She shrugged. "I could just tell. The two of them seemed pretty tight when I'd see them together in the bar."

"I suspected as much," Claire murmured.

"What do you mean?"

"Ben tried to convince me that he and Connor are just acquaintances."

Mia smiled. "So? I did the same thing when you came into the bar last night."

"But you were trying to protect Connor."

"So is Ben."

"I want to believe that, but he's still hiding something from me."

"Maybe he's trying to protect you."

"Maybe, but I'd rather have the truth." Claire's gaze drifted over the square. If the man who had attacked her was out there somewhere, he was well hidden by the crowd. "Did you ever see the two of them argue?"

"Connor and Ben?" Mia dropped her legs to the ground as she turned to Claire. "No, never. Why would you ask that?"

"Marion Palmer told me she saw the two of them arguing outside Connor's apartment a week or so before the murder.

They were having some kind of dispute over a necklace. A medallion, she said. She had the impression Ben was trying to get Connor to do something he didn't want to do. She thought it might have had something to do with India Cortez's jewelry collection."

Mia had gone very still. She said in a strained voice, "Was it a silver medallion with an emblem on the face?"

"I think so. Why?"

"Ben wasn't trying to get Connor to steal that necklace."

"How do you know?"

"Because it had already been stolen by my cousin."

Claire said in astonishment, "What are you talking about?"

"Hector showed me a necklace one night at work. He said he found it, but I never really believed that. I think he took the medallion to give to India. He worked for her for years, doing all sorts of odd jobs around the Compound. Whatever she needed whenever she needed it. He'd drop everything to help her and because of that, she had a soft spot for him. In her own way, she looked out for him. I think Hector wanted to give her that necklace to show his gratitude."

"Was the necklace found in her belongings?"

"She never accepted it. Maybe she knew it was stolen or maybe she thought it too extravagant a gift for someone in Hector's position. Instead, she sketched the symbol on the medallion and later added it to one of her self-portraits. That painting became the centerpiece of her first gallery showing in over a decade. The exhibit made quite a splash."

"So you said last night."

Mia nodded. "Anyway, two weeks after the opening in Austin, Connor moved to San Miguel and went to work at the Compound."

"You said you think he met India at the gallery?"

"I think it's too coincidental to believe otherwise. A few

days after Connor arrived in town, Ben showed up. I don't know how or why, but everything seems to be connected to that medallion."

"So it would seem," Claire said, her mind racing.

"Think about it." Mia's voice was hushed. "Hector showed the medallion to India. She painted it onto her self-portrait. Connor happened upon that portrait at the gallery. Now India is dead and both Connor and Hector are missing."

Claire's heart had started to thud. "Have you talked to Ben about the medallion?"

"He warned me not to mention it to anyone. I'm only telling you because I think what happened to you today is somehow connected." She turned in alarm. "Maybe that's why your bag was stolen. What if someone thinks you have the medallion?"

Claire swallowed, trying to keep a tremor from her voice. "That would explain why he left my phone and wallet." Now that the adrenaline had faded, the old caution had returned, and she was starting to wonder why she had ever thought she could find her brother on her own. "I've wondered why Connor moved to San Miguel so abruptly. It never made any sense to me and he would never give me a straight answer."

"He was chasing that necklace," Mia said.

"But why? Why is that damned necklace so important?"

"You tell me."

Claire shook her head. "I wish I could. The only medallion that ever had any significance to me was buried with my father twenty-five years ago."

Chapter Eleven

Claire spent the rest of the afternoon in the apartment going through Connor's things. She'd already conducted a search the day before, but now she went through absolutely everything, shoving aside any lingering qualms about invading his privacy. She thoroughly examined each and every piece of artwork she could find, searching for implanted clues as to what he might be involved in. The revelation from Mia about her cousin and the mysterious necklace had sparked a renewed frenzy. What was so important about a silver medallion that could lead to the murder of a prominent artist and the disappearance of two young men in their prime?

Hours later, exhausted both mentally and physically, Claire put everything back in its proper place and then stretched out on the leather sofa to rest. She only meant to close her eyes for a few minutes, but when she awakened, twilight had fallen. Fireflies flitted in the garden. She lay motionless and groggy watching the flickering lights in the bushes.

She'd dreamed about her father's murder again and her and Connor's terrified flight across that slippery roof. Her brother had been Ethan back then. She hardly ever thought of either of their birth names anymore. Ethan and Emily Cross had died a long time ago, but every now and then they came back to life in Claire's dreams. For the last two nights, they'd been haunting her sleep, as if San Miguel had triggered something deep in her subconscious.

After a while, she got up and padded back to the bathroom to shower and change clothes. By this time, twilight had deepened and she was getting hungry. She thought about trying one of the quaint restaurants she'd noticed near the square, but instead, she found herself once again at the Crooked Ferret. All the faces from Connor's artwork seemed to congregate there. Maybe she would even spot the man who had lured her into the alleyway earlier, but she wasn't at all sure she would even recognize him. Too much of his face had been obscured by sunglasses and the bill of his cap. And that had undoubtedly been the point.

The parking lot was already filling up with the weekend crowd. A cheery gathering of various ages had settled in at the bar and out on the patio. Mia spotted her as soon as she walked through the door. She greeted her as she would any other customer, but when Claire stepped up to the bar, she lowered her voice so that no one nearby could overhear them.

"I wasn't sure you'd feel like stopping by after what happened earlier." She wiped the counter as she shot a glance out over the crowd.

"I'm fine," Claire assured her. "I was feeling a little claustrophobic in the apartment and needed to get out for a while. A public place seemed like a good idea."

Mia nodded, then said in her normal voice, "What can I get for you?"

"Just a soda. I'm trying to keep a clear head tonight."

"Probably a good idea." Mia filled a glass and garnished it with a slice of lime. She placed the drink on a cocktail napkin in front of Claire. "Menu?"

"How's the club sandwich?"

Mia shrugged. "It's a club sandwich. Not much you can do to dress it up or mess it up."

"Sounds good. I'll have it on the patio." Claire glanced around. "You've got a big crowd tonight."

"Lots of people in town for the festival. Somehow, they always seem to find their way here."

Claire said casually, "I don't see Ben anywhere. Or any other familiar faces besides yours."

"Ben left for Matamoras a few hours ago. He didn't tell you?"

"He texted earlier but he didn't say where he was going." Claire wondered why that bothered her so much.

"He won't be back until late," Mia added.

Claire took a sip of her drink. "What's he doing down there?"

"He wanted to talk to my aunt and my cousins and anyone else who may have seen Hector before he crossed back over the border."

"I hope he has good news for you when he gets back."

"Thanks." Her voice dropped once more. "As for familiar faces, none of the regulars are here tonight and apparently, Lyle is taking the night off."

"What about Sean Greggory? Isn't he a regular?" Claire asked.

Mia frowned. "He hasn't been in, either, and he rarely misses a Friday night. Or any night, for that matter."

"Maybe he isn't feeling well. I saw him earlier at the festival. He had some kind of spell or heatstroke that came on all of a sudden. He looked pretty sick."

"He's got a bad heart from what I hear. All that drinking can't be good for him. I'll have somebody go up and check on him in a bit."

"Probably a good idea." Claire picked up her drink. "I'll let you get back to work. Talk to you later."

Mia nodded and moved down the bar to another customer.

Claire made her way through the crowd to the patio and found an empty table near the railing where she could enjoy a view of the grounds while keeping an eye on the door. She thought about Ben looking for clues in Matamoras. Somehow the notion of him being hours away left a hollow feeling in her chest. Which made no sense. She barely knew the man, and she hadn't yet decided to trust him. But she couldn't seem to stop thinking about him.

...I feel like we have a connection. Am I wrong?

No, he wasn't wrong. Even as mortified as she'd been when she crashed into him at the convenience store, her senses had been fully attuned to him. Those piercing eyes. The charm and quick smile that disguised a simmering intensity.

You're headed for trouble, a little voice chided her.

Maybe she wanted trouble. Maybe she was growing tired of her small life. In truth, she'd been restless for a long time, she just hadn't wanted to admit it. Maybe that was why she'd been so quick to drop everything and rush to San Miguel before she even had any of the facts.

Or maybe she was just killing time daydreaming about a man who intrigued her. Nothing more was likely to come from their connection anyway.

She sipped her drink and surreptitiously studied the crowd as she waited for her food. It was a beautiful cloudless evening. The stars were out. Having lived in the city for most of her life, she'd forgotten what the night sky could look like away from all the light pollution.

Her sandwich came and she ate slowly, postponing the inevitable. She didn't relish going back to her brother's empty apartment. It had now been over forty-eight hours since his last text message. Maybe her trip to San Miguel had been a bit impulsive, but she'd been right to come. Connor was obviously in trouble.

The events of the day started to close in on her—the attack in the alley, the strange sensation outside the walls of the Compound and Gil Bennett's odd behavior in the studio. She had no idea how they were all related, and at the moment, she didn't quite know what to do. Her expertise as a criminal analyst didn't lend itself to the more personal crimes of murder and missing persons. She studied organizations, not people. Maybe Ben was right. Maybe it would be safer and more productive if they worked together.

She thought about calling him. She had his number, and he'd told her to reach out anytime day or night, for any reason. But it was getting late, and if he was on the road, she didn't want to distract him. Besides, no need to make another hasty decision. She had a feeling that engaging his help would have unintended consequences, and she'd already gotten herself in trouble earlier by acting on impulse. *Take the night and think it through.*

Deep down, she knew the decision had already been made no matter the consequences.

FOR THE LAST several miles, the same set of headlights had been tailing Ben. Traffic was routinely light on US 77, but this time of night, the two-lane highway was practically deserted. He was still a few miles out of Corpus Christi. At least another three hours to San Miguel. He was making good time by avoiding the heavier congestion on the interstate, but now he was starting to second guess the wisdom of choosing a rural route. No houses, no cars. Nothing for miles but farmland and coastal wetlands. And the steady glow of those headlights behind him.

He glanced in the rearview mirror for the umpteenth time and wondered if the trailing vehicle was the same car he'd spotted earlier in Matamoras. He and Hector's mother had been seated on the front porch of her modest home when a black SUV had driven slowly past, not once, not twice but three times in the space of an hour. He asked Mrs. Zavala if she recognized the vehicle, but she shrugged and remarked that they all looked the same to her.

The front plate was missing, and the rear plate number was obscured by mud. That in itself attracted Ben's attention because the rest of the vehicle appeared relatively clean. The windows were tinted, and the driver always managed to have his head turned away when he drove by the house. Not at all suspicious. Either someone was watching the Zavala home or Ben was being followed. Now he had his answer.

He sped up and the distance between the vehicles momentarily lengthened until the other car accelerated, coming up so quickly on Ben's bumper that he thought for a moment the driver meant to ram him. He lowered his window and motioned for the car to go around him. The driver fell back, once again matching Ben's pace.

Up ahead, he could see the glow from a well-lit gas station. Rather than signal his exit, he waited until the last minute to hit the brakes and turn sharply into the parking lot. He sat with his engine idling as he waited to see if the car would continue down the highway or turn into the station behind him. The driver went on by, giving Ben a good view of the vehicle. A dark, late-model SUV that looked to be identical to the one he'd spotted in Matamoras.

He thought about pulling back on the highway and coming up behind the vehicle to see if he could get a plate number, but for all he knew, he might be driving into an ambush. Better that he let the driver get on down the road. He eased up to one of the pumps and got out. He still had half a tank, but he decided to fill up so he wouldn't have to make another stop. He wanted to get back to San Miguel as quickly as possible.

The last time he'd been away for more than a couple of hours, he'd come back to Connor's disappearance and Claire's arrival. And that thought made him wonder if she was safe and sound behind the locked doors of her brother's apartment or if she'd taken it upon herself to go out and look for him. Ben hoped for the former, but he was worried about the latter.

Idly, he watched the gallons click over as he pondered their earlier conversation. She'd made it clear that she had no intention of leaving town, and he believed her. She'd dug in for the duration. With Connor still missing, Ben had run out of options. He had to tell her the truth. Keeping her in the dark had seemed like a good idea when she was at home in DC or even better, vacationing overseas. No need to worry her. No need to bring her into their plan. She was safer not knowing. Now she was in San Miguel with no idea of the danger she might be facing. If the car that had tailed him from Matamoras was any indication, someone was getting nervous. His cover might not yet be blown, but his trip had obviously provoked concern.

He finished gassing up and went inside to buy a cup of coffee before finally getting back on the road. He fiddled with the radio, turning the dial slowly until he was able to pick up a Corpus Christi station. He turned down the volume so the music was just background noise. Then he set his cruise control to a few miles over the speed limit and settled in for the rest of the trip.

It was well after midnight and he was getting tired. Five hours each way was hardly a quick trip. But he'd done what he set out to do. He'd talked to Hector's family, some of his friends and even the local authorities. No one had seen or heard from him since he left for San Miguel. No one had noticed anything suspicious about his behavior nor did they know anything about a stolen medallion. Hector was a good guy who would never be involved in anything illegal or dan-

gerous, they said. As far as anyone knew, he'd left Matamo-
ras two days ago and had never arrived at his destination.
No leads, no clues, no anything. Like Connor, it was as if
Hector Zavala had vanished into the thin air.

His mother had been distraught, fearing the worst. She'd
clung to Ben's hand before he left, gazing into his eyes as if
she could peer into his soul. "Mia says I should trust you.
She says if anyone can find my Hector and bring him home,
it's you. Is she right?"

Ben had wanted to disabuse her of those lofty expectations as gently as he could. He wanted to remind her that he
was only one man with limited resources. Instead, he noted
the slight tremor of emotion at the corners of her mouth and
nodded. "I've found people before. I can do it again."

"Mia said you used to be a cop."

"A federal agent. FBI."

That took her aback. "Whatever you think my son has
done, Hector is a good man."

"Mia said the same thing. I'm inclined to believe you."

Her eyes darted past him as if she'd suddenly spied someone lurking in the yard that only she could see. Her focus
was so intense Ben found himself glancing over his shoulder. "What is it?"

"I see him."

A shiver crawled up his spine at the look in her eyes.
"You see Hector?"

She drew a shuddering breath as her trembling fingers
tightened around his hand. "The man you seek hides in plain
sight, but he watches from the shadows. He is cunning and
deceptive and he enjoys inflicting pain." Her voice lowered
to a near whisper. *"Cuídate, Benjamín."*

CLAIRE HAD JUST finished eating when her phone pinged an
incoming text. She thought it might be Ben again or even

Connor. Her pulse thumped as she turned over her phone and glanced at the message. She didn't recognize the number.

We need to talk. Outside. Make sure you aren't followed.

She glanced around the patio. Most of the customers were laughing and conversing, having a good time on this hot June night. A couple were on their phones, but she didn't recognize either of them. She peered through the doors into the bar area before she texted a reply: Who is this?

The answer came back instantly: Mia. Go around to the back of the building. Wait for me at the outside stairs.

Claire motioned for the waiter and handed him her credit card. He returned a few minutes later with the card and her receipt. She put everything away and rose, casually glancing over her shoulder as she made her way inside. Mia was still behind the bar mixing drinks. Claire's first thought was to verify that the text had actually come from her. She wasn't about to be ambushed for a second time that day. Mia caught her eye and angled her head toward the door. Claire answered back with a slight nod before leaving.

Outside, she paused at the bottom of the porch steps as the headlights from an incoming vehicle caught her in the face. She waited until the glare arced away before heading around the corner of the building. The glow from the security lights in the parking lot soon waned. Trash bins and dark alcoves provided too many places for someone to hide. Not for the first time, Claire questioned the wisdom of trusting someone she'd met only twenty-four hours ago. In reflection, how opportune was it that Mia had happened along in the alley when she did?

Claire hurried past all those hiding places. She could still hear laughter from the patio. Despite the crowd, she wondered if anyone would come running if she screamed for help? Would they even hear her over the music and merriment?

She rounded the corner to the back of the building. A wooden staircase led up to a tiny covered landing lit by a single light bulb. Lamplight glowed from one of the windows.

A door opened and closed somewhere nearby, causing her to start. She whirled as Mia came around the side of the building, lifting a finger to her lips when she saw Claire. Then she hurried over to join her at the bottom of the staircase.

"This way," she said in a low voice as she started up the steps.

Claire had no intention of following her up those stairs until she had some idea of what she was walking into. "What is this place?"

"Sean Greggory's apartment. Come on," Mia urged in that same hushed voice. "We don't have much time, and you need to see this."

Claire still held back. "Wait. *Wait.* We can't just break in."

"We don't have to break in." Mia held up a key. "I took it from Lyle's office."

"Won't he miss it?"

"I'll put it back as soon as we're finished. I told you earlier, he's not coming in tonight and Sean isn't home."

"How do you know?"

"I was worried that he might be seriously ill after you told me about his spell at the festival. I started imagining the worst, so I came up and knocked on his door. When he didn't answer, I borrowed Lyle's key to check on him."

Claire said doubtfully, "You're absolutely sure he's not home?"

"Yes, I searched the whole apartment. He has an old beat-up car that mostly takes up space in the parking lot. It's not there."

Claire swallowed her misgivings and followed her up the stairs. Mia fitted the key in the lock and the door swung open with a loud creak. Claire winced and glanced toward the corner of the building, worried the noise would have attracted attention.

"He left a lamp on," Mia said. "It doesn't provide much light, but it's probably best we don't turn on the overhead light."

"What if he comes back while we're inside?" Claire asked.

"I'll stand watch and head him off."

"While I do what?"

"You'll see."

Claire reluctantly stepped across the threshold. The apartment was tiny and modestly furnished with a sagging sofa, a well-worn armchair and a desk piled high with books and papers.

"Over here," Mia said as she moved across the room to the desk.

Claire followed willingly this time because she'd already caught sight of Connor's sketches pinned to a corkboard mounted on the wall. Her gaze flitted over the drawings. "These are really good."

"Why do you sound surprised?"

She shrugged. "My brother's talent always catches me by surprise. Our mother was an artist. Or at least, that's what we were told. I don't remember her."

"I lost my mother when I was young, too," Mia said. "My aunt took me in. Hector and I were raised together. He's more like a brother than a cousin." She opened a drawer and removed a large manilla envelope, which she handed to Claire.

"What's this?"

"That's what you need to see."

Claire gave her a long, scrutinizing look. "You didn't just

come up here to check on Sean, did you? I thought we agreed that you wouldn't put yourself in any risky situations."

"You'll be glad I did when you see what's inside," Mia insisted. "I'll go keep watch while you take a look. But hurry. We're swamped tonight. I can't be late getting back from my break."

Claire waited until the door clicked shut behind Mia before releasing the metal clasp on the envelope flap. She removed a stack of photographs and quickly thumbed through them. They were all of Connor, caught from a distance and apparently unaware of the camera.

She tried to contain her fear and work efficiently, but her hands trembled as she spread the photographs across the desk. They had been taken at different times at the same location—one of the missions judging by the limestone arches and crumbling bell towers in the background. She compared the shots to the pinned sketches on the corkboard, but none of the structures matched the one in the photographs.

Connor's clothing had changed in some of the pictures, but the intense, almost somber expression remained the same. Claire recognized that look of single-minded concentration. He was focused on a task to the exclusion of everything else, including danger.

He appeared to be searching for something. His gaze seemed to be trained on the ground or lifted toward the bell towers. Claire tried to think of a rational explanation. Maybe he was simply studying the architecture to draw, but she didn't think so. His expression was more dogged than curious. More anxious than intrigued.

What on earth were you looking for?

And why had Sean Greggory been following him?

Chapter Twelve

Day Three

Claire got up early, showered, dressed and then stretched out on the couch while she waited to hear back from Ben. She'd hesitated to call knowing that he would have gotten back late from his trip to Matamoras. He may not have seen her text yet. But she wanted to be ready if and when he decided to contact her. The photographs Mia had found in Sean Greggory's apartment had cemented Claire's decision to ask for help. Connor was in big trouble. She felt it with every fiber of her being. If she couldn't go to the local police, then who else could she turn to?

She'd just dozed off when a loud noise startled her awake. She bolted upright on the couch, her heart pounding until she realized that someone was knocking on the door.

She hurried over to the foyer, taking the time to glance through the sidelight before she threw open the door for Ben. "You came." Her racing pulse made her sound breathless.

"As soon as I saw your text. It sounded urgent. What's going on?"

He brushed past her into the foyer, unshaven, bloodshot eyes and looking more than a little dangerous himself. His cane was still absent, she noticed, but his limp was more perceptible than the day before.

She closed the door and waved him into the living room. "I'm sorry for contacting you so early. Mia told me about your trip to Matamoras. Did you get any sleep at all?"

"A couple of hours." He shifted restlessly, his gaze darting about the living room. "What's going on, Claire? Have you heard from Connor?"

"No, not a word." She ran fingers through her own unkempt hair. "But I do have news. Have you talked to Mia this morning?"

"Briefly. I promised her I would call as soon as I got back. Why?"

"Did she say anything about the photographs we found? Or the incident at the festival?"

He gave her a frowning inspection, taking in the tangled hair and the dark circles under her eyes. "Did you get any sleep last night? You look exhausted."

"I am exhausted. But so much has happened, I'm almost afraid to close my eyes."

He took her arm and pulled her down to the couch. "Start with the photographs."

"It's probably better if I show you." She grabbed her phone from the coffee table and tapped one of the photos. Then she used her fingers to magnify the image before handing the phone to Ben.

He studied it for a moment, then glanced up. "It's a picture of Connor. I don't get the significance."

"It's a photograph of a photograph of Connor," she explained. "We found the printed images in Sean Greggory's apartment. Or rather, Mia found them. She took me up to the apartment to show me—"

"Wait, *what?*" His expression was a mixture of concern and incredulity. "You two broke into his apartment?"

"Mia had a key. She went up to check on him because he didn't come down to the bar. And earlier, when I saw him at the festival, he seemed to have some kind of spell. Mia was worried about him."

"So worried that she took the time to search his apartment?"

"I'm not trying to condone what we did," Claire said. "But we found what we found. Just scroll through the pictures and tell me what you see."

He swiped and studied. "They were taken on different days, but same location."

"Exactly. Do you recognize the background?"

He continued to swipe. "Judging by the arches, the terrain and the overall decay of the place, I'm guessing ruins of some kind. Probably the San Miguel Mission."

"That's what Mia said. Have you ever been out there?" Claire asked anxiously.

"No, but I know where it is." Ben glanced up. "The surrounding landscape is pretty rugged. From what I understand, it's a challenging hike."

"According to Mia, the county has been trying to involve the Texas Historical Commission and the National Park Service for years, but there's never enough money and the structure is too far gone to save at this point. There's really no way to make it safe for tourists without demolition. She said the locals rarely go out there anymore because of the danger of collapse."

He lifted the phone and turned the screen in her direction. "Connor obviously went out there."

"On more than one occasion," she agreed. "But why?"

"Maybe he intended to draw the mission for Sean's book."

"I don't think so," Claire said. "He never once looks at the camera. I don't think he had any idea he was being watched, let alone photographed. And another thing. I talked to Sean

Greggory for quite some time at the festival. I'd bet good money he isn't who he claims to be. I doubt he was ever a priest. He told me he'd spent a lot of years traveling through Mexico before settling down in San Miguel."

Ben's voice sharpened. "Mexico? He said that?"

She nodded. "I knew from the start there was something very off about him. I felt it the moment I saw his portrait in Connor's sketchbook."

"I believe you." Ben glanced back down at the phone. "What, specifically, about these images has you so worked up?"

"Other than the fact that Connor was obviously followed and photographed without his knowledge? Or that we found printed images in Sean Greggory's apartment? Look at the expression on Connor's face. I recognize that intense concentration. He was lost in his own world out there. He wouldn't have had a clue that anyone else was about." Claire took the phone from Ben's hand and studied her brother's features. "I think he was looking for something. And I think you know what that something is."

"You're wrong about that," Ben said. "I'm as much in the dark about his trips to that mission as you are. He never once mentioned to me that he'd been out there." His expression was shuttered, but Claire had the impression that he was telling the truth. He seemed taken aback by the photographs. He took the phone from her hand and set it aside. "Forget about the photographs for a minute. Tell me what happened at the festival."

Claire instantly protested. "We can get into that later, but right now I want to go out to that mission and I'm hoping you'll take me."

"Why?"

"I don't want to go alone."

"No, I mean, why do you want to go out there?"

"Isn't it obvious? The place is remote and by your own description, the terrain is rugged. What if Connor went out there alone and he fell or the place caved in on him? Or he was attacked? Or snakebit? I can think of a dozen scenarios as to why he might not have returned from his last trip to that mission and none of them good. I know what you're thinking," she said before he had a chance to respond. "It's a long shot. You think I don't know that? But what if he *is* hurt? What if he desperately needs my help and I don't do everything in my power to find him." Her voice rose in distress. The longer they talked, the more certain she became that time was of the essence.

"Are you sure you want my help?"

"Yes," she replied without hesitation. "But just so you know, I'm going out to that mission with or without you."

He nodded. "In that case, go put on closed-toed shoes. Boots if you have them. Those sandals won't offer much protection from the scorpions."

Scorpions? She shuddered as she hurried to grab her shoes.

CLAIRE WAS SILENT for the first part of the journey. She stared out the window at the passing scenery as her mind kept whirling with dire possibilities. She knew it was improbable that Connor would be at the ruins, just as searching the Compound had been pointless. But she didn't know what else to do.

Ben cut into her chaotic thoughts. "Now will you tell me what happened at the festival?"

She didn't want to talk about the attack. She was too preoccupied, and she'd been over the incident so many times in her head that the last thing she wanted was to recount the ambush. Plus, she knew her actions had been foolish and she was a little embarrassed. But she'd asked for his help and he'd willingly agreed no matter the danger to himself, no matter the strain on his knee from the rugged terrain, no matter what he really thought of her request. She at least owed him an explanation. And maybe it would take her mind off what they might find at the ruins.

She started out with an abbreviated version of the events, but found herself elaborating every time he cut in with a question. When she concluded with her trip to the clinic, she glanced at his profile. He frowned out the windshield as he took it all in.

The first thing he said was, "You're okay?"

"From yesterday? Yes, I'm fine. The NP at the clinic gave me a couple of stitches and a tetanus booster. I'll be good as new in a day or so."

"What about those bruises on your arm?"

"What?" She twisted her arm to have a look. "I hadn't even noticed them until now. He must have grabbed me harder than I thought."

Ben muttered something under his breath.

"What?"

"Nothing. I'm just marveling at the nerve of this guy trying to pass himself off as Connor."

"I know, but I'm not exactly blameless. I knew he wasn't my brother, yet I followed him anyway. It was foolish and reckless, but I couldn't just let him walk away. There had to be a reason why he wore that shirt and why he'd memorized some of Connor's mannerisms. At the very least, he was a clue. In hindsight, the setup seems all too obvious. He wanted to lure me away from the festival and down that alleyway. I should have been smarter and more careful, and that's on me."

Ben shot her a glance. "He attacked you. That's on him. You're not to blame for any of this."

She sat back against the seat and closed her eyes. "What

is going on around here, Ben? Just a week after India Cortez was murdered, two men who worked for her are missing. I don't know Hector so I can't vouch for him. But I am one hundred percent certain Connor has done nothing wrong. The opposite, in fact. I'm really starting to worry that someone has done something to him."

He gave her a pensive look. "Before last night, I'd hoped he and Hector were lying low waiting for the heat to die down."

"And now?"

"A car followed me part of the way back from Matamoras. I believe it was the same vehicle I saw pass by Mrs. Zavala's house at least three times while we sat talking on her porch."

"Did you get a plate number?"

"The front plate was missing and the back one was concealed by mud. Just outside of Corpus, the driver came up behind me so fast, I thought he meant to ram me. I pulled off at a gas station to see what he would do. He went on by. I didn't see him again."

"What do you think he wanted?"

"I think someone is getting nervous. At the very least, someone was curious enough about my trip to Matamoras to put a tail on me."

"Why?"

"I think Hector may have stumbled upon something he shouldn't have."

"The medallion?"

He gave her a sharp glance. "You know about that?"

"Mia told me. She thinks he stole it. She also thinks India may have been murdered because of that medallion." She paused. "Do you know why that medallion is so important?"

He nodded. "I believe so."

"Will you tell me?"

"Yes. But it's a long story and we're almost there. Do you want to hear it now or after we search the mission?"

The impact of what they were about to do hit Claire out of the blue. They were rushing off to the ruins of an old mission where they might find her brother's body. Tears burned behind her eyelids. It was the first time she'd let herself go that far. "We need to search the mission before we do anything else."

He must have heard the tremor of fear in her voice. He said softly, "It'll be okay."

Claire nodded, then turned to meet his gaze. He had that tender look in his eyes again, soft and solicitous. She couldn't remember the last time anyone had been so considerate, not only of her physical well-being, but also her emotional state. She was used to taking care of herself and had always been more than capable of doing so. But she had to admit it was nice to have someone watching out for her. Strange, then, that she would feel lonelier than ever basking in Ben Dornan's kindness.

She turned back to the passing scenery. "Why are we stopping?"

"We have to walk from here," he said.

"Your knee—"

"You let me worry about my knee. Just watch where you step and keep your eyes peeled for snakes."

"And scorpions."

"And scorpions. They grow them big around here."

CLAIRE DIDN'T KNOW what she'd been expecting from the photographs. Marion Palmer had described the ruins as little more than piles of rocks, but most of the limestone walls were still intact, along with the bell towers and the archways that opened into a long, narrow loggia. The roof had collapsed, probably centuries ago, allowing the surrounding landscape to intrude into what once had been a sacred space.

She'd done some research after returning to the apartment the night before. Mission San Miguel had been established in 1757 near the banks of the Medina River. Evidently, the steep arroyo that butted up against the structure hadn't provided enough protection from endless attacks by marauders. The mission had been abandoned ten years after the founding.

Amazingly enough, Claire could see the scraggly offspring of what once had been a bountiful orchard—figs, peaches, persimmons and even pomegranates. The old Spanish missions had been built for self-sufficiency with a church, living quarters, gardens and orchards along with a nearby source of fresh water.

Claire got out her phone and compared the structure to the one in the photographs. "I say we start with the loggia," she said as she nodded toward the arched breezeway. "That seems to be the area Connor was most interested in." She gave him a doubtful glance. "You don't have to do this. I know your knee must be killing you after that hike. I can go it alone from here."

If he was in pain, he hid it well. "No chance. We're in this together, remember?"

She nodded, grateful for his presence, and followed him across a ragged landscape of prickly pear and honey mesquite. The temperature seemed to drop the moment she stepped through one of the arches. The stone along the loggia was chipped and crumbling, and she could smell something dank emanating from the depths of the ruins. Shivering, she turned in a slow circle, her gaze climbing the walls, then dropping to scour the floor and the deep recesses that had once been doorways. *What were you looking for, Connor? And where are you now?*

"I'll take the inside," Ben said. "You search the perimeter."

"Are you sure about that? If the roof goes, I'm a little more agile than you at the moment."

He glanced through one of the doorways. "If the roof goes, agility will be the least of my worries. Besides, I'm wearing boots. Those sneakers won't be much of a deterrent to rattlesnake fangs."

She shuddered. "Okay, I'm convinced. But shouldn't I stay nearby in case you need help?"

"If I need help, you'll know it," he said with a wry smile. "Take a look around, but be careful. Even without the worry of snakes and scorpions, the spines on those prickly pears can be a real menace."

He got out his phone and stepped through the opening, pausing inside to turn on the flashlight. Claire stood outside and watched the trajectory of the beam as he slowly moved it around the space. "All clear," he said, then added. "So far."

She let out a breath as she moved away from the shelter of the loggia. It was still early, but the sun was already hot on her neck and shoulders. She'd left her sunglasses back at the apartment. Making her way around the outside of the structure, she paused now and then to shade her eyes with her hand as she scanned the landscape. She walked along the rim of the gully, peering down the craggy sides and all along the dry bed for any sign of life or movement while simultaneously listening for Ben.

A few minutes into her search, she stopped for a brief respite from the sun beneath the sturdy branches of a bur oak. Just beyond an outcropping of limestone, she spotted something white. Probably wildflowers. Or a piece of trash left behind by a careless hiker.

But the longer she stared, the more convinced she became that the flash of white was the sleeve of a shirt. Her heart

knocked against her chest as she moved to a different location for a better angle.

The body was all but hidden by the dense carpet of ri-
parian vegetation. She could make out a hand, a head, part
of the torso.

She screamed for Ben even as she started down the side
of the arroyo. He must have already been halfway to her because he seemed to appear out of nowhere.

"Down there." She pointed to the outcropping.

He caught her arm. "Let me go first."

She tried to wrench free. "I have to go—"

He held her fast, his dark gaze burning into hers. "Listen.
Listen to me. It may not be him. If it is…just let me go first."

Everything inside Claire wanted to resist, but she closed
her eyes and nodded. "Just hurry."

She watched as he climbed down the outcropping with
little regard to his injured knee. When he reached the body,
she couldn't wait. She started down after him.

He knelt, then quickly stood and backed away. Whatever
he'd found—whoever he'd found—had shocked him.

Claire was almost to him by this time. She could see the
white shirt, the outline of a body. She could even smell the
early stages of decomposition. Her heart was beating so hard
she felt lightheaded. "Is he—"

"It's not Connor."

Relief washed over her, so encompassing she had to bend
over to catch her breath. "Is he dead?"

Ben nodded, his face grim with shock and dread. "It's
Hector Zavala. His throat has been slashed."

WHILE THEY WAITED for the police, they discussed in hushed
voices what to do next.

"It's time to get some help," Ben said. "Until I can make
a few calls, set some things up, we tell Gil Bennett as little

as possible. I have reason to believe he's up to his neck in criminal activity—"

"What kind of activity?" Claire cut in.

"Drug trafficking, is my guess."

"What makes you think—"

"Let's stay on topic," Ben said. "We keep it simple. We came out here to explore the ruins. We say nothing about the photographs. Nothing about what happened at the festival. Nothing about Connor's disappearance."

Claire nodded. "I'm still shaking. I hope I can pull it off."

"You'll be fine," Ben assured her. "It's only natural you'd be rattled by what we found. Just go with it."

Two patrol officers arrived on the scene first, followed by a detective and finally Gil Bennett and the county coroner. The detective spoke to Ben and Claire separately. Claire braced herself for a barrage of questions from Bennett, but he seemed satisfied to let his detective take the lead. After an hour or so of standing in the hot sun, they were allowed to go back to their vehicle.

"Probably best not to leave town," Bennett advised them as they walked away.

Claire cut Ben a look as they headed back to the road in silence. He took her hand when she stumbled and didn't let go until they were safely inside his vehicle. She put on her seat belt then held out her hand as he started the engine.

"Still shaking."

"That's the adrenaline," Ben said. "It'll last for a while. Just relax and take a few deep breaths."

Claire closed her eyes and gulped in air. "When I spotted the body, I was so certain it was Connor."

"For a minute, I was, too," he admitted.

"Poor Mia. She'll be devasted."

Ben nodded briefly and turned back to the road, his expression grim.

They didn't speak again until they pulled up outside Connor's apartment. Marion Palmer stood on the upper gallery staring down at them.

"What's she doing?" Ben muttered.

"Being Marion." Claire waved at her. The landlady didn't wave back. She watched for a moment longer, then went back inside.

Ben turned to Claire, draping one arm over the steering wheel and the other along the back of her seat. "I wish I didn't have to leave you alone, but I have to go see Mia. I don't want her hearing about Hector from someone else."

"No, of course not." Claire drew another breath and released it. "She told me yesterday that Hector was more of a brother than a cousin. His death will hit her hard. She shouldn't be alone."

"I'll stay until she can call someone to be with her. Afterward, I'd like to come back here," Ben said. "We've got a lot to talk about, but I'm not sure the apartment is the best for that discussion." He shot a glance up to the gallery. "We can go back to my cabin if that's okay with you. After everything that's happened, maybe you should plan on staying the night. It'll be safer there."

Claire wasn't so sure that was a good idea, especially in her current state. She felt a little too vulnerable at the moment. She unbuckled her seat belt and closed her hand over the handle, but she didn't open the door. Instead, she spun back to Ben. "Do you think Hector was killed because of the medallion?"

"What, exactly, do you know about the medallion?"

"Mostly what I told you earlier. I know that you and Connor argued over it. I know that Hector likely stole it and that India Cortez added the emblem to a self-portrait that Connor just happened upon at a gallery in Austin. I know that India and Hector are dead and Connor is still missing. What

I don't understand is why. What's the connection? What can be so important about a silver medallion that someone is willing to murder for it?"

Ben gave her a look she couldn't quite define. "You haven't put it together yet?"

"Should I?"

"Maybe not. It happened a long time ago. Twenty-five years to be exact." She could feel his hand in her hair, a feathery touch that sent a shiver up her spine. "The short answer is that the medallion can link a cold-blooded killer to his victim."

Claire put trembling fingers to her lips. "Twenty-five years ago?"

He nodded.

"You can't mean what I think you mean. It's impossible. My dad was buried with his medallion."

Ben slowly shook his head. "He wasn't. It was taken from his body by the man who killed him."

Claire could only stare at him in shock. "That can't be true," she said on a breath. "My mother gave my dad that necklace. She was an artist. She designed the emblem herself. It was something personal to only the two of them. A bond that linked them even in death." She stopped for a moment and tried to regroup. "I was always of the belief—or maybe I wanted to believe—that the medallion went to my dad's grave with him. Why would the killer take it? It couldn't mean anything to him."

"The fact that it meant something to your dad is exactly why Stroud took it."

"Stroud." Claire repeated the name in a soft voice.

"James Stroud. You don't know that name?"

"I was never told the killer's name. Our aunt never wanted to talk about the past. We were never to ask questions about what happened that night. We weren't even allowed to mention Dad's name. We had to leave everything behind when we fled."

"That was for your protection."

"I know that now. She took good care of us, but sometimes I wonder if she was a little too cautious." Claire stared out the window. "I've lived a sheltered life. Always afraid to take risks. At the beginning of my career, I had the opportunity to train as a field agent for the Department of Homeland Security. I told myself I was better suited to the job of an outside analyst. Someone who sits in a cubicle and stares at a computer screen all day. No risk in that. But Connor. He uprooted his whole life to move here because he recognized a necklace in a painting."

"He came because of what that necklace represents," Ben said. "Justice. But tracking James Stroud hasn't been easy, even for the FBI. No one knows what he looks like. He's had twenty-five years of aging and multiple plastic surgeries to create an entirely new persona."

"What about fingerprints, DNA?"

"Nothing on record. He was always too careful for that."

"So what was Connor's plan?"

"To somehow trace the necklace back to Stroud."

"You think *Stroud* killed India and Hector?"

"Yes. Or he had someone do it."

"And Connor?"

Ben fell silent. "I think Stroud was behind the text message that lured you to San Miguel. If Connor knew that Stroud was closing in, he would have gone to ground until he could safely make contact. Stroud would know the quickest way to smoke him out was through you."

"But…how did he get Connor's phone?"

Ben said nothing.

"You don't really think Connor is in hiding, do you? You think Stroud has him."

"That's a possibility," Ben admitted. "But I think Stroud is still looking for that necklace—the one piece of evidence that could be his downfall. As long as he thinks Connor can lead him to it, he'll keep him alive."

"For how long?"

Ben nodded. "That's the worry and that's why I'm trying to call in favors and reinforcements. I have no official capacity to operate here. No backup or tech support. Even so, I'll do everything in my power to find Connor. You have my word on that. Right now, I need you to go inside the apartment and lock the doors. Don't let anyone in until I come back."

She bit her lip. "I still don't understand what this has to do with you."

"That's another long story."

"Is Ben Dornan even your real name?"

"Dornan is my mother's maiden name. I've used it when working undercover for the FBI."

"The *FBI*?" Her brows soared. "So you're not a former cop?"

"I'm still technically with the Bureau, but my future is up in the air at the moment."

"So what *is* your name?"

"Ben Navarro. Raymond Navarro was my father. Does that name ring a bell?"

"I don't—" She stopped herself in mid-denial. "Agent Ray?"

Ben nodded.

Claire tried to swallow past a sudden lump in her throat. "He was the one person our father told us we could trust. He came as soon as we called that night. He brought us down from the roof, wrapped us in blankets and took us back to his house. He had a son about our age named…" She froze again. *Ben.*

He smiled. "So you do remember."

"I could never forget that night. But…you said Raymond Navarro *was* your dad. He's gone?"

Ben's mouth tightened. "He was shot dead in our driveway by the same man who murdered your father."

"Oh, my God." Claire was genuinely stricken. "Ben, I'm so sorry."

"It was a long time ago."

"Yet here you are in San Miguel, I imagine for the same reason as Connor."

He didn't bother to deny it. "You didn't recognize me when we met. After twenty-five years, I wouldn't expect you to. But I knew there was something special about you the minute we collided at that convenience store. The night of the murder…" He trailed away, his gaze dark and mysterious. "You were so scared, trembling underneath that blanket like a frightened rabbit. I've never forgotten you. Or Connor. I was just a kid, but I've always regretted how I behaved that night. I was brought downstairs to try and make you feel less afraid. Instead, I turned on the TV and left you alone while I went into the kitchen to eavesdrop on my parents."

"I don't remember it that way at all," Claire said. "You did make me feel less afraid."

"I'm glad." His touch was gentle as he tucked back her hair. "Go inside. We'll talk more later, I promise."

"Ben." She caught his hand. "I'm sorry I didn't trust you."

"I'm sorry I didn't tell you the truth. No more secrets after tonight."

Chapter Thirteen

Ben picked Claire up at the apartment a few hours later and they drove straight out to the cabin, a beautiful place with a cedar deck that overlooked the crystalline waters of the Medina River. He grilled shrimp and vegetables, and they ate outside in companionable silence with a mild breeze drifting through the Spanish moss that hung from the bald cypress trees. Afterward, they washed the dishes together and then Ben poured them each a whiskey.

Claire eyed the glass. "In my state? I'm not sure this is a good idea."

"It'll help you relax. Make you sleep better."

"The way I feel right now I could curl up in a corner somewhere and be dead to the world in seconds." But she accepted the drink, and they went back out to the deck to watch the sunset.

The sky was a brilliant shade of orange fading to apricot and then lavender. When the light started to wane, Ben lit a citronella candle to ward off the mosquitos.

Claire dropped her head against the back of the chair and sighed. "I could stay out here forever."

"You wouldn't miss the city?"

"At the moment, no. Ask me again the next time I'm attacked or we stumble upon a body." She grimaced as soon as the words left her mouth, her thoughts once again turning to Connor. Where was he tonight? Did he have a view of the same sunset or was he locked away somewhere with no hope of anyone ever finding him?

She took a quick sip of whiskey, hoping the burn would help steady her. She could feel Ben's gaze on her as she concentrated on the river, blinking back sudden tears.

"What do you know about your father's past?" he asked after a few moments.

"I know he was a criminal. A thief. We weren't allowed to talk about the past or even mention his name, but every now and then, my aunt would let something slip. I put a few things together over the years."

"Do you want to know more?"

"I think I have to," she said.

"He was the youngest member of a crew run by James Stroud. They hit high end targets all up and down the east coast. Jewelry stores, banks, riverboat casinos. My dad chased Stroud for years, but he never could get so much as a photo of him, let alone a crew member willing to turn on him. He recruited your dad—he wasn't yet Nathan Cross—when he was in his early twenties. He already had a record. He thought Stroud would be his big break, easy money, but it didn't take long for him to realize that James Stroud was much more than the sophisticated, freewheeling thief he claimed to be. He was a killer, a sadist, a monster who inflicted pain purely for the enjoyment of it. I don't know all the details about how my dad was able to contact yours. They formed a partnership of sorts. Your dad—let's call him Nathan just to make things easier—agreed to help set a trap for Stroud and then to testify against him. In exchange, he would be given full immunity, a new identity and a chance to start over."

"What happened?"

Ben cradled his glass. "Something went wrong. My dad suspected a mole or a leak in the Bureau. Word got back to Stroud and he disappeared overnight. Just vanished without a trace."

"And my dad?"

"He'd kept his word. The immunity deal was still in place, but my dad now knew it was too dangerous to take Nathan into custody. He arranged a new identity—Nathan Cross—outside the Federal Witness Protection Program. A new birth certificate, a new passport and driver's license, new everything. Dad had an old army buddy who worked as a foreman on an oil rig in New Iberia, Louisiana. The kind of job where people come and go and don't ask a lot of questions. Nathan was a hard worker. He was smart and good with numbers. He eventually ended up working in the accounting office for the same oil company, and he met your mom soon after. She died two years after you and Connor were born. But you already know that."

"I don't even remember what she looked like," Claire said wistfully. "I barely remember my dad. But I'll never forget that last night. We had pizza for dinner and watched a movie, some animated film that probably bored him to tears but he never let on."

"He was probably just grateful to have that time with you."

"Something awakened me," Claire said. "I got up and went downstairs with no idea of what I was about to walk into. They were in the kitchen, Stroud and my dad. Stroud had a knife. Mostly, I remember the blood that dripped from the blade."

"Wait a minute." Ben put his hand over hers. "You *saw* him?"

"I only caught a glimpse before I ran, but I heard his voice. He kept saying to my dad over and over, 'Where is it? Where is it?'" She clutched Ben's fingers. "Did he mean the necklace?"

"He was probably looking for a stash of diamonds."

"Diamonds?"

"He always believed that before Nathan disappeared, he stole a cache from their last jewelry heist. Stroud probably needed those diamonds to fund his new identity. If you and Connor hadn't bolted when you did, he would have used you to get Nathan to talk."

A shudder went through Claire as she relived that night. "Dad taught us as soon as we were able to comprehend that under no circumstances were we to talk to strangers. If someone came to the house, we were instructed to hide. He planted burner phones in every room and kept them charged. If someone broke in, we were to grab a phone, crawl out the window and go up to the roof to hide."

"Why the roof?"

"He was afraid someone would be waiting on the ground to grab us. The roof was the least likely place for someone to look."

"He was smart to prepare you," Ben said. "But it must have taken a toll."

"We were so young we didn't know any other lifestyle." Claire got up and went over to the railing to peer down at the water, which had grown dark and mysterious with the setting sun. "I always thought that medallion had been buried with my dad. How did Connor know it had been taken?"

Ben got up and came to stand beside her, leaning a shoulder against a cedar post. "He found a box of letters and newspaper clippings in your aunt's attic after she died. She may not have allowed you to talk about the past, but she kept a detailed record of everything that happened in a journal. Somewhere in there she must have made mention of the missing medallion."

"How did you come into the picture?"

"After reading about my dad's death, Connor managed to track me down. We stayed in touch over the years. Mostly by phone and email. Occasionally, we'd meet in person. He became so obsessed with finding Stroud that he was already primed when he recognized the medallion in the painting."

Claire shook her head in awe. "All these years, he never said a word to me. He never let on that he even thought about the past."

"He didn't want to involve you. He said you'd carved out a nice, safe life for yourself and he didn't want you living in the past. And once he saw that painting, he didn't want to put you in danger."

"And you?"

"To be honest, I thought coming here was a wild-goose chase, but I was bored and frustrated by my injury. Scared to death, if I'm honest, that a career I loved was over. But it turns out, Connor was right all along."

Twilight was rapidly falling by this time. Claire felt simultaneously exhausted and wired by the conversation. She reached back for the whiskey glass and took a long sip. "It's strange, isn't it? Of all the places in the world for Stroud to hide he ended up in San Miguel. Just an hour's drive from where Connor and I grew up. The proximity can't be a coincidence."

"Not exactly a coincidence." Ben picked up his own glass but didn't drink. "According to some of the letters, Nathan had a connection to San Miguel. He'd spent a summer here as a boy and always swore he'd come back. Some of his happiest memories were on the river. Before he died, he wrote to your aunt about bringing you and Connor here someday."

"He never did," Claire said sadly. "And after he was murdered, my aunt was too frightened to bring us."

"Who could blame her?" Ben swirled his drink. "This is

just a guess, but I think Nathan must have mentioned San Miguel to Stroud at some point. Somehow Stroud got it in his head that the diamonds were stashed here."

"Do you think that's what Connor was looking for at the mission?"

"It's possible. But we both agreed a long time ago that there were no diamonds. At least none in Nathan's possession. Another member of Stroud's crew must have taken them."

"So my dad died for nothing."

"Stroud was a vengeful man. He would have come after him regardless."

Claire downed the rest of her drink.

"Easy," Ben cautioned as he took her glass and set it aside.

"I don't want to take it easy. I feel—" Her voice cracked. "I'm feeling pretty vengeful myself at the moment."

"I know the feeling." Ben polished off the rest of his drink. "Maybe we could both do with another," he muttered.

When he turned to go back inside, she caught his arm. "Wait. I need to tell you something. You said earlier that I didn't recognize you. That's true. I didn't. But I remember the boy who went out of his way to show my brother and me kindness on the worst night of our lives."

Ben shook his head. "You give me too much credit. I turned on the TV and left you alone."

"No, you didn't. You came back. Don't you remember? You sat with us. You brought us snacks and toys to distract us. You even showed us your rock collection, which you said was your most prized possession because most of the stones came from your grandfather's farm. You don't remember that?"

"Vaguely."

"Wait here." She went inside and hurried down the hallway to the bedroom where Ben had stored her tote. She rummaged inside until her fingers closed around her good luck charm.

He was still at the railing when she returned. She came up beside him. "Hold out your hand." When he complied, she placed the amethyst crystal in his palm. "You gave that to me before Connor and I were taken away. You said it was for protection. You said I should keep it close, just in case."

He glanced down at the softly glowing crystal, then lifted his gaze to hers. "Wow. Hard to believe you kept it all these years."

"I didn't just keep it," she said. "It goes into my suitcase before every trip. It sits on my desk every day at work. There was a time when I slept with it under my pillow. I may not have recognized you. But I've never forgotten you." She reached up and pulled him down for a kiss.

He responded for a brief moment before pulling away. He searched her face in the deepening twilight. "Are you sure about this?"

"No," she admitted. "That's kind of the point. Being cautious has kept me safe but lonely. I don't want to be alone tonight. And I'm tired of playing it safe."

"Maybe that's the whiskey talking." He rested his forehead against hers.

"Maybe. Or maybe I'm just being honest."

She took his hand and led him inside, down the hallway and into the bedroom. They lay down side by side on the bed, shoulders touching, fingers entwined, speaking in low, intimate tones.

"Tell me something about your childhood," Claire said softly.

"Not a lot to tell. My mother remarried when I was eleven and we moved to Pensacola. My stepdad was in the military. He was a good guy, but I never really warmed up to him. He made my mother happy and that was all that mattered."

"Where did you go to school?"

"Tulane. Prelaw. I was recruited by the FBI right after graduation. I spent a few years in DC before transferring to the New Orleans field office. After that, the field office in Houston." He turned on his side to study her. "What about you?"

"I studied finance at UT. I stayed in Austin for a couple of years before accepting a position with my current employer. I wonder if we were in DC at the same time."

"Seems likely."

"Yet our paths never crossed."

"That we know of."

"True."

He entwined a strand of her hair around his finger. "What about relationships?"

"A couple. They didn't work out. People don't like it when you keep secrets."

"Don't I know it?" She heard a smile in his voice.

She turned on her side to face him. "And you?"

"Nothing too serious. I was married to my work. Turns out, people don't like that, either."

They were both silent for a moment. "Claire?"

"Yes?"

"Are you sure you don't want me to go sleep on the couch?"

"That's the last thing I want. I know what you're thinking. I'm talking too much. It's just…" She paused on a sigh. "I've never been very good at this. You can't have real intimacy without complete honesty, and I've never been able to tell anyone the truth about my past. But you already know my past."

"Your secrets are safe with me," he teased.

"I know," she said in a serious tone.

He leaned over and kissed her. It was gentle at first, then the heat came. Her scalp prickled with the same electricity that zinged down her spine. When they finally broke apart, she whispered, "Did you feel that?"

He pulled her up until they were both on their knees, flinging their clothes to the four corners in between deep kisses. When they fell back against the bed, he rolled so that Claire was on top of him. She pushed back her hair as she stared down at him. "I told you. I'm not very good at this."

He lifted her hips. "Just wait. You have no idea how wrong you are."

Chapter Fourteen

Day Four

"Claire, wake up. Wake up!"

She opened her eyes and squinted. For a split second, she had no idea where she was. Then Ben's face came into focus. He was sitting on the edge of the bed, fully dressed, staring down at her.

She tried to blink away the cobwebs. "What's wrong? Has something happened?"

"Get up and get dressed. Hurry! We've got a lead."

She threw back the covers and scrambled out of bed. "What lead? What's happened?"

"Get dressed!" he called over his shoulder as he disappeared through the bedroom door.

Claire grabbed her bag and dashed to the bathroom. Hopping in and out of the shower, she quickly dressed and pinned up her hair, then followed the smell of fresh coffee out to the kitchen. Ben was seated at the counter with an open laptop in front of him. He pointed to the coffeepot without glancing up. "Help yourself."

She poured herself a cup, then walked over to the counter. "What's the lead?"

"We've finally been able to triangulate Connor's cell phone location. The last activation was a text message."

"Wait a minute? We?"

"I've had some help," he said.

"Should I ask about a warrant?"

"No."

"When was the last activation?"

"Wednesday, 9:45 a.m."

Claire did a mental time zone calculation. "That must have been the text he sent me while I was in Italy. How does that help us exactly?"

"The location is interesting. Come take a look."

She moved around the counter and stood over his shoulder. "What am I looking at?"

"A satellite image of San Miguel and the surrounding area." He pointed to a red dot. "That's where the text originated."

"Okay. And?"

"It's smack-dab in the middle of Lyle Fincher's ranch."

Claire couldn't take her eyes off that red dot. "Why would Connor be all the way out there?"

"We don't know for sure he was ever there, but his phone was." Ben shot her an apologetic glance. "It's not a lot to go on, but it's something."

Claire sat down on a stool next to him. "What do we do now? Can we drive out there?"

"We?"

"You can't expect me to stay behind and do nothing when my brother's life is at stake."

"If we go, it's for surveillance only," he cautioned. "We don't make a move until backup is in place."

"What backup?"

"I'm still working on that."

THEY PARKED A mile from the ranch and went in on foot, taking a position behind a hillside boulder that offered cover and an expansive view of the ranch house and outbuildings. Shortly after their arrival, a flurry of activity commenced. Two men carrying heavy suitcases came out of the house, stored the luggage in the cargo space of a large SUV, then climbed into the front. One of them was tall and wore a baseball cap.

Claire touched Ben's arm. "The one in the black cap. I think he's the guy from the alley."

Ben lowered his binoculars. "Are you sure?"

"No, but he could be."

A few minutes later, Lyle Fincher came out of the house. He spoke to the guys in the SUV through the passenger window, gesturing to some point in the distance. Ben handed the binoculars to Claire and pointed to the sky where a small plane had started to drop altitude with the landing gear locked into place.

She handed the binoculars back to Ben. "What's going on? Why the frenzy? And where is that plane landing?"

"Probably a nearby airstrip. As for the frenzy, I have a feeling Fincher may be getting ready to cut and run. Something must have spooked him."

"Run from what?"

"The cartel, the FBI. His partner."

"Who's his partner?"

"I overhead him and Gil Bennett arguing down by the river the other night. Lyle is involved with one or more of the cartels, and Gil is his fixer."

She turned with a frown. "And you never thought to mention this arrangement to me? What about no more secrets?"

"We've had a few other things going on," he said. "I'm telling you now."

Claire fumed for only a minute before she became engrossed in the tableau unfolding below. Lyle went back into the house and came out a few minutes later with a leather duffel bag. He tossed it in with the other luggage, then climbed into the back seat. The driver U-turned, leaving a thick cloud of dust as they headed toward the road.

Claire shifted to a more comfortable position. "Shouldn't we go down and have a look while they're gone? Connor could be locked up in one of those buildings."

"Just give it a minute," Ben said.

"But if Connor *is* down there and Fincher is getting ready to leave the country—"

"I know." He lowered the binoculars for only a second as his gaze met hers. "We'll find him but we have to do it the right way. Just trust me. I know what I'm doing."

He sounded so calm while Claire's pulse jumped erratically. "Okay. Your way."

Not ten minutes later, a fourth man came out of the house. He went into one of the outbuildings and was gone for what seemed like an eternity to Claire. When the door of the shed finally opened, he came out wiping his hands on a rag.

Claire gasped. "Is that blood?"

"Hard to say." But Ben's mouth had thinned, and there was something in his voice she'd never heard before.

The man went over to an outside faucet, washed and dried his hands, and then he, too, climbed into a vehicle and followed the others.

Claire let out a breath. "What on earth is going on down there?"

"Time to find out." Ben stowed the binoculars in his duffel and pulled out a gun. He checked the chamber and stuffed the weapon in the back of his jeans as he stood. "We go in silent."

She nodded.

They made their way down the embankment, using scrub

brush and mesquite trees for cover. Claire hugged the corner of the outbuilding while Ben went to reconnoiter. When he came back, they went in together.

The dusty shed was close and cluttered. No Connor chained to the wall as Claire had been imagining. Just a bunch of junk scattered all over the place. Nothing of value. Nothing suspicious. So what had kept the man inside for so long?

A pile of moth-eaten blankets had been tossed carelessly onto the floor. Ben toed them aside and then crouched to examine a large metal ring. "Bingo." He pulled on the ring and the floor hatch opened on well-oiled hinges. He peered down into the abyss.

"What is it?" Claire eased up to the edge.

"A tunnel. Probably where they bring the drugs in and out."

"Where do you think it leads to?"

"The landing strip, mostly likely. It's been used recently. The lights are still on." He lowered himself through the opening onto the ladder that was attached to the wall. Claire waited until his head disappeared and then she followed him down.

"You shouldn't be here," Ben said.

"Neither should you, but here we are."

He nodded to the lighted corridor. "That way."

They were about a hundred yards in when the tunnel split. One way remained well-lit, but the other fork had a single bulb beyond which was nothing but blackness. Ben turned on his flashlight and angled the beam down the long passage. It was damp and close inside the tunnel. Claire was already chilled, and now she was starting to get a little panicky.

"Should we turn back?" she asked anxiously.

Ben stood motionless, his head cocked as if he'd picked up on a sound that had escaped her. "Down there." He gestured toward the dark shaft. Claire glanced over her shoulder, reluctant to leave the well-lit tunnel behind.

A few feet in, he stopped again. "Shush."

This time Claire heard a scraping sound, like a chain being dragged across a concrete floor.

Ben turned and put his lips to her ear. "Wait here."

She watched as he disappeared into the darkness. He came back almost at once and motioned for her to follow him. A metal door had been set into the wall just beyond the reach of the light bulb. When Ben tried to open it, the scraping inside subsided and was followed by a weak, "Hello? Is someone there?"

For a moment, Claire thought her heart might flail its way out of her chest. She rushed to the door and placed her hands flat against it. "Connor? Is that you? Can you hear me?"

A long pause. "Claire?"

"Yes! Are you okay?"

"I'm not hurt." Another pause. "Claire, what are you doing down here?"

"I'm with Ben. We've come to get you out."

The jangling sound moved closer to the door. "You need to get out of here. I heard one of Fincher's men say they're going to blow the tunnel."

"How much time do we have?" Ben asked.

"Not long." Connor's voice was stronger now as if he stood just on the other side of the door. "I think Fincher is getting ready to leave the country. Ben?"

"Still here."

"We were right."

"I know."

"Don't let him get away. Whatever it takes."

"Let's worry about that later," Ben said. "How do we get you out of there?"

"There's a shackle around one of my ankles. It's connected to a chain bolted into the wall. I've been trying for two days to get it off. The door is metal. You can't kick it open."

Claire turned to Ben. "Can you shoot off the lock?"

"That's not as easy as they make it look in the movies. Besides, the sound could bring Fincher's men running. We need something to use as leverage. Like a crowbar. And a bolt cutter would be helpful."

"I saw some tools back in the shed," she said. "Should I go back?"

"I'll go," Ben said. "Stay put and keep quiet. If anyone comes down here before I get back, hide."

"Where?"

He angled his flashlight beam toward the darkest end of the tunnel. "Find a corner. Lay low. I'll be back in five minutes."

As soon as he was gone, she heard Connor say her name softly from the other side. She put her cheek against the door. "I'm here."

"Go with Ben. Get as far away from this place as you can."

"That's not happening. I'm not leaving you."

"Claire, please—"

"Shush." She turned her ear toward the corridor. Surely Ben couldn't be returning so soon. He'd only been gone a couple of minutes. She put her lips close to the door. "Someone's coming."

She could have sworn she turned in the opposite direction from the footsteps, but it was hard to distinguish the real sound from the echoes. Easing away from the door, she slid along the wall until she was in complete blackness. She huddled there hoping the danger would pass. The footsteps had gone quiet. No sound at all except for the blood pounding in her ears.

A light came on in her face. Behind the powerful beam, she could see the outline of three men in the corridor. She could only guess at their identities. The tall man from the alley and the sturdier silhouette of Lyle Fincher. The third man remained a mystery, probably one of the guys who had left earlier in the SUV.

The Connor imposter closed the distance between them and squatted. "Hi, sis."

"Cut it out," Fincher barked as he walked toward them. The ballcap guy stood and moved aside. "What the hell are you doing down here?" Fincher demanded. He leaned toward Claire until his face was only inches from her. "You alone?"

She nodded.

Fincher turned to the man in the cap. "Grab her. Take them both up to the house. And find whoever brought her here."

THEY REMOVED CONNOR from his shackles and marched them down the corridor, up the ladder, through the shed and back to the house. Claire fought to keep her gaze straight ahead. Ben was somewhere nearby. She wouldn't give away his presence with the dart of an eye.

They were taken into the great room where their hands were zip-tied behind them and their ankles duct-taped to the chair legs. Claire could see Connor from her periphery. He was bruised and scratched and filthy, but he didn't appear to be badly hurt. He caught her eye and dipped his head as if to reassure her.

Besides her and Connor, there were four people in the room. The three men from the tunnel and Gil Bennett. He'd stormed in a few minutes after their arrival, angry and anxious. His gaze moved from Claire to Connor and then back to Lyle. "What the hell? You had him in the tunnel the whole time you were yapping at me about an arrest? What the *hell* are you up to?"

Claire saw a chance and took it. "It's called misdirection. He wanted you occupied so you wouldn't catch on to what he's planning."

Gil scowled down at her. "What are you talking about?"

"He's getting ready to leave the country. You didn't know that, did you?"

"Shut her up," Fincher demanded.

"No, let her talk," Gil said, his gaze darting back to Claire.

She nodded. "He's already got a plane waiting on the airstrip. He's leaving you to deal with the Feds and the cartel and the murder. You're his patsy."

"I *said* shut her up!"

The guy in the ballcap grinned and grabbed the duct tape.

Connor cut her a glance, giving her a subtle cue. "*Wait.* Ask him about the diamonds."

Gil said in a dangerous voice, "What's he talking about? What diamonds?"

"From a heist years ago," Connor explained. "He's been looking for them ever since he arrived in San Miguel."

"Shoot them both," Fincher screamed.

"No, wait!" Connor flashed another glance, warning Claire to play along. "I know where they are. I can take you to them. Just let my sister go."

"That's funny, because you didn't know where they were two days ago," Lyle said.

"Everyone just shut the hell up!" Gil looked ready to explode. He walked over to Connor. "Where are the diamonds?"

"Let my sister go and I'll tell you. That's the deal."

Lyle grabbed Gil's arm. "There are no diamonds, you idiot. Try to get that through your thick skull. No. Diamonds."

Gil jerked his arm away. "Don't talk to me that way."

"Or what?"

"I told you—"

"Yeah, yeah, you told me." Lyle lifted a pistol and shot Gil between the eyes. The chief of police dropped with a loud thud to the hardwood floor.

Claire stifled a scream as her gaze darted to Connor. *Keep calm*, he mouthed.

Lyle stepped over the body. "After all these years, you still didn't know who you were dealing with," he muttered. To his men, he said, "Take him down to the tunnel and set the charges."

"What about these two?"

Lyle cut a glance in Claire's direction and smiled. "This is personal. I'll handle them myself."

After the two men carried the body out, Lyle walked over to Claire and put the snub nose of the pistol to her temple. "I prefer a knife, but we have to make do the best we can. Last chance, son. The medallion and the diamonds." He fingered the trigger. "I can make it quick or I can make it fun."

"You're wasting your time," a voice taunted from the doorway. "Neither of them knows jack about the diamonds."

Claire thought one of Lyle's men had returned, but instead she watched in astonishment as Sean Greggory stepped through the door. He didn't look sick or drunk. He appeared stone-cold sober and more than a little dangerous.

Lyle whirled. "How the hell did you get in here?"

"That was always one of your weaknesses," Sean said. "You were lax on security because you convinced yourself you were invincible. No one would dare go against the great James Stroud."

Lyle froze at the name. "Who are you?"

Sean merely laughed.

Lyle maneuvered until he had a bead on the newcomer.

He gestured with the pistol. "Tell me who you are before I shoot you between the eyes, too."

"You already know. You're just afraid to admit it."

"Johnny?" The name slipped out in a harsh whisper.

Sean chuckled. "You should see your face right now. Pretty good joke, right? Here I am, living right under your nose for nearly a decade and you never had a clue. You've gotten old and soft, Jimmy." He pulled the silver medallion from his shirt and dangled it in Lyle's direction. "You took this from me once. I wonder if you're man enough to do it again."

Now that the shock was passing Lyle said almost casually, "You forget who you're talking to, old friend. I killed you once. It'll be even sweeter—and slower—the second time around."

"Enough with the catching up," Sean said. "Back to business. The boy's bluffing."

"Like father, like son, eh?"

The comment almost went over Claire's head. Like father, like son... *What?!*

She shot Connor a glance. He was staring at Sean Greggory as if he'd seen a ghost.

Her head swiveled back to Sean. She saw something now that she'd never noticed before. The set of his jaw, the glint in his eyes...

She spun back to her brother. The same jawline, the same dangerous glint...

My God, how had she not seen it before? Even now, she didn't trust her own eyes. It couldn't be true. Her dad was dead. Murdered in cold blood by the man who stood before her.

The conversation had continued while Claire's whole world crashed around her.

"I'm telling you, he doesn't know where the diamonds

are," Sean insisted. "But I do. Let them go and the stash is yours. All of it."

Lyle cocked his head. "How do I know *you're* not bluffing? Maybe this is another of your traps."

"I guess you'll just have to trust me."

"Not likely," Lyle said. "I made that mistake once."

The ballcap guy appeared in the doorway, jolting Claire out of her stupor.

"Get lost," Lyle growled. "I told you this is personal."

The man stepped into the room and lifted his hands in the air. "Sorry, Mr. Fincher."

Ben came in behind him holding a 9mm to his back. "Drop your weapon," he told Lyle.

The older man merely laughed. "Shoot him. See if I care."

"This is the end of the line," Ben said. "The Feds are on the way. Nowhere to run to, Stroud."

"You think he's the only man working for me? All I have to do—"

In the split second Lyle's attention was diverted, Sean rushed him. They grappled over the pistol while Ben dropped the ballcap man with a blow to his head.

A shot rang out and Sean fell back, a bloom of red spreading across his chest. Lyle staggered to his feet and pointed the pistol at the wounded man. "You won't come back this time."

Ben lifted his weapon. "Don't do it," he warned.

Before James Stroud could pull the trigger, Ben took him down with one shot.

Chapter Fifteen

One week later

The days passed, and Claire was still barely able to comprehend the series of events that had brought her to San Miguel. But she was deeply grateful that her brother was apparently no worse for the wear and Sean aka Nathan aka Johnny had already been released from the hospital. Connor was currently seated at the bar in the Crooked Ferret in deep conversation with Mia. Sean had gone up to his apartment to rest. His story—his real story—was nothing short of astonishing.

He'd barely been alive when Agent Raymond Navarro arrived on the scene that night. In addition to whisking the twins to safety, he'd arranged for Nathan to be transported to a clinic run by a doctor that he knew from his army days. The doctor agreed to treat him as a John Doe. He even provided the body of another John Doe to be buried in Nathan Cross's grave.

The recovery was slow and painful. In addition to his internal injuries, Nathan's face had been slashed so severely that the scars would attract too much attention once he left the clinic. When he was able to travel, the doctor provided the name and address of a plastic surgeon in Mexico. For fifteen years, Sean Greggory wandered through the Mexican countryside chasing the ghost of his old nemesis. After years of fruitless searching, he planted his own rumor with some of James Stroud's former crew members. The diamonds, it was whispered, had been stashed in a place called San Miguel, Texas.

He settled in to wait for Stroud to turn up. But the same procedures that had made Nathan Cross look less of a monster and more like a disgraced man had also made James Stroud unrecognizable. Nathan had all but given up. Then his medallion made an appearance in the unlikeliest of places.

Everything Claire had learned in the past few days was still rambling around in her head as she and Ben walked down to the river. The bottle-green water looked cool and inviting. She was tempted to take off her sandals and wade in.

"What's going to happen to him?" she asked as she perched on the edge of a warm rock. "He still has a criminal record."

Ben came over to sit beside her. "His immunity deal is still in place. He upheld his end of the bargain. And helping take down one of the FBI's most wanted—and my dad's killer—will go a long way in his favor. The man's a hero in my book."

"What about the diamonds?" Claire asked.

Ben shrugged. "What diamonds?"

She lifted a brow. "Just like that? The slate wiped clean?"

"If there were ever any diamonds, they're probably long gone by now. Most of them anyway. He's paid for his mistakes, Claire. I say let him have a little peace. He's earned it."

"It's just so strange," she mused. "I don't even know what to call him. Johnny, Nathan, Sean."

"Why not just call him Dad? He's still in there, you know. The man who loved and raised you for the first seven years of your life…the man who gave up his whole world to protect you and Connor. That man is still there."

"I know that. I do. But I'm not like Connor. The two of them have already planned a trip to Mexico when Sean heals. I'm more reserved. I need time to sort things out."

Ben slid his hand down her thigh. "You weren't reserved last night. Or the night before or the night before that."

Claire shivered at his touch. "I'm not reserved with you. But you're different."

"Which brings up another interesting question." He kept his tone light, but his gaze turned intense. "What's next for us?"

She sighed. "I'll be heading back to DC in a couple of days."

"Why rush back? I still have the cabin for another month. There's plenty of room for two."

"Tempting for sure, but I'm out of vacation days. I have to get back. And maybe a little distance is what we need right now. Maybe we need some time to process. To figure out whether this—you and me—is real."

"Or…" He entwined his fingers with hers. "We could throw caution to the wind and see where it takes us."

"Quit my job? Just like that?"

"Not quit, transfer. Connor told me your company has an office in Houston. He said you'd been talking about moving back here for years."

"That's true." She got up and walked back to the water's edge, already putting distance between them.

Why was she resisting so hard? Claire wondered. True, she could get hurt. True, she could be running from nothing more than a summer fling. But it was also true that she could be turning her back on the love of her life.

Ben came up behind her, planting a kiss in her hair before he moved to her side. He took the crystal amethyst from his pocket and placed it in her palm. "You left this back at the cabin." He closed her fingers around it. "Twenty-five years ago, I gave this to you for protection. Now that James Stroud is dead, maybe it's time to let it go."

Claire held on tightly. The keepsake had meant the world to her all these years, but maybe Ben was right. It was time to let go of the past. Throw caution to the wind and live in the here and now.

"You said yourself, you're tired of playing it safe," he reminded her.

She smiled. "I did say that, didn't I? Only for you would I ever have the courage to do this."

She tossed the stone in a high arc over the river. A split second before the crystal splashed against the surface, a dozen tiny rainbows danced across the facets.

* * * * *

COLTON'S WILDERNESS RESCUE

KACY CROSS

Chapter One

Contrary to popular opinion, Sabrina West did not in fact hate all men. Mostly she didn't think about them. Unless they went out of their way to be misogynistic, condescending, rude or career-limiting.

Then she made it a point to earn every one of the unflattering names they called her behind her back. *They* being the particular subset of male creatures she worked with.

Dispatch shot her a concerned glance as she strode into United States Forest Service headquarters, letting the heavy glass door slam behind her with an angry clunk. Kirk Bonner—one of the *they* in question—had pushed her last button, and it wasn't even 8:00 a.m.

"You assigned yourself to search the Peavine area?" she asked as she stormed into the briefing room.

It wasn't really a question. She never had to ask if Bonner had done something specifically to irritate her.

The man lived to best her, belittle her, beat her. Too bad for him that he never succeeded.

Bonner glanced up. The fluorescent lights cast harsh shadows across his face as he leaned over the topographical map spread across the conference table. Three other rangers huddled around him, hanging on his every word like he was some kind of forestry wizard instead of just another officer gunning for the same promotion she wanted.

"Of course I did," he replied, his annoying drawl dripping with manufactured concern. "That terrain is brutal. Especially this time of year."

"I can handle Peavine." She kept her voice steady as she approached the table, boots thudding against the linoleum. The January cold had followed her inside, but the heat of righteous indignation made her wish she'd shed her heavy coat. "Unless you're suggesting there's something about that terrain that makes it more manageable for an officer with a Y chromosome?"

Bonner's eyes widened with fake innocence. "Come on, West. I'm just looking out for your safety. That area's full of deadfalls and rockslides waiting to happen. One wrong step—"

"Exactly why this situation calls for assigning the most experienced officer to that region." She placed both palms on the table, mostly to keep from punching the smug smile off Bonner's face. "That would be me. I've logged more wilderness hours than anyone else in this room."

The other rangers shifted, finding sudden and intense fascination with the map they all should know like the backs of their hands but probably didn't. Only she'd grown up breathing Dark Canyon's wild air, learning its moods, absorbing the energy of the stone and sky.

Bonner's jaw tightened, but before he could respond, Marcus Reynolds's deep voice cut through the tension.

"West is right." Marcus stepped into the room, his weathered face impossible to read. Just like her father's had been—which made working for this man familiar but not easy. "She knows that territory better than anyone. As you've all read in the alert that went out, we've got three separate hiking parties who haven't checked in this morning—a father and

son near south Elk Ridge, a solo hiker who started at Woodenshoe Trailhead and a couple who were supposed to camp
at Peavine last night. Time is critical with this weather system moving in. Rain'll be here soon."

Sabrina suppressed a smile as Bonner's face reddened.
She didn't need her boss's validation any more than she'd
needed her father's, but it felt good anyway—even if accepting it made her feel like that eager-to-please kid all over
again, the one who'd never quite measured up.

"I'll take Peavine," she reiterated firmly, already mentally cataloging her gear. The unusually snow-free January
had lulled some hikers into a false sense of security. They
didn't understand how quickly conditions could turn deadly
up there, especially when the temperature dropped.

Bonner opened his mouth to object, but Reynolds was already discussing the other search zones. Sabrina studied the
map, memorizing the coordinates while adrenaline hummed
through her veins. This was what she lived for—the challenge, the urgency, the chance to prove herself against the
wilderness and anyone who doubted her.

Let Bonner play his games. She had a job to do, and doing
it better than anyone else was the surest path to that promotion. She wasn't about to let any man stop her from claiming what she'd earned.

"Gear up and move out in fifteen," Marcus ordered.
"Check-ins every thirty minutes. And people?" He paused,
making eye contact with each of them. "Be careful out
there."

The gear room smelled of sweat and pine, familiar scents
that centered her. Sabrina pulled her emergency pack from
her locker, examining each item methodically. New batteries in the flashlight, fresh supplies in the first aid kit, extra
radio battery, emergency shelter. Check, check, check.

"Going to be nasty up there."

She glanced up to find Pete Holloway watching her from the doorway. The officer's dark eyes held none of Bonner's condescension—just genuine concern. Pete was a good guy, a rare one. Married fifteen years to his high school sweetheart, he treated Sabrina like a fellow officer instead of eye candy in a uniform.

Unlike some other guys she could mention. Most of her colleagues fell into one of two camps—the flirty types who figured they should at least give it a go and the ones who'd already been shot down.

Two guesses which category Kirk Bonner fell into.

"Weather system's moving in fast," Pete continued. "They're saying high winds by afternoon."

"All the more reason to find those hikers quickly." She shouldered her pack, double-checking the radio clip. "You headed to Woodenshoe?"

Pete nodded. "Keep your head on straight up there, West. Peavine's no joke even in good conditions."

"Thanks, Pete. You be careful too."

He'd always acted like he'd never noticed she had boobs under her uniform, a rarity in this male-dominated world of treacherous terrain, extreme elements, and breathtaking elevations. Though sometimes it got really old never meeting anyone who appreciated *all* of her assets. It wasn't like she started out trying to chop off all the male extremities in a mile-wide radius. Was it her fault none of them could hack it?

The last guy she'd dated had tapped out after three months, claiming she was too intense, too focused, too much. *Too bad.*

Sabrina wasn't about to dial herself back just to make some man comfortable with her strength. What she really wanted was someone who matched her in every way. Who was man enough from the first moment that it never occurred to him to feel threatened. A guy who could keep up, be a companion. Make her feel like being feminine might have some pluses in certain situations.

A unicorn, basically. So she'd be single for the next seventy-five years. It was fine. Watching her parents go through a bitter divorce had cured her of any happily ever after dreams long before the reality of the dating pool had.

The cold bit through Sabrina's heavy coat as she jumped into her Forest Service vehicle, then navigated it up the winding access road. Heavy cloud cover turned the sandstone rock ahead a grayish color.

She'd learned to read these canyons like other people read books, each shadow and contour familiar. But wrong. Everything should be draped in white by this late in the season. Even the air felt off, heavy with potential energy that made her skin prickle.

She tried to shake it off.

Her radio crackled. "West, what's your position?"

"Approaching Peavine Canyon access point," she responded calmly, even though Bonner's voice alone chafed against her skin. "Beginning segment sweep from the northwest quadrant. Over."

"Let me know if you need backup."

She rolled her eyes. Bonner was something else. "Copy that. I'll radio Reynolds if I need support."

The road ended at a small turnaround. Beyond, the wilderness yawned, stretching as far as the eye could see, both stark and beautiful at the same time. Sabrina grabbed her pack and stepped out into the crisp morning air.

Now she could breathe. Finally.

The vast open space of Dark Canyon called to her soul. Out here, she wasn't Officer West or the product of a broken home—she was simply herself, fierce and free. Part of the land, part of the sky.

A red-tailed hawk screamed overhead, the sound echoing off the canyon walls. She tracked its flight, noting the wind direction. The missing couple—Jason and Sarah Miller, according to their backcountry permit—were supposed to have made camp in the sheltered valley two miles into Peavine Canyon, a logical choice for its protection against the wind and for its proximity to seasonal water sources.

She pulled out her GPS unit and marked her starting coordinates. The Millers were experienced hikers, according to their permit application, but experience didn't always translate to good judgment. Sabrina had seen too many seasoned outdoorsmen make rookie mistakes, especially when unusual conditions lulled them into complacency.

The first mile of trail showed no signs of recent passage—no scuffed rocks, no disturbed vegetation, nothing to suggest anyone had come this way in the past twenty-four hours. She documented her observations into her field notebook, keeping her notes concise. Detail work like this bored some officers, but Sabrina liked everything about her job.

She liked being good at it more than anything. Even in this small, likely insignificant area of note-taking. That's what integrity and excellence meant—doing your best despite the lack of an audience.

Bonner could take a lesson.

She'd be sure to teach it to him when she got the district ranger position and became his boss.

The trail wound through stands of juniper and piñon pine before opening into a rocky stretch that required careful navigation. Each step carried her deeper into the canyon, the walls rising steep and unforgiving on either side. The Millers' planned route would have taken them through here yesterday afternoon.

A splash of color caught her eye—a granola bar wrapper wedged between two rocks. The wrapper was fresh, the foil still bright. Someone had passed this way recently. She photographed it to mark its location and condition before retrieving it with gloved hands. No one liked to think about the possibility of a search mission turning into an investigation, but it happened.

She grabbed her radio. "Dispatch, West checking in. Found signs of recent hiking activity along the main trail. Continuing northwest."

"Copy that." The dispatcher's voice crackled with static. "Bonner reports contact with target subjects at Elk Ridge. He's bringing them in now."

Of course he was. Biting back a grimace, she switched off the radio with more force than necessary and pressed on. Now she had double the reason to prevail in her search.

The trail grew more challenging as it climbed, loose rubble making each step treacherous as it shifted beneath her boots. Each step required her full attention. She picked her way carefully across a particularly exposed section, very aware of the steep drop-off to her right.

Not because it scared her. Because it didn't.

This was the stuff she lived for. The sharp edge of danger, the breathless pulse of knowing one wrong move could change everything—it made her feel alive in a way few things could.

Clouds were closing in, thick and ominous, painting the sky in shades of gray that matched the rock around her. She needed to find these campers before the weather turned and the canyon became even more unforgiving. Another fifteen minutes in, she still hadn't found any definitive sign of the Millers. She paused to radio her position, scanning the jagged ridgelines and shadowed slopes below.

A glint of metal flashed up on the ridge where no metal should be. Or people.

Maybe the Millers had climbed higher for a better view of the canyons. Or maybe it was nothing. Another scrap of foil caught in the wind.

A responsible searcher would stick to the trail, continue the grid search pattern and trust the process. But her gut, her finely honed instincts, whispered otherwise.

She shifted her weight, testing the stability of the narrow ledge she stood on. The ridge was higher, steeper, the approach riddled with loose scree and blind turns. A fall here wouldn't just hurt—it could kill her.

But what if she ignored the glint only to find later that she could have saved the Millers by investigating? Besides, the view from the ridge was spectacular and she'd never backed down from a challenge.

Her pulse kicked up a beat.

"West checking in," she said into her radio. "Following up on possible evidence off trail. Will report findings in fifteen."

"Negative, West." Dispatch's voice crackled. "You need to maintain your assigned route—"

She clicked off. If Reynolds wanted to reprimand her later, fine. But she wasn't about to let Bonner get the upper hand. The promotion they both wanted *should* go to the best candidate. Her. But she'd always had to prove herself by being twice as good.

Always. Even now, in this moment.

The rock face offered plenty of handholds, but the sandstone was brittle, prone to breaking away without warning. Sabrina tested each grip carefully before committing her weight, hyperaware that she was alone up here.

No backup, no safety net.

Her father's voice echoed in her head: *Pride makes you careless, and careless gets you killed.*

She pushed the thought away and kept climbing. Bonner had found his missing group; she'd find hers. Period.

Near the top, the terrain leveled off into a small plateau, offering a sweeping view of the canyon below. The glint turned out to be a bracelet, thin silver catching the weak sunlight filtering through the clouds. Sabrina moved closer, her pulse quickening as she spotted something else partially hidden behind a boulder.

A woman's body lay crumpled on the ground, blonde hair fanned out like a halo against the dirt.

She wasn't moving, her limbs spread at odd angles.

Sabrina sprinted toward her, already reaching for the first aid kit at her belt. Two fingers pressed against the woman's neck confirmed what she'd feared—no pulse, skin cool to the touch.

Heart on jackhammer mode, Sabrina cataloged the woman's features. Early twenties, delicate build, wearing only jeans and a light sweater. No coat, no hiking boots, no gear. Definitely not Sarah Miller, who was a brunette, according to her permit photo.

Blinking, Sabrina tried to recall if she'd ever seen this woman around Dark Canyon but came up blank.

"Dispatch, this is West." She kept her voice steady despite the adrenaline surging through her system. "I've got deceased human remains near marker—"

The ground shuddered beneath her feet, cutting off her words. A deep rumble filled the air as the rock itself seemed to come alive around her, tumbling and wheeling.

Earthquake.

Not uncommon in this region, but the timing couldn't have been worse.

Sabrina lunged for more stable ground as loose rock began to cascade down the cliff face. The radio squawked with voices she couldn't make out over the sound of shifting earth. She pressed herself against the canyon wall, her throat tight as a shower of rock and debris rolled and bounced over the body she'd just discovered.

A woman. That body was a woman, a person. A dead one, but she must have people who cared about her. Who would want to know what had happened to her. Plus, she hadn't wound up out here in the wilderness by herself, not this far out with no coat.

If she'd been the victim of foul play, the body held all the evidence.

And now she was disappearing under tons of unstable rock.

Hands shaking, Sabrina palmed her radio again. "Dispatch, come in. We have a situation. The quake triggered a major rockslide." She swallowed hard, steadying her voice. "The body is now under significant debris. I need search and rescue, excavation equipment—"

Another tremor hit, smaller but enough to send more rocks tumbling. Sabrina flattened herself against the wall, breathing in the acrid dust. The plateau she stood on felt suddenly precarious, like a table missing a leg.

Any wrong move could bring the whole thing down. On her.

She would be buried, just like the Jane Doe she'd found. Only she'd be alive when it happened.

"West. Come in. Repeat. Are you okay?" Dispatch's voice crackled through static.

"Copy. I'm here," Sabrina acknowledged hoarsely.

"Do not attempt recovery alone. We're locking on your GPS coordinates now. Search and rescue is en route. Along with Dark Canyon police officers."

Sabrina stared at the fresh rock fall, memorizing every

detail. Someone had brought that woman up here. Maybe the same someone who had killed her. And now Mother Nature was helping cover their tracks.

Not on her watch.

Chapter Two

Noah Colton screeched to a stop at the small turnout near the coordinates he'd been given for the search site in Dark Canyon Wilderness, landing sideways in the clearing that probably wasn't meant to be a parking spot. But if you weren't coming in hot and spraying a shower of gravel to announce that you'd arrived to get the party started, what were you even doing with your life?

Besides, driving fast and furiously had its perks, but it wasn't his job. And he'd been itching to get out into the field from the moment he'd received the call.

A body hidden by a rockslide was exactly the kind of challenge that made his blood pump faster. Search and rescue work wasn't the same rush as investigative journalism, but he loved it.

Maybe not as much, but it was close. He'd made his peace with walking away from chasing stories. Mostly. When his mom had gotten sick, he'd dropped everything and come home to Dark Canyon with no regrets.

Noah made it a habit to never look back. All the good stuff lay forward.

Dancer stood at high alert in his travel carrier, picking up on his energy like always. The golden lab might as well be the other half of his brain. They'd worked seamlessly together from moment one.

The second Noah opened the carrier door, Dancer sprang from the back seat of the truck, sidestepping in excitement. That's how he'd gotten his name—he did this funny dance step crossover move when forced to hold back.

They understood each other. Noah didn't like boundaries either.

Grabbing his gear, he trekked to the scene, a long haul in the biting cold, well accustomed to people's tendencies to *never* disappear near the road. Once on-site, he surveyed the scene, his mind chopping through what he knew.

A dead body in Dark Canyon meant questions that needed answers. The kind that used to drive him halfway around the world in search of the truth.

If only…but that wasn't why he was here. SAR was his job now. Find what was hidden, uncover the land's secrets. No room for mistakes when lives were at stake.

Though this would be a rare one for him, already knowing from the outset that this was a recovery effort, not a rescue. That alone accounted for why his attention had veered even slightly from the mission.

The weather had turned nasty since the earthquake, clouds heavy with promised rain. Not ideal conditions for scent work, but Dancer had delivered in worse. Noah pulled out his radio to check in with incident command, documenting the deteriorating conditions. Everything by the book— scene contamination was already a concern with the number of personnel moving around.

"Command, Colton on site. Need immediate perimeter control and photo documentation before search begins. Over."

"Copy that. Establishing fifty-foot perimeter now."

His gaze snapped to the woman pacing near the fresh evidence of a rockslide.

Hello. What have we here?

She had to be Officer West, the one who'd discovered the body before the earthquake hit. Yes, okay—she was the only female in the entire group, but that wasn't why she'd instantly commanded his attention.

Energy crackled off her as she moved. And the way she moved…efficient. Commanding. The woman possessed serious presence and it hooked something inside him. Noah found himself picking up his pace to reach her, Dancer matching his stride.

"Officer West," he called out. "I understand you have a difficult recovery situation for us."

She turned, and Noah's breath caught. He'd been expecting capable. He hadn't been prepared for the fire in her blue eyes or the way she sized him up with the same hungry intensity he saw in the mirror every morning. She was all throttle, no brakes.

Her gaze swept him from head to toe in kind, and she didn't bother to disguise the fact that she appreciated what she saw. *Likewise, Officer West. Likewise.*

The air between them sizzled.

Oh. Boy.

"Colton." Her gaze sucked him in and they stared at each other. "Related to Jacob?"

"My brother." He nodded once, because of course she'd be acquainted with National Park Services personnel. His brother was the reason he had a job.

"That's a tick in the pro column, then," she said, with an eyebrow lift. "He's one of the best they've got at NPS."

"I have another brother and some cousins running around Dark Canyon, too," he threw in, just in case that counted toward an invisible tally that would land him her phone number later.

Because he was definitely asking her for it.

"Thanks for coming out so quickly." She gestured over her shoulder, all business now. "I can show you the approximate location, but the rockslide changed the landscape. I'm not even sure where to start."

Perfect. This was what he did best—solving puzzles. Just not the kind that led to hard-hitting exposé pieces. "That's what Dancer's here for. But first, walk me through exactly what you saw before the earthquake hit."

He pulled out his field notebook, the waterproof one with the pencil that wrote on anything, wet or dry.

Officer West eyed his setup. "I have that same one," she commented with a thread of appreciation. "The rest of these yahoos like their electronic tablets, but I'm old school."

Noah grinned. "Never needs charging and works even if you end up in the river."

"Which happens more often than you'd think."

Oh, yes, he did like this woman a whole lot. "Exactly what I was about to say."

Her answering smile put a very nice hum in his gut. He scrubbed at his beard to refocus his attention on the job at hand. Plenty of time for flirting later.

"Here's what you can write down in your notebook. I was searching this area for missing hikers when I spotted something reflective." She pointed to a section of rock and debris. "The body was there, partially hidden behind that outcropping. Then the earthquake hit."

The investigative journalist in him wanted to pepper her with follow-up questions: Had she identified the body? Did there appear to be foul play involved? Any history of other bodies turning up in the area?

But that wasn't his role anymore. Focus on recovery. Leave the investigation to others.

Noah studied the rockfall pattern, already mapping potential search grids in his mind. The slide had created an unstable cone of debris—they'd need engineering support before any excavation could begin. But first, they had to pinpoint the location.

USFS personnel and some other uniforms—cops—milled around near the rockslide. One of them, a beefy guy in a USFS uniform that matched Officer West's in style strode over, clearly having overheard what they were talking about.

"West, we've accounted for all registered hikers," he said, bracing his hands on his hips. "Are you sure you actually saw a body? The earthquake could have affected your perception of things."

Wow. Talk about lack of professional courtesy. Not to mention a severe inability to read the room. Noah had known this woman for all of fourteen seconds, and even he could see she didn't miss much.

Officer West pivoted to face the man, her chin lifting. Somehow, she managed to drop the temperature with nothing more than the disdain dripping from her expression. Which was saying something, considering the already frigid weather.

"The victim wasn't a hiker, Bonner. She was wearing regular shoes and a light sweater." Her voice sharpened with razor precision. "But please, don't let that stop you. Continue explaining to me how I don't know the difference between a rock and a dead body."

Noah hid a smile, secretly cheering her on, because *dang*.

The guy she'd called Bonner clenched his teeth. "Just remember, resources are limited. Let's hope this isn't a wild-goose chase."

Oh, no, he had *not* just spoken for Noah without permission. "Since the resources are me and my dog, you might want to step that back a notch before I decide you calling me limited was an insult."

Officer West crossed her arms, a grin on full display because she didn't seem to be the type to hide much of anything. "You heard the man. Step back. And then do it again until you're inside your vehicle. This is a one-woman show."

Okay, that decided it. Noah officially had a raging crush on Officer West.

It was a little surprising that he'd never met her before, but he worked with NPS all over the state, not solely in Dark Canyon, so he traveled a lot. Jacob worked as a special agent for Parks Services, and had often called Noah in for his recovery expertise, which he'd spent four years building to fill the void that walking away from journalism had left.

Noah clicked his radio to the search channel. "Command, Colton on scene. Beginning search setup. Need updated terrain stability report and scene documentation before we start the grid."

While uniforms moved to establish the boundary, Noah ran Dancer through his pre-search routine. The lab's disciplined focus helped center him. He had a job—find what was lost, bring closure. Not chase down leads or expose corruption. Just because this scene had fired up his old investigative instincts didn't mean he had to listen to them. Right now, anyway.

Though watching Officer West document notes in her field notebook with such precision made those instincts sing. There was something about her…he couldn't put his finger on it but whatever it was made everything inside him sit up and take notice.

It was a siren's song that he felt powerless to resist. Mostly because he didn't want to.

"Officer West, I'm not done with you," he called. Not by a long shot.

"What else would you like to know?" She kept a professional distance, but her energy filled the space between them. Her straight-backed posture and clipped tone screamed military background.

Why was that sexy? He'd never have called that a preference before, but it suddenly felt extremely necessary to add to his list.

"Tell me more about the body and where it was the last time you saw it before it was buried. Then Dancer will work a grid pattern from your original vantage point." He nodded toward his partner, who sat at his side in ready-to-go mode. "He's certified in human remains detection. The rockslide actually works in our favor—might have trapped scent evidence we can use to pinpoint the location."

"The victim was female, early twenties, blonde," Officer West snapped out with clinical meticulousness, as if she'd been poised to spit out this information. "Wearing jeans and a light sweater—completely inappropriate for the conditions. No hiking gear. Body was partially concealed behind that outcropping." She indicated a now buried section of rock. "I spotted a silver bracelet first, reflecting sunlight."

He should really find out her first name. Though he could get on board with calling her Officer West for the foreseeable future.

Noah documented each detail in his search log while part of his mind spun theories. A young woman in regular clothes didn't end up dead on a mountain by accident. The journalist in him itched to start digging, connecting dots.

It sucked to have to keep reminding himself that he had a specific role here, and it wasn't that. The investigation would have to be left to others.

Even if it killed him a little.

That was the real issue—he'd been telling himself he was fine with leaving that life behind, but this incident had started spinning a completely different narrative.

One he didn't want to ignore.

While the incident commander coordinated with the terrain engineers, Noah worked with Officer West to establish a precise grid pattern based on her original sighting. She moved with the efficiency he remembered from working with his best field contacts—anticipating needs, thinking three steps ahead.

His world had gotten smaller since coming home to care for his mom. More controlled. Not by choice but definitely by design. He was here for his family.

Officer West made him think about what it felt like to shed all of that, to strap in for a wild ride with an intriguing woman at his side. To seek for himself, instead of relying on Dancer to do the heavy lifting.

"Command, beginning grid search from Officer West's initial position," he reported, pushing the thoughts away. "Dancer, hunt."

The lab moved out in a particular pattern, nose working methodically. Noah had trained him to indicate from a distance once he caught scent of human remains, preserving the scene for evidence collection. Four years of working together had honed their partnership to near telepathy.

He'd never worked with a partner before this one, but he liked it.

"Your dog's impressive," Officer West said, watching Dancer work. She'd positioned herself to document the search pattern without interfering. "That level of discipline takes serious training."

"He's a natural." Noah kept his attention on his partner so he didn't react to the way the very atmosphere hummed with her presence. "Found him at a shelter if you can believe it. Their loss. My gain. And the state of Utah's, since he became one of the best SAR dogs around."

That was how life worked sometimes. Like how his mother's illness had cost him his previous life but given him another. Everything was a trade-off.

But sometimes, cases like this came along and it seemed cruel that he'd lost everything. Including his mother.

Dancer's posture shifted subtly—a change only Noah would notice after countless hours working together. His nose worked faster as he quartered back across his pattern.

"He's got something." Noah clicked his radio. "Command, possible indication in grid seven. Standing by for confirmation."

Officer West took an unconscious step forward before catching herself. The intensity in her eyes spoke to him at a bone-deep level. She wanted to be in the middle of things, not standing on the sidelines. He knew the feeling.

"Multiple spots," Noah noted as Dancer's pattern tightened. "The slide probably scattered evidence. We'll need to map it carefully before we start excavation."

Officer West was already documenting coordinates. "I can provide my exact position when I first spotted her. Help establish the original location."

Noah had just opened his mouth to ask her to do that, and she'd read his mind again. Dang, he did like being on an identical wavelength with Officer West.

Dancer barked sharply—his trained alert that meant absolute certainty.

"Call it," the incident commander's voice crackled over the radio.

Noah looked at Officer West, recognizing the satisfaction in her expression. She'd known the victim was here. And unless he missed his guess, she'd very much like to rub her colleague's nose in it.

Actually, he'd like to see that too. No one had asked him to pick a side, but he'd landed on Team Officer West the moment the tool had opened his mouth and proven he had a Neanderthal brain.

"Grid seven confirmed," Noah reported. "HRD positive indication at multiple points. Scene is hot—full recovery protocols in effect."

As the recovery team moved in to begin mapping the site, Noah found himself studying Officer West's contained energy. She reminded him of himself before life had forced him to change course. When he'd known exactly who he was and what he was meant to do.

Maybe that's why he couldn't quite ignore how she made his blood sing with possibility. She embodied everything he'd walked away from—the thrill of the chase, the drive for truth, the certainty of purpose.

Dancer nudged his hand, grounding him in the present. In who he was now.

"Good boy," Noah murmured, scratching his partner's ears. Focus on the job. Do what you came for.

But watching Officer West in her element, her movements precise and measured despite the electric energy coursing beneath her professional demeanor, Noah knew in his bones this would not be the last time he saw her.

He wasn't one to look before he leaped, especially not when it came to a woman who intrigued him as much as Officer West. Sure, he had a string of broken hearts in his rearview mirror—all of them his own. Came with the territory when you careened into everything sideways, no holds barred. That was the one lesson he'd learned from his mother's death—the clock was ticking for everyone on this earth and no one knew when their time would be up.

So he'd vowed to make the most of life while he could, no apologies. He wasn't about to start now.

Chapter Three

Afternoon shadows stretched across the canyon as Sabrina watched the recovery team begin their careful work. *Watched* might have been too generous of a word. She maintained a peripheral awareness that other people besides Noah Colton existed in the world. But she doubted she could name anyone else working at the recovery site at gunpoint.

Where had this guy been hiding?

The temperature had dropped another few degrees, but she barely noticed. Her attention was locked on the man directing the operation with authority that was so sexy, it defied logic.

He kept shooting her secret glances that hummed along her skin. It didn't hurt that Jacob's brother had gotten every ounce of the Colton charm and then some; plus, it came wrapped in a delicious candy shell that she could easily envision taking a bite out of. Repeatedly.

She should probably be doing something professional, but honestly, Noah didn't seem like he needed any help, so it kind of worked in her favor to sit back and enjoy the view.

"Engineering team confirms ground stability in the primary search area," Noah reported into his radio, his voice carrying that same wicked edge that had burrowed beneath her skin the moment she'd first heard it. "Beginning evidence documentation. Need photo team on site."

The way he handled the scene—professional, but with enthusiasm she didn't often run across—intrigued her. She'd seen enough SAR operations to understand that Noah operated on a whole different level. A cut above.

He cared. She could feel it in the set of his jaw and the way he kept his body turned slightly into the scene instead of away from it. It was a subtle tell, but he was *invested*.

A lot of people just did their job, no extra effort. This guy wasn't clocking in another day at the office. For one, Noah never took his eyes off his lab, even if someone spoke to him. That dog mattered to him.

"Would you like me to find you a task, Officer West?"

Noah's gaze lit on hers, his out-of-the-blue question carrying a hint of amusement that put a slight curl on her own lips.

Shockingly.

Men usually didn't have a prayer of making her smile, even when they tried to. But this one had noticed that she felt at loose ends, even while running his incredibly intricate operation. Points to Noah Colton.

"I'm fine watching. Just don't want to miss the moment when I should take my victory lap." She matched his tone, keeping things light. "You know, for when you prove I'm not crazy and there's actually a body under all that rock."

He turned to face her fully, and that spark she'd felt earlier flared again. The man topped her by several inches, which she normally didn't consider a plus, but there was something about Noah that made her feel very feminine, and she didn't hate it.

Also shocking.

"I never doubted you. Neither did Dancer." A small smile played at the corners of his mouth. "We're the ones who count."

"Agree with that."

"Besides—" he gestured to where his dog maintained position at the edge of the search grid "—I trust my partner's nose, and it's saying there's something here to find. You don't seem like the type to waste everyone's time and energy, so I'm putting my money on your instincts over your colleague's opinions any day of the week."

The compliment pricked at something in her chest, which was ridiculous. She didn't need validation from any man, especially one she'd just met, no matter how much he oozed appeal. One recovered body would be all the vindication she needed.

Moving on.

"Speaking of which," she said, redirecting to safer ground, "what's your timeline for recovery?"

"Depends on how deep she's buried and what the engineers say about maintaining stability as we start to dig." He consulted his notebook, where he'd documented her initial report. "The fact that you saw her partially concealed behind that outcropping before the slide works in our favor. Suggests she might be in a relatively protected pocket."

His quiet competence was extremely attractive. Most men she worked with tried to impress her with bravado. Noah just…did the job. Incredibly well.

Stop obsessing over the pretty man.

"The sooner we can get to her, the better," she said, fighting the urge to move, to do something besides stand there. Especially if it would help her refocus. "I'm worried the weather won't hold."

"I'm not going to let you—or her—down." Noah's gaze settled on hers, and it was like slipping into a warm bath at the end of a long day. "Dancer is the best. We're not leaving here without the truth."

"Is that what we're doing?" She couldn't help but push

on this intriguing glimpse into Noah's mind. Also known as not shoving their association back into the professional realm. Oops. "Discovering the truth?"

"Always." He paused as Dancer let out a sharp bark. "Excuse me."

Sabrina watched him jog over to his partner, their silent communication fascinating. The dog's alert posture shifted slightly, nose working the air, and Noah immediately radioed the change to the recovery team. They worked seamlessly together, mapping out the grid so they could finish the job. Find the truth.

Truth. Noah had dropped the concept into the conversation without apology and she found that she liked thinking of search-and-rescue efforts as uncovering the truth. She'd never really put that together before, but what was SAR if it wasn't meant to provide answers? Someone cared about the missing person. Family members, law enforcement officials, the coroner. They all had a stake in the results of Noah's efforts.

And eventually, together, they'd all figure out the truth of why a lone woman ended up out here in the unforgiving wilderness.

Sabrina wanted those answers too.

That was the thing to focus on here, not the tall drink of water directing everything.

The afternoon wore on and Sabrina tried to stay out of the way. Eventually, Noah ceded control of the grid to the recovery team, and the digging began in earnest. The engineering and stability experts had done their jobs well in securing the site, so the pile of rock and silt gradually began to diminish.

Noah drifted closer to Sabrina, his smile easy and pointedly directed at her. "Not much longer now."

She nodded, savoring the rush of knowing that he'd sought

her out. He probably shouldn't have. She probably shouldn't
have hoped he would. This was an intense search-and-rescue
operation, not a bar, but she didn't make it to social events
too often anyway. Where else was she supposed to meet intriguing men but in Peavine Canyon while the temperature
hovered near freezing?

Besides, bar flies didn't interest her. Noah Colton did.
Why should she apologize for it?

"Is this like, a normal Tuesday scene for you, or is a rockslide a one-in-a-million call?" she asked, genuinely interested in any glimpse he wanted to give her of himself, his
job and his world.

"It's not my first rockslide," he said, his expression sobering. "But I much prefer this one to the last one. The victim was still alive when he was buried. It didn't end well."

"That must be a tough part of the job," she said. "Knowing that sometimes it's just search, no rescue possible."

"It's all just establishing the truth," he reminded her with
a head tilt. "Sometimes the truth is more painful and difficult than we would prefer, but it still has to be told."

Oh, so he had a side of emotional maturity with his blin-
dingly gorgeous face? Yes, please. "Well said."

Noah gestured toward the dig site. "If the engineer's cal-
culations are correct, we'll find your Jane Doe after they
remove this next layer. Dancer called that spot early on and
never wavered, though some of the team seems to think the
rockslide might have spread the scent around."

It was a delicate way of saying there might be more than
one recovery site. Rockslides didn't always keep the body
in one piece.

"That's where you'll find her." She pointed to where the
rock face had sheared away. "The initial quake triggered a
cascade effect. Multiple slides from different points. But the

area where she was lying is flatter, not inclined, so I still think the body didn't shift much."

He studied the pattern she indicated, head tilted slightly. "Good eye. You know this area well?"

"Grew up here." It was so rare to meet someone who didn't know her life story—and even rarer for her to voluntarily share. Mostly because she was out of practice. "Dark Canyon's been my backyard since I could walk."

"That explains a few things." When she raised an eyebrow, he clarified, "You seem at home out here. As if...well, I'm not much of a poet, but you mesh with the land."

Her pulse kicked up at the observation and she felt ridiculously flattered for some reason. It wasn't a pretty compliment, the kind most women would expect from a hot guy they'd just met. But Sabrina wasn't most women.

And Noah Colton was definitely not a run-of-the-mill hot guy.

"Part of the job," she murmured, because what else was she supposed to say? *Thank you for noticing that I'm singularly well suited for the life I've carved out for myself here? Good on ya for being more observant than most men?*

"No." His gaze never flinched, and she found herself enjoying the idea of getting lost in it for a good long while. "Those guys are here for the paycheck. You're here because this is who you are."

"Got it in one," she said, impressed and not at all ashamed of letting him know it. "I could say the same about you."

He inclined his head. "Could you?"

Shrugging, she tried to read the change in his demeanor, but despite having spent the last couple of hours studying him, she hadn't quite learned enough to understand what button she'd inadvertently pushed. "Sure. I mean, you've obviously unlocked expert level on your SAR skills. I've been around other teams before, and you're wearing a whole different set of skins."

His quick smile added another check in the pro column. "Ah, well, if I've achieved master gamer status in your book, that feels like high praise indeed."

"Don't you feel like you're out here making a difference? As opposed to checking off another call?" If she'd missed the mark and Noah didn't have quite the depths she'd sensed, she'd be very disappointed.

"I do," he assured her and a shadow crossed his expression. "I'm just not quite used to thinking of this stage of my life as making a difference."

"Now you've done it." She jammed a hand down on her hip. "You have to tell me everything. Don't leave anything out."

"Maybe we'll save that for our second date," he said with a laugh.

Well, she did like the sound of that. Enough that she didn't take offense to him shutting down the personal nature of the conversation. "I didn't mean to pry."

"You didn't. No offense taken here." He held up a hand. "SAR is my life now."

"And you're good at it." She gestured to his dog, which seemed to be a far safer topic of conversation. "Dancer's impressive."

"He's the best partner I could ask for." Pride and something deeper colored his voice. "Never questions my judgment, never argues about jurisdiction and works for kibble."

She laughed, happy they were back on somewhat even ground. "Sounds perfect."

"Almost." His eyes locked on hers again, that spark arcing between them. "I'm still trying to teach him to talk so we can hold a conversation. SAR work gets lonely sometimes."

The words hung in the air between them, no way to mistake the innuendo that he'd deliberately dropped into his tone. They were both interested, and neither of them seemed to be too concerned about hiding it.

Lovely. Lack of pretense shot right to the top of Noah's list of good qualities.

"How did you get started with Dancer?" she asked, genuinely interested but also not about to pass up an opportunity to continue interacting with this man, given that he'd so nicely dropped the bait in her lap.

Noah grinned. "It was Jacob's suggestion, actually. I needed a career change, and he knows a guy working out of Salt Lake City. Put us in touch. I started working with his trainer and the rest is history."

"Sounds like it was meant to be."

Some things obviously were.

"Officer West!" Bonner's voice shattered the moment. "Command needs your initial incident report."

Noah's expression shifted to neutral as Bonner invaded their little circle for two. Three if you counted the dog, which meant no room for jerkwads with huge egos.

"I heard you, Bonner." She shot him a scathing glance, mostly because he'd interrupted but also because his face made her skin crawl. "You didn't need to come all the way over here."

"Sorry to break up the party," Bonner sneered, his expression bordering on glee, as if he'd guessed exactly what was going on between Noah and Sabrina and thought it would be fun to put a damper on everything. "Figured you were too busy flirting to give it proper priority, so I thought I'd speed things along."

"You're such a big help," she muttered. If you replaced *help* with *tool*.

"I'll let you get to work," Noah said with a loaded glance that told her he'd guessed exactly what Bonner had been up to. "Officer."

"Sabrina," she murmured as Bonner gave her a pointed stare. So what? She could give the SAR expert her first name if she wanted to. "I'll be back."

She forced herself to walk away at a measured pace, very aware of Noah's gaze following her. And Bonner's. Who didn't leave. She wouldn't put it past him to feel out Noah's intent just to be a thorn in her side.

But as she glanced back at Noah, something pinged inside her. This was a beginning. No question. The beginning of what remained to be seen. She didn't have a great track record with the handful of men she'd dallied with over the years. Which was fine. If Noah ended up being yet another in a string of fun guys who backed off after figuring out they had zero prayer of keeping up with her, better to discover that right out of the gate instead of later.

Meanwhile, they both had a job to do.

The recovery operation continued as the sun sank toward the horizon, painting the canyon walls in deep orange and red. Floodlights clicked on, casting harsh shadows across the scene. Sabrina finished her report and found herself gravitating back to where Noah coordinated with the engineering team.

That's when the first telltale flash of beige caught her eye. The excavation team paused as a distinctive patch of human skin appeared beneath the rubble. Finally.

Noah turned to Sabrina, his natural enthusiasm spilling over into the space around them. "There's your Jane Doe. Exactly where you said she'd be."

Why this guy seemed as excited to prove her right as she was to get her vindication, she couldn't quite fathom. But she appreciated it.

"Thanks for helping me prove it," she told him.

"Now comes the good part. The investigation," Noah clarified as they both watched the team switch to hand tools in order to avoid triggering another rockslide.

"Not my jurisdiction," Sabrina said flatly, and he nodded.

"Mine either." But she could hear the wistfulness in his voice. "I'm sure the Dark Canyon folks assigned will do the case justice."

A young woman had died up here alone in the cold. Someone definitely needed to find the answers. Normally, Sabrina would be happy to pass that job off to the experts and dust her hands of the situation. She'd done her part.

But something about this situation tugged at her. Maybe because Noah remained so clearly invested in the outcome. Or maybe just because she'd been involved from the very beginning. It was hard to distance yourself from something you had such a big stake in.

"West." Her radio crackled with Marcus Reynolds's voice. "I need you on the perimeter to ensure the site stays as clear as possible. Now that we have a body, this is a crime scene. Assist as needed."

"On it." She nodded at Noah, who smiled.

And then she didn't see him again before she was finally able to call it a day.

Chapter Four

Normally, Noah would call himself a master multitasker. He had to be in order to handle the intricacies of search and rescue. And investigative reporting too, for that matter.

The problem was that he wasn't supposed to be thinking about a certain dead woman while simultaneously running Dancer through advanced certification sequences and mentally composing an article about K-9 training innovations.

Okay, that wasn't the problem. If those were the only things on his mind, he'd be golden. But a certain blonde USFS officer had wound her way into his very molecules and dug in.

Sabrina.

Yesterday, he'd gotten busy and she'd drifted away from him at the recovery site, then he'd lost sight of her. It had gotten late, and Dancer needed some downtime before he burned out, so Noah had bugged out of there, regretfully, without Sabrina's phone number.

And calling up the USFS office to casually ask for her felt pathetic. Especially since she hadn't sought him out either.

Also pathetic? Hanging out at the K-9 training facility in hopes of running into her.

The training facility sprawled behind the main police building, a complex maze of specialized areas designed to challenge both dogs and handlers. From his position near the covered break area, Noah could see officers coming and going from the department's main entrance.

What he could not see was a reason why Sabrina would darken the door of the police station, but it was all he had. No one would question him if he spent the entire day here. Multitasking. Allegedly.

"You're kind of a disaster today," he told Dancer as they lined up for another practice run. His partner gave him a look that clearly said Noah was the disaster in this partnership. Fair enough. The dog had never met a task he couldn't focus on completely.

Meanwhile, Noah's attention could generously be called split.

Because after a long dry spell of not being an investigative reporter, all of a sudden, a story had dropped into his lap.

Coincidence? It didn't feel like it. He hadn't given up investigative reporting because he felt done with it. More like it was on hold. Now that he'd been presented with a mystery to solve, a story to pursue, he could admit the vague restlessness he'd been experiencing lately would only be addressed by diving into the reason a body had turned up in the Dark Canyon Wilderness.

Something about the whole situation made his blood rush, the way it used to when he was on the verge of breaking a story wide open.

Officer West had more than a little to do with that too.

"Let's run the advanced recovery sequence," he told Dancer, pushing thoughts of fierce female officers aside. For the moment. "Hunt."

Dancer moved with fluid precision through the complex scenario they'd set up, following the scent trail Noah had laid earlier. This was the kind of work that had earned them their reputation—deliberate, technical and precise. The dog paused at a junction of crossing trails, nose working the air before confidently choosing the correct path.

"Nice work," Noah murmured. He should be taking notes. The article he was supposed to be writing was all about these advanced discrimination techniques. Instead, his mind kept overlaying the search grid from yesterday's recovery, mapping how the victim's position related to the natural terrain.

The laptop waited on a nearby table, his article notes a jumble of false starts and trailing thoughts. He pulled it open while Dancer took a water break.

Advanced scent discrimination requires a careful balance of instinct and training. The handler must—

Must what? Follow the evidence? Trust their gut when patterns emerge?

The case of why a dead woman had ended up buried under a pile of rock had all the hallmarks of something bigger. His cursor blinked as his old instincts rose to the surface. He had a whole folder of articles he'd written about similar cases. Young women found in remote locations, staged to look like accidents.

"Got a minute?" Steve from the K-9 unit interrupted his dangerous train of thought. "We could use your expertise with Kelly's new shepherd. He's struggling with scent differentiation."

"Sure." Noah closed the laptop before he could fall deeper into that research hole, actually grateful for the distraction.

The other handlers were good guys, completely dedicated to their specialized training routines. He needed to focus on his day job until he had time to really dig into the story forming in his mind. There was actual work to do, the kind that paid the bills, but not if he slacked off chasing a few leads that didn't exist yet.

Kelly, a newer freelancer from Telluride, stood with her young shepherd in the complex trails area they used for discrimination training. The dog had potential—great nose, solid work ethic—but Noah could see the tension in his body language. Whatever was throwing him off had been building for a while.

"Walk me through what's happening," Noah said, shifting into teaching mode. Complex search problems were his sweet spot—when he could focus on them. Dancer sat at attention, always ready to demonstrate proper technique.

"He keeps losing the trail," Kelly explained, frustration evident in her voice. "Does great with simple tracks but fails when we add crossing patterns. Gets distracted by older scents."

Now this was familiar ground. Noah pulled out training aids from his vest. "Let's break it down. Dancer, show them the sequence."

His partner's ears perked up. They'd developed this demonstration over years of working with new teams. Noah laid out scent articles in a pattern, explaining each step. "The key is building their confidence with discrimination. Let them work it out instead of trying to force the issue."

Dancer moved through the sequence with practiced ease, showing how to work crossing patterns without losing the primary scent. The shepherd watched intently, and Noah could practically see the wheels turning in the younger dog's mind.

Kelly shifted closer than strictly necessary as Noah demonstrated the pattern layout. Her light floral perfume invaded his space.

"You make everything look so easy," she said, her smile bright and wide.

She'd been dropping hints for weeks that she'd like to get coffee sometime. Honestly, he couldn't put his finger on why he hadn't taken her up on it. Kelly's long brown hair curled up at the ends, and she always wore subtle makeup that accented her eyes perfectly, as if she'd spent a long time in front of the mirror perfecting her look.

In short, exactly his type. Beautiful. They had K-9 handling in common. And it would be easy. Not a lot of effort on his part.

Maybe that was the problem. Falling into a casual relationship with a pretty woman who would do all the work didn't sound very appealing.

He wanted passion. Fire. Explosions. A reason to wake up every morning and an even better one to draw him to bed each night. He wanted intense.

Sabrina's fierce blue eyes appeared in his mind's eye again, and just thinking about her put a hum in his gut. Poor Kelly couldn't hope to compare.

Dancer moved through the sequence with practiced ease, showing how to work crossing patterns without losing the primary scent. The shepherd watched intently while Kelly used the opportunity to brush against Noah's arm as she asked another question about scent discrimination.

His phone buzzed. Excellent.

He bobbled it out of his pocket like a stupid, eager teenager when, normally, he ignored the thing. Real interaction floated his boat most days, but right this second, he was thrilled to have a distancing mechanism. "Apologies, let me get this."

It was a text message from Jacob.

Mark's gone AWOL again. Not answering calls. I'm worried about him.

Noah's chest tightened. Mark had been different since quitting the Army—quieter, more withdrawn. Now this mysterious security job? Something was definitely up with his older brother, and that sat like a rock in Noah's gut.

The Coltons looked out for each other. Always had. He'd moved back to Dark Canyon to be closer to his family. He should be more on top of what was going on with them.

"Sorry," he told Kelly, ignoring her flirtatious smile. "Need to handle something with my brother. Give me five?"

Her disappointment was clear, but Noah was already moving toward the break area, typing out another message to Jacob:

Noah: Have you tried stopping by his place?

Jacob: He's never there.

Noah: I'll track him down this week.

He'd been so busy lately he hadn't checked on Mark in person. That needed to change.

"Sorry," he told Kelly, deliberately halting a solid six feet away from her as he pocketed his phone. "Family stuff. Where were we with the training sequence?"

Her smile dimmed slightly as she registered his distance, but at least she didn't close the gap. "The crossing patterns?"

Dancer nudged his hand, grounding him like always. Noah was here to help with training issues, and he owed it to her to be present. He smiled in a way that hopefully conveyed, *Never going to happen*, without being too insulting.

She gestured to where her shepherd paced, eager to try again. "You were saying something about confidence."

"Yeah. Watch how Dancer processes each intersection." He set up a new pattern, more complex this time. "See how he slows down, really works the scent before committing? That's what we want to build."

The next hour passed in a blur of demonstrations and adjustments. Kelly's shepherd began to show improvement, his movements becoming more deliberate as he gained confidence. When the training sequences grew a little more rote, Noah left her and her dog to run through their paces solo, which allowed his mind to wander back to those old case files still buried in his laptop.

A few years ago in Colorado, a woman was found in hiking territory wearing city clothes. The official ruling had been accidental death, but something about the scene had never sat right with him. He'd started digging, found similar cases in Utah and Wyoming, but his mom had gotten sick before he'd finished that story.

"Earth to Noah." Steve's voice broke through his thoughts. "We're breaking for lunch. You coming?"

"No, I've got a few things to catch up on." Like the article currently stuck on a blinking cursor because he couldn't focus on basic training protocols when his brain kept spinning bigger stories. "Thanks though."

After Steve and the others left, Noah pulled up his notes. Maybe if he approached it from a different angle. Write about how working with new teams kept the training fresh. But his fingers had their own ideas, opening that folder of old articles instead.

The similarities were there. He wasn't imagining them. The clothing, the locations, the careful positioning that looked just a little too perfect.

Dancer's head settled on his knee with a soft whine. That dog would be an excellent therapy dog if he ever lost his desire to hunt. But for now, he played the part of Noah's best friend exceptionally well.

Movement near the main building's entrance caught his eye. Officer Sabrina West strode out of the police department, her purposeful energy drawing his attention like a magnet. Even from this distance, he could see the fierceness and sheer *presence* that had hooked him yesterday.

"Dancer, heel," he called automatically, launching himself out of his chair to stride toward Officer West before she vanished again.

As he strode toward the parking lot, the lab fell into perfect heel position because, unlike his handler, he actually had some chill. Noah tried to moderate his pace to something that didn't scream, *Desperately chasing after a woman*, but he had a feeling he wasn't quite pulling it off.

She must have sensed him coming because she glanced over her shoulder well shy of the first row of cars. Intense blue eyes locked on him, her smile edged with something he'd like to call *pleasure*.

She was happy to see him.

And he liked being the one to put that expression on her face.

"Officer West," he called, letting his own pleasure lace the phrase with warmth. "Fancy meeting you here."

"So, this wasn't an ambush?" she asked, amusement practically dripping from her voice. "The way you came after me felt very focused."

He lifted a brow. "I'll own that. There was no way I was letting you slip away a second time."

"Is that what I did?" Now she was outright laughing at him. "Or did I finish up a grueling fourteen-hour shift and look around to see if I could locate the intriguing SAR expert I'd just met, only to find an empty canyon?"

Noah crossed his arms, his grin widening. "You looked for me?"

The once-over she gave him put a hard flutter in his gut. "Of course. How else would you have had the opportunity to ask me to dinner?"

"Let me correct that grievous oversight immediately. Phone, please." He held out his hand and curled his fingers in a gimme motion.

She didn't hesitate, pulling it from a utility pocket in her pants, which was far sexier than he was expecting. "Are you entering your phone number so we can exchange text messages for a few days?"

"No, I'm entering my phone number so you can text me your address. I'm picking you up at seven."

She laughed again, taking her phone back. "Bold. Efficient. I like that."

"Life's too short to waste time playing games. I'd like to get to know you better." He shrugged. "Why bother pretending otherwise?"

Something flickered in her gaze that gave him the distinct impression she appreciated the sentiment. Good. They were starting out on the same page. Always an excellent place to be.

"Any dietary restrictions or preferences I should know about?" he asked.

"If it fits on a plate, I eat it." Making a show of tapping on her phone, she glanced up as his buzzed. That same intensity that had drawn him yesterday sparked between them. "See you at seven then."

Chapter Five

Sabrina couldn't remember the last time she'd been this excited about a date.

Actually, she couldn't remember the last time she'd gone on a date, but it had been warm outside. Over the summer maybe?

Her usual approach involved showing up in whatever she happened to be wearing, most often because she'd left work late.

But here she stood in front of her closet, actually caring what she put on. Actually wanting to make an effort.

That was new.

She surveyed her options: little and none. A shopping maven she was not, but she had a few things she'd picked up. For emergencies. And this counted as one.

"Best outfit it is," she muttered to herself, pulling out a sweater dress in deep blue that hit mid-thigh. Paired with boots, she'd strike the right balance between looking like she'd tried and looking like herself.

Not that Noah Colton seemed like the type to care what she wore. The way he looked at her in uniform had sparked something she hadn't felt in a long time. Maybe ever.

Of course, coming in hot with her best look meant she didn't have a second-date outfit waiting in the wings, in the event she wanted to up her game. Possibly that wouldn't be necessary. But she'd lay odds on a shopping trip in her future.

Her phone buzzed. Noah. Or rather, Sexy SAR Expert, the contact name he'd entered when he'd keyed in his number to her phone.

It was too cute to change. And kind of a fun way to keep their blossoming attraction under wraps. The only way someone would know who Sexy SAR Expert was would be to ask her...and then admit they were paying attention to her text messages.

Sexy SAR Expert: I'm five minutes away.

Her phone time flipped to 6:55 p.m. Nice. A punctual guy who also kept her informed.

The flutter in her stomach was definitely anticipation. And maybe a touch of recognition that tonight could be the start of something fun. Fun because that's all it could ever be. She'd long given up on finding her unicorn guy.

But Noah felt like an excellent Mr. Right Now.

She'd just slipped on her second boot when the doorbell rang exactly at 7:00 p.m. on the dot. Not that she'd expected anything less from a guy who handled search-and-rescue operations with precision and flair.

Though she did wonder if he'd waited outside her door for a few beats specifically so he could hit the buzzer at exactly the top of the hour. It felt like a detail he'd strive to get right.

She started to fling open the door and hesitated for split second. What if Noah didn't live up to the hype her brain had manufactured? Odds were high he'd disappoint her, given the track record of those who'd come before.

She didn't want him to fail the test. Never mind that she had no idea what test she hoped he'd pass. Perfect guy? Most likely to keep up with Sabrina West in a single bound?

Spoiler alert: he was neither.

Noah Colton equaled a fun time and a free dinner. Unless he'd really pulled one over on her and she decided to cut her losses during their first drink.

Stop being silly.

When she opened the door and spied the tall hunk of perfection on her front step, her breath caught.

He'd cleaned up nice. Really nice. His dark hair had some texture to it, but not enough to be called styled, and the windblown look *worked* for him. The unkempt facial hair was still there, thank goodness, because she'd been having some pretty intense fantasies about that scruffy beard. But he'd traded his SAR gear for dark jeans and a ribbed Henley that hugged his shoulders. Mouthwatering. She wanted to feel those shoulders under her fingertips, just to see if the muscles were as well defined as they looked.

Yeah. Good call on wearing her best outfit.

"Hi." His eyes lit up as they traveled down her dress to her boots and back up again. The heat in his gaze put a matching warmth in her chest. "You look incredible."

"You dress up pretty well yourself." She stepped out, pulling her door shut behind her. His truck sat in her driveway, and he'd parked at an angle as if too eager to get out the door to straighten up.

That made her feel giddy.

"I know a place that matches what you're wearing." He opened the passenger door for her, which did something to her insides. "Unless you had somewhere specific in mind?"

"You're the boss of this venture." As she settled into the seat, Noah's clean wintery scent engulfed her, and she might never exit the cab of this truck. It was too delicious. "I'm curious to see what kind of restaurant you think matches this dress."

His answering grin sent another flutter through her stomach. "The kind that makes me think about how hungry I am."

Oh, this date was starting off on exactly the right note. "I like that answer."

The drive was short, which was good, because the anticipation crackling between them made small talk feel anticlimactic. He pulled into the lot of the Stone House, Dark Canyon's nicest restaurant. She'd driven past it a hundred times but never been inside.

"I hear they have decent steaks," Noah said as he opened her door, his tone casual but the appreciation in his gaze anything but. "Am I allowed to say I'm glad you're not a vegetarian?"

"Well, I hope so. Because I'm glad too."

He held out a hand to help her down from the truck, and it was on the tip of her tongue to inform him she could handle vaulting a couple of feet to the ground. But shut her mouth, because duh.

Noah Colton was a gentleman. She didn't meet many of those. Granted, it might be because she radiated a *back off* vibe ninety-nine percent of the time. Had she been warding away this kind of treatment all along? Maybe guys like Noah were thick on the ground and she'd been missing out, thanks to her highly capable vibe.

But she didn't think so.

Besides, she had no interest in other guys opening doors and treating her like she was special. With Noah, it worked. She couldn't wait to see what happened next.

She put her hand in his. An electric zing crackled across her skin as he helped her slide to the ground. The thing was, he didn't back up to give her room, so there was a lot of sliding against his extremely solid torso.

Awareness sizzled between them, taking on shape and weight.

"I seem to be somewhat trapped against the seat," she murmured an instant before his mouth descended on hers.

Noah. Was. Kissing. Her.

Time shuddered to a halt as he dropped her into a swirl of sensation, his lips speaking to her as clearly as if she could hear his voice. And they were saying things she had no idea she'd wanted to hear.

His hands framed her face as he deepened the kiss, and she melted into him, every ounce of first-date jitters evaporating like morning mist in the canyon. Noah kissed like he did everything else—with abject enthusiasm, incredible skill and absolute authority.

This was a man who knew how to kiss and made no apologies about the timing. Or the lack of warning.

He just…swallowed her.

The interior of the truck was cool against her back, a stark contrast to the heat building between them. His shoulders did indeed feel solid as rock beneath her fingers, but just as she got good and ready to explore the rest of him, the kiss wound down.

Noah's thumb traced her jawline as he pulled back just enough to look at her, his eyes darkening with his own reaction.

"I'm not going to apologize." His voice slid into places inside that could wholly benefit from hearing it a lot more in much more intimate circumstances.

"Please don't," she murmured. "Apologies are for mistakes."

"I've been thinking about doing that since I first saw you."

"You mean when I was covered in dirt from the rockslide?" Her attempt at light humor came out breathless.

"Even then." He brushed his lips against hers again, softer this time but no less intense. "Especially then."

She curled her fingers into his shirt, torn between yanking

him back for round two and pushing him toward the promised steak that was all the way inside the building. "You always kiss your dates before the appetizers?"

"Never been tempted before. I have recently become a convert of the idea though. We might make it a thing from now on. Just between us." His grin simultaneously made her want that mouth on hers again and for him to keep talking, because she did like the way his mind worked.

"I've never let a guy help me down out of a truck before," she admitted freely. "Can we add that to our thing?"

His grin turned wolfish. "I insist." He stepped back—darn it—but kept hold of her hand. "Come on. I'm starving, and you look too good in that dress to spend the whole evening crammed into the passenger side of my truck."

"The dress comes off, you know." Flirting with him was so easy, the words just came out all by themselves.

The look he gave her sent another wave of warmth through her midsection. "Trust me, I'm aware. But we have to save something for later. Distract me with a story. I want to hear all about how you ended up working in Dark Canyon Wilderness."

The host's gaze widened slightly as they walked in. No doubt they looked a little rumpled, Noah's shirt slightly askew, her lips reddened and chaffed. As thoroughly as she'd been kissed, she hoped it showed all over her face.

They followed the host to a corner booth, and Noah slid in next to her instead of across. Bold. But after that kiss, space felt pointless. She didn't even want to maintain a respectable distance. Why put up pretense?

"So." He picked up his menu, but his eyes stayed on her. "Where do you want to start? Work history? Favorite climbing spots? Most dangerous area of the canyons?"

"You're assuming I have stories."

"Please." That grin again, making her stomach flip. "The

way you handle yourself out in the elements? You've got stories."

She laughed, appreciating how he'd segued to a subject near and dear to her heart instead of jumping into small talk about stuff that didn't matter. "Most guys try to avoid discussing my job."

Because it scared them that she could take care of herself, she'd always assumed.

"Most guys probably bore you to tears." He set down his menu. "I can tell you're someone who doesn't shy away from dangerous situations. You live for this stuff as much as I do."

"The thrill of being one false step from death?" She tilted her head, studying him. "Is that what drew you to SAR work?"

Something flickered in his expression. "Among other things. But we were talking about your stories first."

Their server appeared with water glasses, and they quickly ordered—both choosing steaks, both medium rare. Noah's eyebrows lifted at her order.

"Let me guess." She took a sip of water. "Most women you date prefer well done."

"I don't usually pay attention to what my dates order." His knee brushed hers under the table. "But I'm paying attention to everything about you."

Heat crept up her neck at his intense focus. "In that case, you've probably noticed I don't like to waste time either. So tell me about your most dangerous rescue."

"Trying to avoid talking about yourself?" The amusement in his voice told her he knew exactly what she was doing.

"Maybe I just want to know what kind of trouble you get into when you're not pulling bodies out of rockslides."

"Oh, I get into all kinds of trouble." He shifted closer, his thigh pressed against hers now. "Last month, I had to race up Mount Peale in a thunderstorm to reach some stranded climbers. Lightning was cracking all around, and the rain made every step a gamble. Nearly lost my footing a few times before we finally spotted them."

"The west face in that weather must have been a nightmare," she remarked. "Were you able to approach from the south ridge, or did you have to navigate the northern ascent?"

His eyebrows lifted in surprise. "You're familiar with the ridge?"

"Race you to the top sometime?" The offer slipped out naturally. She wasn't usually one to make future plans on a first date, but this was not a typical first date. At all.

His eyes sparkled with the same fierce joy she felt when tackling a challenge. "Now that's my kind of second date."

The server arrived with their steaks and salads, and they fell into an easy rhythm of sharing stories between bites. Noah described SAR operations that made her pulse race, while she told him about her favorite climbing routes—the ones that weren't in any guidebook.

"No wonder you spotted our victim," he said after she described a particularly hairy solo climb. "You know every inch of that terrain."

"Speaking of which." She leaned forward, dropping her voice. "What's your take on how she ended up there? There was something off about the whole scene, and I think we both know she wasn't hiking."

Noah practically lit up, as if he'd been waiting for her to segue to this exact subject. "The position seemed staged, like someone wanted her to be found eventually."

"Like a message?" Sabrina toyed with her fork, the steak forgotten as her mind raced through possibilities. "But for who? That area isn't exactly prime hiking territory this time of year. Any time of year, really."

"Exactly." Noah's intensity ratcheted up a notch, which was saying something, given that it seemed to be his default mode. "Someone chose that spot deliberately. Someone who knew the terrain well enough to understand it would be found, but not immediately."

"By someone who regularly patrols that section." She met his gaze. "Like me."

"Have you worked that region long?"

"My whole career." A thought struck her. "But Bonner tried to take that zone. He was so weird about it. Kind of underhanded, actually."

"The guy who horned in on our conversation?" Noah's expression sharpened with interest. "The one who questioned whether you'd actually found a body?"

"The very same." She sat back, mind whirling. "He was so insistent about taking that search zone. I didn't think much about it at the time—he's always trying to weasel his way into the more challenging assignments."

"And now we know there was actually something to find." Noah's knee pressed against hers, grounding her racing thoughts. "But we also know there's more going on here than a simple case of exposure. Those clothes, that location…"

"The staging," she finished. The energy between them had shifted, professional fascination merging with personal attraction in a heady combination. "I've never had someone to really talk through an odd case with before. Most of the guys I work with—"

"Aren't interested in your theories?" His mouth quirked. "Their loss. Your instincts are spot on."

She laughed. "Careful. Complimenting my professional skills will get you everywhere."

"Good." He caught her hand where it rested on the table, his thumb brushing over her knuckles. "Because I have a lot more where that came from. You're an impressive person, Officer West."

The heat in his gaze made her lungs hitch. Among other things.

"Speaking of professional observation," Sabrina said, hoping to take it down a few notches before she forgot they were in a public place. "I've never seen SAR work like what you did out there. The precision, the control. Most teams I've worked with aren't nearly as methodical."

His eyes lit with genuine pleasure at the compliment. "SAR requires a specific mindset. You'd be good at it."

"You think?" She tilted her head, studying him. "It would look good on my résumé, actually. I need an edge for the district ranger promotion I'm gunning for. Would it be hard to get certified?"

"Not for you," he said confidently. "You strike me as the type who excels at anything you put your mind to."

That might be the prettiest compliment a man had ever given her. She tried not to let it go to her head, but *dang*. Noah Colton knew the way to a girl's heart.

"You're giving me lots to think about, Colton," she said with a saucy smile. "Especially since I'm up against Bonner for the promotion. I would like nothing more than to see him crushed under my heel."

"Now I understand why Bonner went out of his way to get in your face at Peavine." Noah rolled his eyes, which made her grin.

"He thinks the position is his by divine right or something." She shook her head. "But SAR certification would definitely help my chances. Especially since no one else in my unit has those skills."

"I could put you in touch with my trainer." The way Noah angled his whole body toward her set off sparks in her midsection. "Though I warn you, it's intense. Long hours, complicated scenarios, complete dedication. But somehow, I don't think that would scare you off."

"Please." She grinned. "You had me at 'intense.' I'd love

to learn from whoever trained you and Dancer. Your partnership is impressive."

She'd never had that with anyone. Or even owned a pet. Too much responsibility. On both counts.

"Having the right partner makes all the difference. I'd be happy to help you get started, go through some basics together. Show you the ropes."

"That would be fabulous."

They'd gone from zero to sixty in nothing flat. She should be backing way up, playing this nonchalant, aloof. Something other than sitting here grinning at this man who had just volunteered to spend a *lot* of time with her.

Noah made it sound like fun. That was a neat trick.

Sabrina glanced around, suddenly realizing the restaurant had emptied while they'd been lost in conversation. Only one other table remained occupied, and the servers were starting to give them pointed looks.

"I think we're about to get kicked out," she said with a laugh.

Noah checked his watch and his eyebrows shot up. "We've been here three hours."

"Flew by." She wasn't ready for the evening to end. Not when every moment with Noah felt like discovering a new section of the wilderness she'd never explored, each turn revealing something more intriguing than the last.

Their server appeared, smile strained. "We'll be closing in five minutes."

"Message received." Noah handed over his credit card and focused on Sabrina once the server left to close out their tab. "Care to continue this conversation somewhere else?"

The invitation hung between them, loaded with possibility. Any other time, with any other guy, Sabrina would have called it a night. Better to leave them wanting more, that was her usual strategy.

But nothing about Noah felt usual.

"There's a nice walking trail around the pond across the street," she found herself saying. "Unless you're scared of the cold?"

His answering grin held a challenge. "I can handle it."

The man was singing her tune, all right, but she wasn't sure she could trust the feelings flooding every inch of her body. Yeah, it had been a while, and frankly, she'd never hesitated to jump right into something, even if she didn't know exactly where she was going to land.

Minutes later, they strolled along the moonlit path, shoulders brushing. The night air held a bite of cold that made Sabrina glad she'd worn boots instead of heels.

"You know what I think?" Noah's voice broke the comfortable silence.

"About the case or about this?" Whatever *this* was.

"Both." He caught her hand, pulling her to a stop. "I think we make a good team. And I don't know about you, but I'm nowhere near done with this date."

Chapter Six

Sabrina in a uniform took his breath away, but Sabrina in that deep blue dress with her eyes sparkling counted as a near religious experience. Because he'd put that expression on her face. Several times, actually.

It wasn't just that he considered her a knockout, though she was. Incredibly beautiful with a wild edge that matched the reasons a sunrise over the mountain put an ache in his chest. There was something else about this woman that had hooked him instantly. Intelligence. Fierceness. A *presence* that said she never did things halfway.

They were the same.

How baffling to realize this late in his life that the perfect woman for him wasn't his opposite but his complement.

That might have been something he should have figured out a long time ago. It explained why all of his other relationships had fizzled after a few months. They'd all been, well, boring.

Sabrina, on the other hand, she exhilarated him. Constantly. He'd never been so tempted to back a woman into his truck and see how hot he could make her burn.

Except he hadn't been kidding when he'd told her he wanted to save something for later. Much later. He did like anticipation as an appetizer.

And judging by the glimmer in her gaze, he wasn't alone.

"Shockingly, I don't seem to be ready to call it a night either," Sabrina admitted, moving closer as they stood on the edge of the half-frozen pond. She shivered, her hand trembling slightly in his.

"Cold?"

She shrugged. "Not enough to break up the team."

Nearly everything she said made him smile, but that widened his grin to the point of ridiculous. "You feel it too?"

"Sure. I think you finished my sentences a couple of times at dinner. The question is, what are we going to call ourselves? Team Saboah? Nobina?"

She'd combined their names.

Something in his chest twinged, and he nearly put his hand over it until he realized it was his heart. And cluing her in that she'd crawled right inside would not do for a first date.

Maybe the second one.

"Either works." He cleared his throat. "You choose."

"I appreciate a man who takes suggestion well." She actually looked pleased, which did not help whatever was going on inside him. "What will our first order of business be?"

He bit his tongue before he said, *Get married and live happily ever after.* Definitely not first-date material...or second. He needed to reel it way back before he scared the living daylights out of her.

"The case," he said instead. Which was what they should be talking about.

What he *wanted* to talk about.

This was his shot at getting back into the investigative journalism game. He could feel it. None of this had happened randomly. Not meeting Sabrina. Not being called to the site in Peavine Canyon, when the USFS could have tapped a dozen or more SAR teams.

Not this feeling that he was at the edge of something spectacular whenever he locked gazes with this woman.

"I covered a case in Colorado a few years back," he said, his mind warming up, testing out underused muscles as it started spinning connections. "Young woman found in hiking territory wearing city clothes. It was ruled accidental death, but something never sat right about the scene."

"Similar to our Jane Doe?" Sabrina's focus sharpened, and he liked that look on her way too much.

"Too similar, maybe. I started digging, found other cases in Utah and Wyoming with the same pattern." He ran a hand through his hair as the circumstances rushed back, reminding him why he'd never written that article. "But I had to drop the investigation."

"You think our Jane's death could be connected?"

"The staging is similar. Deliberate placement in outdoor recreation areas, victims in street clothes rather than hiking gear." The pieces were starting to align in his head, and he welcomed the opportunity to move on from why he hadn't finished the investigation—and the fact that she hadn't asked. "I still have my research files. And contacts in law enforcement across three states."

"While I have access to Forest Service incident reports." She nodded, clearly following his train of thought. "We could cross-reference similar cases, look for patterns."

This. This was exactly why he'd broached the subject with her. She would be a fantastic partner; he could already tell. "My journalism background plus your insider knowledge of the area and department resources? We'd make a great investigative team."

"You were a journalist?" Her confusion cleared instantly. "That's why you seem so sharp and detail-oriented. I couldn't put my finger on it, but you don't miss much."

Noah had never felt so flattered in his life. "Guilty."

She snapped her fingers. "That's why you wanted to team up—to solve this case. So you can write about it."

"Yeah. In a nutshell. How does that work for you?"

"I'm in. Completely. As long as we keep it quiet."

It was only after she agreed that he realized how much he'd wanted her to say yes. To everything. Sweet relief eased the tight set of his shoulders.

Her expression turned thoughtful. "The police won't appreciate unofficial interference in an active investigation."

"I'm good at working behind the scenes." The thrill of the hunt was already humming in his veins. "And you know how to work the system from the inside."

"We'll need to be careful though." She glanced around the moonlit park. "If there really is a pattern, if Jane Doe's death is connected to other cases—"

"Then we could be dealing with something bigger than either of us expected." The protective instinct that had been growing all evening surged again. "Are you sure you want to get involved in this?"

The look she gave him could have melted steel. "Try to stop me."

Her fierceness hit him right in the chest. Noah found himself leaning forward, drinking in every word as she laid out her thoughts about the case. The way her mind worked, jumping three steps ahead, connecting dots others might miss—it was intoxicating. When she mentioned being anxious to dig deeper, to find real answers, his whole body hummed with recognition.

He couldn't have dreamed up a more perfect scenario. Here was this incredible woman who matched him not just in attraction, but in drive and intelligence. The chance to work with her, to combine business with the pleasure of her company, it felt like fate.

"What do you say to taking Dancer out in the morning?" he asked. "We can take a stroll through Peavine Canyon. Maybe find something the recovery team missed."

"Yes." No hesitation. "I see that poor woman's face when I close my eyes. If we can help get her some closure, that would be icing on the cake."

He could already tell Sabrina was the charge-ahead type, the kind who would push aggressively for answers. It suited his style perfectly.

Watching her eyes light up with plans and possibilities, Noah finally understood why he'd ended up back in Dark Canyon after leaving his globe-trotting journalism career. Why life had steered him here, to this moment.

To Sabrina.

Good grief, she was magnificent. Standing there in the moonlight, fearless, ready to dive into whatever to find the truth. Every cell in his body urged him to pull her close, to show her exactly how he was feeling, she called to him at a basic level.

But she deserved his honesty first.

"I should warn you." He stepped into her space, drawn by the energy radiating from her. "I'm kind of a whirlwind. It's a lot for some people. I've been called Hurricane Noah more than once. My tendency is to start out at category five and only get more intense. It feels like that won't be a problem for you, but I'm going to need your express consent to baptism by fire."

She grinned. "Are you trying to scare me off, or is this just the welcome spiel everyone gets?"

"No one else was asked to apply."

"Good." She stuck out her hand. "Because I don't do anything halfway either. And I don't like sharing."

The space between them crackled with possibility. He was on the edge of something all right—an opportunity to soar or crash spectacularly. But he'd be doing it right alongside Sabrina.

It felt like fate. Like step one of an amazing journey.

When he finally kissed her, everything shifted, and then it felt like falling. Into what, he couldn't wait to find out.

NOAH HAD NEVER been one to sleep late, but after the best first date ever, the bed seemed unnaturally empty despite the fact that he'd slept alone in it every night of the four years he'd lived here. It was far too easy to imagine a certain fierce blonde in the space next to him.

Since she wasn't here, he got started on the day early. Before dawn.

Sabrina had agreed to meet him at Peavine this morning, and he could think of literally nothing he'd like better than to see her ASAP. Probably he could have found something to occupy his time besides cooling his heels—literally—out in Dark Canyon Wilderness while he waited on her to arrive, though.

But he found himself headed in that direction anyway, his body still on high alert from both the kiss and from being poised on the threshold of possibly getting his life back.

He hadn't wanted to think about it too hard. This investigation—it could literally change everything for him. Allow him to reclaim lost pieces of himself, pieces he'd only very briefly acknowledged losing.

It was too difficult to think about otherwise.

So he didn't. He didn't regret spending time with his mom before she'd passed and never would. As the gulf between then and now stretched, he could see shifting his life again. Drifting away from Dark Canyon gradually as he immersed himself in investigative reporting again. This Jane Doe mystery could be the beginning, but there certainly weren't a wide swath of those types of cases thick on the ground around here.

He'd end up traversing the globe again if he had his way and make no apologies about it.

Which he wasn't quite ready to admit to anyone. Not until he found out if he still had the chops. That's why Jane Doe mattered so much. She was a chance to warm up with a few graceful practice dives before he tried the ten-meter platform.

The sharp bite of January air put a spring in his step and whetted his appetite to see Sabrina again. It was an odd thing to associate frigid temperatures with a woman who burned as hot as Officer West, but it was definitely a thing. Maybe it was the contrast.

When he drove around the bend to pull into the turnout near the canyon, a brown Forest Service vehicle sat parked, its driver leaning against the door with her arms crossed in a casual slouch that indicated she'd been waiting a while.

Noah grinned and swerved into the spot behind her, spraying gravel in his haste to hit the ground running. Which he did so he could sweep her up in a hello kiss.

The moment his lips touched hers, his body settled, as if he'd slid into a favorite pair of jeans. Not to say the kiss wasn't the best kind of magic. Her essence, the things that made her Sabrina, that exploded inside quicker than a lit fuse on dynamite.

But the recognition of this being *exactly* where he should be…that he felt at a bone deep level.

It was like this was a missing piece too, one he'd never registered the absence of until it slotted into place.

She pulled back well before he was done. Way before he'd had his fill.

"Hello to you too," she murmured, her fingers threading through the scruff at his neck that he hadn't had time to get trimmed in months. "Is that my reward for beating you here?"

"Absolutely. And when I'm the first to arrive, I expect the same in return."

Her smile widened. "That seems fair. Hope you've had your coffee, because I've been going over the scene in my head since we talked about it last night. There something I want to check."

"No coffee needed here." He shook his head, warding off the disappointment that she didn't want to say hello a bit longer. For like an hour. In his truck with the heater blasting. "Caffeine just wears off. I run on adrenaline and hope."

She lifted a brow. "That's a new one for me. Hope for what?"

"You know. That the next adventure is just around the corner. Or the next answer. The next experience that might be unlike anything I've ever done before." He shrugged. "It's all fuel."

Nodding slowly, she gave him a once-over that tingled his toes. "Just when I think you can't get any more intriguing. I like the way you approach life, Colton. It's refreshing. But fair warning. I drink coffee, and you'll pry it from my cold, dead fingers."

He laughed and released her with reluctance, but only because Dancer sat patiently in his crate waiting to be liberated, and the dog had been cooped up long enough. He jogged back to the truck and released the lab, who picked up on his energy, prancing as he kept his perfect heel position—even with the line of Noah's jeans, like he'd been taught.

"We're both ready to roll," he told Sabrina and, yeah, he might be prancing a little too. "Lead the way."

She moved with confidence through the difficult terrain, obviously familiar with every twist of the rocky path. He didn't have any trouble keeping up with her, and frankly, he enjoyed the view. There was something extremely affecting about Sabrina anyway, but put her against the backdrop of a rising sun, craggy peaks and expansive sky?

His chest hurt every time their gazes connected.

He loved every second of whatever was happening between them. And he had just enough working brain cells to understand that, generally, people didn't fall in love at first sight.

It happened though, right? Why couldn't this be his epic love-at-first-sight story?

Near the area where the excavation team had sifted through the rockslide debris, Sabrina climbed a few feet up, away from the trail, and shaded her eyes as she evaluated the surrounding area.

"This is what I wanted to see. Most people stick to marked trails," she said, gesturing at the rugged landscape ahead. "But whoever dumped Jane here had to have carried the body from somewhere without a lot of eyes."

"Or they know the area well enough to navigate at night," he suggested, earning a glimmer of approval in Sabrina's expression.

"Right. There are old hunting paths, game trails that locals use. We should check those."

Noah had learned to trust his instincts during investigations, and right now they were telling him to follow her. Dancer seemed to agree, perking up as Sabrina pointed out a barely visible track between two rock faces.

"It's going to be rough going," she warned, but her eyes sparked with a challenge that he couldn't imagine not rising to. "These paths connect to different access points, but they're not maintained. Hunting season's been over for months. Are you up for this?"

"Trying to scare me off, or is this the welcome spiel everyone gets?" he asked with a wink.

She laughed and then very quickly proved her point. The woman was a machine.

They spent excruciatingly long minutes scrambling over rocky outcrops and navigating steep inclines. The winter wind picked up, driving bitter cold through Noah's coat, but Sabrina never flagged, pushing forward, a leader in every sense of the word as she glanced back occasionally to tell him to watch his footing. Her knowledge of the terrain kept them moving, even as Dancer struggled to pick up any scents in the harsh weather.

Noah's legs burned from the effort, but witnessing Sabrina in her element made up for it. She navigated through the wilderness like she'd been born amongst the scrubby vegetation, shadows and stone. Each time she pointed out another hidden path or concealed vantage point, he found himself more impressed.

"Hold up," he called as Dancer's posture suddenly changed, nose working the air near the edge of a steep drop. Years of working together had taught him to read every subtle shift in his partner's movements.

The dog had picked up something.

Dancer led them to a particularly thick section of sagebrush, nosing around its base with increasing focus.

"We need to check this out," Noah called to Sabrina, kneeling with care so he didn't disturb anything.

She joined them, dropping into a crouch to peer into the brush where Dancer indicated.

"What is that?" She pointed to a dun-colored strip of fabric.

Noah found a stick and pushed aside the drooping branch of the sagebrush. "It's a baseball cap."

Her sharp intake of breath told him she'd picked up on the importance of the clue.

Caught in the closure were several strands of bleached blonde hair.

"Is that…hair?" she asked. "It's the exact same shade as Jane Doe's."

Their eyes met, electricity arcing between them.

"She might have been wearing it, but whoever dumped her here didn't realize they'd lost it." Or a hundred other explanations that got his senses humming.

This was a huge find. A clue that told him his instincts had been right—there was a story here.

The fierce triumph in Sabrina's expression made every freezing hour worth it. She already had her evidence camera out, documenting the find from multiple angles with precise, thorough movements.

Noah watched her work, emotions jockeying for position in his chest. Here was someone who understood how to embrace the thrill ride of life. Who matched him step for step, in every way that mattered. Especially in relation to uncovering the truth, investigating until every avenue had been explored regardless of the effort.

What were the odds he'd meet someone like her by chance? Zero. This was something else, something he intended to jump into very fast and very thoroughly.

Chapter Seven

Sabrina had seen enough evidence collection teams in her career to know they operated like well-oiled machines. But she'd never watched one meticulously photograph and document a dusty baseball cap while standing next to a guy she couldn't label.

Was this a date? Did she introduce Noah as her boyfriend? Sexy SAR Expert?

Thank God no one had asked her. Though as the morning sun climbed over Dark Canyon's jagged peaks, it occurred to her that any given member of Dark Canyon's police department staff might already know Noah. If they did, they'd assume he'd arrived on the scene in an official capacity, especially since Dancer sat right by his left leg.

Well, didn't he have an official capacity? He certainly wasn't here because she'd invited him—*he'd* been the one to issue the invitation. The fact that she knew exactly what he tasted like and wished she could kiss him again right now had nothing to do with baseball caps, Jane Does, homicide investigations or evidence.

That was on her. She'd mixed business with pleasure, no one else. It was screwing with her, thinking about how unprofessional it was. How she always had to think about people's—men's—perception of her.

Ugh. This uncertainty was not going to work.

Noah worked for her, though, every inch of his glorious hard body and messy hair. Their conversation during dinner had been off the charts. Never had she felt so *seen* before. He understood her, recognized her drive without it feeling like he wished she'd throttle back a little.

Maybe she could get over herself and just worry about the investigation and not that everyone here knew her mouth watered when Noah shot her secret smiles.

They'd found a legitimate piece of evidence. Probably. It was on the PD to prove that, unfortunately, but she had enough brain cells not dedicated to Noah to start thinking through how to get her hands on that part of the investigation too.

That's what she needed to be focusing on. Work. This was her job, her identity, and Noah was…a fun addition. She knew these canyons, every twist and shadow, every game trail that wandered off the beaten path. Yet somehow Noah had shown her a new way to approach them, approach how she interacted, not just in the way he worked with Dancer but in how naturally they'd fallen into step together.

She'd never been much for teamwork. Not that the guys in her department gave her the impression they wanted to partner with her. Sure, she did her share of growling and barking when they approached her. It was easier that way. No one to disappoint or be disappointed by.

But Noah made her think about everything differently. The way he anticipated her movements, matched her pace without trying to outdo her—it was unbelievably sexy.

Even now, as they watched the evidence team work, she found herself hyperaware of his presence, the solidness of him at her shoulder making her feel oddly secure.

Which was ridiculous. She'd never needed anyone to make her feel any way before.

The evidence team moved with practiced efficiency, photographing the baseball cap from multiple angles before carefully documenting its position in the brush. Yellow evidence markers dotted the ground, creating a precise grid around their find. The blonde hairs caught in the closure had generated particular excitement—they couldn't have asked for better proof that Jane Doe had been brought through here.

More than that though, the location told a story. This wasn't a hiking trail, not even close. Someone had brought that woman up here deliberately, someone who knew these back routes as well as Sabrina did.

Who? No one she'd ever met.

The unknown pieces of this mystery nagged at her. She wanted answers, both for Jane Doe—and closure on her untimely death—and for Noah. Because it seemed important to him and Sabrina found herself wanting to please him.

"Your dog's got quite a nose." One of the police department's crime scene techs nodded toward Dancer, who sat at perfect attention beside Noah despite the surrounding activity.

It was a nod to Noah's SAR skills and maybe a subtle thank-you for calling it in. Some of the uniforms got testy when external teams overstepped or didn't respect jurisdiction, which was exactly why she'd insisted they bring in the proper departments.

"He's the best," Noah replied, but his gaze shifted right back to Sabrina. As if he preferred looking at her instead of the view.

And having a man like Noah's attention was going to her head.

"West."

She turned to find Marcus Reynolds striding toward them, his expression carved from the same stone as the canyon walls. That was a look she rarely saw on her commander, and she didn't want to see it now.

He'd gotten wind of her find. Obviously. And had come all the way up here to see why one of his officers was tied up with a police investigation instead of handling her regular patrol duties, no doubt. She had a feeling he intended to ensure she heard exactly how far outside her lane she'd drifted.

"Sir."

He crossed his arms. "Care to explain what's going on?"

At least he was giving her the opportunity—and hopefully the benefit of the doubt. She gestured to where the team worked. "Dancer indicated a baseball cap during a training exercise and we noticed hair caught in the closure. It appears to match our victim's."

Not exactly a lie. Noah had been the one to mention bringing Dancer out here. And SAR dogs did have to go through regular training exercises, which she'd learned while researching how one went about getting SAR certified before going to bed last night.

Reynolds's weathered face didn't give away much as he surveyed the scene, but she caught the slight narrowing of his eyes that usually preceded a thorough dressing down. "Training exercise? You're supposed to be patrolling the south rim. Looking for evidence falls under local PD jurisdiction."

The reprimand stung, but she'd been dealing with male authority figures her entire life. She knew the drill—stand straight, maintain eye contact, don't show weakness.

"With all due respect, sir—" she started, but Reynolds cut her off.

"Respect would be following the chain of command." His voice dropped lower, the way her father's used to when he was particularly disappointed. "We have protocols for a reason. Your job is to protect and monitor forest resources, not conduct investigations."

Heat crept up her neck. She'd followed her instincts and found actual evidence. That should count for something. But he was right—this wasn't her jurisdiction. As a Forest Service officer, she should have suggested the search area to the police department and let them handle the investigation.

But before she could defend herself, Noah stepped forward.

"Commander Reynolds." Noah's voice carried that perfect blend of authority and respect that seemed to come naturally to him. "I take full responsibility. I asked Officer West to help me run through some advanced tracking techniques. Given her knowledge of the local terrain, she was the ideal candidate to assist with Dancer's training."

Her first instinct was to bristle—she could handle Reynolds on her own. She'd been managing difficult men her entire career. But something about Noah's presence at her shoulder calmed her. It said they were in this together and he'd never abandon her. Which shouldn't feel so good.

Reynolds's attention shifted to Noah, his expression skeptical. "Training? Or were you hoping to stumble onto evidence related to our Jane Doe?"

"Both." Noah didn't flinch under that hard stare. "Officer West mentioned her interest in SAR certification. As someone who regularly works with law enforcement, I know how valuable those skills can be. When she agreed to help with today's training exercise, I saw an opportunity to evaluate her aptitude while covering ground that might be relevant to the police investigation. It's just smart to run a training exercise in an area where there might be something to find, sir."

Reynolds's skeptical look said he wasn't completely buying it, but Noah's explanation had given him a way to over-look the protocol breach without losing face. "Is that right?"

"We understand the jurisdictional concerns," Noah said, answering the real question Reynolds was asking. "That's why Officer West immediately called in the evidence team when Dancer alerted. She followed protocol to the letter."

Sabrina held her breath. She hadn't asked Noah to cover for her, hadn't expected him to step between her and Reynolds's justified anger. The surge of emotion that rolled through her caught her off guard. Usually, she hated when men tried to fight her battles.

But Noah hadn't rushed in to save the damsel in distress. He'd merely repeated what she'd already told her commander, supporting her position. Complementing her. Like they were a real team and he'd always have her back.

Was *this* what true partnership felt like?

Reynolds crossed his arms. "SAR certification? Is that what this is about, West? Using an active investigation to pad your résumé?"

"No, sir. Though I won't deny the certification would look good for the district ranger position. But mainly—" she glanced at Noah, drawing her next words carefully from a heartfelt place deep inside "—I've seen how effective SAR teams can be. How they make a real difference. That's something I want to be part of."

It wasn't until the words left her mouth that she realized how true they were.

Yes, the certification would help her career. That was the obvious reason, the first one that came to her after Noah casually dropped the suggestion in her lap during dinner. But watching him work with Dancer, seeing the strong bonds between them—it stirred something in her. A longing she hadn't even known was there.

Reynolds studied her for a long moment. "You understand the commitment involved? SAR certification isn't a weekend course. It's months of intensive training."

"I understand, sir." What was she if not committed to her place in the world? "I've actually been considering joining a volunteer SAR organization."

That got his attention. "Have you?"

"Yes, sir." She straightened her shoulders. He didn't have to know she'd only started thinking about the next steps after certification this morning while waiting on Noah to show up.

Reynolds's expression shifted slightly. Was that approval? "The department has been looking to expand our K-9 capabilities. Budget's always been the issue, but a certified volunteer handler within the ranks would be great."

Hope fluttered in her chest. Maybe she hadn't screwed everything up after all. And maybe her late-night research wasn't just wishful thinking.

"I can put together a training schedule," Noah offered. "One that won't interfere with her regular duties."

Reynolds nodded slowly. "Have you started the application process?"

"Not yet, sir." Sabrina met his gaze steadily. "But I will. Today."

"See that you do." Reynolds's tone carried a warning, but his eyes had softened slightly. "And, West? Next time you want to investigate something off your assigned route, clear it through proper channels first."

"Yes, sir."

As Reynolds walked away, Sabrina sucked in a lungful of air. Noah's hand brushed her lower back so briefly she might have imagined it, but the warmth of that touch spread through her whole body.

"You okay?" he asked softly.

"Better than okay." And she meant it. For the first time

in her career, she felt like she was choosing a path not just to prove something but because she genuinely wanted it. "Though we should probably actually do some training now that we've committed to that story."

The evidence team finished their collection, carefully bagging the cap while Noah filled out his portion of the chain of custody forms. She should probably be heading back to her regular patrol route, but she couldn't quite bring herself to walk away.

"I have some training scenarios mapped out," Noah said as the last police vehicle pulled away. "If you're interested in getting started right away."

Reynolds had drifted toward his own vehicle but still stood within earshot. Interesting that he hadn't ordered her back to work yet.

"I'm not big on waiting once I decide to do something." She caught Noah's answering grin, and heat crawled up her neck.

"I've noticed that about you." His voice carried that same edge that had drawn her in from the beginning. The one that said he saw right through her professional facade to the woman underneath who craved adventure as much as he did.

"When's your next training session?" Reynolds called, his meaning clear. Get back to work, but not without sorting out the details first.

"Tomorrow morning," Noah answered smoothly. "Assuming Officer West is available."

"She'll be there." Reynolds strode to his vehicle. "Keep me updated on your progress, West."

She watched Reynolds walk away, knowing she'd dodged a bullet. If he'd really wanted to make an issue of her overstepping into police jurisdiction, he could have written her up. The fact that he'd accepted Noah's explanation and even supported the SAR certification idea felt like a gift she'd better not waste.

She was really doing this.

She watched Noah interact easily with his dog, her mind spinning with possibilities. The things she'd been reading about SAR work suddenly felt more real, more achievable. And the career advantages weren't lost on her either. She mentally tallied the points in her favor—her wilderness experience, her physical conditioning, and now potentially SAR certification.

Bonner wouldn't know what hit him when the selection committee met.

Still, something tugged at her. Noah and Dancer's seamless partnership spoke to a part of her she usually kept locked away. The part that sometimes got tired of doing everything alone, of being fiercely independent because she had no other choice.

Sometimes it sucked to never have anyone.

But it also sucked to have someone and then find out he couldn't handle it when she brought the thunder. So she'd gotten used to counting on one person—herself.

"Hey." Noah's low voice skated across her skin. "What's going on? You seem distressed."

His gaze hooked hers, warm and not the slightest bit intrusive. He brushed back a strand of hair as if he did that kind of thing often, both paying enough attention to notice hair out of place and casually touching her.

She liked both.

"Just thinking about what Reynolds said. About the commitment involved." She hesitated, then decided to be honest. "I guess I wasn't sure I was ready to take that leap before. It's not just the training. It's—"

Well, that she could barely spell *commitment*, let alone fathom the requirements for it.

"Learning to rely on a partner?"

"Maybe." She matched his steady gaze, daring him to make something out of it. Hoping he would, if for no other reason than to give her an outlet for the steam building inside.

He just shook his head. "You're already aces at that. If I thought you'd have a single lick of trouble bonding with an SAR dog, I wouldn't have suggested it."

Jamming a hand down on her hip, she eyed him. "What are you babbling about? How do you know I'm already good at working with a partner?"

"Because you work with me, Sabrina," he told her gently, drawing her hand into his and raising it to his mouth in a gesture that should have been weird but felt so natural, as if his lips had been made for that hollow near her thumb. "We're a good team. Don't bother to deny it. You feel it too."

Her face did a thing without her permission that probably looked like agreement to him. She might have even nodded against her will.

Oh, who was she kidding? It was dumb to pretend she didn't know exactly what he was talking about, even if she couldn't quite reconcile the truth herself. "Yeah. Okay. You might have a point."

"Faint praise." He laughed, totally unfazed. "Obviously I have some work to do to get you to see it my way. Challenge accepted."

Good grief. This guy.

"Maybe less than you think." She tilted her head, studying him. "If any other man had stepped in like that with my commander, he'd be on the ground bleeding out. Since you're still in one piece, we're gonna chalk that up to whatever this thing is going on between us. I don't hate it. You had my back when it counted."

"That's what partners do. Dogs and human ones." The

words carried weight, even though his tone stayed light. "I'm a totally separate package from the SAR cert training, by the way. You have my offer to help regardless of what happens between us. But I'm selfish enough to hope that you take me up on everything I'm offering."

"What's that?"

He spread his hands wide with a flourish. "You see it, it's yours."

That sounded remarkably like a label. "Can I write Sabrina across your forehead with a Sharpie?"

His brow lifted. "No. Too public. What goes on between us is no one else's business. Pick a spot I can cover up and the answer is yes."

She'd been kidding. But there was something so elemental about his total willingness to be claimed that she couldn't quite dismiss the idea from her mind.

All of this heaviness should have given her pause. Instead, she found herself taking a step closer. "Maybe we'll save that for next week."

"It's a date," he said, his voice rasping deliciously.

"Does that mean you're going to teach me all your SAR secrets?" she asked, trying to lighten the suddenly charged atmosphere.

His answering grin did funny things to her insides. "Every single one. Your next day off. It's mine."

"I'll be there." The promise came easily now, weighted with possibility.

She had no illusions about what she was getting into. SAR certification would demand everything she had—physically, mentally, emotionally. It would mean long hours, brutal conditions and learning to be a permanent part of a team.

That she could handle.

But could she handle everything Noah would demand of her? She had a feeling she'd barely scratched the surface of what the man was capable of, and not just the stuff that was SAR-related.

He had depth he'd only barely begun to show her, of that she had no doubt. The roller coaster still had screamingly steep drops visible on the horizon, and the train had barely left the station.

Good thing she liked thrill rides.

Chapter Eight

Noah stared at his phone, thumb hovering over the messaging app where he'd opened the text thread with Sabrina. Then he closed it again and threw his phone on the bed near his left leg.

It was nearly midnight. Only a horribly insensitive person texted a girl at midnight.

Or one who had zero game and might as well let the girl write her name on his forehead. It wasn't like he'd fooled anyone, least of all Sabrina, about how hard she'd hooked him.

What a great word for the riot of sensation in his chest. *Hooked.* Yeah, he'd done his fair share of flopping around on the dock, gasping for air as Sabrina's laser-sharp blue eyes pierced him like a harpoon.

Somehow, the phone ended up in his hand again, just like it had the other dozen times.

Maybe he could check in with her really quick and then he could sleep. She'd kept pace with him on their date night and then popped up at Peavine bright and early. Maybe she wasn't the type who needed a lot of sleep either.

Wouldn't *that* be a great thing to have in common?

Miss me yet? he typed and immediately backspaced. How old was he, fourteen? Geez.

Did you get the SAR application link I sent you? Delete. That made it sound like he was checking up on her as if *she* was fourteen and couldn't tap a link.

Dancer lifted his head from his bed in the corner of Noah's bedroom, ears cocked at a sassy angle. Even his dog knew something was up.

"Don't judge me," Noah muttered. "I lasted six whole hours after she left the evidence scene. That shows remarkable restraint."

He typed again: Can't stop thinking about our case.

Innocuous. Easy to ignore if she didn't want to talk. Definitely not a lie. Well, it was not even remotely the extent of what he'd been thinking about, but she didn't need to hear that she'd dominated his thoughts as he ate dinner alone, because even he knew you didn't push to have dinner two nights in a row.

He hit Send before he could second-guess himself.

The message status changed to Delivered, then Read almost immediately. Three dots appeared as she typed back.

Sabrina: Took you long enough.

A grin spread across his face as he replied: You're thinking about it too?

Sabrina: Among other things.

He sat up. Like what?

Sabrina: Where I want to sign my name in Sharpie.

Something extremely dangerous knifed through his midsection—the urge to grab his keys and hightail it over to

Sabrina's house so she could try out a few places until she found the right one.

Dangerous, because he didn't want to mess this up.

And he had a very bad feeling it could tip either way. As if the slightest wrong move might send Sabrina scampering off, and he very much wanted to play his cards exactly right. Only a fool would blindly rush ahead without mapping out the lay of the land first.

Noah: Officer West, are you flirting with me?

She replied with a laughing emoji. And then: A girl doesn't get an offer to sign her name on a hot guy every day. You can't blame me for taking the suggestion and running with it.

He grinned and replied: Just to be clear, when I said I needed to be able to cover up your signature, I meant with my sleeve. So like, you can sign my wrist, for example.

This time, she replied with the mad emoji, the red one with the pouty face. I was hoping for a bicep at least. Maybe one of those amazing shoulders.

Noah: You think I have amazing shoulders? All this time, I just thought they were for holding up my shirt.

The eye-roll emoji flashed onto his screen. Somehow he hadn't pegged Sabrina as an emoji texter but he liked it. Her texts felt very stream-of-consciousness, and he was nothing if not an avid student of what went on inside her fascinating brain.

He wanted to know everything: what she thought about, what she dreamed of, her favorite colors—because someone like Sabrina did not have just one, or he'd be very disappointed.

Sabrina: Spare me the false modesty. What do you bench, like 150?

200. Delete. Good grief, was that really how he wanted to impress a woman? Instead, he replied: A better question is why we're not talking about the case.

Sabrina: Because that was a flimsy excuse to text me and we both know it?

That made him laugh out loud. In that case, you should just call me so we can talk all night.

His phone lit up with a call notification instantly, Sabrina's name flashing across the screen. His heart slammed against his ribs.

Man, this woman was doing a number on him. He hit the Answer call icon.

"New phone, who dis?" he deadpanned.

"Angelina Jolie," she retorted with a laugh that unfurled inside him. "I thought my lawyers told you to delete my number."

"That is literally the best response to that question I have ever heard."

"More where that came from." She paused. "We can talk about our case if that's really what you want to do."

Our case. He liked that. Liked how naturally she'd slipped into being his partner in this investigation. "We can talk about whatever you want. The case was just an excuse, because you see right through me, apparently. I couldn't stop thinking about you."

A soft intake of breath carried through the line. "I'm still not used to the way you lay it all out there. Most guys are not so direct."

"Life's too short not to be." He leaned back in his chair, savoring the way just talking to her made everything feel more vibrant. "Besides, I have a feeling you appreciate honesty."

"I do. And since we're being honest—" she paused for a heartbeat "—I've been staring at my phone for the past hour wondering if it was too late to text you."

His heart did a slow roll in his chest. "Great minds think alike."

She didn't give him a second to absorb the implications. "Thanks for the SAR application. I started working on it."

Her voice sounded scratchy and low, as if she might be lying in bed too. He did enjoy that visual. "Good. I didn't want to ask in case it felt like hovering."

"I'm allergic to hovering. If I start to feel itchy, I'll let you know." Her tone held a smile that made him wish he could see her face.

Maybe he'd suggest FaceTiming tomorrow night.

"So, the training manuals, study guides and full history of the SAR program weren't too much?" He'd maybe gone a little overboard with the supplemental material he'd attached to the email. But he'd never been accused of doing things half-heartedly.

"You forgot to mention the case studies."

She was laughing at him. But he didn't mind. "I'm ridiculous. I straight-up admit it. I just want you to succeed. So you can show up Bonner and hit him where it hurts."

"Oh, I like you a whole lot," she said, drawing out the *o* in *whole*. "You're speaking my love language."

"Vengeance and retribution are my favorite vices," he informed her, even as his gut responded to the texture coming through the line loud and clear. "Especially when it ensures a tool like that gets what's coming to him."

How was this so *easy*? It felt like they'd had a million conversations like this, late at night when the rest of the world had faded away. He'd never had such a genuine connection with someone before.

Best of all, she seemed to feel it too. Right? She was flirty and engaged, and she'd been the one to call him, after all.

"Seriously though. The case studies were really interesting. That was a thoughtful addition to the mix," she said.

"I figured you're the type who likes to be prepared."

"You figured right. There's a case here about a rescue in Cataract Canyon. Reminds me of something that happened last spring."

"Yeah?" He settled deeper into his chair, anticipating a good story. "Tell me about it."

"Flash flood caught some kayakers off guard. Water came up so fast they barely had time to get to higher ground, but they were trapped on this narrow ledge with the river rising." As she talked, he could feel the rising tension. Had been in many situations exactly like the one she described, where you could lose the rescue in only a few seconds. "I was first on scene. Had to figure out how to get them down before the ledge collapsed."

"What did you do?"

"Improvised a rope system using my vehicle as an anchor point. The tricky part was getting the first line across to them. The current was brutal." She paused. "Everyone said I should wait for backup, but I knew we were running out of time."

"So you went for it anyway."

"Had to. Sometimes you have to trust your gut, you know? Even when everyone else thinks you're crazy."

Noah's chest tightened with recognition. How many times had he followed his instincts on a story, chasing leads others dismissed? "I know exactly what you mean. Back when I was reporting, I'd get these feelings about cases. Couldn't always explain why, but I knew there was more to the story."

"Like our Jane Doe?"

"Yeah." He uncrossed his legs, energy humming through him. "It's the little details that don't quite fit. This kind of thing is never isolated. When you dig, you start to find patterns. Connections. That's what I loved about investigative reporting, and sometimes—" He broke off before he said something disloyal, something he couldn't take back. "Let's just say I miss it."

"Why did you stop?" Her gentle voice carried no censure, just genuine curiosity.

Memories of his mother's illness pressing against his chest.

"My mom got sick. Cancer. I came home to help take care of her." The words came easier than he expected. Something about Sabrina made him want to share the parts of himself he usually kept locked away. "She was always my biggest supporter, you know? Used to say I had a gift for finding truth in the darkness."

"Sounds like a great mom."

"She was." He swallowed hard. "It's hard to believe she's been gone four years."

"I'm sorry." Simple words, but he could hear the genuine empathy behind them. "So, you stayed in Dark Canyon for your family? After?"

It was a great question, one he'd only recently started re-examining himself.

"Partly. I found SAR work through my brother Jacob, discovered I had a knack for it." He glanced at Dancer, sleeping peacefully now. "Plus, I met a really great dog who needed me."

Sabrina laughed softly. "Love at first sight?"

"Something like that."

Her phrasing made him want to ask her if that meant she believed in love at first sight. Especially between people. Because he'd recently starting thinking he might, and it would be amazing if she didn't think he'd fallen into a vat of loony juice for thinking along those lines.

"What about you? What keeps you in Dark Canyon?"

"Besides the obvious stellar working conditions and highly supportive environment for female officers?" Her sarcastic laugh got his back up, because he hated that she had to fight for a rightful place in her world. "The wilderness is in my blood. My father was military, we moved constantly when I was young. But every summer, my mom would bring me here to stay with my grandparents. It was the only place that ever felt like home."

The longing in her voice resonated deep in his soul. "Must have been hard, always being the new kid."

"It taught me to be self-reliant. How to prove myself over and over." Steel threaded through her words. "My father had…let's call them high expectations. Nothing was ever quite good enough. That's why I have to push so hard. Be the best. It's stupid. He'll never know or care if I excel every single day or fall on my butt."

"It's not stupid," he countered fiercely. "You have amazing drive. I recognize it at a soul-deep level. It's impressive, and it means we're a good fit, because I won't leave you behind."

"As if, Colton. I'll always be in the front."

He grinned. "Fine by me. That's a better view anyway."

She laughed, followed by a telltale sniff. "How did you do that?"

"Do what?"

"Make me feel like I can tell you anything." She shifted, and he could hear rustling that made him think of her getting comfortable in bed. "I don't usually talk about my dad."

"I'm a good listener. It's a necessary skill when you depend on leads and tips to get an investigation going." He sank down a bit in his own bed, liking the idea of being in the same place at their respective houses while they talked. "Also, I like learning interesting things about other people. When my mom got sick, it changed my whole world. I dropped everything to come home—my career, my life, all of it. And I've never regretted that choice. But sometimes it's nice to feel like my old self again."

"Why didn't you ever pick it back up again?" she asked in the pause.

"I don't know," he admitted quietly. "I write articles occasionally, mostly for SAR publications."

"I recognized your byline," she informed him dryly. "In the stuff you sent. It was riveting. You know that's not what I'm talking about. You need to get back into the game. It's important. You're going to solve the Jane Doe mystery and write about it, and I'm going to help you."

"You already agreed to help," he reminded her, amused that she'd latched onto his quest with such ferocity. "Are you all out of noble causes?"

"Yeah, actually," she shot back. "You clearly need someone to support you as you ease back into your journalism self. I'm happy to be that for you."

Well, first of all, he didn't ease into anything. And second of all, *dang.* His heart squished out between his ribs and melted into a puddle on the floor.

"Why?" he murmured, a little blown away with what was happening between them.

"Because you need someone in your corner." Her voice held an edge that he wanted to know more about. "I hear you when you talk about your stories. It's your passion. You miss it, but you don't do it, and I suspect you never went back to that life because it feels selfish."

He started to protest and then closed his mouth, letting her point ping around inside him. "I didn't realize I was getting free psychoanalysis with this phone call."

"Tell me I'm wrong."

"I can't. But it's not the whole truth. SAR is important. I can't just give that up, stop doing the work Dancer and I are extremely well suited for. It would be a waste."

And he did feel selfish for wanting his old life back when it meant not being here for his family. His dad was single and alone for the first time in decades. Mark had something going on that didn't seem good. He couldn't just walk away.

Plus, it made him sad to think about passing Dancer off to someone else. He couldn't in good conscience drag a trained SAR dog along as he traveled—by plane mostly—to far flung locales. There was probably some guilt in there too about something he didn't feel like examining at the moment, now that Sabrina had ripped open this wound.

"So, we'll work on the Jane Doe story for now," she told him soothingly as if she really did get it, "and then see what's what."

"Do you bulldoze everyone like this?" he asked with a laugh meant to cover the quaver in his voice.

"Please. Like you can't take it."

He could. Gladly. Because it meant they were building something. "I'm not threatened by a strong woman. Bring it."

"The fact that you aren't is the only reason we're having this conversation," she said, the teasing note from a moment ago gone. "It's not that common, you know. For a man like you to be okay with a woman like me."

"A smart, sexy woman in uniform who can beat me in a foot race? Oh, no. Not that," he said lightly. "I like who you are. It's not that common here either to find someone who isn't exhausted by me."

"Same. I'm used to being out front alone. It's nice that you haven't thrown in the towel yet."

This was not the conversation he'd been expecting, but it

was absolutely the one he wanted to be having. They were a matched pair. She felt it too and it was making him giddy.

Which could also be a function of the late hour.

"I'm sorry you've been exposed to the toxic side of my gender."

"Not just at work." She paused. "I…don't date that often either. Or for that long. I mean, second dates are not so much a thing in my world."

Good. That left the door wide open for him to walk right through, and he did like the sound of that.

"Their loss," he said, pulling it from a place deep inside where there was only truth. "I'll make you a deal. When we get married, you can carry me over the threshold."

She laughed like he was kidding. "Maybe we'll just walk through together. That feels more like our speed."

If she could make wedding jokes without flinching, things were going way better than he'd dared hope. It was going to be impossible to wipe the smile off his face tomorrow.

"Yeah." He paused, choosing his next words carefully. "This is the first time I've felt like staying in Dark Canyon isn't a sacrifice. Like maybe I'm still here for another reason."

"Careful, Colton." But her voice held a smile. "You're getting dangerously close to fate territory."

"Is that a terrible thing? To think of forces bigger than ourselves being at work?"

Her soft laugh warmed him. "I'm not one to cede control to the whims of fate. But I'll allow that it feels like we were meant to meet."

He'd take it. Noah glanced at his bedside clock and blinked. "How is it already two in the morning?"

"What?" She must have checked her own time because she groaned. "I have to be at work in four hours."

"Me too." But he made no move to end the call. "Though I'm tempted to suggest we just stay up."

She yawned. "Some of us need actual sleep instead of running on pure adrenaline and hope."

He laughed, remembering their earlier conversation. "One day you'll appreciate that about me."

"I appreciate it now." Another yawn. "We should probably be responsible adults."

"Probably." He couldn't stop smiling. "Though for the record, I'd much rather keep talking to you."

"Same." The simple admission carried more weight than a thousand pretty words.

"I can't wait to see you again. When's your next day off?"

"Saturday."

Four days from now. Ugh. "That's way too long."

"Call me tonight, then," she told him. "I'll answer."

They said goodbye and hung up reluctantly. At least on his side.

Noah lay awake, his mind spinning. He couldn't remember the last time he'd felt this kind of connection with someone. The kind that made him want to share every thought, every dream, every piece of himself.

He'd never felt it. That was the thing. This was uncharted territory, and he could barely stand to wait for the next stage.

Chapter Nine

The National Park Service Investigative Services Branch took over any potential homicides that occurred on federal land—standard procedure. Noah had been waiting for Dark Canyon PD to transfer Jane Doe's case for a week now, but they'd taken their sweet time getting around to it, waffling about whether they had enough evidence to call it a potential homicide.

Like there was some remote chance she'd ended up dead in Peavine Canyon by accident.

Fortunately, the fine folks in blue got their act together and did Noah a huge favor by handing the case over to NPS at 8:00 a.m. the next morning, which meant he hit the door of his brother's satellite IBS office at 8:15 a.m. on the dot.

But only because it took him an extra four minutes to feed Dancer, or he would have been even earlier.

The scent of industrial cleaner and public service coffee hit his nose as he strode through the building. Smelled like old times, when he lived in places like this, begging for someone with a hot tip to give him five minutes.

This time, he had the best leg up possible.

His brother's office door stood open. The man himself sat at his desk, tapping at his keyboard as he stared at the screen.

Noah crossed his arms and leaned on the door. "Never expected to see you end up as a desk jockey."

Jacob glanced up, his expression shifting from focused to resigned. "That's Agent Desk Jockey to you. I wondered how long it would take you to show up."

"Longer than it should have since I had to hear from Misty at DCPD that they'd lobbed you the ball." Noah collapsed into the visitor's chair, ignoring his brother's eye-roll.

"Leaning on your high school girlfriend for info? That's pathetic, even for you." Jacob pointedly stared at his screen as if Noah had interrupted a critical task.

"It would have been old news if you'd been the one to tell me."

That earned him a glance from his brother. "Now, why would I have done that, pray tell? Do you have information regarding this case that the agent assigned to investigate should be aware of?"

"Well, now. That's a great question." Noah eased back in his chair and crossed his arms with a grin designed to get under Jacob's skin. "How would I know what you are and aren't aware of if you won't talk to me about the case?"

Jacob's mouth flattened.

This was an old comfortable routine that they fell into after five seconds in each other's company—Jacob playing the part of the big brother who followed all the rules, living his life on the straight and narrow and having zero chill, while Noah poked at him with varying results.

It was fun. For Noah. Jacob, on the other hand, usually ended up looking like he did in this exact moment, as if he wanted to punch a wall. Or his brother.

Maybe they could save that for another day when Noah didn't need to be on Jacob's good side.

He held up his hands in surrender. "Okay, peace. I'm sure

you already read the report. Me and Dancer got the call on your Jane Doe. So, really, I'm here to help you. Anything you want to know about the scene, I'm your guy."

The look his brother gave him said he didn't believe Noah's capitulation one bit. "Is there something missing from your official report?"

"No," he replied honestly. "It's accurate. But that doesn't mean we can't shoot the breeze and maybe stumble over something that would be of value to you. Like my insight honed from years of investigative reporting."

"And there we have it, folks." Jacob shook his head, but he didn't look as perturbed as his tone suggested. "You want to write a piece on her."

All at once, Noah had a flash of unease. This was his brother. They had few secrets from each other, had gone through their mother's death together, a difficult season that would break a lot of people. To say they were close would be an understatement.

And Noah wanted his brother to bless the idea of him jumping back into investigative reporting. So far, it didn't feel as much like the slam-dunk collaboration he'd expected.

"Is that so terrible?" he mumbled, struck all at once that Jacob might not be that thrilled with the idea.

Writing stories had pulled Noah away from Dark Canyon once and would likely do it again. Would his brother hate losing the close ties their family had created once Noah had returned?

Jacob tipped his head. "It wouldn't be the worst thing to have someone with your skills looking into this."

Hope flared in Noah's chest even as the compliment pleased him. "So there is something to look into."

"There's always something to look into." Jacob rubbed his temples. "What brought all this on? I thought you were happy with search and rescue?"

"I am," he interjected quickly. "I love it. Love making a difference. Dancer is more than a dog, he's my buddy. This is not a quest to give up the life I've built here."

But wasn't it? He'd been dreaming of chasing leads again, of scouring social media for tips on hot spots, hopping a plane to Syria, Myanmar, the Philippines—wherever he could find signs pointing to human rights violations, the effects of environmental disasters, or civil war, because those made the most impactful stories.

Noah rubbed at his eyes and sighed. "Let me start over. I got a SAR call, only the victim was already deceased. We found our Jane Doe and the excavation team pulled her out. The officer who called it in had this way about her, I can't explain it. But she was adamant that there was something off about the scene, convinced the victim had been dumped there. It got my senses humming. The fact that you've got the case now says my instincts—and Officer West's—aren't off base."

For whatever reason, his brother's gaze had equal parts interest and evaluation as he zeroed in on Noah. "Officer West, huh."

"What's that supposed to mean?"

Jacob smirked. "I know that look. What kind of way did Sabrina have about her?"

His rib cage got tight and did a thing that felt like a Roman candle had gone off in his chest. Was he that transparent? "I forgot you knew each other. Yeah, I met her and she's amazing. Why wouldn't I notice that?"

"Uh-huh."

What was this all about? Noah shifted in his chair, crossing his arms again, which did not make him more comfortable. "We went on a date. Is that what you were fishing for? I like her. Is this really what you want to talk about when we have a Jane D—"

"Be careful, Noah," his brother interjected quietly. "You have a tendency to make a fool of yourself over a woman. I like Sabrina too. But you have to see how this is going to end."

"Happily?" he threw out, because come on. No one had a crystal ball. Was there something wrong with hope? With thinking positive and assuming the best possible outcome of a relationship instead of the worst?

"It's going to end with a jagged scar where your heart used to be," his brother said flatly.

Noah scowled, fingering the area in question as if he could already feel the phantom beating. "Are you sure this isn't more about you than me?"

His brother cracked his neck and rubbed at it as if Noah might be causing him pain. "Don't be obtuse when I'm trying to look out for you. You have a tendency to take a flying leap into everything, and I'm just saying maybe check the water before you do a cannonball."

The genuine concern in Jacob's voice deflated some of his bluster. Because yeah, that was not wrong.

But still, Noah wasn't a teenager anymore, mooning around over a succession of girls in his class. That was the last time his brother had witnessed Noah's feelings splattered all over the floor when said girls inevitably shoved off—some with a great deal of drama.

No, he hadn't gotten any better at protecting himself, but so what? What was the point of life but to experience it? Highs and lows.

"What if I have checked the water and Sabrina seems on board with cannonballs?" he asked with only a tiny curl of smugness to his smile. "We talked for hours last night."

The wedding joke sat fresh on his mind. A woman didn't laugh at a subject she had a fundamental aversion to, right?

"Great. I hope it works out, I really do. I'll repeat, I like

Sabrina." There was a qualifier coming, no doubt. "She does her job well and she's generally considered competent. But you have to know she has a…reputation."

"Watch it." Noah was half out of his seat in Sabrina's defense before Jacob could throw his hands up in protest.

"Not *that* kind of reputation. The opposite. She eats men for breakfast and stomps their bones into dust on her way out the door. You don't mess with her. Everyone knows that." His brother ran a hand through his hair, but it didn't settle the simmer in Noah's blood that *this* was the conversation they were having. "Some of the guys call her Mantis. You know, because the females eat the males?"

"I know what you meant," Noah said. Spit out, more like, and if he could have punctuated the phrase with a shiv, he would have. "And that's about the biggest load of horse manure I've ever heard you repeat. You know better than that. She's a living, breathing human being who has to fight for her place in her chosen profession every day. Anyone who wants to take a shot at her methods can come talk to me."

Jacob managed to look slightly chagrined. "I don't disagree that sometimes people exaggerate, and obviously, I've never had a problem with her. All I'm saying is be careful. Make sure you're on the same page before you offer up your heart still beating. Just in case there's a tiny smidge of truth."

As if. Sabrina was warm, engaging. Sexy. A fabulous kisser. And she had brains for miles. Her text messages amused him. Her strength inspired him. And sure, they hadn't known each other that long, but he did not get a praying-mantis vibe from her. At all.

Toward Bonner, yes. She'd sever his head in a New York second and feed it to him if he so much as looked at her wrong, but after seeing the tool in action, Noah would not only help her dismember Bonner, he'd volunteer to drive there and back.

Sabrina and Noah, on the other hand, had a *connection*.

"What do you know about it?" Noah challenged and gave Jacob's bare left hand a pointed glance. "I must have missed the part where you're half of a successful couple, which gives you the right to slap a Relationship Expert label on your forehead."

"Not me." Jacob's expression shifted so fast that Noah blinked. "Dad."

The topic whiplash caught Noah crossways. "What about Dad?"

"Exhibit A on what happens when you let someone in. Give them the power to hurt you."

Jacob's point crashed over Noah's head like a fifteen-foot wave at the height of a tropical storm. Noah had learned everything about how to approach life from his dad. They both jumped in wholeheartedly, and his dad had been wrecked when his wife died.

They all had been.

What Jacob was not so subtly telling him was to think about how soul crushing it could be to lose someone—for any reason.

Was that what he wanted to sign up for?

Sure, that was taking the negative approach, the one he'd literally just told himself he wasn't going to believe, but stuff did happen in relationships. Feelings died—or people did.

As strongly as Noah felt about Sabrina, he could see the wisdom in stepping back for a minute and doing exactly as Jacob suggested. Take time to evaluate. Make sure Sabrina really was on board before letting his thoughts stray toward something more permanent.

Which sucked.

"I'm starting to regret coming by this morning," Noah muttered and jerked his head. "So, what am I supposed to do, just never date?"

"As you pointed out, I'm not the relationship guru," his brother countered wryly. "I don't do relationships for a reason. You have to make your own way. All I'm saying is if it wasn't a woman who doesn't seem too invested in the long term, we wouldn't be having this conversation."

"It's certainly not the conversation I planned to have," Noah muttered, and shook his head. "But I get it. I'll be careful."

Would he?

Maybe. Now that his brother had planted these doubts, it was all he could think about. Sabrina had mentioned a couple of times that men didn't stick around too long, but he'd never thought to question why that was.

But what he did know was that he wanted to fall in love. Get married. Have a family of his own. He had no idea if Sabrina would be the one, but it certainly had felt like he should be exploring the possibility. That's what relationships were about. Jacob was missing out.

"Can we talk about the case now?" Noah asked. Okay, it was more of a grumble.

"No." His brother crossed his arms. "It's an active investigation. I know zero about it, especially since I got the case five minutes before you darkened my door. If you want to write an article, I can't stop you. But I've got no official statement on the matter at the moment."

Ugh. Figured this would be a waste of time. "Fine. But you have to promise me you'll let me know if you find out anything. It would mean a lot to me."

And now he'd laid out his second big secret.

Secret was the wrong word. Sabrina knew he wanted to get back into investigative reporting, just like she knew he was interested in her. What he hadn't quite reconciled was how much he wanted both.

Jacob had seen it though.

"I'll see what I can do," his brother said with a nod. "And that brings us to the next order of business, since you're still here instead of letting me get back to work. Dad's dating again. He's been seeing Susan Baylor."

The words burrowed into Noah's gut painfully. Dad *dating*? Dad dating *Susan Baylor*?

"What are these words coming out of your mouth?" Noah shook his head, hard. "Dad had a wife. Mom. Why in the world would he be dating anyone, least of all Susan Baylor?"

"Because he's lonely and it's been four years?" Jacob said it like it should be obvious.

"But… Susan Baylor?"

If he kept saying her name, there was a possibility it might eventually make sense.

But that didn't seem to be happening.

"Yeah. Susan," Jacob said with a grim nod.

Noah squeezed the bridge of his nose. "We're talking about the same woman who lives next door to Dad and used to help Mom sew Halloween costumes?"

His mind flashed to memories of his mother and Susan bent over the sewing machine, laughing as they created his Han Solo costume. The image unleashed stuff he usually held very close to the vest because he didn't like breaking down in front of people.

But it was Jacob. His brother had seen him at his worst and probably would again.

"It's weird, I know." Kicking back in his chair, Jacob scrubbed a hand over his face and peered at Noah.

"How long has this been going on?" Noah asked hoarsely.

"A few weeks now. I found out last Friday but haven't had a chance to process it myself, let alone figure out how to talk about it." Jacob's expression softened. "You okay?"

"I don't know." Noah let his face fall into his palms. Four years since they'd lost Mom. It felt like yesterday and a lifetime ago. "I mean, logically, I want Dad to be happy. But Susan?"

"Yeah. Look, that's not even the concerning part." Jacob pulled up to his desk and lowered his voice. "Her ex-husband is making trouble again."

Noah's jaw tightened. Everyone knew about Susan's ex, Ken Baylor, the former lieutenant governor whose political career had ended in scandal. "What kind of trouble?"

"Harassment mostly. Nothing we can prove yet." Jacob's expression darkened. "But he's unstable. Has been ever since the divorce. I've got some friends at DCPD keeping an eye on things, but—"

"But you're worried," Noah said. "What did Mark say?"

"Can't get ahold of him." Now Jacob looked truly troubled. "He's gone dark again. Won't answer calls, hasn't been home in days. This security job he landed—something feels off."

Noah's chest tightened. He'd meant to check in with his brother. Had made a mental note of it when he'd gotten Jacob's text about it a few days ago. And then forgot. "Define *off.*"

"Like he won't say who his employer is." Jacob's phone buzzed and he glanced at the screen. "I have to get back to work."

That was Noah's cue to move on to the next item on his agenda today.

A surprise for Sabrina.

But now he wondered if he was overstepping. If he should be reeling things back, not charging forward.

That wasn't who he was, how he operated. Which didn't mean he couldn't try to find some balance. Nothing wrong with calling a woman, with asking her out. Giving her presents. He didn't have to fall in love with her instantly, especially not if she wasn't looking for anything serious.

If nothing else, that was the advice he planned to take from Jacob. He'd feel her out. Scope the lay of the land, so to speak. At the end of the day, he had to try.

Chapter Ten

Sabrina's office chair squeaked as she double-checked her SAR application. Everything looked perfect, each box ticked, every field filled in. She had enough experience with bureaucracy to know that one mistake would bounce her application back, delaying the whole process.

She needed this win. Kirk Bonner had already put in his application for district ranger, and he'd beat her out for this job over her dead body. Sure, he had more years of service, but she had more time in the wilderness. And if she had something extra—like SAR expertise—that could only help. Right?

"Got a minute?" Marcus Reynolds stepped into her office doorway, rapping against the frame.

"Yes, sir." She stifled the urge to click out of the application and to a more innocuous screen. It wasn't like he'd caught her doing anything wrong, but she still wasn't sure how she felt about the SAR application.

What if she got rejected?

Reynolds glanced at her screen, just like she'd known he would. "That your SAR application? It's a good plan. I was going to encourage you to apply, but I see you're already on it. Not that I'm surprised, but if I'm being honest, it felt like your interest in SAR might have a little more to do with Colton than the skill set."

"I'm not looking to add another notch to my bedpost," she shot back with a withering glare. Just in case the thought had crossed his mind.

The look he gave her said that she was the only one who had gone there. "That's no one's business but yours. And Colton's. Just keep it out of the office."

"SAR appeals to me. I like dogs. I like the idea of being someone who can help in emergencies. And I figured it couldn't hurt to add to my résumé, you know, to give me an edge."

Reynolds perched on the edge of her desk, a rare casual move from a man who normally didn't delve into buddy-buddy routines. "If you're worried about Bonner, don't. He's got seniority but lacks leadership skills. Innovation. Adaptability. SAR is a perfect example of forward thinking. The kind of thing that will look good to the selection committee."

Wait, was he…was her boss actually saying what she thought he was? That he might be putting his weight behind her instead of Bonner, if asked?

"Plus," he continued, "Colton's an excellent trainer. If you're going to do this, it's helpful that you already have an in with him. The Coltons are good people."

"I don't want this to seem like I'm just getting certified for promotional advantage." She bit her lip. The other reason—Noah—probably didn't need to be added to the mix, not after she'd flat out denied her interest in him.

"No one is going to think that." His smile let her know he understood her concerns though. "Anyone who's met you understands that if you're going to do SAR, you'll go all in. You don't have another speed."

He stood, as if realizing he'd extended his usual gruff

demeanor past its normal limits. "Turn in that application ASAP."

"Yes, sir." She watched him leave, her head spinning. Had her boss just indicated the promotion was hers to lose? Why hadn't he said anything before?

And since when did his belief in her matter so much?

Her phone buzzed.

Sexy SAR Expert: Come over tonight? Have something to show you.

All thoughts of promotions and advancement fled. After their conversation last night, her skin had hummed for hours. Today hadn't diminished the buzz at all.

Noah was so different she hardly knew what to think. Not bad different, not yet anyway. She wasn't the type to moon over a man, yet here she sat, fingers hovering over her phone like a giddy teenager texting with the hot guy in her English class.

Sabrina: What time?

Sexy SAR Expert: Now? Unless you're still working.

She glanced at the time on her phone. Her shift had technically ended an hour ago. She'd only stayed to finish up the application.

Sabrina: Send me the address.

Fifteen minutes later, she pulled into Noah's driveway on the outskirts of Dark Canyon, excitement bubbling in her stomach. And something else she had no idea what to call.

She'd spent hours reliving that first kiss in the parking lot. The unexpected one. The others had been good too, but the way he'd jumped in before they'd even taken a step toward the restaurant, as if he couldn't wait to get to the next stage *spoke* to her.

When Noah opened the door, her stomach did a little dance. His worn jeans hugged solid thighs and a faded T-shirt highlighted his shoulders, reminding her exactly what that muscle definition felt like.

His hair killed her. He wore it a little long, messy and made for a woman's fingers.

She made a fist so she didn't actually reach out. Though she had a feeling he wouldn't think twice about it if she did. It was liberating to think she could go with her natural tendency to fling herself off the cliff with no apologies if she wanted to.

"Hey." His smile widened as he took in her uniform with a once-over that set her insides on simmer. "Come straight from work?"

"You said 'now.' Here I am." Could he tell she'd broken the speed limit multiple times to get here? That her whole body had hummed in anticipation the entire way?

She stepped inside, cataloging details of his home. Neat but lived in. Training gear organized near the door. Dog toys scattered around.

A furry blur launched itself at her from the hallway. Not Dancer. This dog was chocolate brown and slightly smaller. And way more enthusiastic.

"Sabrina, meet Ripley." Noah's voice carried a tinge of something she couldn't quite identify. "She's been looking for the right partner."

"Ripley?" Sabrina stared at the chocolate lab who had plastered herself against Sabrina's legs, tail wagging furiously.

Noah's grin widened. "She's perfect for SAR work. If you like her."

"She's what?" The pieces clicked together in Sabrina's mind. "A SAR dog? For *me*?"

She'd only just completed the application. Was it even legal to start working with a dog?

"Offering you a potential partner." He crouched down next to them, scratching behind Ripley's ears. "She's young, smart and has the right temperament for search work. My trainer spotted her at a shelter last month. She's been waiting for the right handler."

Which was her?

Sabrina sank to her knees, letting Ripley snuffle her hands. The dog immediately rolled over, exposing her belly. Adorable. Was it possible for your insides to actually melt?

"I thought we were going to talk about the case. You don't waste time, do you?" She meant it to sound teasing, but her voice came out all wrong. And she had no idea what emotion had clogged it.

"Life's too short to wait when you see the right fit." Noah's hand brushed hers as they both petted Ripley, and it wasn't an accident. "And you two? Definitely the right fit."

He wasn't wrong. Already Ripley had climbed right inside Sabrina with those soulful brown eyes and eager energy. But this was a huge step. A dog meant commitment, responsibility. Stuff she hadn't fully reconciled in her head yet, figuring she had time.

"I just turned in my SAR application today," she said slowly. "I haven't even been accepted to the program yet."

"You will be." The certainty in his voice made her look up, meeting his concentrated gaze. "Besides, you can get certified outside of the partner program you applied to, if for some reason you don't get a slot. There are all kinds of volunteer organizations, especially in this area. Take the dog, get acquainted, and we'll figure out what the next steps look like together."

Heat bloomed in her chest. Both from his faith in her and the realization that he'd been thinking about her future, planning this surprise—with the full intent of being right by her side the whole way.

"This is—" *Crazy.* Fast. Overwhelming.

But when had she ever shied away from the deep end? She was just used to being the one at the rudder, the one everyone else was telling to slow down.

But she couldn't stop smiling as Ripley wriggled closer, clearly having decided Sabrina belonged to her now. "I've never even had a houseplant. What if I'm not cut out to own a dog?"

"Well, first of all, Ripley will be your partner, not just a pet." His hand settled warm on her shoulder. "It makes a difference, trust me. You automatically step up when you think about her like that. But I have a good feeling about this."

Dazed, Sabrina glanced up and blew out a breath. "Okay. Where do we start?"

Noah grinned. "You're gonna need some supplies."

They quickly made their way to the pet store.

"We'll get the basics to start." Noah grabbed a cart at the entrance like a man on a mission. "Food, bowls, leash, treats for training."

"That doesn't sound too bad." Sabrina followed him, Ripley prancing between them on her borrowed leash, still glued to Sabrina's side. The car ride had been…interesting. Full of man and dog, a combo that shouldn't have been so appealing.

But definitely was.

"Oh, we're just getting warmed up." He steered them toward an aisle filled with what looked like every dog product ever invented. "SAR dogs need specific gear. We'll start with the essentials and build from there."

"There's more than essentials?"

His answering grin made her stomach flip. "You have no idea. Wait until we get to the specialized training equipment."

"I think my credit card just whimpered."

"Good thing you're getting that promotion." He winked, then held up two different leashes. "Standard or retractable?"

"You're the expert." She gestured for him to choose.

Normally, she'd be all over making her own decisions, getting out in front, proving she could handle whatever got thrown in her lap.

But there was something really great about having Noah around. He made her feel supported instead of defensive. And she couldn't quite figure out how he'd done it.

"Standard. Better control during training." He added it to the cart, then grabbed a matching collar. "You might like to switch later on, but at the beginning, the retractable ones can be dangerous if the dog lunges unexpectedly."

"Voice of experience?"

"Dancer taught me that lesson early on." Noah crouched to measure the collar against Ripley's neck. "Your girl here is about the same size he was at this age."

Your girl. The words sent a little thrill through her as Noah handed her the collar and nodded to Ripley. She bent down and tried it on the dog, Ripley sitting perfectly still as if she understood the importance of the moment.

"She really likes you," Noah commented, scratching under Ripley's chin. "Dogs are excellent judges of character."

"What if I'm terrible at this?" The question slipped out before she could stop it.

And, no, she definitely wasn't used to being this vulnerable in front of a guy. Noah never made her feel like she had to pull punches, though, or be anything other than herself.

It was doing a number on her.

He stepped close enough that she had to tilt her head back to meet his gaze. "You won't be. But even if you struggle at first, I'll be right here to help."

"Why?"

"Because I want to." His gaze turned molten as they stared at each other, undercurrents rippling the space between them.

There was something super hot about a guy who didn't shy away from tough questions. Who seemed so genuinely earnest in his responses, as if it had never occurred to him that he could lie or hedge.

But then he cleared his throat, shattering the moment as he turned back to the shelves. "Food and water bowls. Stainless steel lasts longer than plastic."

They worked their way through the store, Noah explaining each item as it went into the cart. She watched Noah confidently selecting supplies, explaining each choice with the expertise she usually insisted on having herself. The strange part wasn't that she was letting him lead—it was how natural it felt to trust his judgment. When was the last time she'd trusted anyone's judgment but her own?

Ripley watched the proceedings with keen interest, occasionally bumping Sabrina's leg as if reminding her that all of this was really happening.

"Do I want to know how much this is going to cost?" she asked as the pile grew.

"Consider it an investment in your future." He tossed in a rope toy that made Ripley's tail wag so hard, she nearly fell over. "Besides, wait until you see the bill for her first vet visit."

"Are you trying to scare me off?"

"Never." His hand brushed the small of her back as they rounded the corner to another aisle. "Just being honest about what you're getting into. A SAR dog is a serious commitment."

That was a word she didn't throw around very often.

"Good thing I don't scare easy." She meant it to sound confident, but her voice wavered slightly as she internalized that this was in fact one of the scariest things she'd done.

And she wasn't pushing back.

Noah's gaze met hers unflinchingly. "That's one of the things I like best about you."

AN HOUR LATER, they stood in Sabrina's living room surrounded by shopping bags. Her credit card might be smoking slightly, but Ripley's obvious excitement made it hard to regret a single purchase.

"Where should we start?" Sabrina surveyed the pile of supplies, thinking how her normal MO would be to google the answers.

But she didn't have to with Sexy SAR Expert in the house. They'd spent hours together over the last few days. Shouldn't she be ready for him to go? She wasn't though. Not by a long shot.

"Food and water station first." Noah held up the stainless-steel bowls they'd chosen. "Kitchen?"

She nodded, leading the way. Her house suddenly felt different with Noah in it. Smaller. More intimate. And not just because of his height—his presence filled the space, which of course made her realize how empty it normally was.

That rode shotgun in her chest, with far more weight than the dent in her credit card.

"This corner would work." He indicated a spot near her breakfast bar. "Easy to clean if she splashes."

"When," Sabrina corrected as Ripley wriggled across her carpet, familiarizing herself with every inch. "Pretty sure it'll be *when* she splashes."

Noah's laugh curled her toes. "Fair point. We'll get you a mat too."

"Add it to my tab." She crouched to help him arrange the bowls, very aware of his proximity. "I had no idea dogs needed so much stuff."

"Just wait until we start training." He bumped her shoulder playfully. "The equipment list for SAR work is twice as long."

"You're really going to help me with all of this?"

His hands stilled on the water bowl. "Of course. For as long as you want."

Their eyes met and that spark flared again, the one that had been present from moment one. Noah was close enough to kiss, his gaze on her lips making it clear he was thinking about it too.

Ripley chose that moment to wedge herself between them, almost knocking Sabrina off-balance. Noah's hand shot out to steady her, warm against her waist.

"Thanks." She caught her breath, trying to ignore the flutters taking flight inside at his touch. "We should probably finish setting up before it gets too late."

"Right." But he didn't move away immediately, clearly enjoying being close to her too. "Where do you want her bed?"

They worked together to arrange Ripley's space, Noah explaining the importance of establishing routines early. The dog followed them from room to room, investigating each new addition to the house with enthusiasm.

Noah moved through her space like he belonged there, rearranging her carefully maintained independence to make room for Ripley. For himself. The strangest part? She wanted him to stay, to keep filling up her empty corners with his presence.

Everything was upside down.

"She's going to need a lot of exercise," Noah said as they

set up her crate in the spare room. "Daily runs, structured play sessions. SAR training will help, but she's got tons of energy. Just like you."

Sabrina raised an eyebrow.

"It's a compliment. You two are perfectly matched in that department." His grin held an edge that made her pulse skip. "I have a feeling you'll keep each other busy."

Finally, everything had a place. Sabrina collapsed onto her couch, suddenly exhausted. Ripley immediately hopped up next to her, laying her head in Sabrina's lap as if she'd been doing it for years.

"She's already claimed you." Noah settled on Ripley's other side, his arm stretching along the back of the couch behind them. "Look at that face. She knows she's home."

Home. Such a simple word, but it squeezed something in Sabrina's chest. She'd never thought of this place as a home. Her apartment was spare, functional. A place to sleep between shifts. Work had always been her focus.

Now she had dog beds and toys and a cabinet full of supplies. A living creature who would depend on her completely. Never mind that Ripley had ties to her job. It didn't feel like an assignment.

This was totally new ground. And she didn't know how to feel about the way Noah threaded through everything.

"You're quiet all at once." Noah's voice held a note of concern. "Did I overstep?"

"No." She scratched behind Ripley's ears, smiling as the dog's eyes drifted closed in bliss. "Just realizing how big of a change this is."

His fingers brushed her shoulder, the touch sending warmth through her whole body. "You don't strike me as the type to back down from challenges."

Even the fact that he knew that about her kind of made the point.

"This is different." She gestured to Ripley, to the evidence of their shopping spree scattered around her living room. "This is a lot of reality. I paid an exorbitant pet deposit. It doesn't feel like there's room for backsies."

"Scared?"

The question could have sounded mocking. Instead, his tone held simple curiosity, as if he genuinely wanted to understand what she was feeling.

"Terrified," she admitted. "But also excited. I'm not sure I've ever felt that way about anything before."

"That's exactly how you should feel about the best things in life." His hand settled more firmly on her shoulder. "The trick is not letting the fear stop you from going after what you want."

Their eyes met over Ripley's head, and Sabrina had the sense again of being on that roller coaster, cresting over the first hill at that point when the world opened up. You could see forever and you forgot for a moment that the bottom was about to drop out.

She should probably grab onto something. The way Noah had blazed into her life, upending everything in the span of forty-eight hours—that probably wasn't going to stop.

And she didn't see herself tapping the brakes. Not yet. There was too much to discover here, too much exhilaration to experience.

Besides, Noah wasn't asking her to marry him. He'd given her a dog. And a potential leg up with the selection committee. Nothing more. She could handle this.

"Thank you," she said softly. "For Ripley. For all of this."

"Thank you for not shoving it all back in my face." He leaned closer, his breath warm against her cheek. "For being exactly the woman I thought you were. One willing to take a chance on something great."

When his lips met hers, Ripley huffed and wiggled off

the couch, apparently done with being squeezed between them. Sabrina barely noticed, too caught up in the way Noah kissed her—like he'd been thinking about it since their last kiss, like he couldn't wait another second to taste her again.

Like she was exactly what he wanted.

She could get used to this.

Chapter Eleven

Noah's truck tires squealed as he skidded between the lines and shuddered to a halt in the parking lot at the training course near his house. It was probably time to replace his tires, which he had to do about every six months the way he drove, but oh well.

It was finally Saturday, Sabrina's day off. And she'd be here for her first SAR training session in exactly fifty-seven minutes.

Yeah, his steps might be a little lighter than normal because of it. So what?

The sun wouldn't make an appearance for a while yet, so Noah shoved a headlamp over his ball cap. The beam caught chunks of ice crystals in the frosted grass, making them sparkle like someone had scattered diamonds across the field.

It was like a fairy world. Perfect.

Jacob's unsolicited, unwelcome and one hundred percent not wrong advice had been pinballing around in his chest, looking for a place to land since the NPS office ambush the other day. It was times like these—when he wanted to believe that something mystical and maybe a little implausible might happen—that he wished he could push everything his brother had said out of his brain.

But then he remembered the string of women he'd dated over the years, all of whom had run screaming for the hills when he laid it on too thick. He was a romantic. Why did everyone have a problem with that?

Well, Sabrina hadn't proven to be one of them. Not yet. And he needed to spend time with her to find out if they were on the same page.

He wanted to spend time with her. So it all worked out in the end.

Dancer sat at perfect heel position while Noah laid out basic equipment—long leads, training bumpers, scent articles. This would be the first test of Sabrina and Ripley's partnership. And his skill in matching them.

They'd all pass. He had no doubt.

Headlights swept across the field and his pulse kicked into overdrive as Sabrina's USFS vehicle pulled in five minutes early. Looked like someone else had been eager to get here too.

She emerged in black workout leggings and a purple fleece jacket that hugged her athletic body. The blue dress had been his favorite look on her until now. The sun chose that exact moment to peek over the mountain ridge behind her, creating a halo effect that belonged in one of those Renaissance paintings of angels.

It was a sign. This thing between them had the blessings of the heavens. Who was he to ignore *that*?

"Officer West, I hardly recognized you in your civilian clothes," he joked as she jogged over, Ripley bounding at her heels with enough enthusiasm to power a small city. "Ready to start your SAR journey?"

"Oh, I already started. I've been up since four." Her smile took on a glittering edge. "Fair warning. I studied everything. Stand back for the best trainee you've ever seen. Ripley and I are gonna tear the place up."

She bounced on her feet like a prizefighter, throwing fake punches, and it would not surprise him at all if she did sock him in the gut.

"Whoa, there. Let's leave the violence to the professionals," he said, throwing up his hands in mock surrender. "There's no first day test. This is just a warm-up until you get accepted into the SAR program."

She slanted him a look. "Are you telling me to reel it back in?" She said it like she'd spit out the nastiest phrase on the planet.

All at once, he felt precarious, as if he'd wound up on the edge of an abyss, only to realize at the last second that he'd almost stepped out into nothingness. "I would never say that to you."

"It sounded a lot like you were." A fine thread of indictment ran through her tone.

Mayday! He needed to wave a white flag, pronto, but with style and enough sincerity that they didn't have to go through this again.

"Hey," he murmured softly and held out his hand. "Come here."

She eyed his outstretched hand. And then eyed him, giving him serious vibes as if she might leave him hanging. But then she rolled her shoulders and slid her hand into his, fingers tangling.

Pulling her close was easy. She fit up against him, even as bristly as she was, which needed to go, like yesterday. Noah brushed a thumb across her cheek, his other arm firm in place at her waist, letting his smile communicate exactly how much he'd been looking forward to getting her in exactly this place, her heat warming him nicely on this frosty morning.

"This is me," he told her. "You want to ace this course

your first time out? Do it. You want to beat every time me and Dancer have ever put up? I'll hold the stop watch."

Her gaze still snapped with challenge. "Yeah?"

"Yeah." He didn't look away. And wouldn't, no matter how hard she tried to freeze him out with her icy blue eyes.

It was important to him that she knew he could take it.

"Because it sounded like you were saying the opposite."

"Rookie mistake," he countered easily. "It was meant to relax you so that you didn't put so much pressure on yourself. Ripley is new. She might be a disaster the first time and that's not a reflection on you."

Slowly, her spine had started to relax and the ice in her vibe got a little less arctic. "Isn't it? You picked her for me. She's already got the seal of approval. I'm the untried one here."

Was that what this was about? He resisted the urge to kiss away the slight downturn to her lips. Though he knew he could if she'd let him, she needed to hear his words, not be distracted.

"If you want to prove to yourself that you've got what it takes, I'm gonna release you and stand back so you can crush it. I'll take lots of pictures. But there's nothing for you to prove to *me*. I already think you're amazing."

She blinked, confusion and a billion other emotions battling across her face. "You do?"

Man, she was killing him.

This was Sabrina West in full vulnerability mode, and he did not mistake it as anything other than a huge gift that she'd let him see this glimpse into her soul.

"I do," he murmured and that's when he brushed his lips across her forehead.

That turned her polar ice caps into puddles. Her whole body just…unspooled, going slack against him, her lithe frame feeling like heaven against his as he took her weight, hefting her even closer with the arm she'd never removed from her waist.

He counted that as much of a win as the rest.

Because what was this but another sign? Jacob's warnings had some merit, sure, but Noah had never felt like this with another woman. As if he could fly. As if he could help *her* fly. That's what he'd seen his whole life between his parents—two people united in everything, supporting each other, loving each other, *understanding* each other.

"Sorry," she murmured against his heavy fleece pullover. "I forgot for a second that you're not normal."

He had to laugh at that. "I've never felt so oddly complimented in my life."

"Are we going to like, do any dog stuff or stand here all day?" she asked him, her own arms tight around him. "Because I'm trying to figure out which one I'd pick, and right now, it's stand here."

He rested his head against hers, enjoying their height difference. "Standing here is very nice, I completely agree. But I already know you're a champion hugger. I want to see what you do with Ripley."

"Kay." She levered her face up to his and pressed a long kiss against his lips that he had to fight to keep chaste.

This was her show. He was just here for the moral support.

Finally, she stepped back. "All right, crisis is over. Show me everything."

That was it? Their first fight and it was just…done? Man, he could get used to this. And how well he'd handled it, if he did say so himself. Before he could get busy patting himself on the back, he had more important things to do, like dog stuff.

"First things first." He gestured to where Dancer sat demonstrating perfect form, patiently waiting for the humans to get their act together. "The foundation of SAR work is the bond between handler and dog. Everything builds from there."

Sabrina nodded, her gaze on him in that way she had that made him feel like the only person in her world. "You and Dancer have that. I noticed it right away."

"We'll start with proper heel position." He demonstrated with Dancer, explaining how the dog should stay on the left side, shoulder aligned with the handler's leg. "Consistency is crucial in the field. It builds trust, creates a rhythm between you. That's how you create a bond."

She summoned Ripley to her side and the dog pressed against her leg instantly, looking up with complete adoration. Yeah, he'd made the right call. Ripley needed someone extraordinary, who could match her drive, her enthusiasm, her fierce heart.

And vice versa.

"Like this?" Sabrina asked.

"Exactly like that." He moved behind her, his hands settling on her hips to adjust her stance slightly, his fingers lingering because, man, she felt good. "You want your weight balanced, ready to move in any direction."

She glanced over her shoulder as his fingers traced up her sides, her sharp intake of breath telling him that she'd noticed his position. And how nicely it worked. "Is this a training session or an excuse to get your hands on me?"

"Both?" He pressed a kiss to her cheek, just because he could. "I'm excellent at multitasking."

She laughed, the sound skating across his skin. "I see how you are. This is a ploy, isn't it? To keep me from learning so I can't beat your times." She snapped her fingers. "Less flirting, more training."

"Yes, ma'am." But he kept one hand on the small of her back as he moved beside her to demonstrate the hand signals.

"These commands need to be crystal clear and consistent. Your dog has to trust that you'll always give the same cues."

"Trust," Sabrina repeated, something flickering in her expression. "That's not something I have a lot of experience with. Giving it or accepting it."

"It'll come in time. The right partner will be patient with you."

Their eyes met and held. Which made it really easy to see that she got the point, and it wasn't solely specific to dog training.

She gave a tiny nod that was barely perceptible, but he saw it. He saw a lot of things. First and foremost, that Jacob could jump in a lake with his warnings.

This was real and was happening.

They spent another hour working on various commands, Noah using every excuse to adjust her form, which doubled as its own secret language.

"Ready to try something more challenging?" he asked, already planning their next sequence. Their next date. The next year as she earned her certification and became an SAR specialist. They could work together. They could travel places together so he could write articles. Be one of those nauseating couples who are so in love that people don't want to be around them.

The whole thing unfolded in his head so easily that he couldn't stop imagining it.

Sabrina's answering grin held a wild edge that called to him. "Bring it, Colton. We can handle anything you throw at us."

However, by the beginning of the third hour, Sabrina started to regret her flippant proposition that she could handle whatever Noah put on her plate. The guy didn't have an Off switch.

Normally, she'd be all over it, especially something like

this SAR thing with such high stakes, which she really wanted to get right.

But everything had ratcheted up to a whole other level of intense, thanks to the subtext Noah had dropped into the mix.

This wasn't merely SAR training. She and Ripley were *bonding*. Learning to trust each other. They were building a partnership—a permanent one.

Noah guided them through basic obedience work, each exercise building on the last. They practiced sits, stays, heels—what Noah called their foundation. He kept throwing around these twenty-dollar words that must be second nature to him. But she'd never done anything like this, something that required her to do more, be more and, above all, consider the long term.

Not to mention that nebulous concept of *trust*. There was some fine print that she'd totally missed in all her research and video watching.

But despite all the stuff going on inside her, the sheer overwhelm of the responsibility and commitment required for this SAR dog partnership business, it was going well. Really well. Ripley responded to Sabrina's commands like they'd been working together for years. It was something else.

That other thing jockeying for position in her chest was pride. In herself. In Ripley. And, yeah, in Noah too. Because he'd made this happen. He'd seen the potential and then put in the work to push both dog and woman to this place.

If she didn't already have a thing for him, that would have done it.

Also, no one had told her how sexy it was to watch a competent guy in his element. It was very distracting. How she'd retained a word of what the man said, she'd never know.

"The most important command is the emergency recall," Noah explained, setting up a longer distance exercise. "When you call your dog off a track, they have to respond instantly. Lives could depend on it."

His hands settled briefly on her shoulders as he positioned her, still with the same casual familiarity, as if he'd been doing it for ages.

"Like if the terrain suddenly becomes dangerous?" she asked, leaning into his touch because this easy intimacy they'd developed worked for her.

"Exactly." Noah's voice got so animated when he explained things. It was adorable. "Natural hazards, human threats—SAR work isn't always safe. Your dog has to trust your judgment completely."

There was that word again. *Trust*. The concept made her chest do funny things—that subtext again. He was doing it on purpose, calling her out, making her think about how little she trusted anyone except herself.

It was doing a number on her.

Especially after the way Noah had handled her intensity that morning. He'd been…perfect. He hadn't tried to change her or rein her in. Just accepted her exactly as she was. Even when she'd completely overreacted, which she could admit now.

Finally, a guy who got it.

But she kept waiting for the other shoe to drop. For this perfect guy to turn out to be not so perfect—just like all of the other ones who had zero staying power.

Maybe if she learned to trust her partnership with Ripley, she could figure out how to do it with a guy. Eventually.

"Show me," she said, thrilled to have an excuse to segueing into her new favorite activity, watching Noah do anything.

Four hours passed like four minutes. Sabrina's muscles burned from running Ripley through recall exercises, but dang if she wasn't nailing every single one. She had this. They had this. Noah made it feel less like work and more like the best kind of game—one she was absolutely crushing.

Who knew having a hot guy for a trainer could be this much fun? And that was the thing about Noah. He made everything fun. It was part of his charm.

"You're both picking this up faster than anyone I've ever trained." Noah's praise sent a shower of sparks through her chest.

It was nearly miraculous how he actually appreciated her drive instead of being threatened by it. She couldn't get over how perfectly suited they were for each other. It was like the universe figured she needed a break from the usual guys and dropped a whole different species of male in her lap.

"Ready for something new?" he asked.

"Always."

"This one's about scent discrimination." He pulled what looked like small canvas pouches from his pack. "SAR dogs need to learn to identify specific scents and ignore others. Even the most tempting ones."

She watched him demonstrate with Dancer, admiring the way his shoulders moved as he planted the scent articles. Dang, this guy was crafted finer than anyone she'd ever met. As if her exact specifications in a perfect male had been plucked from her subconscious.

"The real trick is teaching them to stay focused when there are distractions," Noah explained, laying out what looked like beef jerky near one of the pouches. "Most dogs would go straight for the food, but watch this."

Dancer moved through the course with laser focus, ignoring the treats to indicate the proper scent article. The quiet pride in Noah's voice as he praised his partner made something squeeze in Sabrina's chest. They had the bond she needed to replicate with Ripley. It seemed nearly impossible to imagine being at that place. Her—the woman who spent twenty-four seven making sure everyone knew she could do it all herself.

"That's incredible," she said, meaning it. "How long did it take to get to that level?"

"Months of work." He grinned. "But the bond you build during training? Worth every second. Nothing better than having someone you trust completely at your side."

"Ripley's turn?" She needed to move, to do something besides think about the weight of his words. "Let's see if we can match that focus."

"Start her about twenty yards back." He positioned the scent articles differently. "Remember, you're her anchor point. She'll take her cues from your energy."

To her surprise, Ripley worked the scent problem perfectly, bypassing the food to indicate the proper article. Pride bloomed in Sabrina's chest, fierce and unexpected.

"See?" Noah's hands settled on her shoulders again, thumbs working the knots she hadn't realized had formed. "You're a natural at this. At all of it."

She nearly groaned in pure bliss.

How did he know the right things to say and do? It was like he could read everything about her written on her skin or something. The idea of being that transparent sent a tiny warning flicker through her brain, but his fingers felt too good to pull away. Everything about him felt too good. The way he touched her, the way he looked at her, the way he seemed to actually see her.

She couldn't figure out why this was a problem. But it might be soon enough, as they inevitably drifted apart.

"I have excellent taste in teachers," she said with a laugh, because that at least was true.

"You have excellent everything." His voice dropped lower,

sending shivers down her spine that had nothing to do with the January cold. "I've never met anyone like you, Sabrina."

Her pulse fluttered at his pretty words. But this was just Noah being Noah—intense about everything, even her.

"Flatterer." She leaned back against his chest, savoring his warmth. "Trying to make sure I come back for more training?"

"Trying to make sure you know exactly how amazing you are." His lips brushed her temple.

When this thing between them fizzled out—which it surely would, given how hot and fast they'd burned from the start—she'd really miss this way he had about him. How good he made her feel.

She planned to savor it all for however long the fun lasted.

"Keep telling me and maybe it'll sink in," she told him and stepped back. "I have plans tonight. Is this a good place to stop?"

"Yeah, it can be. I was hoping to take you to dinner though." Noah didn't hide his disappointment. Yet another odd aspect of him that she couldn't get used to. He never pretended or pulled punches.

Which was exactly why they worked. Why it was different from all those other relationships that had crashed and burned when guys couldn't handle her full-throttle approach to life. He'd tell her if aspects of her personality bothered him or if he was getting tired of her.

That was the great thing about Noah. They were on the same page. They were both having fun while it lasted.

"Sorry, I promised my mom I would drive over to visit. She's in Durango," Sabrina explained. "I usually spend the night."

Noah's grin widened. "That's an acceptable excuse for ditching me. Call me tomorrow night so we can talk until dawn again."

"It's a date."

Her own smile didn't fade as she hightailed it to her vehicle so she could get home to do the umpteen things required to travel with a dog. How had she gotten so lucky as to meet a great guy who was happy spending time with her? No agenda, no pressure, and he seemed to really get her independent streak.

Maybe Noah Colton had more in common with a unicorn than she'd expected.

Chapter Twelve

Noah threaded his fingers through Sabrina's as he led her through the National Park Service building to Jacob's office. She didn't protest, but the look she slanted him dripped question marks.

"I haven't seen you since Saturday," he murmured and brushed a thumb over hers. "I missed you."

"So you said," she said, giving him a smirk. "Several times. Both on the phone and when you picked me up this morning."

But she didn't seem to mind an extra dose of touchy-feely, nor did she push him for any further clarification. Which was good. Because he didn't know how to explain the sudden urge to ensure everyone—especially Jacob—knew she was with him.

This rush of possessiveness wasn't his normal vibe at all. And he didn't think he'd be the type to listen to emo songs and eat a gallon of ice cream while his girlfriend visited her mother either, but here they were.

Sabrina had upended everything inside his skin. He kind of liked the way it unbalanced him. Shouldn't all great experiences do that?

"Your brother's going to kill me for bringing you along," Sabrina said, matching his stride as they rounded the corner.

"Probably." Noah's grin widened. "But what are little brothers for if it's not showing up unannounced at an official interagency meeting. Besides, Jacob likes you. So I'm counting on you to smooth things over."

Maybe in more ways than one. He'd be lying if he said he didn't hope his brother could see him with Sabrina, see how great they were together and get over himself. Jacob would readily admit his warnings had been unfounded.

And the way things were going, Noah fully expected Sabrina to be by his side a whole lot more at family events and Thanksgiving and such. It would be nice if Jacob was already on board.

They reached Jacob's office door, the buzz under his skin different this time. Better. Because he wasn't trying to get information for his article alone, but was here with someone who'd fiercely insisted that he should do the thing he loved, that it was important to reclaim what he'd lost.

Noah had a speech prepared for when his brother realized Sabrina hadn't come alone. Three actually, ranging from "I ran into her at the door" to "She kidnapped me and forced me to drive." Hopefully one of them would convince his by-the-book brother to bend a little.

He pushed open the door, speech number one locked and loaded as he guided Sabrina over the threshold.

Jacob glanced up from his desk. "Officer West, right on time." When his gaze narrowed and zeroed in on Noah, he held up a hand. "Are you a packaged deal now?"

Noah grinned. "I figured my invitation got lost in the mail. I forgive the oversight."

"I take it you two know each other," Sabrina deadpanned, which earned a solid laugh from Noah. Jacob actually cracked a smile. "Nice to see you, Agent Colton. It's been a while."

Jacob stood and extended his hand to Sabrina, holding it

a touch too long for Noah's taste. "Whatever this joker told you to get you to bring him along for the ride, it's all lies."

"Hey," Noah protested, crossing his arms hard over his torso as he tried to ignore how jealous that innocuous handshake among colleagues had made him. "I brought her, not the other way around. The gentlemanly thing to do when you find out your brother has information about a case you happen to be interested in."

"Yeah, always the gentleman." Jacob snickered. "I'll just call someone to escort you out."

Noah sighed. Obviously, Jacob wasn't in a charitable mood, though why Noah had thought his brother might be willing to throw him a bone, he had no idea.

"Agent Colton." Sabrina stepped in front of Noah smoothly, angling her body so he was almost hidden behind her. "As you're aware, SAR played a key role in recovering our Jane Doe. I'm certain it wouldn't be a breach of protocol if the specialist sat in on our interagency briefing."

There were a lot of heavy, suggestive glances going on between Jacob and Sabrina, which made Noah a little squirrelly, but she was pleading his case, so he kept his mouth shut.

Jacob folded his hands, eyebrows raised. "Are you officially requesting the SAR specialist's presence, Officer West? As a lead officer responsible for the coordination between our departments?"

Beaming, Sabrina nodded vigorously. "Why, yes, Agent Colton. I am. How kind of you to ask."

"Fine." Jacob waved a hand dismissively as if he didn't really care one way or the other. But then he eyed Noah. "Don't make me sorry."

"Not a chance, Agent Colton," Noah said with just a smidge of sarcasm that was one hundred percent warranted as he parked himself in a chair just in case his brother changed his mind. Though it wasn't bolted to the floor. Jacob could still kick him out, so that felt like not so much of a safeguard.

Really, he needed a bag to hold the remnants of his heart, which had liquefied and poured out all over the floor at Sabrina's feet.

She'd gone to bat for him. For no reason other than because she knew this case was important to him.

That more than anything should prove to Jacob that his relationship with Sabrina was not a disaster waiting to happen.

Jacob settled behind his desk, shuffling papers in a way that seemed designed to make Noah twitch. His brother had perfected the art of antagonizing him over the years.

"Our victim's name is Annie Ross." Jacob's gaze fixed on Sabrina as if he truly meant to pretend Noah wasn't there. "Fingerprints matched an arrest record from two years ago."

Noah's fingers tightened around Sabrina's before he realized he'd reached for her hand again. She squeezed back, and that tiny gesture steadied him.

They were finally getting somewhere.

"Prostitution charge," Jacob continued, his voice carefully neutral. "Her residence on record at the time was a small town here in Utah called Wilson. After that, she disappeared. No job history tied to her social, no phone, no address. Just…gone."

The words hit Noah like stones dropping into still water, ripples of possibility expanding outward. His investigative brain fired up, connections forming. They were dealing with a woman who'd erased herself.

Or been erased.

"Time of death?" Sabrina asked, her officer voice a stark contrast to how she'd bantered with Jacob moments ago.

"Medical examiner puts it at twenty-four to thirty-six hours before Officer West found her." Jacob's gaze slid to

Noah for a brief second. "Cause of death appears to be hypothermia."

Appears to be. Noah caught the careful phrasing, Jacob's penetrating stare alluding to more than what he could say out loud, saw Sabrina's slight head tilt that said she'd noticed too. His brother was throwing him a bone after all. Huh.

He opened his mouth to ask a follow-up question, but Jacob's phone buzzed. His brother glanced at the display and something in his expression shifted. The name Mae Copeland flashed on the screen.

"Need to take this. Test results from the lab," Jacob said shortly, his tone painfully casual.

Test results? The look on his brother's face did not scream, *I'm taking a call from a colleague!* The opposite in fact.

Was Jacob dating one of his coworkers? And he'd had the nerve to read Noah the riot act about being careful. Noah shook his head, his mind still on Annie Ross, the more important mystery here. A woman had vanished from the system only to reappear dead on a mountain.

And he'd landed center stage in the lead role on this story.

Jacob stepped into the hallway, phone pressed to his ear. Through the glass in the door, Noah watched his brother's shoulders relax, his usual rigid posture softening. Interesting.

Maybe their father dating Susan had rattled something loose in all of them.

"Is your brother seeing someone in the lab?" Sabrina murmured, following Noah's gaze.

"You noticed the less-than-professional vibe too?" He turned to study her profile, still caught off guard by how naturally she fit here, in this moment, reading his brother just as easily as he did.

"Definitely. That is not his typical smile." Sabrina nodded toward the glass. "Which is so unlike him. He's normally so by the book."

Noah studied Sabrina with piqued interest. "You think it's a bad idea to date someone you work with?"

The look she gave him had plenty of subtext. "Everyone thinks that at some point. It's just a question of how convoluted it gets before you clue in that it's a terrible idea."

"We work together," he reminded her, suddenly struck that they should have had this conversation a long time ago. Was she breaking one of her cardinal rules for him? What did that mean?

"That's different. You freelance. So next time I need an SAR specialist, I can call someone else. Voilà. Now we don't work together."

Blinking, Noah processed that. It was a throwaway comment, one Sabrina didn't even seem to realize had tripped him up. But it had. How would they work search and rescue together after Ripley was trained if Sabrina didn't even plan to call him next time she needed him in an official capacity?

"Noted."

Jacob came back in the room then, stalling the conversation. But not the churn in Noah's chest.

Jacob tucked his phone away with the kind of deliberate care that suggested he knew exactly how much he'd revealed and didn't know what to do about it. "Where were we?"

"Annie Ross," Noah supplied helpfully. "You were about to tell us everything you know about her."

"I was not." But there wasn't much heat in the denial. "Though I suppose you're going to find ways to dig into this no matter what."

"I will." Noah grinned. "You know me."

"That's what worries me." Jacob sank into his chair, leveling his gaze at Noah. "I can't tell you in an official capacity that I think there's something fishy about Annie Ross's death. I can't tell you in an official capacity that she wasn't reported missing or that I find that suspicious. What I am telling you is that this is still an active IBS case and I'm continuing to work on it. I've given Officer West all the information I have gathered thus far on this case. The interagency briefing portion of our day is over."

Noah sat on his hands to keep from hugging his brother. Because that would be weird. Jacob might throw a lot of bluster around, but obviously he trusted Noah to get to the bottom of a case that he himself couldn't pursue in the same way, not officially.

"Thank you, Agent Colton," Sabrina said, springing to life to play her part in the very carefully orchestrated proceedings that Noah wouldn't have believed his brother capable of if he hadn't witnessed it with his own eyes.

There must be something huge under the surface for the rule-loving oldest Colton brother to be so on board with all of this. It was almost enough to forget that his girlfriend had just dropped a very casual bomb on him about never working together.

Noah stood and snagged Sabrina's hand to help her to her feet because he wanted to and he could. Plus, it was a statement, one he liked making, especially since he knew dang well that Sabrina wouldn't let another male on the planet treat her like this.

He had a feeling she knew it wasn't because he didn't think she was capable of using her own two feet to get out of a chair. It made him feel like a million feet tall that she let him.

Before he could follow Sabrina out of Jacob's office, his brother stopped him with a head jerk.

"Dad called earlier. He's having dinner with Susan tonight."

The change of subject caught Noah off guard as he glanced at Sabrina through the open door, wondering if his brother expected him to shut it. "Already? I mean, again?"

"Apparently it's a regular thing now."

Something in Jacob's tone made Noah's chest ache. Their last conversation about their father's dating life hung between them. About how watching someone you loved move forward meant accepting that life didn't stand still.

Even when you wanted it to.

"Good for him." The words felt strange in Noah's mouth. But he meant them. "Mom would want him to be happy."

Probably. It was hard for him to project that when the idea of Sabrina dating someone else made him insane. Even if something happened and Noah wasn't here on this earth any longer, it hit wrong.

But neither did it thrill him to think about her sitting around being sad all the time. So he got it. Kind of.

"Yeah." Jacob's gaze drifted to where Sabrina stood in the hall quietly observing their exchange. "Mom would."

The weight of unspoken meaning pressed against Noah's ribs. Their mother had always pushed them to chase their dreams, to grab onto happiness with both hands. Even at the end, she'd worried more about them than herself.

"Speaking of family," Jacob said, "have you heard from Mark?"

"Radio silence." Noah scrubbed a hand over his face. "I went by his place twice, but he didn't answer the door. It's... a difficult situation."

"Tell me about it." Jacob's expression darkened. "I'll go by on my way home. We have to keep trying. Right now, Annie Ross is my priority."

And Noah's. Just like that, they were back to business.

But Noah caught Sabrina watching him with quiet sympathy. Maybe some understanding.

As they walked back out into the parking lot, Noah squinted against the bright sun, setting off the headache that had been brewing.

"You okay?" she murmured. "I didn't know your dad was dating again."

Because he hadn't mentioned it. Talking about it made it real.

He blew out a breath. Like keeping it under pressure in his chest and not dealing with this new reality had caused Jacob to keep quiet about the situation. "It's new and weird, and I'm still processing."

She slipped her hand from his and lifted it to his face, spreading her fingers across his cheek. "Process all you want. Out loud if you need to. Until then, let's talk about Annie Ross instead, because apparently, your brother has given his blessing for us to do that."

Yeah, along with a pointed reminder that the Colton family had its issues. As if ensuring that Noah would have that in the front of his mind as he investigated where Annie Ross had been for the two years no one had heard from her.

He slid Sabrina's palm to his lips and kissed it, pulling her into a hug that washed through him. She was here. For now, that meant he wasn't going anywhere.

They needed to talk about a lot of things. If nothing else, to get on the same page, because as much as he hated to admit it, his brother did have a point about that. Look at how differently Sabrina viewed working with someone she was dating.

What else were they not aligned on?

But at the moment, he didn't want to talk about that. He wanted to get cracking on Annie Ross. Dark Canyon's mysteries weren't going to solve themselves.

And he had a feeling there was so much more going on here than one woman's lone death indicated.

Chapter Thirteen

Cold wind bit through Sabrina's coat as she studied the convenience store's grimy facade. One of the fluorescent letters in the Open sign flickered, mirroring her pulse.

Her heartbeat was erratic partially because she couldn't quite believe they'd managed to track Annie Ross to this place. Hopefully. It was a lead Noah had scared up with some magic that she hadn't pressed on too hard, unsure she wanted to know the answers.

Also, her pulse never quite settled around Noah anyway, but apparently the dodgy nature of this area geared him up to stick closer to her than normal, his shoulder brushing hers as they surveyed their target.

He hadn't mentioned his father dating Susan once since they'd left Jacob's office the other day. In fact, it felt like he'd gone out of his way to avoid the subject. It was weird to have noticed and even weirder for her to care—emotional crises weren't her thing, and besides, sharing that kind of stuff wasn't what they were doing here.

But Noah shared everything. Honestly, she'd call him an oversharer. His quiet felt wrong, like the atmosphere over Dark Canyon when you could see storm clouds gathering over the horizon.

"Ready to see what we can find out?" he asked, that familiar energy humming beneath his words despite the shadows in his eyes.

She nodded, fighting the urge to lean into his warmth. She'd been doing that too much lately—gravitating toward him, treating him like a shelter she hadn't realized she'd needed.

It felt like a problem. Like she'd started depending on him. But she couldn't seem to take a step back.

The bell jangled as they entered. An elderly clerk barely glanced up from her crossword puzzle, her smile widening as she met Noah's gaze. He had that effect on people. Women mostly, but even a straight guy wouldn't be able to ignore Noah's dazzle.

"Annie Ross," Noah said, sliding his phone across the counter to show the clerk their victim's photo. "Did you know her?"

His voice carried that same forced lightness it had since leaving Jacob's office, like someone trying too hard not to be swallowed by an emotional quagmire. She knew that technique. Had perfected it under her father's exacting standards.

Should she ask him about it? It was getting harder and harder to remember that they weren't a couple. That they were just two people hanging out and seeing how things went. Sure, they jumped in when the other needed someone to have their back, but that was a proximity thing, not a feelings thing.

She was here to solve a case, get some closure for Annie Ross, and hope it helped Noah find his way back into writing articles.

End of story.

The clerk's weathered face creased. "Poor thing had a tough time of it. She was a sweet girl, though. Always took the worst shifts nobody else wanted."

Of course she did. Sabrina's chest tightened. With no social security activity, it was patently obvious Annie had been scraping by, working off the books, probably desperate for cash. What must her life have been like to resort to such measures?

That's why it was critical to rely on no one but yourself. Eventually, everyone flaked out or disappointed you, leaving you to fend off the wolves. Better you learn how to do that early, or you ended up in Peavine Canyon dead.

"When did she leave?" Noah's voice carried that same authoritative tone he used with Dancer. It seemed to work well on people too.

"About six months ago? Just stopped showing up." The clerk shrugged. "Happens a lot with the younger ones. Can't blame them—midnight shifts are rough."

"Did she ever mention where she lived?" Sabrina asked, pen poised over her notebook. Action felt safer than dwelling on Annie's desperate choices.

"Some apartment complex off Miller Street. Lived with friends from the system, she said. A couple of girls." The clerk's gaze turned quizzical. "Did something happen to her?"

Sabrina let Noah handle that one, his smooth deflection buying them a graceful exit. Outside, the wind had picked up, carrying the sharp bite of approaching snow. Perfect weather for nothing but cuddling up by a fire with Noah and a blanket.

Which was why they were tromping around in the freezing conditions, chasing leads. Otherwise, she'd get soft. This was *necessary* for multiple reasons.

"Miller Street." Noah was already pulling up a map on his phone, the screen's glow catching the planes of his face. No trace now of the vulnerability she'd glimpsed in Jacob's office. She should be relieved. Instead, her chest ached like she'd let him down.

"The cheapest one," Sabrina said with certainty, shoving the feeling aside. "A building with the broken security door and no cameras."

His answering smile hit her sideways. Because it wasn't his normal one. "Lead the way, Officer West."

She did, because forward motion was the only defense against thinking about things she shouldn't be. Like how to fix Noah so they could get back to having fun. And that thought made her feel worse, because what was he, a trained monkey?

The drive to Miller Street stretched under weighted silence. Noah stared out the window, clearly somewhere else entirely. She should say something. Ask about his dad, about Susan.

But what if she got it wrong? She'd never had a relationship before, never wanted one, never practiced how all this type of stuff worked. What if she pushed when he needed space or stayed quiet when he needed to talk? She was better with physical challenges. Give her an impossible climbing route over relationship navigation any day.

Noah would talk if he felt like it.

The apartment complex matched her prediction exactly. Peeling paint, cracked concrete, sheets hanging in windows instead of curtains. A maintenance worker slouched against the wall, cigarette dangling, looking about as welcoming as a rattlesnake guarding its den.

Noah shifted closer to her as they approached, walking side by side. She wished he'd take her hand like he had in the parking lot of Jacob's office, but he didn't.

"We're looking for this woman's apartment," Noah said as he showed the picture again, projecting that easy charm that seemed to work on everyone. "Her name is Annie Ross."

Except it didn't work on snake-den guy, whose expression

didn't change. He took a long drag from his cigarette, eyes narrowing. "Don't know nobody by that name."

Was this guy for real?

Sabrina stepped forward, letting her official USFS attitude fill the space between them. "Then you won't mind if we check the rent records. Unless you'd prefer that we take it up with your boss. I'm sure he'd loved to be dragged into a simple matter like this one after you refused to cooperate with a law enforcement officer."

The worker's face shifted. Message received.

"Unit 3C," he muttered. "But I ain't got a key. Manager's gone for the day."

Noah glanced at her, silently communicating that she should continue.

"Call him." Sabrina crossed her arms and gave the worker a look. "This is official business."

"Can't. He's at his kid's recital or something." The worker took another drag. "Try tomorrow."

Yeah, that wasn't happening. Annie's trail was already ice cold. They needed in that apartment now.

"What about maintenance access?" Noah asked, shooting the guy a half smile. "Surely you have override keys for emergencies. Burst pipes, that kind of thing?"

The worker's hesitation told her they were onto something. She recognized Noah's strategy now—good cop to her bad cop. They hadn't even planned it. Just fell into sync like they'd been working together for years instead of days.

"Look," Noah continued, "we can do this the easy way— you let us in, we're out in twenty minutes. Or we can call it in, wait for a warrant, have a whole circus of officials crawling over this place for hours. Your choice."

She bit back a smile. He made it sound so reasonable. Like he was doing the guy a favor instead of threatening to rain bureaucratic red tape all over his parade.

The worker muttered something unflattering but straightened up. "Fine. But you didn't get the key from me."

"What key?" Noah asked innocently as a ring of jangling metal appeared from the worker's pocket.

They followed him up three flights of creaking stairs. The whole building smelled of stale cigarettes and desperation. Their footsteps echoed off concrete walls painted an institutional shade of yellow that reminded Sabrina of her elementary school cafeteria.

A door cracked open down the hall as they passed, then quickly shut. Through the thin walls, Sabrina could hear the murmur of a TV, someone's music, a baby crying. Life going on behind closed doors. But there was something else—a watchfulness. As if she could feel eyes tracking them through peepholes.

The maintenance guy caught her noticing. "Folks here like their privacy," he said with a shrug that wasn't quite casual. "Kind of an unwritten rule. Nobody asks questions. Nobody causes trouble."

"Sounds peaceful," Noah commented mildly.

The worker snorted. "Yeah. Real peaceful. That's why the old lady in 2B sits by her window all day, calling neighbors if she spots certain cars pulling in. Why half these units got extra deadbolts that ain't on the lease. Privacy ain't about peace."

Sabrina's gut twisted. She knew what that meant. This was the kind of place you ended up when you needed to disappear. When running was safer than staying.

A woman emerged from the stairwell, caught sight of them, and immediately reversed direction. The maintenance guy didn't even blink.

"We're not here for them," she said quietly. "Just Annie."

Something in her tone must have registered, because the worker nodded slowly. "Unit 3C," he repeated, softer this time. "Think the blonde one moved out a few weeks ago. Real quiet-like. Middle of the night."

Sabrina's stomach swooped. They were getting somewhere.

The door to 3C looked identical to all the others lining the dingy hallway—cheap wood with peeling numbers, deadbolt showing signs of recent replacement. But something about it raised the hair on her neck.

The worker's key stuck slightly in the lock. "Dang thing's always screwy." He jiggled it with practiced motion until the mechanism clicked.

"We've got it from here," Noah said smoothly, already palming a twenty that appeared from nowhere.

The worker hesitated, looking between them. "You'll lock up after?"

"Scout's honor." Noah's easy smile got him nowhere with this guy. But Sabrina appreciated it.

"Whatever. I'm on break." The worker disappeared down the stairs, taking his cigarette stench and Noah's twenty with him.

Noah gestured to the door with an exaggerated flourish. "Ladies first?"

"Such a gentleman." She rolled her eyes but couldn't quite suppress her answering grin. Sometimes his ridiculousness was exactly what a moment needed.

The apartment door swung open on protesting hinges. Stale air carried traces of cheap air freshener and abandonment. The walls created three distinct living spaces in the cramped quarters—mattresses lay in the living room, in the converted dining room and in the actual bedroom. There were signs of a hasty departure everywhere.

"They left in a hurry," Noah murmured, examining scattered papers near the door. He held up an envelope. "The mail's still coming. But it's all addressed to Camille Lancaster. Utility bills, bank statements and a hospital bill from last month. That's pretty recent."

Sabrina frowned. "Nothing for Annie?"

"Doesn't look like it. Everything official is in Camille's name." He held up a rental agreement with Camille's signature at the bottom.

"Did the maintenance guy get it wrong?"

Noah shrugged. "Could be. Might have been trying to give us the brush-off."

Frustrated, Sabrina moved through the space with measured steps, cataloging details. Three coffee mugs by the sink, one chipped but carefully glued back together. A bulletin board covered in job listings, red circles around anything paying cash. A stack of applications filled out in different handwriting.

What a far cry from most people's world, where companies had websites and electronic submission processes. Everything here screamed, *Leave no trail!*

The kitchen told its own story. Store brand everything, except the prenatal vitamins lined up on the windowsill. Those were name brand, likely handed out by a free clinic. Three different kinds of peanut butter and a bottle of barbecue sauce but barely any real food.

Her throat tightened. She moved on.

The bathroom revealed more. Two different brands of shampoo—cheap stuff and one pretty bottle of an expensive brand, probably a gift. Makeup scattered across the counter, some high-end items mixed with drugstore brands. Little touches of luxury in a life stripped down to basics.

Noah appeared in the doorway, his presence filling the small space instantly. He even smelled good.

"Found something interesting," he said, holding up a photo. Three young women squeezed together for a selfie,

Annie in the middle. All smiling. All looking incredibly young.

"Happiness looks different in hindsight," she muttered, more to herself than Noah. But his hand settled warm on her shoulder, and she let it stay there. Just for a moment.

"Annie must have been crashing here unofficially. Smart, if she was trying to stay under the radar," Noah said and went back to the living room to continue his search.

The bedroom was last on Sabrina's list. Clothes still hung in the closet—cheap polyester uniforms from various service jobs. A dress that must have been for interviews, price tag still attached. Something sat behind all the clothes.

Her hands trembled slightly as she pushed hangers aside. It was a small shelving unit. And it was full of baby supplies. Diapers, wipes, tiny clothes still with tags attached. An unopened crib box leaned up against the back wall of the closet. Someone had folded a pink blanket with painful precision.

She'd expected evidence of Annie's life, maybe clues about where she'd gone. Not this punch to the chest that felt like free fall without a rope.

Never in a million years had she imagined Annie might have had a child somewhere. One who was wondering where her mother was.

The keening sound that came out of her mouth barely sounded human.

"Sabrina?" Noah's concerned voice carried through the apartment as he came into the bedroom. "You okay?"

"Fine." The word came out sharper than intended, but the last thing she needed was him cluing in that this whole scene was getting to her. "I was just…surprised."

He crossed the room to look over her shoulder. His sharp inhale said he understood exactly what they were seeing.

"A baby," he said softly. "Or one on the way."

She nodded, not trusting her voice. The perfectly folded

blanket blurred in her vision. All that careful preparation, that hope for the future. Left behind, just like Annie.

Noah settled his arm around her waist, pulling her in for a comforting hug. She should shake him off, maintain some distance before he figured out that she was fighting back emotions she didn't know how to name.

Instead, she relaxed against him. Just for a minute. Let his solid presence anchor her against the wave threatening to sweep her under.

She straightened, stepping away before he could burrow deeper under her skin. Though she feared it was far too late. "We need to find Camille Lancaster. She might know what happened."

He caught her arm as she turned to leave. "Sabrina."

She couldn't look at him, not with the evidence of somebody else's shattered dreams surrounding them. Would the coroner find that Annie had been pregnant? Or had one of the other girls living here been the mother of the baby?

"I'm fine." Two could play the silent game. "Let's just focus on the case."

She'd learned early that vulnerability was just another word for target. Some things were better left unexamined, like the way finding evidence of a family in chaos hit her sideways.

Or why it bothered her so much that he wouldn't talk about his father dating Susan.

She wasn't supposed to care about that part. Just like she didn't want him digging around in her emotional reaction to this scene, he probably had zero interest in exposing his own weaknesses.

But watching Noah process his emotional landmines in silence felt wrong. Like watching someone tackle a dangerous route without proper safety gear. She knew better. But opening that Pandora's box meant admitting how much she'd started to invest in him. In them.

She pulled out her phone. Time to do what she did best—charge ahead and let momentum carry her past the dangerous emotional swamps that threatened to drag her under.

Behind her, Noah started methodically photographing the baby supplies. They worked in silence, documenting the scene with practiced efficiency. Her camera clicked through shots of the bulletin board, the job applications, the careful collection of prenatal vitamins. Each photo was a brick in Annie's life, hopefully building a whole that would help them understand how she'd ended up dead on a mountain in clothes that didn't fit her surroundings.

"Receipt," Noah called from the kitchen. "Food delivery from two weeks ago. Three meals."

"She wasn't alone," Sabrina replied, examining a stack of magazines by the bed. Parenting guides, all of them. Some pages dog-eared, others marked with sticky notes. "They were planning for this baby or helping care for it. All of them."

The weight of that settled between them. Three women, one baby, a collection of dreams folded as carefully as that pink blanket. Now one was dead, possibly murdered. It wasn't a stretch to assume the others might be in danger.

Was that why they'd left in such a hurry?

"We need to find them." Noah's voice carried steel beneath the quiet. "Before—"

"I know." She did. The clock was ticking, and not just for their investigation. Somewhere out there, a baby might need help. "We will."

His answering nod felt like a promise. One she actually believed he could keep.

That was the dangerous thing about Noah Colton. He

made her believe in impossible things. Made her want to reach for them.

Except they were just supposed to be investigating Annie Ross's death. Not building a relationship.

Chapter Fourteen

The tiny exam room at Doctor Richie Colton's veterinary practice smelled of antiseptic and wet dog—thanks to Ripley, who'd decided to splash in every puddle on their way in. And because Sabrina couldn't bring herself to be the bad guy while Ripley beamed up at her with those fudge-colored eyes, she'd let her get away with it.

It wasn't a crime. And this was her first dog. First vet visit. First a lot of stuff. She got a pass.

"Up," Noah commanded, patting the metal exam table, and Ripley executed a perfect jump without hesitation. Show-off. Not that Sabrina minded. They'd been crushing their training sessions lately.

"Your girl has perfect form," Noah said with a wink, sliding an arm around her waist.

Noah was the most easily affectionate guy she'd ever met, by a mile. Most people gave her a lot of distance, but not this one. She kind of liked it. Reminded her that being prickly with everyone had earned her a lot of loneliness.

Who knew withdrawing her quills would lead to such a great time? Though lately she'd started thinking Noah had done a lot to dissolve those quills versus her making any kind of conscious choice.

"She's smart." Sabrina leaned into him, because why not?

His shoulder was right there and he was warm. "Unlike her owner, who let her play in puddles before her vet visit."

"The techs have seen worse. One time, Dancer rolled in something dead, and they told me I had to bring him in after-hours." His fingers traced circles against her hip. "Uncle Richie made me hose him off in the parking lot first."

"Uncle Richie sounds wise."

Noah grinned. "Sometimes family has its perks, but most of the time, they just treat you like family."

The door opened and Dr. Richie Colton strode in, somehow managing to look both distinguished and approachable in khakis and a crisp blue button-down under his white coat. He had the same eyes as Jacob and Noah. His weathered face creased into a genuine smile the moment he spotted Noah.

"If it isn't my favorite nephew." He clapped Noah on the shoulder, then turned a keen eye on Sabrina. "And you must be Sabrina West. I hear you're Ripley's new partner."

"Yes, sir." She caught herself straightening and fought the urge to salute. Force of habit when dealing with authority figures.

"None of that around here." Richie's warm eyes crinkled at the corners. "We're all family. Though this one—" he jerked a thumb at Noah "—nearly lost his Colton card when he put a frog in my coffee during a family camping trip. He was seven."

"It was a toad," Noah protested. "And you never proved it was me."

"Like father, like son." Richie winked at Sabrina. "Sam pulled the same stunt when we were kids."

The easy banter knocked something loose in Sabrina's chest. Her own father had never been the type for pranks or fond remembrances. Everything was serious. In fact, she couldn't remember a time when her father had taken her on vacation or even said the word *frog* out loud.

"Well, let's take a look at our girl." Richie moved efficiently through Ripley's exam while keeping up a steady stream of conversation, asking about their training progress and Noah's latest search-and-rescue operation. He had a way of drawing out information without making it feel like an interrogation.

"Perfect health," he pronounced after checking Ripley's teeth. "Noah mentioned you're starting SAR certification?"

"Yes, s—" She caught herself. "Just beginning the process."

"Breezed through the application." Noah's voice carried that note of pride that did funny things to her insides. "She'll have her certification in no time."

"That's our Noah." A woman's voice drew their attention to the doorway, where a striking brunette leaned against the frame. "Always the cheerleader."

She carried herself with the kind of polished grace that made Sabrina's muddy boots and brown uniform feel extra ugly—which they were, even without the contrast.

"Sassy." Noah's grin widened. "Sabrina, this is my cousin, Uncle Richie's daughter."

"Sabrina West? Officer West? I can't believe I'm meeting the great officer herself." Sassy paused to mock-fan herself. "Noah talks about you all the time. Nonstop. Even if you ask him nicely to pick another subject. Any at all."

Heat crawled up Sabrina's neck.

"Ignore her." Noah squeezed Sabrina's hip, completely unfazed by his cousin calling him out. "Sassy owns the gallery downtown."

"The one with all the incredible landscapes in the window?" The words slipped out before she could stop them.

"You know my gallery?" Sassy pushed off the doorframe, instantly warming. "I've got some new pieces coming in next week. You should stop by—I'd love to get your perspective on the local scenery."

It was such a natural invitation. These people made everything feel natural. Easy.

Like family.

The thought hit her sideways, leaving her slightly off-balance. What did she know about family, about being part of something like this? Nothing. They made it seem easy because they'd all grown up in this environment, where people cared about each other and spent enough time together that they'd heard about the woman Noah was dating.

She hadn't even mentioned Noah's name to her mother.

"Maybe." She focused on scratching behind Ripley's ears. "If I can find time between training sessions."

"As your current training instructor, I think we can work something out," Noah teased.

Great. Now she didn't have a ready excuse. Nor did she have a good reason why she'd been looking for one. It was just…a lot to be absorbed into this family dynamic. They'd just folded her right in, like it was the most natural thing in the world.

Like she belonged here.

The door opened again, this time admitting a tech with a question for Dr. Colton. The interruption gave Sabrina a moment to breathe. Because she needed one.

"Speaking of family," Sassy said when the tech left. "What's going on with Mark? He hasn't been answering my texts."

Something in Noah's expression shifted. "I wish I could tell you, but you're not the only one he's ducking."

"Sam mentioned he still hasn't given anyone a reason why he suddenly quit the Army." Richie's weathered face creased with concern. "Do we need to be concern—"

"Jacob and I are handling it." Noah's tone carried an edge

Sabrina hadn't heard before. "We'll let you know if we need anything."

The undercurrent of worry in the room felt familiar. She'd sensed it at Jacob's office too, though she hadn't known what it meant then. Now the picture was clearer—the Coltons closed ranks around their own. Protected each other.

Must be nice. Did Noah have any idea how lucky he was?

"Well—" Sassy's bright tone didn't quite mask her unease as she changed the subject "—you two should join us for lunch. Giuseppe's has outdoor seating. Ripley can come too."

For a moment, Sabrina let herself imagine it. Lunch with Noah's family, listening to the stories, learning more about what Noah had been like as a kid. Being a part of this dynamic, these people, for a little while longer.

The surge of want in her chest terrified her.

This wasn't what she did. Families were full of other people who weren't her. She and Noah were having fun. That's all this was supposed to be. If Noah wouldn't set the record straight, she had to be the one to set the boundaries.

"Thanks, but I should get back to work." She managed a smile and stuck out her foot. "Still breaking in these new boots."

It sounded pathetic out loud. Noah's slight frown said he wasn't totally on board with her excuse either, and that didn't bode well for someone who should have been the one to decline on her behalf.

He didn't push though, just helped gather Ripley's paperwork while trading goodbyes with his family. Sassy hugged her, which threw her for a loop. What was with these Coltons and their easy affection? Did they not get the memo that she could double as a porcupine?

The drive back to her place stretched under weighted silence. Noah kept shooting her careful glances that she pretended not to notice.

"Any word on Camille?" she asked finally, desperate to think about anything besides how much she'd enjoyed his family. And how she'd had to push back.

He sighed. "Dead end so far. No activity on her social security number, no new address. She's gone completely dark, just like Annie did."

"That can't be a coincidence."

"My thoughts exactly." His hands tightened on the wheel. "But without more evidence, we're stuck. I've got some contacts checking into similar cases in neighboring states, but it'll take time."

Time they might not have, if there really was a baby involved. The thought of that carefully folded pink blanket haunted her.

"We'll figure it out." She meant it to sound confident, but her voice wavered slightly.

Noah reached across the console to tangle his fingers with hers. "Of course we will. We're partners."

Her chest tightened. That's what scared her. How easy it was to want the bigger meaning behind that concept, to want to be the person his family thought she was.

But she wasn't built for that. Her father had made sure she understood early that no one was in her corner. That she had to fight for every inch, every piece of her place in the world. No one could be trusted not to take it from her, especially not men.

"Hey." Noah squeezed her hand as he pulled into her driveway. "You okay? You got quiet after we left."

"Just thinking about the case." It wasn't entirely a lie. "Seems like we hit nothing but dead ends."

"We'll get there." He lifted their joined hands to brush a kiss across her knuckles. "I've got a few more leads to chase down. Maybe they'll pan out."

Normally, she loved his charm and optimism and casual

affection. Right this minute, it felt dangerous. Like something that could crack her wide open if she let it.

She needed space. Just a little breathing room to get her head on straight. To reel everything back until this thing with Noah became fun and uncomplicated again.

"So, I was thinking," she said, her throat raw for some reason. "Ripley needs a little more focus. I love that you're taking time out to work with us, but I think it'll be better if we find someone else for a bit."

Noah's face scrunched up as he processed that. "Okay. Did I do something wrong?"

"Yeah, you're distracting," she said with a hollow laugh that he hopefully didn't notice. "We spend more time kissing than training. I want to get my SAR certification and not have to redo everything in a few weeks when I realize Ripley and I are behind."

"Oh, I see. I'm too sexy for you on the training field." He laughed, thankfully seeming to buy her excuse.

It wasn't an excuse. It was the gospel truth. Just not the whole reason.

"I know a guy," he continued with a nod. "I'll get you in touch with him."

Sabrina blew out a breath. Crisis averted. She could lay low without Noah cluing in and focus on SAR training. Like she should be.

"AGAIN." NATHAN BRADLEY'S command lacked the warmth that always colored Noah's voice. "Your dog's form is sloppy."

Ripley's form was not sloppy. She'd executed the recall perfectly, just like Noah had taught them. But apparently Bradley had different standards.

"Good girl," Sabrina murmured as she gave Ripley the

release command. The lab's tail drooped slightly, picking up on the tension that had been building for the past hour.

This had seemed like such a good idea in the car the other day. Get some distance, gain some clarity, focus, focus, focus. Except she missed Noah and she had a feeling Ripley did too.

Noah would have noticed the dog's flagging enthusiasm immediately. Would have called for a water break or switched up the routine. He'd have noticed Sabrina's mood too and would have kissed her frown upside down by now. Twice.

Which was exactly why she was working with Nathan Bradley, a guy who did nothing for her at all with his mountain-man beard and barrel-shaped chest. So his methods were different than Noah's. Good. That's what she and Ripley needed.

"Reset." Bradley's tone held an edge of impatience. "And this time, make sure she stays in proper heel position. I don't know what kind of subpar training you've been doing, but—"

"Her training has been excellent." The words snapped out before Sabrina could stop them. "She's crushing the certification requirements."

Bradley's eyebrows shot up. "According to who?"

Noah.

Heat crawled up her neck as she bit back a defense of Noah. Because that's who Bradley was really criticizing, and it wasn't accurate or fair. But she wasn't working with Noah, and besides, they weren't a couple. He didn't need her speaking up for him.

Her phone buzzed in her pocket, and she pulled it out without thinking about how Bradley would react.

Sexy SAR Expert: Got a possible lead on Camille. Call you later?

Her heart did a stupid little flutter. Great. This distance idea had really worked out. Instead, her brain seemed determined to fixate on Noah and the lack of his presence.

Except maybe that was the problem. Giving herself space had started to feel less like a smart choice and more like a defense mechanism. Against what? A fantastic guy who had done nothing but treat her like a queen?

"Would it be possible to get back to work soon?" Bradley's dry voice interrupted her spiral. "We're never going to resolve the problems with Ripley's training at this rate."

Sabrina gritted her teeth before she snapped at Bradley again. Noah would have texted her that question while standing next to her. As a joke. Apparently joking wasn't allowed while training with Nathan Bradley. Neither was fun.

Noah had fun without trying. It was just part of his nature.

She jammed her phone back in her pocket without responding to him. This was getting ridiculous. *She* was ridiculous.

"Reset," she told Ripley, who immediately moved to heel position. Perfect form, no matter what Bradley claimed.

For the next hour, she threw herself into the training. Focused on the technicalities, on proving that she and Ripley had what it took. That she didn't need anything. Or anyone. Sabrina West would get SAR certified and be the best of the best.

But with every correction, every clipped command from Bradley, a voice in her head that sounded suspiciously like Noah's whispered that if he was so fun, why had she backed off? Noah's middle name might as well be Fun, so what was the real problem here?

Her phone buzzed again right after she and Bradley wrapped up.

Sexy SAR Expert: Dancer says Ripley is ghosting him.

Despite everything, she smiled. Noah had a way of doing that—cutting through all the crap with his ridiculous charm.

That was exactly it, wasn't it? He made everything so easy. So natural. Like being part of his family, part of his world, wasn't a big deal. It could even be considered fun.

Ripley bumped against her legs, brown eyes full of concern. Even her dog knew something was wrong.

"Good job today." She scratched behind Ripley's ears, ignoring Bradley's pointed comments about their form. "Sorry I subjected you to that."

What was she doing? Running away from the best training partner she'd ever had because…what? Because his family liked her? Because he made her want things she'd convinced herself she couldn't have?

Because she was scared?

All at once, she had a minor epiphany that felt more like the onset of a migraine. All those relationships that had fizzled out—had she been the cause?

All this time, she'd been convinced she'd never met a guy who could keep up with her. Had she been running too fast to make it worth their while to catch up?

Was she doing that with Noah?

Sexy SAR Expert: Everything okay? You've been quiet today.

Her throat tightened. Even through text, he noticed. Cared. What was she doing?

They were having fun. They'd never stopped having fun, and then out of nowhere, she'd freaked out over nothing and pulled the rug out from under the best thing that had ever happened to her.

Ripley whined softly, still picking up on her mood.

"I know, girl." She sighed. "I'm being stupid."

She was. Noah hadn't breathed a word about picking out furniture together. He was just being Noah. A thrill a minute, funny and genuine. Not terrifying at all.

Sabrina: Training ran long. I miss you.

There. That wasn't so hard.

Sabrina: We should go away together for the weekend.

Okay aliens had possibly taken over her body. But she sent the text anyway.

Chapter Fifteen

Never let it be said that Noah Colton turned down a challenge. Especially not one issued by a gorgeous woman who suggested they "blow off some steam" by going rock climbing in Moab. As if he needed an excuse to watch Sabrina do anything, but he had a feeling she'd scale vertical walls as if gravity was more of a suggestion than a law.

He was here for that.

The fact that she'd initiated this little adventure did a number on his insides. If a number felt like hope mixed with a healthy dose of terror—which pretty much summed up falling for Sabrina in general.

He'd thought something was off. After the visit to Uncle Richie's vet practice, Noah had gotten the distinct impression she'd hit some kind of wall, or rather she'd slammed *him* up against one. It was hard to misinterpret how she'd ducked out of lunch with his family, citing new boots that needed breaking in. Or switching to a different SAR trainer because, apparently, Noah was "too distracting."

Right. As excuses went, that one had been pretty inventive, but he'd heard a few in his day. Classic distancing protocol. He recognized it a mile away, even as she effectively sliced up his heart in the process.

But then she'd texted him out of the blue with this suggestion to go away for the weekend, as if nothing was wrong and he'd been moping around like a big baby.

Paranoid. That was his problem. Stupid Jacob and his warnings.

The January sun hadn't yet crested Moab's towering red rock formations. Dawn painted the desert landscape in watercolors, but the bite in the air promised another frigid morning. Perfect sending temperatures, climbers called it. As if there was something perfect about frozen fingers and chattering teeth.

Then again, watching Sabrina sort through her rack of climbing gear, maybe there was. She had that look in her eyes—the one that said she was already five moves ahead and planning her victory dance when they reached the summit. Pure intensity wrapped in a package that did more damage to his equilibrium than leading his hardest route ever had.

Yeah, he had it bad for her. And could see no reason to stop the momentum. This slow slide into her was the best part of falling in love, and he had zero intention of missing it.

Jacob was cynical, that was his problem. This wasn't like Noah's past relationships—the ones that had burned bright and fast like magnesium flares, leaving only smoke and regret. This was different.

Sabrina was different.

She was his *match*, his mirror, his perfect complement. The way she approached everything—fearless, focused, fierce—sparked something inside him he'd thought died alongside his mother when he'd traded war zones for SAR zones. Every time Sabrina pushed her limits, took on a new challenge, refused to back down, it reminded him that some stories didn't need a byline to change your life.

She'd already started sorting through the pile of quick draws they'd need for the multi-pitch route ahead. The early light caught her hair, turning it to white-gold against the red rock. As if he needed more reasons to stare.

"You planning to stand there all day checking your gear?" she called. "Or are we actually going to climb something?"

"Just admiring the view." He moved to help her organize their gear, drifting into her space because he couldn't stay away from her. The sharp scent of climbing chalk mixed with something uniquely Sabrina—sunshine and adrenaline and the kind of trouble that made a man forget about self-preservation. "Besides, you know what they say about proper preparation."

"That it's for people who don't trust their instincts?" She flashed him that million-watt smile that he wished he could pocket somehow. "Come on, Colton. Stop stalling."

They set off, trading leads up increasingly difficult routes, showing off for each other without shame. Every time Sabrina flashed a particularly technical sequence, pride bloomed in his chest. And every time she turned that smile his direction, his blood hummed with the need to taste it.

"Eyes on the wall, Colton." Her voice floated down from above, threaded with laughter. "You're supposed to be belaying me, not checking out my—"

"Form?" He grinned up at her. "I'm a trained professional. I can do both."

Her answering laugh carried on the wind. "That's what I like about you. You're not afraid to admit when you're busted."

"I don't scare easily."

He watched her execute a particularly graceful sequence that had his mouth going dry. The way she moved—fluid and precise, every placement deliberate—made him think dangerous thoughts about other ways she could move in much more intimate circumstances. She flowed up the rock face like she'd been born for it, finding holds he would have missed, linking moves into a dance that bordered on art.

The route they'd chosen was a Moab classic—three pitches of sustained climbing up an exposed arête that caught the morning sun. Technical face climbing gave way to a series of delicate crimps, the kind of moves that required absolute trust in your own strength. Noah had climbed it before, but watching Sabrina work her way up the crux pitched made it feel brand new. Like listening to your favorite song in a remix that was better than the original somehow.

They eased into a rhythm that felt natural, as if they'd been climbing together for years instead of hours. Every shared anchor brought them closer, every gear exchange an excuse to brush hands, to share space, to be in this bubble where nothing else existed except rock and sky and possibility.

She was three-quarters of the way up a particularly difficult pitch when it happened. One minute she was flowing through a delicate sequence of crimps, making it look like a ballet instead of 5.11 climbing. The next, her foot slipped on a barely there edge and she cursed.

Noah's heart stopped, then revved into overdrive as she caught herself with characteristic grace. But he'd seen it—that flash of real fear in her eyes before her game face slammed back into place.

"You okay up there?" He kept his voice casual even though his pulse was still doing its best impression of a jackhammer.

"Of course." But she didn't immediately start climbing again. "Just testing the rope."

"Right. Because that's something you do regularly."

"Are you throwing sarcasm at me right now? That's what you're going with?" The laugh in her voice didn't quite mask the slight tremor. "Bold strategy, Colton."

He wanted to pull her down and wrap her in his arms until that tremor disappeared. But somehow he didn't think she'd appreciate him making a big deal out of this. She'd take it as him fixating on a weakness.

Which he wasn't. This was him fixating on nearly watching the woman he loved plunge to her death before his eyes. And if there was anything in the world that could have solidified his feelings for her, that was it.

Safety ropes failed. Guarantees failed. Cancer snuck up and robbed you of happily ever after. It changed things. Sped up his timeline for how long he'd planned to give Sabrina to get comfortable with the fact that he wanted a life with her.

They climbed until the sun started its descent toward the horizon, painting the red rock in deeper shades of crimson and gold. Noah had packed food along with his gear so they didn't have to wait to eat.

"One more pitch?" Sabrina's eyes held that particular gleam that meant she was plotting something. "Before we lose the light?"

He made a show of checking the angle of the sun. "Normally I'd say yes, but I have a better idea."

Her eyebrow lifted in that way that did dangerous things to his equilibrium. "Better than climbing?"

"There's this spot I know." He focused on racking gear, definitely not thinking about how he couldn't wait to get to a place where he could put his hands on her. "Perfect for watching the sunset. I packed dinner."

"I like the sound of that." She wet her lips, the gesture drawing his attention like a magnet.

He forced his gaze back to her eyes. At least until they weren't in a precarious place. "Ready for phase two of this adventure?"

"Lead the way, hotshot."

This was what he'd missed most about journalism—not the bylines or the accolades but that feeling of being exactly where you were meant to be. Of everything clicking into place like tumblers in a lock. Sabrina gave him that same feeling times about a thousand.

The spot Noah had chosen sat high enough to catch the last rays of sun but protected them from the wind that picked up as evening approached, thanks to the rock face against their backs. He spread out a blanket while Sabrina dug through his pack, making appreciative noises at his food choices.

"Real silverware?" She held up the fork with a grin. "You did plan this."

"You're worth it." He settled beside her, close enough that their shoulders brushed. "I kind of thought something was going on with you. I'm glad I was wrong."

Sabrina set down the fork carefully, her gaze trained on it as if it held the secrets of the universe. "What? Why in the world would you think that?"

"You know, because of the ridiculous new boots excuse?" They could laugh about it now. And talk about it so he understood why she hadn't wanted to go to lunch with his family.

"Oh, ha-ha, yeah." She smiled but it didn't quite reach her eyes. "The whole thing just caught me off guard. I'm not used to people inviting me to go places just to be nice. Next time I'll figure out a better exit strategy so you're not embarrassed by my inadequacies."

Ah. She'd come up with an off-the-cuff excuse because she'd mistakenly thought the invitation hadn't been genuine. That made him feel so much better.

"Embarrassed is the last thing I was," he said mildly. "And Sassy wasn't asking because she's nice. More like so she could grill you for information to tease me about mercilessly later."

"So it's a good thing I bowed out. Noted," she said, and the weird vibe vanished. "Maybe next time I'll go. I'm sure your family would like to hear how you squealed like a little girl when that squirrel ran across your foot."

"Hey," he protested, throwing his hands up to ward off the memory. "That thing looked rabid and, man, was he fast. He could have crawled into my pants and taken up residence in no time flat."

"Oh, poor baby," she crooned, laughing as he tried to grab her for some punishment he'd yet to define in his head. "Eat first. Mess around later."

Or now. He'd never wanted to eat less in his life, but he pushed back the urge to yank her into his arms so he could kiss her senseless. Glancing at his watch, he lifted his brows. "So, in like four or five minutes?"

She pushed him playfully. They ate in comfortable silence as the sun sank toward the horizon, painting the sky in impossible colors. Stars winked into existence overhead, impossibly bright against the darkening canvas of twilight.

"If this is you trying to impress me, you might have succeeded." Sabrina's voice held a touch of wonder as she stared at the canopy of light appearing above them.

"What?" He scoffed to cover the hitch in his throat at her admission, as if he'd done something meaningful. "You've seen the sky at night before."

She scooted closer, nudging his arm until he lifted it to snuggle her close. "Not like this. It makes you feel the power of the infinite."

"Like anything is possible." Noah nuzzled her neck where it most smelled like Sabrina in the wild and then murmured in her ear. "Is it later? I feel like it's later."

Slowly, languorously, she let her head fall back against his shoulder as she stared at him, the starlight reflected in her gaze. "It's later."

Sabrina's lips met his. Sweet and searching at first, like

she was asking a question. He answered by threading his fingers through her hair, angling her head to deepen the kiss.

She made a sound in the back of her throat that shot straight through him. Her hands found his shoulders, memorizing the muscles there before sliding down his chest. The nip of her fingertips sent sparks racing across his skin.

Gradually, the kiss built into something more. Something that tasted like fire and honey and destiny. This was nothing like their first kiss, the exploratory one meant to see how much chemistry they had. Or the ones since then, tame ones in public, stolen ones when they should have been training.

This kiss exploded with promise. Potential. All of this energy had to go somewhere, or he'd spontaneously combust.

Noah lost himself in the silk of her hair, the sweet curve of her waist under his palms. When she pressed closer, fitting herself against him like she belonged there, his control splintered.

"Noah." His name on her lips was nearly his undoing. "Take me back to the hotel."

He didn't need to be told twice.

After a tense, very careful descent, they packed everything in the car in two minutes flat. Made it to the hotel a few miles away in less than that. Never had Noah been so grateful for his skill behind the wheel, especially when it came to parking sideways.

The hotel room door had barely clicked shut before Sabrina was in his arms again, her mouth finding his with unerring accuracy. Noah caught her close, walking her backward until she hit the wall. She made that sound again—the one that had been driving him crazy—and wound her arms around his neck.

He wanted to go slow. To savor every moment, memorize every touch. But Sabrina was already tugging at his shirt, her hands leaving trails of fire across his skin. When she rocked against him, his control frayed dangerously.

"Wait." He caught her hands, pressing them against the wall above her head. "Let me look at you."

She was gorgeous in the low light, all flushed skin and bright eyes. Her hair had come loose from its stubby pony-tail, spilling to her shoulders like pale gold. But it was the trust in her expression that undid him completely. The way she let him pin her there, vulnerable and open in a way he'd never seen before.

His heart expanded painfully in his chest.

"You're incredible." He brushed his lips across her jaw, down the curve of her throat. "Do you know that?"

"Less talking." She arched into him, chasing more contact. "More kissing."

"I like it when you're demanding."

He obliged, capturing her mouth again. This kiss was different—deeper, hungrier. Her hands broke free to tangle in his hair, and he let his own roam freely. Learning the dip of her waist, the curve of her hip. The way she shivered when he found sensitive spots.

Everything about her called to him. The soft sounds she made. The way she moved against him. How she gave as good as she got, matching him touch for touch until they were both breathless.

When she finally pulled back, her eyes had gone dark with desire. But there was something else there too. Something that looked a lot like the emotion currently trying to crack his ribs open from the inside.

"Noah." She traced his face with trembling fingers. Like she was memorizing him by touch.

"I'm here." Always. Forever. He turned to press a kiss to her palm. "Tell me what you want."

"You." The word scraped from her throat. "Just you."

His heart did something complicated in his chest. Because what was this but a huge step toward something real and lasting? Something she wanted too.

"You have me." He poured every ounce of feeling into the words. Into the kiss that followed. "All of me."

And then she took everything he had to give, turned it around and gifted him the same miraculous energy over and over again until he couldn't breathe with how much he loved this woman.

When neither of them could possibly be any more sated, Sabrina curled against his chest as they lay splayed on the king-sized bed that might not have any sheets or pillows left. His brain had stopped working after the third time she'd rocked his world.

Everything felt like a dream—the climbing, the sunset, the way Sabrina had come alive under his hands.

The way she'd trusted him with pieces of her soul.

Emotion swelled in his chest, too big to contain. She was everything he'd never known he needed, all fire and softness wrapped in one irresistible package. How had he gotten so lucky?

"You're staring at me again." Sabrina's sensually rough voice sent shivers down his spine.

"Can't help it." He pressed a kiss to her shoulder, savoring the way she melted against him. "You're the best thing that's ever happened to me. I've completely fallen for you, Sabrina."

She went still in his arms. Too still.

Chapter Sixteen

Time crystallized, sharp as the edge of a granite cliff face in winter. Sabrina's lungs seized, every molecule of oxygen frozen in place.

"You're, um, what?" she wheezed, her throat closing as the mattress turned into quicksand, trapping her in a quagmire she'd never seen coming.

"I'm in love with you, Sabrina," Noah repeated, probably not as harshly as it sounded to her. But the words raked through her, impossible to unhear.

The pause lengthened, gaining teeth, the way it did right before a storm hit the canyon, when the air crackled with doom and destruction, and the smart move was to get off the mountain before lightning struck.

But there was nowhere to go. No escape route, no backup plan, no clear path down.

"You can't be." Good grief, was that her voice?

Noah's brows knitted. "What? Why not?"

"Because," she ground out hoarsely, her throat feeling like she'd swallowed glass, "that's not what we're doing here."

And he wasn't supposed to make her feel like this—exposed, raw, as if he'd stripped away more than just her clothes.

"It's most definitely what we're doing here. Sabrina—"

But he reached for her then and she couldn't. Could. Not. Do. This. *No.*

She needed air. Space. Room to think past the buzzing in her head that sounded suspiciously like warning bells. The sheet tangled around her legs as she scrambled back, nearly falling off the bed in her haste.

Noah didn't try to stop her. Just watched with that intense gaze that never wavered, never faltered, never changed. Because he'd always looked at her like that. And she'd missed the signs. Had never even thought to question how much of that intensity burned for *her.*

"Sabrina." His voice carried that same whatever it was that had drawn her in from the start.

It burrowed beneath her skin, inexplicably calming her.

And that was exactly the problem. She didn't need him to do that. She didn't need him at all. Or anyone. The minute you depended on someone else was the minute they proved you shouldn't have.

"Stop doing that," she ordered, backing away. "Stop saying all that stuff."

Her hands trembled as she grabbed for her clothes, scattered across the floor like confetti for a party that she hadn't realized she'd been invited to.

"Okay." Noah's quiet acceptance somehow made it worse. He should be angry, frustrated, something. Not this infinite patience that made her feel like she was the one being unreasonable. "We can talk about something else."

A harsh laugh escaped her. Not because it was funny but because…well, she didn't know what it was. She'd never been in this place before, where it felt like she needed to claw her skin off so she could breathe.

"I don't think that's how this works," she muttered, shoving a hand through her hair, wishing it was tied back, but Noah had pulled her rubber band out long ago and she had no idea where it was. "You don't just move on to a new subject after…" She waved a hand in a big, erratic circle. Which pretty much summed up everything.

"Dropping an emotional bombshell on you?" His lips quirked slightly. "Tell me what you'd like me to do instead then."

Whirling, she yanked her shirt over her head, needing some kind of armor. Even if it felt about as effective as tissue paper against a rockslide. "Why am I the one who has to decide?"

The bed creaked as Noah sat up, keeping his distance. Smart man. "Because you're the one who matters."

The room just sort of tilted then. But there was nothing for her to grab onto to steady herself against the onslaught of Noah. Her heart just…liquefied.

What was *happening*?

She wrapped her arms around herself, cold despite the warm room. This was exactly the kind of thing she hadn't signed up for—the way he said these impossibly romantic things as if they were simple facts.

As if loving someone came as easily to him as breathing.

"You matter too," she whispered so softly that it was a wonder he heard her, but the softening around his mouth told her there was nothing wrong with his hearing.

"That's why I'm still here."

The catch in his voice undid her. Such simple words. They shouldn't make her chest ache like she'd taken a hundred-foot whipper fall, the rope catching just before impact.

"You shouldn't be." She paced to the window, then back. The room suddenly felt as confining as taking the wrong turn into one of the inaccessible canyons, walls pressing in, no obvious escape route. "You should be running away as fast as you can."

"Because that's what everyone else does to you?"

Yeah. Exactly, Sabrina thought to herself.

His gaze burned into her back, but she didn't dare glance at him. Whatever magic trick he thought he was going to pull to make this okay wasn't happening.

"Because all this emotional stuff isn't what we're doing here. We're having fun. That's all."

Fun was safe. Fun didn't require vulnerability or trust or any of the hundred other things relationships demanded. Fun didn't plunk her down at a crossroads where she had to choose to give up Noah or wait around until he inevitably decided she was too much.

Of course, given the current state of things, Noah didn't feel like so much of a flight risk all at once.

She was the one who got that role.

"Well, I don't know about you, but I am having fun." His voice remained steady, but something flickered in his expression. "Okay, granted, not right this second. But only because I kind of thought this would play out a bit differently."

She squeezed her eyes shut. "I have to know. How did you think this would play out?"

"With a lot less panic and a lot more kissing." His brow quirked. "And in my head, neither of us were dressed."

He still wasn't because he hadn't moved from where he'd sat back against the pillow, calmly taking whatever she threw at him. The guy had definitely found his calling with a profession that required meticulous patience and the ability to avoid tricky spots liable to crumble underneath him.

Also, Noah without a shirt should come with a warning label: "May cause unavoidable distraction."

"Maybe getting dressed is a good idea," she muttered. "And I'm not panicking."

Very much.

"I was talking about me," he countered, and she shot him

a look. "What, you think because I'm not wailing and gnashing my teeth that this conversation is easy for me?"

Yeah, she had thought that. He was so unflappable, so strong and capable. It wasn't like she could hurt him.

Could she?

The walls closed in tighter. Her heart thundered against her ribs like it was trying to escape. This was exactly why he should have kept things casual, uncomplicated. No one got hurt that way.

Especially not Noah.

Oh, man. How had they gotten to a place where she was the one who had the power to hurt this amazing, sensitive, beautiful man?

Because she hadn't seen him coming. Not even a little bit. This had all happened one tiny step at a time. That first date. Training with Ripley. Working the case together. All those late-night phone calls where she'd told him things she'd never told anyone.

When had he become so essential to her daily rhythm?

"I can't do this." The words tumbled out before she could stop them. "I didn't—this kind of thing is not me. Relationships, feelings, all of it. I told you that."

"Did you?" Noah's head tilted. "I remember you saying men couldn't keep up. That relationships fizzled out. But I don't remember you saying you didn't want one."

Oh, she so had. She'd made it crystal clear that she didn't trust easily, that she didn't do commitment. Probably. Maybe.

Though now that she thought about it, she couldn't pinpoint exactly when she'd spelled it out. She'd been too busy letting him teach her how to work with Ripley, too caught up in stolen kisses between training sessions.

Too wrapped up in how easy he made everything feel.

"Same difference." The words felt hollow even to her own ears.

"No." He shifted to the edge of the bed but didn't stand. Still giving her space while refusing to back down completely. Classic Noah to read her so well that he figured out what she needed before she did. "It's not. And you know it."

Heat pricked behind her eyes. She blinked hard, hating how he could slice through her defenses with nothing but quiet certainty. The same way he approached everything—confident, steady, unflinching.

She'd never met anyone like him. That was the problem.

"What do you want from me, Noah?"

It came out far less demanding than she'd have preferred.

"Nothing you're not ready to give." The simple honesty in his voice hit her like a falling rock, impossible to dodge. "I just wanted you to know where I stand. That's all."

"That's all?" Another sharp laugh escaped her. As if his words hadn't just triggered an avalanche that threatened to bury everything she'd carefully constructed. "You drop this bomb on me and act like it's no big deal?"

Her fingers itched for something to climb, some physical challenge to tackle. Anything to escape the intensity of his gaze, the way he seemed to see straight through to all the dark places she tried to keep hidden.

"It is a big deal." He ran a hand through his hair, making it stand up in ways that shouldn't make her heart clench. "But if you're afraid, it doesn't have to change anything you're not ready to change."

She stared at him, trying to make sense of what he was saying. This wasn't how it was supposed to go. He was supposed to get angry, push back, prove that he was just like all the others who didn't have any intention of sticking with her no matter what.

Instead, he just sat there, radiating that impossible patience that made her want to throw something at his head. Or kiss him. Maybe both.

"I'm not afraid." The denial felt like chalk dust on her tongue, dry and bitter. Her father's voice echoed in her head: *Fear is for the weak. Winners don't show weakness.*

His eyebrow lifted. "No? Then why are you halfway to the door?"

She glanced down, realizing she had unconsciously shifted toward the exit, her body already plotting an escape route she hadn't consciously chosen. Heat crawled up her neck. "I don't run from things."

"Exactly." Something knowing flickered in his eyes. Like he'd been waiting for her to arrive at this exact point, the sneaky jerk. "So, why start now?"

The question sliced through all the barriers she'd tried to place between them. He was right—running wasn't her style. She tackled everything head-on, at full speed, screw the consequences. It was her trademark, her defining characteristic.

Except this felt different. Scarier than any exposed ridgeline or technical climbing sequence. At least with those, she knew the rules. Keep three points of contact. Check your gear. Trust your training.

But there was no training manual for this. No safety gear to check. Just Noah and his steady presence and these impossible feelings that threatened to sweep her away like a flash flood.

"I don't know what you want me to say." The words came out small and fragile as a spider web.

"Say you'll stay." He held out a hand but didn't move closer. Another classic Noah move—offering connection while letting her choose whether to take it. "Say we can keep being us, keep having fun, keep figuring this out together. That's all I'm asking for."

She stared at his outstretched hand. The same one that had guided her through SAR training, steadied her on climbs, traced fire across her skin.

It would be easy to take his hand. She wanted to.

She didn't move.

"Just like that?"

"Just like that." His voice held absolute certainty, the kind that could weather any storm. "No pressure. No timeline. No expectations beyond what you're ready for."

"But you just said…"

"That I've fallen for you. Yeah."

He shrugged, the motion drawing her attention to those shoulders she'd been mapping with her hands not so long ago. Those capable shoulders, broad enough to hold up under the weight of a woman who was most definitely freaking out.

"So, what?" she asked. "We just go on like it's fine that you're in love with me and I have no idea what I'm supposed to be doing?"

He smiled. "I have some ideas about what you could be doing, if you'd like to hear them. Otherwise, yeah. I'll be over here in love with you, and you'll be over there figuring out what you want to do about it."

"That's not fair to you," she protested.

"Let me worry about that. I'm a big boy. I can handle my own feelings."

Something inside her chest cracked. Just a hairline fracture, but she felt it all the same. Because that was Noah in a nutshell—giving her exactly what she needed without demanding anything in return. He knew how to handle her moods and personality quirks. Somehow.

His hand remained steady between them. An offer, not a demand. Like everything else about him.

Good grief, she'd never had a chance, had she?

"Sabrina, do you want to stay or go?"

She should say *go*. Should walk away before this got even more complicated. Before the hairline crack in her chest spread into a full-blown fissure that she couldn't patch.

But her feet wouldn't move.

The truth lodged in her throat—she did want to stay. Wanted to keep having this whatever it was with him. Wanted his laughter and his steady presence and the way he made her feel like she might not be broken after all, that he might be the only person in the world who truly got her.

"If I stay, I'm probably going to screw this up," she warned him.

"The woman who always wants to be the best at everything? I highly doubt it." He wiggled his fingers in her direction. "Though, if you want to let me win, I'm totally okay with that."

A reluctant laugh rumbled from her throat. So it was working again, apparently. "You're ridiculous."

"Part of my charm." His grin widened, familiar and devastating.

Maybe they didn't have to figure everything out right now. Maybe she could just stay. See what happened when she stopped fighting so hard against the inevitable pull between them and let it happen. To hear him tell it, he was fine with that.

His hand remained outstretched.

She took it and the earth didn't split open.

Noah tugged her closer, but didn't try to pull her down to the bed. Just drew her between his knees and rested his forehead against her stomach, quiet for a long beat before he murmured, "Thank you."

He was trembling.

Oh, man, *she'd* done that to him. Her heart did a slow dive to the floor. "For what?"

"For not running." His breath was warm through her shirt, settling inside her chest. "For giving us a chance to figure this out."

She threaded her fingers through his hair, letting the moment, the connection, unfold inside her.

Maybe this was what trust felt like.

Or maybe she'd just set herself up to fail. And maybe she'd take Noah down with her.

Chapter Seventeen

Noah had witnessed a lot of stunning moments in his respective careers. Revolutions igniting with a single spark. A perilous rescue. Cities falling to their knees. Tense moments when he couldn't see Dancer and had to run on faith.

But none of them compared to successfully navigating the most difficult and critical negotiation of his life.

She'd stayed.

One minute, Sabrina had both feet out the door, and then the next—well, he still wasn't sure what had truly happened, not before or after she'd taken his hand.

All he knew was that she had. She'd stayed in that hotel room in Moab, and somehow, they'd managed to do exactly as he'd suggested: move on. Sort of.

Everything was fine as far as she knew. On his side, he had no idea what he was doing.

At least his premature declaration hadn't ruined everything. There'd been a moment when he'd been one hundred percent convinced it would go the other way. Okay, several moments. Worst conversation of his life.

And the best. Because she'd stayed.

It changed everything and nothing at all. She was still Sabrina—fierce and commanding and as unpredictable as a flash flood through Dark Canyon Wilderness. But now he got it. They weren't at the same place. Not for the reasons Jacob had tried to warn him about though. This wasn't a case of a Noah hanging his heart out to dry for a woman who was just passing through.

This was a love match in progress. Or would be as soon as she got over whatever was holding her back. He just had to hang on until she realized he wasn't going anywhere. Until she understood that he meant what he said and said what he meant. She could trust him.

Except she didn't quite yet. Okay. He could live with that. He was used to jumping in with both feet and dealing with the splash damage later.

He skidded into a turn out off 191 and headed south from Dark Canyon, just shy of the Navajo Nation border. He didn't venture this direction often, as this part of the state didn't have a whole lot of anything but a bunch of flatlands. They called this area White Mesa for a reason. You could see for miles.

Sabrina had opted to meet him here, citing a "work thing" for why he couldn't pick her up—which may or may not be legit—but as long as she came, he'd take her whatever way got him into her orbit.

Dancer's head appeared between the seats, his cold nose bumping Noah's ear. "Yeah, yeah. I know. She'll be here. I'm not worried."

Jacob's cryptic text messages about suspicious activity in this sector would get her here if anything would. His brother wouldn't send him a breadcrumb about the Annie Ross case without good reason. Had Noah shamelessly forwarded the text to Sabrina in hopes she'd want to join him? Yes. Had Noah shamelessly suggested using it as a training vehicle for Ripley? Also yes.

Maybe Noah by himself might have been enough to tempt

Sabrina into hanging out with him. But today wasn't a day he felt like testing that. And fortunately, he didn't have to.

Sabrina's USFS vehicle pulled in just as Noah grabbed his gear. He hadn't realized how tight his shoulders were until they relaxed—slightly—as she hopped from the driver's seat. They were supposed to be figuring it out, but mostly that had consisted of not talking about it and dodging the slight strain that hovered around the edges of everything.

Which he needed to fix. Immediately.

"Bet Nathan Bradley doesn't combine training sessions with fun stuff like chasing leads in a murder case," he called, keeping it light until he could figure out how to get through this wrinkle between them.

"Nathan Bradley wouldn't know fun if it bit him in the—" She cut off as Ripley bounded over to greet Dancer. "Let's just say his teaching style made me appreciate yours more."

"My methods are unconventional but effective." He jammed his hands in his pockets to keep from reaching for her, which was difficult. But he did it. "Speaking of unconventional. Jacob wouldn't give me any information about his tip. This could all be for nothing."

Her eyes lit with that spark that he'd missed. "Would he do that? Give us a tip that wasn't legit?"

"And take an opportunity to be a pain in my rear? Absolutely."

"You guys don't fool me. I can tell you care about each other." Suddenly, she gave him a pointed look. "Why are you way over there? Do I not warrant a proper hello these days?"

Noah blinked and got his wits in order a second later, eating up the space between them, then scooping her up in his arms.

They locked gazes. Instantly, the weird tension dissolved.

She snuggled up in his embrace where she fit like she'd

been made for this spot, settling his nerves and his heart in one shot.

"Hey," he murmured as he nuzzled her cheek. "How's it going?"

She laughed and it rumbled against his chest. "Fine. And you?"

"I missed you."

"It's been like two days since you saw me. And you saw a lot of me then," she reminded him as if he needed reminding of the good parts of that trip to Moab.

Never one to shy away from laying it all out there, he pulled back and searched her impossibly blue eyes. "I can never see enough of you. But I didn't want to crowd you."

Sabrina's gaze grew sober. "Which I appreciate. It's important to me that you realize I'm the one figuring stuff out, not you. But you don't have to stop being you. I'm pretty partial to you."

That sent a dizzying wave of sparklers through his chest. "Then I'm going to kiss you and you better like it."

She met his mouth without hesitation, but everything was different. Noah had never kissed Sabrina with the knowledge that he was in love with her shimmering between them. Sure, *he'd* known, almost from the very beginning, but she hadn't.

Now that she did, it changed things. Softened them. Everything felt more wondrous, exploratory. As if she might be using this very moment to work through what it might be like if she let herself fall.

The beauty of it, of her, stole his breath.

Obviously, he hadn't needed to hold back. So he poured all of his feelings into the kiss, telling her without any words how much he admired her, how he loved the snap, crackle and pop she always brought into the room.

Or onto the mesa, rather. A cold wind whipped across his ungloved hands as he spread them across her back, wishing he could pick her up and deposit her in the front seat of his truck so they could find a dozen ways to warm each other up.

But he didn't. He stepped back because they were here for a reason. Annie Ross.

"That was a pretty good greeting, Colton." Mischief crept into her expression. "But I suspect you can do better. We'll test it next time."

In the meantime, she was going to kill him. "I could do better now, but I was distracted by the fact that we're outside in January and not here to let me show you how much I missed you."

Her brows lifted. "Now you have me intrigued as to what you would have shown me. So probably you should switch gears to why we are here."

Noah outlined what he'd inferred from Jacob's text, which was nothing concrete, but enough weird reports to justify some creative location scouting disguised as SAR training.

"We can only assume it somehow connects to Annie Ross," he said. "Or at least that's the hope."

"Let's hope it's *not* like Annie Ross." She nodded toward where Ripley and Dancer waited at perfect attention. "I'd rather the dogs find someone alive. Basic search pattern to start?"

They fell into an easy rhythm, working the dogs through increasingly complex sequences. Noah found himself watching Sabrina more than the actual training. She'd taken to SAR work like she'd been born for it, her competitive streak melting into genuine passion for the work.

He could relate. Some things just got into your blood.

Like the way she moved with such fluid grace, anticipating Ripley's needs before the dog even shifted position. Or how her whole face lit up when they nailed a particularly tricky sequence. The woman had intensity programmed into her DNA, same as he did.

They were a match. He could feel it in his bones. Did she?

"Earth to Noah." Her voice snapped him back. "You're supposed to be watching Dancer's nose work."

He grinned at her eye-roll. "Don't need to. Your form is perfect. Unless you'd prefer an unbiased opinion. You're welcome to go show it to Nathan Bradley."

"You're not letting that go, are you?"

"Not a chance."

But before he could really get going with the Nathan-related teasing, Dancer's posture shifted. Just a tiny change that most people wouldn't notice. But Noah knew that particular realignment of muscle and bone, the way his partner's entire body switched from training mode to something else entirely.

"Dancer?" The lab's head came up sharply, nose working the air in that precise pattern that meant business. Real business. "What've you got, boy?"

Ripley picked up on Dancer's change instantly, her own stance morphing to mirror his intensity. Noah's pulse picked up. Two dogs alerting like this? Not a coincidence.

"Is Ripley copying him, or did she pick up something too?" Sabrina asked.

Noah kept his eye on the dogs, his old instincts hummed to life, the ones that used to keep him alive in much more dangerous places than Dark Canyon. "I think door number two. Dancer, show me."

The lab moved with deliberate purpose, each step calculated as he led them deeper into the scrubby vegetation, Ripley a quarter of a length behind him. Dawn had barely started making an appearance, which meant visibility was low. Perfect time for someone to think they wouldn't be spotted.

Sabrina fell into step beside him, her voice pitched low. "What do you think it is?"

"I don't know." He kept his own voice down, letting the

dogs work. "But if Jacob's tip is right, we might be about to discover what the definition of 'suspicious activity' is. Dancer doesn't get worked up over nothing."

They pushed forward in silence, following the dogs' lead. The terrain out here near the Navajo lands wasn't mountainous, but it had its own dangers: washed out gullies hidden by brush, loose rock and the occasional predator.

Though, frankly, he was worried about the human variety more than the animals.

They weren't the only people to come this way.

Noah automatically cataloged details with the precision that had earned him accolades across the globe. Broken branches. Disturbed ground. Signs of recent vehicle activity where there shouldn't be any.

Someone had definitely been out here. Recently.

The first hints of smoke teased his nose—just a whisper, but enough to set off warning bells. It was not the friendly kind of smoke that meant someone had a campfire going. This smelled like burning plastic and charred wood, a toxic, acrid aroma of an unnatural, destructive fire.

Dancer's urgent bark confirmed he'd scented it too.

"You smell that?" Sabrina was already moving faster, Ripley tight on her heels.

"Yeah." Noah's pulse revved into overdrive even as his brain snapped into journalist mode.

Remote location. Dawn timing. A whiff of accelerant under the smoke.

Someone did not want their fire discovered until it was too late.

What had Jacob's cryptic text gotten them into? Noah resisted the urge to shuffle Sabrina behind him, mostly because it would be hard to walk and shield her at the same time, but also because she'd probably just hustle around him again.

Yeah, he knew she could take care of herself. But still. He liked her in one piece and he did *not* like the way this whole scenario sat in his craw.

"You know what this reminds me of?" he muttered as they pushed deeper into the scrubby vegetation after the dogs. "That time in Yemen when my local contact insisted we follow his 'reliable source' into questionable territory."

"Do I want to know how that ended?"

"Probably not."

The dogs led them around a white rock ledge big enough to obscure their view, and there it was—a ramshackle cabin that might have been someone's hunting getaway once upon a time. Now it blazed against the predawn sky like an angry beacon.

Sabrina already had her radio in her hand, bless her.

"Dispatch, Officer West, over." Sabrina's voice carried an edge of steel. "I have a visual on a structure fire in sector seven, coordinates—" She rattled off numbers. "Request immediate relay to local emergency services, over."

As she clicked off, she glanced at him.

"How long?" Noah asked.

"All the way out here? Probably fifteen minutes."

Okay. Good. That was all they could do for now.

Dancer's barking shifted into that particular tone that meant only one thing. The sound hit Noah's bloodstream like ice water.

"What?" Sabrina's gaze flitted between him and the dog. "Why does your face look like that?"

"Dancer. He only barks like that when he scents a human," he said, his throat drier than if he'd gargled with a handful of the broken rocks underfoot.

"Friend or foe?" she murmured, her expression suddenly wary. "You think the fire bug might still be around here? Or are we dealing with something more sinister?"

He scrubbed at his face, calling Dancer back to heel. Honestly, he hadn't gotten that far, but he wasn't sacrificing his dog to a criminal's itchy trigger finger if she was right. "Getting caught by the arsonist feels pretty high on the sinister scale. I was more worried about finding another Annie Ross."

"We don't have a choice. We have to see what he's indicating."

Noah nodded, clenching both hands into fists, because the desire to pick up Sabrina and forcibly take her back to her truck had just gotten worse, not better.

Sabrina fell into step beside him as they followed Dancer's lead, Ripley matching the lab's focused intensity, clearly wanting in on the action.

The trail led straight through the brush to the burning house. Because of course it did.

Noah's gut did a swan dive. "Someone's in there."

He'd barely gotten the words out when sirens screamed in the distance. But distance was the problem. Judging by the way the flames consumed the weathered wood, they didn't have that kind of time.

Whoever was in the house could already be struggling with smoke inhalation.

Heavy boots pounded through the underbrush as a team of firefighters in full gear burst into view. The last one stopped short, pulling off his helmet and face shield as he zeroed in on Noah.

It was his cousin Ryan. Thank goodness.

"You called this in?" Ryan's voice carried that edge of command that had laced a million Thanksgiving and Christmas conversations. "What's the situation?"

Noah grabbed Ryan's arm, his fingers barely able to grip the heavy fire-resistant fabric of his cousin's turnout coat. "Someone's inside the shack. Dancer's sure."

Ryan's eyes narrowed as he jammed his helmet on his head and peered at the burning shack through his face shield. "Location?"

"Near the front door, based on his alert pattern."

Ryan didn't hesitate. Just adjusted his oxygen mask and charged the building like he did this every day. Which he probably did. Coltons always seemed to be headed toward danger instead of away from it.

Time ceased to have meaning as they watched Ryan disappear into the smoke. Noah's muscles flexed to follow; after all, he was a Colton too. But he forced himself to stay put. This was Ryan's territory, just like SAR was his, and Jacob owned the Annie Ross investigation.

Though he'd managed to break off a chunk and hand it to Noah and Sabrina, hadn't he?

Noah's mind spun through the facts they had. Remote location. Deliberate fire. Suspicious timing. He had a feeling this story was about to break wide open.

When Ryan emerged from the smoke several pulse-pounding moments later, he was carrying something. An unconscious woman. Hopefully she was unconscious. The alternative meant they'd been too late and Noah refused to accept that.

She was barefoot and wearing a thin shirt and pants. No coat. The similarities to Annie Ross were remarkable.

That's when he noticed her bound wrists and ankles.

This was no accident. Someone had tied up this woman and left her to die in that fire.

"Medical, now!" Ryan's voice carried an edge Noah had never heard before, and that was saying something for a guy who bled confidence and authority. "And law enforcement. This is way more than solely a structural fire."

Right on cue, a vehicle marked with the insignia of the Navajo Nation Police rolled up as if they'd been waiting in the wings. The lone officer emerged with the kind of fluid efficiency that said he routinely inserted himself in active emergencies.

Great. Because jurisdictional squabbles were exactly what this situation needed.

The officer's shoulder bore the distinctive yellow, red and forest-green patch of the tribal police, and pinned to his uniform shirt was a name plate that read C. Benally.

"This scene requires tribal involvement." Benally's quiet voice somehow cut through the chaos. "Given the proximity to Navajo lands and the nature of the incident, we have concurrent jurisdiction."

The local uniforms who'd shown up with the firefighters bristled. Noah recognized the tension—jurisdictional disputes were never simple when multiple agencies had legitimate claims.

One of the officers waved off the Navajo cop. "This is county land—"

"With clear connections to an ongoing investigation in my department." Benally's tone could have frozen lava.

Noah glanced at Sabrina and he could tell she'd picked up on the careful wording too. This fire and the unconscious woman may be connected to a Navajo Nation PD investigation. Which meant it could actually connect to the Annie Ross case as well.

"I'll need statements from everyone." Benally's sharp gaze landed on Noah and Sabrina. "Starting with you two since you're the only civilians here. What are you doing out this close to Navajo land at dawn?"

Oh, this was going to be fun to explain. *Well, you see, my brother at IBS gave me a tip and we decided to come tromp all over your crime scene.*

Before Officer Benally could make good on his threat to force them to make statements, the scene devolved into the usual jurisdictional dance as more vehicles arrived. Tribal police, the San Juan County sheriff, crime scene units, additional medical support. Everyone wanted a piece of the action, and no one wanted to give ground.

Politics. Some things never changed, no matter what continent you were on.

But Noah's focus had narrowed to the woman being loaded into the ambulance. To the rope marks on her wrists. To the growing certainty that they'd stumbled onto something bigger than a simple rescue.

There was something to discover here, no doubt. He'd unearth the truth. Meanwhile, there was an unconscious woman who hadn't gone the way of Annie Ross, thanks to them. Her story—the part they knew—deserved to be told.

Chapter Eighteen

Noah watched the ambulance carrying the lone survivor of the fire disappear into the growing light of the day, his brain spinning. The scene around him buzzed with activity—firefighters securing the area, law enforcement documenting evidence, Officer Benally questioning witnesses with his stoic expression never wavering—but Noah barely registered any of it.

All he could see was how close they'd come to finding another body. If Dancer hadn't picked up the scent when he did, if he and Sabrina hadn't followed Jacob's tip out here, all of this would have ended up much, much worse.

Granted, they'd just watched his cousin carry an unconscious woman from a burning building, a woman whose wrists and ankles had been bound. Circumstances were certainly bad enough.

His gaze sought out Ryan, who stood conferring with his team near the smoldering remains of the cabin. His cousin's face was smudged with soot, a stark reminder how close he'd come to the flames.

And his expression was nothing short of haunted.

"You okay?" Noah called when Ryan finally broke away from his crew.

Ryan crossed to Noah, running a hand through sweat-dampened hair. He'd yet to set his helmet down, carrying it around with a white-knuckle grip that spoke volumes about his mental state. "Been better. If you guys hadn't found her when you did…" He broke off, jaw clenching.

"But we did." Noah studied his cousin's face. Ryan had been a firefighter for a decade. He'd seen plenty of rescues, plenty of casualties. This one had gotten under his skin. "She'll make it?"

"They think so." Ryan's gaze tracked to where the ambulance had disappeared. "Smoke inhalation, some burns, other injuries I don't want to think about. She's still unconscious. But she was breathing on her own when they loaded her up."

The tension in Ryan's voice raised the hair on Noah's neck. "You've seen worse. What's different about this one?"

Ryan's gaze filled with something raw. And enough rage to level a city block. "The restraints. Someone tied her up and left her to burn. Who does that?"

"The same kind of person who dumps a body in Peavine Canyon," Noah muttered without thinking.

"What?" Ryan's head snapped up. "What body?"

Ugh. Noah's mouth had run away with him. His cousin wouldn't know about Annie Ross and probably shouldn't know. He hesitated, weighing how much to share. But Ryan had that look—the same one from when they were kids and he and Jacob got into it over who would be the captain of the pirate ship or bat first in the lineup.

Ryan had won at least half the time.

"A woman's body turned up in Peavine a few weeks ago," Noah explained. "Young, no ID. Left in a place she had no business being, dressed all wrong for the terrain."

"Like my victim. *Our* victim. The victim," he corrected hastily, and cleared his throat as his expression darkened. "You thinking there's a connection?"

"Maybe." Noah chose his next words carefully. "The circumstances feel similar. Remote location, signs of foul play."

"Am I reading you right that you're taking more than a casual interest in this?"

Ryan knew about Noah's history as an investigative reporter but not that he'd picked it back up. "Yeah. Feels like it might be time to see if I've still got the chops, you know?"

Better leave it at that. It wasn't like Noah had impressed anyone with his stellar deduction skills thus far. The only reason he had any leads on this case was due to sheer luck and providence.

"Keep me posted?" The gravity of Ryan's tone clued him in that this wasn't an offhand request. "About anything you find out."

Noah shot him a small smile. "Am I detecting a similar lack of casual interest?"

The look on his cousin's face dried up any remnants of humor. "She barely weighs a buck-o-five, dude. I could feel her ribs as I carried her out of that hole where they'd left her to die. She had this fragileness about her, but she hadn't given up yet, so she's stronger than she looks. I—" he scrubbed at his neck sheepishly "—I can't not be invested at this point."

Yeah, no joke. Ryan was going to get whiplash as many times as he kept glancing toward the road where the ambulance had gone, but the protective edge in his voice told the real tale. Noah recognized what it meant because he felt it every time Sabrina walked into a potentially dangerous situation.

Like this one.

"I get you. So, just a thought, maybe head to the hospital and see if she's okay?"

Ryan nodded. "Yeah. Yeah, okay. Good plan."

Sabrina caught his gaze from across the clearing, where

she was talking to one of the local officers. Even from this distance, she twisted him up in knots that had nothing to do with the case and everything to do with how badly he wanted to wrap her up and keep her safe.

Not that she needed his protection. Sabrina West could handle herself in any situation, as she proved time and time again. But after what they'd just witnessed, after seeing exactly what kind of evil they were dealing with, who could blame him for wanting to have his eyes on her as much as humanely possible. Twenty-four seven, preferably. Just so he'd know she was safe.

Ryan cleared his throat.

"There's something else." His cousin shifted closer, pitching his voice low. "The way she was positioned in there. It wasn't random. It's standard protocol, we always clear the front rooms first. Whoever did this wanted her found."

A chill crawled down Noah's spine. "What do you mean?"

"She was placed in the front room, no furniture around her, few walls." Ryan's jaw tightened. "Deliberate. It's the best way to ensure someone dies of smoke inhalation so the body doesn't burn beyond recognition. They wanted us to find her. To see what they'd done. After the fact, once it was too late."

"Or maybe they wanted her rescued." The words felt hollow even as Noah said them.

"Fire was staged. Multiple points of origin but controlled." His expression hardened as he laid out the concepts of how someone had orchestrated a woman's murder. "They knew exactly what they were doing. How the fire would spread, how long before we'd respond, even how we'd approach the building."

"That's horrific," Noah muttered, his brain committing the details to memory against his will.

"It's a message." His gaze locked onto Noah's. "Watch

your back, dude. If you're digging into something connected to this, you might not like what you find."

Noah's phone buzzed in his pocket and he glanced at it. Jacob. Perfect timing.

"Will do," he told Ryan. "But you do the same. And seriously—let me know the second she wakes up?"

Ryan nodded once sharply, rage still visible in the lines of his face as his gaze drifted back to the road where the ambulance had disappeared. "Find whoever did this, Noah."

The raw edge in his cousin's voice spoke volumes, and it said he wouldn't let anyone near that poor unconscious woman again. Ryan was already invested in this woman's story.

Just like he was invested in Sabrina's.

Because he recognized that look in Ryan's eyes. The one that said you'd found something worth fighting for, worth protecting at all costs. Worth changing your whole life for, if that's what it took.

Noah's phone buzzed again. He hit the button to answer. "Tell me you have something."

"Maybe." His brother's voice carried that careful neutrality that meant he was choosing his words with precision. "Got the preliminary autopsy results on Annie Ross. The medical examiner found evidence she'd given birth recently. Within the last few months."

That carefully folded pink blanket they'd found in the apartment. All those baby supplies hidden away in the closet. Not waiting for a baby to be born—waiting for one to come home.

"You're sure?"

"Medical examiner confirmed it. Hormonal markers, physical evidence, the works." Clicks fired off in the background. "No sign of the child though. We're expanding the search parameters, checking missing-persons reports, looking for any recent infant abandonments or safe haven drop-offs."

"But nothing yet." It wasn't really a question. If they'd found the baby, Jacob would have led with that.

"No. And it's interesting what pops when you're searching missing persons." More clicks. "Camille Lancaster, Annie's roommate? She was reported missing two weeks ago. Complete radio silence—no phone activity, no credit card usage, nothing."

Noah's mind spun through the implications. Another woman vanished without a trace. Just like Annie had. And then they'd found her body.

"And, Noah?" Jacob's voice tightened. "The ME found trace evidence under Annie's nails. Signs of a struggle. She didn't go quietly."

Oh, man. It hit Noah in the gut with a chaser that made his throat hurt. Had Annie Ross died trying to protect her baby? Was that what this was all about?

"Can you send me your findings? Is that allowed?" he asked, already mentally cataloging connections. "There has to be a connection to all three of these women."

"Three?"

"We did your investigative dirty work this morning." Noah quickly filled his brother in on the morning's near tragedy. "So I need whatever you got that can help me make this case."

"Already compiling it. But watch yourself, Noah." Jacob paused. "If there is a connection, it's not a good one."

Both of the Coltons were on that kick today apparently, as if Noah hadn't survived war zones and violent protests. But that didn't make it a bad suggestion.

"Yeah, I got it." Noah's gaze sought out Sabrina again, something fierce and protective rising in his chest. "I'll be careful."

He hung up just as Sabrina reached him. The morning sun caught her ponytail, turning it white. His heart did that thing it always did when she was near—expanded until his ribs ached with the need to pull her close and never let go.

"You okay?" she asked, sliding her hand into his.

He twined their fingers together, anchoring himself in her touch. "Annie Ross had given birth recently. Medical examiner confirmed it."

Sabrina's sharp intake of breath told him she'd made the same connection he had. "The baby lived at the apartment with them."

"Yeah." He tugged her closer, needing her warmth to fight back the chill of what they'd discovered. "No sign of the baby yet. Jacob's expanding the search."

"They wanted the baby." It wasn't a question. Trust Sabrina to read between the lines of what he hadn't said. "And now Camille's missing too."

The words hung between them, heavy with implications. If the criminals responsible for all of this had killed Annie to get the baby, why? Illegal adoption ring?

He itched to find out. There was a baby somewhere out there separated from his mother against her will. And another woman who might have known the truth had vanished into thin air.

And then came the third woman, bound and left to burn. How did she fit in? Was she pregnant too? The connections were there, hovering just out of reach. Noah could feel the shape of the story forming, even if he couldn't quite grasp it yet.

"Can we go somewhere that doesn't smell like smoke?" Sabrina asked softly. "Somewhere we can sort through all of this."

Relief flooded through him. He didn't want to let her out

of his sight, not with the shadow of what they'd discovered hanging over them. "My place? I'll make coffee."

Her smile warmed him from the inside out. "Only if you add an extra scoop. Your coffee is weak, my guy."

By the time they reached his house, the sun had fully crested the horizon. Dancer and Ripley bounded straight for the training yard, their energy seemingly unaffected by the morning's events. Must be nice. The dogs always seemed to snap back much sooner than he did after a difficult rescue.

Inside, he moved through his kitchen on autopilot, measuring coffee grounds while Sabrina sank onto his couch. She looked so right there, curled up in the corner like she belonged. Which she did. She belonged here, with him, filling up all his empty spaces with her fierce light.

He never wanted to let her go.

"Here." He pressed a mug into her hands, then settled beside her. Close enough that their shoulders brushed, but not crowding. "I made it extra strong and with an ungodly amount of sugar. I still can't believe you drink that stuff."

"I still can't believe you call the stuff you drink coffee. Eventually I will succeed in my plot to make you a convert." She shifted closer, snuggling up against his side, which was way better, but he hadn't wanted to push.

He wrapped an arm around her shoulders, drawing her in. The familiar scent of her shampoo swirled together with traces of smoke from the scene.

It was sobering. A reminder that no one was guaranteed tomorrow or even the rest of today.

"You're unusually quiet," she commented. "Thinking about the connections between all of these women?"

Among other things. Like how to keep her here in this exact spot where he could feel the pulse point in her neck under his fingers.

But he could tell she wanted to talk about the case. "I keep coming back to the staging. Ryan said she was positioned deliberately, where first responders would find her quickly."

"Unlike Annie. Who was hidden away until I stumbled on her."

"Exactly. Different methods, different goals maybe." His fingers traced idle patterns on her shoulder. "Ryan thinks they left the Jane Doe today as a message."

"What kind of message involves leaving someone to burn alive?" She shuddered slightly.

Noah pressed his lips to her temple as comfort to both of them. "The kind meant to warn people off. Show what happens if you don't play by their rules."

"You think there are rules to this?" She pulled back enough to meet his gaze. "What, like some kind of organized operation?"

"Has to be, doesn't it? Multiple victims, different locations but similar circumstances." He feathered the hair near her ear, unable to stop touching her. "Young women disappearing without a trace, then turning up in remote places. A baby is missing. Could be human traffickers."

"Except traffickers don't usually kill their merchandise," Sabrina stated flatly. "Unless…"

"Unless what?"

"Unless they're making examples. Showing what happens to people who don't cooperate." Her voice dropped lower. "Like mothers who won't give up their babies."

The implications settled cold in Noah's chest. "Or friends who might know too much."

"Like Camille." Sabrina pushed closer, as if seeking shelter from the darkness of their theories. "This is going on here, in Dark Canyon, Noah. Whatever the answer is, this is where we live. We have to stop it. How can we when we don't know anything about the people responsible?"

"I don't know." He gathered her closer, and she came

willingly, melting against him like she needed this connection as much as he did. "But we'll figure it out. Together."

She hummed against his neck, the sound doing dangerous things to his equilibrium. "I like the idea of figuring things out together."

If that wasn't a positive sign, he didn't know what was. His heart expanded, pressing against his ribs with everything he felt for this woman. Having her here, in his space, trusting him with her fears and theories—it felt right. Perfect. Like everything finally clicking into place.

"You know what I like?" He traced her jaw with his thumb, tilting her face up to his. "This. Us. The way you fit here."

Her smile was soft, edges blurred with exhaustion and leftover adrenaline. "Yeah?"

"Yeah." He brushed his lips across hers, gentle as morning light. "I think better when you're here."

She made a sound low in her throat and pressed closer, deepening the kiss. Heat sparked between them, but tempered with something else. Something that felt like coming home.

When they finally broke apart, she stayed close, forehead resting against his.

"I *am* better when you're here," she whispered, like it was a confession.

The words lodged in his chest like sunlight. This was her figuring it out, in real time. Choosing to let him in, to trust him with her heart. Ever since that night in Moab when she'd stayed despite her fears, he'd felt them moving toward something real. Something lasting.

Having her here now, tucked against him after a rough morning, the dogs playing together, it felt like everything clicking into place. Like his whole life had been leading to this moment, this woman, this perfect certainty that they belonged together.

Why weren't they doing this every day?

"Move in with me."

The words slipped out before he could stop them. Not how he'd planned to ask—he'd actually had plans involving dinner and maybe some strategic usage of both dogs' best begging faces. But watching her in his space, the way she fit so naturally into every corner of his life, the question just bubbled up, impossible to contain.

He'd never balked at jumping without a parachute before. Why start with this?

Except instead of enthusiastic agreement with this very solid plan, Sabrina's spine went ramrod straight.

"What?" Her voice came out strangled.

"Move in with me," he repeated and thought about getting down on one knee, but he hadn't bought a ring yet, and that kind of proposal did deserve the right circumstances. "You like my house, right? You know Ripley loves the backyard and Dancer. I want you here. All the time. In every part of my life."

Her expression froze. "Noah—"

"I know it's fast." He reached for her hands. "I know we haven't really talked about what happened in Moab. We can though. Anytime. What we can't do is waste any time getting on with the rest of our lives. Nothing about us has been slow. Why start now?"

"Because." She yanked her hands free, wrapping her arms around herself. "Because this is the opposite of giving me a chance to take a breath. You promised you'd give me space to figure this out, not push me into a corner and throw up a steel wall so I can't escape."

Wow. That was a visual he had not seen coming. He

blinked as she scrambled off the couch, backing away. From him. As if her metaphorical steel wall might be in his pocket.

What in the world?

All his earlier certainty crumbled, leaving him off-balance and feeling like he'd walked out onto a thin beam over a deep gorge and the wood had started to crack. "Sabrina, what's happening right now? If you're scared, it's fine. We can work this out tog—"

"Stop." The word came out sharp. "Do not say, 'together.' I'm starting to think that word means something different to you than it does to me."

He forced himself to breathe, to stay still when everything in him screamed to go to her. To fix this. To reframe the words that had shattered their perfect moment so that she understood that he was offering her *paradise*, not a cage.

She paced to the window, then back, that restless energy he loved about her now burning with something that looked a lot like panic. "I can't move in with you. Just like that. As if everything is fine and we're not still at very different places emotionally."

"Okay." He kept his voice calm even as his pulse tried to break a world record. "We can slow down. Table this discussion for later."

"No. No discussion, Noah." Her voice hitched. "You want to have fun, let's have some fun, but moving in together is something else, something I did *not* sign up for."

"How is living together all of a sudden the opposite of fun?" He couldn't help asking, even though her expression said he really didn't want to know the answer. "I'm pretty sure I'll still want to have fun while we're cooking together or watching a movie together."

She just shook her head, that wild look still in her eyes. Like she was searching for an escape route but couldn't quite find one.

The sight pierced him somewhere vital. Because he'd put that look there. She wanted to escape from *him*.

"You're missing the point. On purpose, I suspect," she said, arms crossed. "Why do we have to change anything? What's wrong with living our totally separate lives and seeing each other when we feel like it? Why do we have to put labels on things and drag feelings into this—"

"Because I love you, Sabrina," he said and spread his hands wide to show her that he was offering himself to her, no holds barred.

"You might think you do, but you don't," she snapped, her voice rising with each word. "Love isn't pushing your agenda down my throat when I already told you I'm not cut out for this."

The accusation whacked him in the solar plexus, sucking everything out of him as if he'd fallen onto concrete. She didn't believe him. She was *questioning* the authenticity of his feelings. "That's not true. At all."

"It is true. You don't want me, Noah. You want the experience of being in love. Of having this epic romance. I'm just convenient because I happen to be here. Any woman would have done the trick."

"You think that in my head women are *interchangeable*? How can you say that?" His stomach hurt. Everything hurt.

"Because it's true." She wrapped her arms around herself, backing toward the door. "You're so caught up in the idea of finding this great love story that you don't even see that I can't give you what you want."

"I see you, Sabrina," he said around the eight ball in his throat. "I see how fierce you are, how dedicated. How you push yourself to be the best at everything. I see your strength and your vulnerability. And I love all of it. All of you."

"Noah, please." She shut her eyes for a beat, but he could

still see the anguish carved into her expression. "Accept that I can't do this. I can't be your perfect romance novel ending."

"That's not what I'm asking for."

"Isn't it?" Her laugh held no humor. "You're already planning our happily ever after, and I'm still trying to figure out how to be around you knowing that you have all these feelings I don't have."

The words landed like shrapnel, embedding themselves in places he couldn't reach. Jacob's warnings echoed in his head: *You have a tendency to make a fool of yourself over a woman.*

Had he really been so blind? So caught up in his own feelings that he'd missed how much he was overwhelming her?

"Sabrina." He tried one more time, even as she reached for the door. "Please. We can slow down. Just don't leave."

"We tried that once. It didn't work. Now I have to take the space I need." She wouldn't meet his eyes. "I can't think when you're looking at me like that. Like I'm breaking your heart."

"Aren't you?"

But she was already gone, the door clicking shut behind her with devastating finality. Noah sank onto the couch, his legs watery and unreliable.

Was she right? Maybe he had been more in love with the idea of them than with the reality. Maybe he'd built this whole thing up in his head while she'd been trying to tell him all along that she wasn't there yet.

Maybe she never would be.

The silence of his empty house pressed in around him, broken only by Dancer's concerned whine. Noah buried his face in his hands, trying to breathe through the ache in his chest.

He'd thought they were writing their story together. Turns out, he might have been the only one holding the pen.

Chapter Nineteen

The incident report on Sabrina's desk had zero chance at holding her attention. She'd read the same paragraph eight times and still had no idea what it said. Something about trail maintenance blah blah blah.

As if that mattered when her entire world had imploded because a man had the audacity to order her to move in with him. No asking for Noah Colton. Just—*Live here. I love you. We're going to do everything together!*

Where was her agency in all of this? Why did he get to say what happened? Where was her right to demand they go back to having fun, the way their relationship had started?

She bristled again, holding on to her anger, because if she let it go...well, she didn't want to think about that.

Noah should have known better. Everyone knew better. She had standards, boundaries and a firm policy against letting anyone think they could waltz into her life and tell her what to do. Even if he'd given her a huge leg up toward her promotion by selflessly working with her and Ripley. And giving her the dog in the first place.

Speaking of dogs, Bonner drifted in her direction, a deceptively casual expression on his face that didn't fool her for a minute.

"Well, well. If it isn't Officer West, actually at her desk

for once instead of playing with dogs and SAR experts." His voice grated across her nerves like sandpaper on a sunburn.

She didn't look up. Her emotions simmered pretty close to the surface, and it might not take much to lose it completely. Which would result in a fist through Bonner's face and disciplinary action for her.

Though honestly, the fact that she had all this stuff seething behind her rib cage was Noah's fault. She'd been doing just fine before he showed up with his gorgeous smile and his thing about honesty and his complete inability to understand that some people weren't built for happy ever after.

"Some of us do actual work around here, Bonner." She deliberately kept her tone bored. Unaffected. He'd never clue in on her turmoil.

"That's what I hear." His tone dripped false sympathy. "Though I also heard your boyfriend's not training you anymore. Trouble in paradise?"

Her pen snapped in her grip, spattering ink across the report. Perfect. Just perfect. Like she needed one more sign from the universe that her life was spiraling.

"Don't you have something better to do?" She grabbed a tissue to clean up the mess, still refusing to meet his gaze. "Like actually patrolling your sector?"

"Already done." He leaned against her doorframe, radiating smugness like a cat who'd found an injured bird. "Even checked out that suspicious activity report near where you found your body. Nothing there, of course. Waste of time, just like I told Reynolds it would be."

That got her attention. "What suspicious activity?"

"Oh, you didn't hear?" His grin widened, showing altogether too many teeth. "Someone reported movement up there last night. Lights where there shouldn't be any. Probably just kids messing around. I did a thorough sweep of the area this morning. All clear."

Thorough. Right. Bonner's idea of *thorough* meant a cursory drive-by, if that. And lights in Peavine Canyon after dark? That wasn't kids. Not in January, and not that far from the road. But Bonner wouldn't know the difference between suspicious activity and his own reflection in a mirror.

"Really?" She kept her voice carefully neutral even as her pulse picked up. "You checked the whole area? Including the upper ridge?"

"Please." He waved a dismissive hand. "I know how to do my job. Unlike some people who need their boyfriend to help them get ahead."

The dark satisfaction in his voice made her stomach turn. He'd heard about her and Noah. Probably through the gossip machine that passed for interagency communication around here. And he was loving every second of her personal drama, the tool.

If there was anything she hated, it was her personal life being trotted through the office like some kind of game. She was a professional. No one had a reason to doubt her.

"If you're done throwing all that swagger around," she said with perfect calm that she definitely didn't feel, "I have work to do."

He lingered another moment, probably hoping for a reaction, then finally pushed off the doorframe. "Have fun with your paperwork, West. Maybe if you're a really good girl, they'll let you have my desk when I leave for the district office. You know, after I get the promotion."

Fortunately—for him—he waltzed off then, or she would have rounded this desk to take great satisfaction in rearranging his face.

She waited until his footsteps faded before slumping back in her chair. Her hands trembled slightly as she tried to salvage the ink-stained report. What was it about men and their need to stake claims on everything? Territory, promotions, women's hearts. As if they had some divine right to plant their flag wherever they wanted.

Not that Noah was anything like Bonner. He at least truly cared, which somehow made it worse. Because caring led to feelings and feelings led to love and love led to...

Nope. Not going there.

Instead, she focused on what mattered. Suspicious activity near Annie's site. And Bonner had brushed it off without a second thought.

He hadn't seen the baby supplies hidden in that apartment. Hadn't connected the dots between Annie and the woman they'd rescued from the fire. Didn't know what she and Noah had discovered about missing women and—

The ache in her chest flared. She couldn't think about Noah. Not now. Not ever, preferably, though that was about as likely as Bonner developing actual investigative skills.

But she could do her job. The job she'd been doing long before Noah Colton whirled into her life and flipped everything over with his gale force winds. He'd even told her to expect Hurricane Noah to roar onshore at any moment.

And what had she done? Made huge assumptions that his admittedly thrilling personality meant they were a good match. All intensity, all the time, no apologies.

Gah, she had to stop thinking about this and go do something with a chance of distracting her.

Decision made, she grabbed her gear. Bonner might not care about suspicious activity in her canyon, but she did. And she had a partner who could help her investigate. One who wouldn't complicate everything.

RIPLEY'S TAIL WAGGED the moment Sabrina collected her from the department's K-9 kennel. The dog had adapted well to staying there during Sabrina's shifts, though she missed having her around the way she did at home.

She missed a lot of things lately. Not that she'd admit that to anyone, especially not herself.

Dogs didn't gossip, so she'd found her companion for the day. They also didn't try to move you in with them or make grand declarations that turned your entire world inside out. They were happy with belly rubs and treats and the occasional game of fetch. No expectations. Exactly what she needed.

"Just us today, girl." The words felt hollow as she loaded Ripley into her vehicle. "Think you can work without your boyfriend?"

The lab's tail drooped slightly at the mention of Dancer. Great. Even her dog was going to make her feel guilty about this. Ironic. Ripley was her longest relationship and she was screwing it up too.

The drive to Peavine Canyon normally got her pumped to be out in the wilderness. This time, not so much.

Peavine was where she'd met Noah. All of this just reminded her of him, the way he jumped into absolutely everything, danger, love, rock climbing, kissing—ugh, she could have done herself a favor and not thought about that.

She'd done the right thing walking away. She had. Because the alternative was letting Noah catch up, and she'd never recover when it inevitably fell apart. And it would have fallen apart. Everything did. Men didn't stay. They told you what to do, ignored your right to choose and then disappointed you.

The mantra felt emptier with each repetition, but she clung to it anyway. No man she'd ever met had been any different, starting with her father and ending with Noah.

The morning sun painted the red rock cliffs in shades of flame as she parked in the small turnout. Late January air bit through her jacket, sharp enough to steal her breath. Or maybe that was the memory of Noah's face when she'd walked out—that devastating mix of hurt and confusion that haunted her every time she closed her eyes.

At least he'd looked surprised. As if he genuinely hadn't seen it coming. Which just proved her point that he didn't really know her at all. Anyone who truly loved her would have known she'd freak out.

Focus. She was here to work.

Ripley bounded ahead as they climbed toward where she'd found Annie's body. The rockslide had changed the terrain, creating new patterns of shadow and stone that she cataloged with practiced efficiency. Recent footprints marked the sandy soil—Bonner's cursory inspection, no doubt. He hadn't even bothered to check the upper ledges where someone could easily observe the whole canyon.

Men like Bonner were exactly why she was better off alone. All of them thought they could handle her, talk to her like she was an idiot who couldn't figure out her own mind. Even the good ones. Maybe especially the good ones, because they actually believed their own press.

Something caught her eye—a flash of white against the red rock. Paper?

She moved closer, careful of her footing on the loose scree. A torn piece of notebook paper fluttered from where it had snagged on a thorny bush. The edges were weathered but the writing remained legible.

Friday 8 p.m. Same place.

Her pulse quickened. The paper was relatively fresh—the ink hadn't faded despite exposure to the elements. Someone had been here recently.

More signs jumped out at her from this new vantage point. Cigarette butts that hadn't had time to weather. The remains of a small fire, carefully hidden behind an outcropping. Someone had been hanging out in this area.

Why? It wasn't a designated camping site, and from this

vantage point, you could see the trail easily, but anyone hiking it wouldn't see you.

Better question, how did this connect to Annie Ross and that missing baby? Because there were no coincidences, not in Dark Canyon Wilderness in January.

Movement caught her attention—a figure picking his way down the opposite slope. Male, average height, wearing jeans and a heavy jacket. No backpack, no proper hiking boots. But definitely dressed for the cold.

Tourist who'd wandered off trail? Or something else?

The back of her neck prickled as he drew closer. There was something off about this guy, something that niggled at her. She didn't recognize him, but she definitely recognized his kind.

He had cruel eyes that didn't smile.

Ripley's head came up sharply, a low growl rumbling in her chest. Sabrina put her palm on Ripley's head to steady the lab. And also to ensure she could use hand signals to direct the dog if necessary.

"Beautiful morning for a hike." The man's voice carried across the distance—so carefully casual that it raised every alarm in her head. "Though I didn't expect to find anyone else out here."

"This area is closed for investigation." She kept her tone professional, even as she noted how he angled his approach to cut off her exit route. "USFS jurisdiction. I'm going to need to see some ID."

"Investigation?" He widened his eyes to the point of ridiculous. Geez this guy was a terrible actor. "Should I be worried? The other officer said the area was clear. Just this morning."

Bonner had talked to this guy and didn't get the slightest sense of anything being wrong? That tracked.

"Policy requires a second sweep." She shifted her weight,

ready to spring into action as she spied something metallic poking out of his pocket. "ID. Now."

"Now, why would you need that?" Another step. "When we both know you shouldn't be asking questions about things that don't concern you."

The menace in his voice was unmistakable. She was out here alone. Even Bonner didn't know she'd retraced his steps. Things had just gotten dicey.

Her mind raced through options. The path behind her led deeper into the canyon—risky with unstable conditions, but she knew every twist and turn. The route ahead was blocked by her unwelcome visitor.

She could get away. But he would follow her. How well did he know this area?

She had to call someone. Send a message. Something.

"Last chance." She unclipped the radio, making sure he saw the motion. "ID or I call this in."

"You're not touching that radio." His hand disappeared into his pocket.

Ripley didn't wait to see what he reached for, lunging forward, teeth bared, her bark echoing off the canyon walls.

It gave Sabrina the split second she needed. She turned and ran, letting her muscle memory of the terrain guide her feet. Ripley followed her, thankfully, instead of sticking around to defend them both. The path ahead branched— left toward an exposed ridge, right into denser vegetation.

A shout behind her, followed by the sound of pursuit. She veered right, ducking under low-hanging branches. The route was treacherous, loose rock waiting to betray unwary steps, but she'd walked it a hundred times.

Her pursuer crashed through the brush behind her, his heavier footfalls telling her exactly where he was. Not a local then. Someone unfamiliar with the canyon's tricks.

She could use that.

The path ahead split again. The left fork led to a dead end—a box canyon with sheer walls. The right wound deeper into the wilderness. But there was a third option, one only visible if you knew exactly where to look.

Sabrina veered left, hearing her pursuer's footsteps follow. The box canyon opened before her, its walls rising steep and unforgiving. She sprinted toward the back wall where a narrow crevice split the rock face.

She could hide in there and call Noah. She'd heard from Dispatch that he was in the area doing a training exercise but had ignored it obviously.

A rock whizzed past her head, missing by inches. No. Not a rock. A bullet. That guy had a gun.

She didn't look back, just pushed harder, Ripley tight on her heels. Her lungs burned as she pushed herself faster, the rough ground threatening to betray her with every step.

The crevice loomed ahead. She turned sideways, sucking in her breath as she squeezed through the narrow gap. The shadows swallowed her, cool darkness replacing harsh sunlight.

Her pursuer's curse echoed off the canyon walls. He was too big to follow.

He could still shoot into the cave.

Sabrina kept moving, hopefully out of range, feeling her way along the familiar passage. The cave opened up ahead, providing enough space to catch her breath. Ripley pressed against her legs, still alert but no longer growling.

She'd bought herself some time. But she was also trapped.

That guy would wait her out, she had no doubt.

Her radio crackled with static—no signal this deep in the rock. Her phone showed the same. No way to call for backup.

No way to call Noah.

He would have come out here with her in a heartbeat if she'd alerted him to what Bonner had said. Except she'd walked—run—away from Noah, and now she no longer had him to count on. How many times had he been her backup? How many times had she done the happy dance in her heart when he called her his partner?

That was exactly the problem. She couldn't afford to need anyone that much.

A tremor shook the ground, sending loose rocks skittering across the cave floor. Ripley whined softly.

"It's okay, girl." Sabrina reached for the dog, but it was hard to say whether she was comforting Ripley or the other way around. "Nothing to worry about. That was just a baby quake."

The words had barely left her mouth when a second tremor hit—harder, longer. The cave walls groaned ominously.

Then the world exploded.

The roar of falling rock drowned everything else as the aftershock ripped through the canyon. Sabrina dove for the back of the cave, pulling Ripley with her as debris rained down.

When the dust settled, the entrance to the cave had vanished behind a wall of broken rock.

She was trapped. Like, actually trapped, not just unable to leave without running into the guy with a gun.

And no one else knew she was out here.

Chapter Twenty

Darkness had a texture. Sabrina had never noticed that before, but trapped in this cave with only the sound of falling rocks and Ripley's anxious breathing, she could feel it against her skin. Heavy. Suffocating. As impenetrable as the walls she'd built around herself.

"Just breathe." The words disappeared into the blackness, swallowed by the tons of rock pressing down around them.

She'd experienced a lot of tight spots in her life. Literal ones, where she'd wedged herself into cracks in the rock face that barely accommodated her shoulders. Metaphorical ones, where she'd had to prove herself over and over to men who thought she didn't belong in their world.

This was both. And neither. Because she'd never been this kind of trapped before.

The dust hadn't fully settled from the rock fall that had sealed the cave entrance. It was *dark*. Like really dark, the kind that crawled through your eye sockets and made you imagine you could see light, creating patterns that didn't make any sense. Just like nothing in her life made sense anymore.

Was this what surrender felt like? Having absolutely zero control over anything?

She'd lost control the moment she'd spotted that guy on

the trail. Everything after had been pure reaction—running, hiding, getting trapped. A series of choices that weren't really choices at all.

Like how she always ran. From everything.

The thought hit her like falling rock, impossible to dodge. Her specialty was running. From her father's disappointment. From relationships. From Noah.

Bad time to be thinking about him. He would have spotted the guy with the gun before she did, probably. Working together, they could have handled it.

Instead, she'd charged ahead alone. Like always.

Alone was how she did things, and she'd get through this cave in that way too. Well. Alone except for the dog.

Ripley whined softly, and Sabrina forced herself to breathe through the band of pressure squeezing her chest. "We're fine. This is just another problem to solve."

The words echoed off the cave walls, mocking her. Nothing about this was fine. She was trapped in a cave with unstable geology during an earthquake that may not be done, no way to call for help, and an armed man outside who clearly didn't want her asking questions about Annie Ross.

A tremor shook loose more debris, sending pebbles skittering across the cave floor. The sound burrowed into her brain, taking root alongside the dozens of other thoughts she'd been avoiding.

She didn't need Noah. She didn't need anyone.

Even in her head, the words rang hollow.

"Stop it," she ordered herself, but the darkness seemed to press closer, amplifying every breath, every heartbeat, every doubt she'd pushed away.

This was exactly why she worked alone. Other people complicated things. Made you doubt yourself. Made you need them.

Another tremor rattled through the canyon. A larger rock

broke free, rolling into the cave based on the sound, landing inches from where she stood. Ripley's growl held an edge of fear that matched the ice forming in Sabrina's veins.

The temperature was dropping. How long before the cold became a real problem? Before the dust in the air made breathing difficult? Before that guy with the gun decided to start digging through the debris to reach her?

Before someone noticed she was missing?

Would anyone notice? She'd made it such a habit to work alone, maybe no one would think twice about her absence. After Bonner had thrown his weight around, she'd come straight out here to do whatever she could to best him, not a word to anyone.

A tremor shook the cave, dislodging more debris. The temperature had dropped at least ten degrees since the rockslide sealed them in. Or maybe that was just her blood running cold as reality sank in.

She was going to die in here because she couldn't stop running long enough to let anyone catch her.

Ripley pressed closer, offering warmth and comfort she didn't deserve. The lab hadn't hesitated to follow her into this trap, trusting her judgment completely. Just like Noah had trusted her with his heart.

And what had she done with that trust?

The same thing she always did. Push away anything that threatened to matter too much.

Her father's voice echoed in her head: *Showing weakness is the same as admitting defeat.* She'd lived by those words, turned them into armor, used them to justify keeping everyone at arm's length.

Even the one person who'd never tried to change her.

She had to do something other than sit here in her own misery. Minutes bled into each other as she worked her way around the cave's perimeter, testing for weaknesses, fingering the walls for any crack that might let in fresh air. Her hands ached from scraping against rock, but she kept going.

She'd always been good at the physical challenges. It was the emotional ones that tripped her up.

Ripley bumped her leg and Sabrina took a long moment to be grateful she wasn't alone. There was something to be said for taking chances on something new and scary that ended up being great.

For her. Not for the dog, who was terrified and counting on her owner to fix this. She had a responsibility to get them both out of here safely. Then she could wallow in regret.

If she and Ripley actually survived.

"It's okay, girl." She kept her voice steady as Ripley pressed against her. The lab's anxiety vibrated through both of them. "We're going to figure this out."

How, she had no idea. There were no cracks in the walls, no light. This particular crevasse had exactly one entrance.

Which was now blocked by several tons of rock.

She slumped against a semi-straight wall, trying not to panic. Or think about Noah. But it was hard not to give in as the minutes stretched and her brain seemed determined to put memories of his smile on repeat.

Plus, he was really warm. She would give anything to be pulled into his embrace right about now. Maybe for more than the warmth.

"I don't need anyone." Darkness swallowed the words as her own voice betrayed her, cracking on the lie she'd told herself a thousand times.

Ripley's tail thumped against her leg, calling her on it.

"Okay, fine. Maybe I do." The admission scraped her throat raw. "But needing people is dangerous. They leave. They disappoint you. They make you question everything you thought you knew about yourself."

Like how Noah made her question whether being strong meant being alone.

A rock crashed somewhere in the darkness, the sound amplifying her pulse. How long had they been in here? An hour? Two? Time stretched like a rubber band ready to snap.

The cold seeped deeper into her bones, but she couldn't stop shivering long enough to think. To really examine why she always chose the hardest path, the one that led exactly where she was now.

Alone in the dark with no backup plan.

Noah would have come up with one. He always had contingencies, always thought three steps ahead. Even when it came to them, to their relationship. He'd led with his heart, full speed ahead, no apologies.

Move in with me.

She'd panicked. Pushed back. Run away.

But why?

The answer lurked in the darkness, patient as the mountains themselves. Waiting for her to finally face it.

Because Noah scared her more than any treacherous canyon or sheer rock face ever had. More than her father's disappointment or Bonner's snide comments or any of the physical dangers she'd faced in this wilderness.

Noah loved at the same intensity she competed. All in, no holds barred, full commitment to the goal. He didn't just want to be part of her life—he wanted to be her partner in everything.

And that terrified her.

Because what if she wasn't enough? What if she let him in and he discovered that beneath all her fierce independence, she was just a woman who'd never been good enough for anyone?

Her father had taught her that lesson early. Excellence

was the minimum requirement. Anything less meant failure. And failure meant watching the people you loved walk away.

So she'd made sure no one got close enough to matter. Until Noah.

Noah, who'd charged into her life like the hurricane he'd warned her about. Who matched her competitive streak with his own brand of intensity. Who saw past her walls to the woman underneath and loved her anyway.

Who'd never once asked her to be anything other than exactly who she was.

Fresh pain lanced through her chest that had nothing to do with the cold or lack of oxygen. She'd been so busy protecting herself that she'd missed the obvious truth—Noah wasn't trying to box her in, direct her life, take away her independence. He was offering to share her adventures, amplify her strengths, weather her storms.

He was offering partnership, not possession.

And she'd thrown it back in his face because she'd been too scared to admit even she could see the difference.

The darkness pressed closer, heavy with revelation. She'd spent her whole life proving she didn't need anyone, convinced that independence meant isolation. That letting someone in meant giving up control.

But that wasn't what Noah wanted. He'd never tried to take control—he'd offered to share it. To be her backup when she needed it, her cheerleader when she didn't. To love her through all of it.

"I really messed up." The words felt like gravel in her throat. "I had everything and I ran away from it instead of exploring it. Instead of taking it as a new challenge."

Ripley whined softly.

"I know, girl. I know." She buried her fingers in the lab's fur, anchoring herself against the truth she couldn't escape. "I'm an idiot. The guy literally says, 'I'm intense and I don't apologize for it,' and I somehow miss that it would apply to everything. Even me."

Noah didn't just keep up with her—he challenged her to be better. Showed her that vulnerability could be strength. That letting someone in didn't mean letting them take over.

That love wasn't a cage at all. It was a choice.

And she'd chosen wrong.

The realization broke something loose inside her chest. A wall she'd built so long ago she'd forgotten it was there. The one that said she had to do everything alone or it didn't count.

She didn't want to do this alone anymore.

The truth of it shocked her, but not as much as the peace that followed. Like finally accepting that sometimes the best route up the mountain wasn't the hardest one.

Sometimes the best path was the one that led to where you wanted to be, even if that wasn't where you thought you were going.

If she ever got out of here, she'd tell Noah that. Tell him everything. How she'd been so focused on protecting herself that she'd missed the obvious truth—that he made her stronger, not weaker. That his intensity matched hers perfectly. That she'd been afraid of losing control when, really, she'd been afraid of letting him love her.

She wanted to tell him that she loved him back.

Had probably started falling during that first kiss in the parking lot when he'd shown her exactly who he was—someone who didn't waste time playing games, who dove in with his whole heart and who trusted her to catch him.

She hadn't been ready to catch him then. But she was now.

If she survived this cave, this cold, this darkness that pressed against her skin like all the fears she'd been running from, she'd find a way to make it right. To show Noah that she understood now. That she was done running.

That she chose him. Chose them. Chose the adventure of discovering what they could be together instead of the safety of being alone.

Another tremor shook the cave, longer this time. More rocks fell, the sound drilling into her bones. The temperature kept dropping, but she barely noticed.

She was too busy planning what she'd say to Noah when she saw him again. How she'd explain that she finally understood what he'd been offering all along—a chance to soar higher together than either of them could alone.

Ripley's sudden attention shift startled her from her thoughts. The lab's entire body had gone tense, nose working frantically in the darkness.

"What is it, girl?" Sabrina's pulse quickened. Had the man with the gun found another entrance? Was something worse coming?

But Ripley wasn't growling. She was whining softly, pawing at something near the cave-in. The sound of her nails scratching against rock echoed in the confined space.

"Ripley, come back." Fear squeezed Sabrina's chest. Another cave-in could kill them both.

Instead of obeying, the lab continued her frantic investigation, moving with the purpose Sabrina recognized from their training sessions. This wasn't random—Ripley was working.

She crawled toward the sound, her hands outstretched in the darkness. "What did you find, girl?"

Her fingers encountered Ripley's fur, then the rough edge of stone, and beyond it, the faintest whisper of fresh air. A crack, barely wider than her wrist, had opened in the rockfall. Too small for a human, but maybe—

"You brilliant dog." Hope surged through her veins. "Show me."

Ripley needed no further encouragement. She wiggled

closer to the opening, her body language signaling the excitement she displayed during their SAR practice.

The next few minutes passed in a blur as Sabrina carefully widened the crack, just enough for Ripley to squeeze through. She'd never been so grateful for all those hours spent training the dog to find missing persons, to navigate difficult terrain, to seek help.

"Find Noah," she whispered, pressing her face close to the crack. "Bring him back here."

Ripley hesitated, torn between her training to stay with her handler and the command to seek help.

"Go, girl." Sabrina's voice broke. "It's okay. I'm counting on you."

With a final whine, Ripley squeezed through the narrow opening, her movements sending a small shower of pebbles cascading down. Then silence.

Sabrina pressed her eye to the crack, straining to see anything in the darkness beyond. Nothing. But somewhere out there, Ripley was running through the canyon, seeking help. Seeking Noah.

Please, God, let that be true. Don't let the man with the gun see her. Fly, Ripley, fly.

She settled back against the wall and wrapped her arms around herself. The cold penetrated deeper now, but the spark of hope burned brighter. Ripley knew what to do. She'd been trained for this.

It was time for Sabrina to trust her partner, just as she needed to trust Noah. To believe that sometimes, salvation came in the form you least expected.

All she had to do now was survive until rescue came. And when it did, she'd be ready—for everything.

Chapter Twenty-One

Noah squinted against the morning glare, his clipboard notes on the junior handler's technique with his Malinois forgotten in his hand. The early session was wrapping up, but his gaze was on the jagged peaks beyond Peavine Canyon, visible in the distance. The mountains stood sentinel against the horizon, uncompromising and unforgiving—a physical reminder that beauty could be painful. This training spot offered the perfect blend of varied terrain and accessibility, but that's not why he'd chosen it.

He'd chosen it because it hurt to remember, and he needed to cauterize the gaping wound Sabrina had left behind.

"You with us, Colton?" Steve's voice carried across the training field, a knowing edge to his words.

"Yeah." Noah forced his attention away from the view and back to the clipboard. "Just evaluating Sandra's retrieval pattern."

Steve's eyebrows went up. "Which would be great if Sandra hadn't finished her run ten minutes ago."

Busted. Noah scrubbed a hand over his face, feeling the growth he'd neglected to trim this morning. Or yesterday. The last few days had blurred together in a haze of work and not thinking about Sabrina, which was like trying not to think about breathing when someone was holding your head underwater.

The harder you fought it, the more it consumed you.

"I'm good," he said, though no one had asked. "Just distracted by that new water retrieval technique I want to try with Dancer later."

Steve nodded, clearly not buying it but kind enough not to push. The man had seen enough shattered hearts in this line of work to know when to leave the broken pieces alone. The other handlers had started packing up, their dogs already loaded into various vehicles. The early morning training had been Noah's idea, a desperate attempt to keep his mind and body moving at such a punishing pace that there'd be no room for the tsunami of emotions threatening to tear him apart from the inside.

So far, it wasn't working. At all. So now he was exhausted *and* heartbroken.

Dancer bumped his leg, a gentle reminder that at least one relationship in his life remained rock solid. The lab's eyes held that quiet understanding that made him both man's best friend and Noah's emotional lifeline.

"Don't you start," Noah murmured, but scratched behind the lab's ears anyway. "I'm not pining. I'm processing."

The dog's answering look could only be described as skeptical. That was the problem with having such an intuitive partner. Dancer could see straight through the lining Noah had constructed around the raw, bleeding heart he was pretending didn't exist.

"All right, wrap it up!" Noah called to the remaining stragglers. "We'll pick this up Thursday at the lake."

He should feel proud. The new handlers were showing real progress, and the local SAR units would benefit from having more certified teams in the field. His program was working. His life was moving forward.

And if he kept telling himself that, maybe it would start to feel true.

The truth was, he'd like to be writing the article he'd started. The one about Annie Ross. But every time he sat down at his keyboard, nothing productive happened, that was for sure. And until he could figure out how to get through that quagmire of grief, nothing on the investigative reporting front would be in his future.

A sharp bark caught his attention—not Dancer's familiar voice. His head snapped up, scanning the tree line at the edge of the training ground.

A chocolate lab burst from the underbrush, coat matted with dirt, sides heaving. The moment his brain processed it was Ripley, a cavity formed in his chest, as if all his blood had suddenly decided to pool in his feet.

Something was very, very wrong.

The dog sprinted straight for him, barking frantically. No leash. No Sabrina.

"Ripley!" Noah dropped to one knee as the lab skidded to a halt in front of him, whining and pawing at his legs. "Where's Sabrina?"

The lab barked again, turning in circles before darting a few feet away, then back to him. Classic alert behavior. She was trying to lead him somewhere.

His blood turned to ice in his veins as his mind painted a thousand possible scenarios, each worse than the last. If Ripley was here alone, clearly on a mission, something had happened to Sabrina. Something bad enough that she'd sent her dog for help instead of calling on the radio.

Or maybe she couldn't call.

That thought knocked the air from his lungs like a sucker punch, the image of Sabrina alone and hurt flooding his system with adrenaline so potent it nearly made him dizzy. He'd seen what terrible things could happen to people alone in those canyons. Had recovered the broken bodies left behind when nature reminded humans who was really in charge.

That was *not* happing to Sabrina. He was not losing her to the wilderness.

"Steve!" Noah's voice cracked like a whip. "Get emergency services on standby. Possible SAR operation. Full team."

He was already moving toward his truck, Dancer at his heel and Ripley circling, her anxiety like a living thing between them, a third creature formed of pure fear. "Where is she, girl? Show me."

Ripley barked and took off toward the main road, then circled back, clearly distressed. Noah's mind raced—Ripley had come from the southeast, the direction of Peavine Canyon. The same canyon where they'd found Annie Ross. The same place Sabrina patrolled most frequently.

"I know where she is," he said, yanking open the truck door. Dancer leaped into the back seat, and after a moment's hesitation, Ripley jumped in beside him. "Good girl. Take me to her."

The drive was a blur, tension coiling tighter with each passing minute. Ripley grew more frantic the closer they got to Peavine, practically throwing herself against the window.

"We're going to find her," he promised the anxious dog, whose brown eyes—so like Sabrina's that it physically hurt to look at them—seemed to understand every word.

Noah finally skidded sideways into the same turnout he'd parked in the first time he'd met Sabrina. The moment Noah rounded the truck, Ripley burst through the door he'd barely opened, nose to the ground, already tracking. This was what she'd been trained for—to find what was lost, to lead the way when all other signs failed.

Noah grabbed his emergency gear, cursing himself for not bringing more. His field vest held the basics: first aid kit, water, radio, protein bars. But if Sabrina was seriously injured—

No. He couldn't think like that. One crisis at a time.

"Dancer, heel. Ripley, show me."

He followed the chocolate lab up the same trail where he and Sabrina had once found Annie Ross's body. His mind cataloged details with professional precision even as his heart thundered against his ribs. Fresh footprints. Signs of a struggle. A spent shell casing that made his blood run cold.

Someone had fired a weapon here.

He unclipped the radio from his belt. "Command, this is Colton. I'm tracking a possible injured USFS officer in Peavine Canyon, sector seven. Evidence of firearms discharge. Request immediate backup."

The radio crackled. "Copy that, Colton. Units en route. ETA fifteen minutes. What's your situation?"

"Following service dog to possible location. Target is Officer Sabrina West. No contact yet." His voice remained steady despite the fifty-ton elephant sitting on his chest. He'd done this before. Dozens of times. Find what's lost. Bring them home.

But never when the lost person was more precious than his own life.

Ripley's path veered suddenly into denser terrain, away from the main trail. Noah followed, noting how the dog moved with singular focus. Not random. She knew exactly where they were going.

When the path opened into a box canyon, his heart plummeted like a rock thrown from the highest cliff. The back wall was almost completely obscured by a massive pile of broken rock. Fresh rock. A rockslide.

The universe had a sick sense of irony sometimes. How many times had he thought about Sabrina being walled off, unreachable? How many metaphors had he constructed about her barriers, her defenses, the walls she built to keep everyone—keep him—at a distance? Now here he was, faced with an actual, physical wall of stone between them. The cosmic joke would have been funny if it wasn't so terrifying.

Ripley ran straight to the pile, pawing frantically at a small opening near the bottom, her barks taking on a desperate edge—the sound of pure panic that transcended species, that primal cry that said someone he loved was in danger.

"Sabrina!" he shouted, running now, his voice tearing from his throat like it was being ripped out by force. "Sabrina!"

A faint sound came from behind the rocks—so faint he might have imagined it, might have created it from the desperate hope that threatened to crack his ribs from the inside.

Except Dancer heard it too, immediately alerting on the same spot Ripley was working, and Dancer never, ever gave false alerts.

"Sabrina! Can you hear me?" He dropped to his knees, pressing his face toward the small opening Ripley had found, gravel digging into his skin in a way that registered as nothing more than background noise compared to the thundering of his own heart.

"Noah?" Her voice was small, strained, but so unmistakably her that his chest physically ached, like someone had reached in and squeezed his heart in a vise. "Are you really here?"

"It's me." Relief made his voice crack, splitting open all the raw emotion he'd tried to bury. "Are you hurt? Can you move?"

"I'm okay. Cold. Can't get out." She sounded exhausted, each word carrying the weight of hours spent alone in the darkness, trapped and uncertain. "The earthquake—"

"I know. Help is coming." He was already assessing the rock pile, looking for any way to reach her, his SAR training kicking in even as his emotions threatened to swamp everything he knew about trying to do this on his own. "Hang on."

Hang on. Such a simple phrase, and yet it carried every desperate plea he'd ever made—to her, to himself, to God. *Hang on. Don't give up. I'm coming for you. I'm here.*

The radio crackled again, and he updated command on her status. The response was swift—search-and-rescue teams, paramedics, equipment for extraction—all en route. But minutes mattered in cave-ins. With the temperature, the air supply, the risk of further collapse, every second counted.

He couldn't wait.

Noah studied the pile, his mind working through the geology. The earthquake had triggered the slide, but the rocks looked stable enough now. The opening Ripley had used was too small for a person, but if he could carefully remove some of the smaller rocks above it…

"Sabrina, I'm going to try to widen this opening. Stay back from this wall." He kept his voice calm, professional. "Talk to me so I know you're okay."

"I'm here." A pause. Then, so softly he barely registered it, she whispered, "I can't believe you came."

She hadn't thought he would. She'd been trapped alone in this cave wondering if he would come to save her, if he cared enough. What was left of his heart shattered.

But he couldn't think about that now.

"Of course I came." He began carefully removing rocks, stacking them to the side. "Did you think I wouldn't?"

Her answering laugh held no humor. "After how I left things? I wouldn't have blamed you."

"That's not how this works." He grunted as he shifted a particularly heavy stone. "That's not how I work."

Silence stretched from the darkness behind the rocks until she finally said, "I know that now."

The quietness in her voice made something catch in his

throat. But he couldn't dwell on it, not when she was still trapped and in danger. He worked methodically, muscles straining as he cleared away enough debris to create an opening just large enough for her to crawl through—if she could reach it.

"Sabrina, I've got an opening here, about two feet wide. Can you see any light?"

"A little." Her voice sounded closer. "Everything is spinning."

Oh, man. Hypoxia already? That was so, so not good. Panic clawed at his gut.

Another tremor hit, a small one, but enough to send fresh panic through Noah's veins. Loose rock skittered down, threatening to undo his progress.

"Sabrina!" *Answer, answer, answer.*

"I'm okay." Her voice was shaky, like a radio signal just on the edge of range. "But I think that made things worse in here."

The sound of sirens wailed in the distance, a cavalry that felt an eternity away. Help was coming, but they might not have that much time. Every instinct in his body screamed at him to get her out now while she was still conscious and coherent—the same instinct that had once sent him charging into a collapsing building in Syria to pull out a family trapped by crossfire, the same instinct that made him who he was, for better or worse. The man who never waited when he could jump feet first into the fire.

There was no choice here. There never had been.

"I'm coming in." The decision crystallized in his mind with perfect clarity, like a diamond formed under impossible pressure.

"What? You can't. It's not…stable." Her voice drifted in and out.

He was already shimmying through the opening he'd created, flashlight clenched between his teeth, his body figuring out on the fly how to make itself small, how to become fluid against unyielding stone. The passage was tight—painfully so—but he pushed through, ignoring the sharp edges tearing at his clothes and skin.

Pain was temporary. Regret lasted forever.

And then he was through, on the other side, the beam of his flashlight cutting through the darkness like a blade to reveal Sabrina's wide eyes, reflecting back all the fear and relief and something else that made his chest constrict.

She looked smaller somehow, huddled against the far wall, arms wrapped around herself like she might fall apart otherwise. Her uniform was covered in dust, her face smudged with dirt.

But she was alive. Breathing. Whole.

The sight of her hit him like a physical force, a tsunami of emotion that threatened to sweep away all the careful distance he'd tried to maintain.

"Noah." His name on her lips carried a weight he couldn't quite define—part prayer, part disbelief, part something that might have been longing if he let himself believe it.

"Hey." He moved toward her carefully, mindful of unstable ground, completely unconcerned about the metaphorical ground between them that could be just as treacherous, if he cared.

Which he did not.

When he reached her, his hand rose of its own accord to brush dirt from her cheek, needing to touch her, to confirm that she was real and not some desperate hallucination his mind had conjured. "You scared me."

She caught his hand, her fingers ice-cold against his skin, like she'd absorbed the chill of the stone around her. "Did Ripley…did she find you?"

"She did." He smiled despite everything, despite the part

of him that was still bleeding from her rejection, still raw from watching her walk away. "That dog was not about to let you go without a fight."

Something shifted in her expression, too complicated to read in the dim light, layers of emotion that would require time and better illumination to fully decode. "I didn't know if you'd know…or if she'd be able to lead you."

"I will always find you." The words held more force than he intended, raw with the emotions he'd been trying to contain, spilling out now like water through a cracked dam. He couldn't stop them any more than he could stop breathing. "Always."

It wasn't just a promise. It was a declaration. A truth etched into his bones that no amount of hurt could erase.

Her breath hitched, and for a heartbeat, they just stared at each other, everything that remained unsaid hanging in the dusty air between them.

Then another tremor shook the cave, jolting them back to reality.

"We need to go." Noah turned, scoping out their exit route. "They've got equipment coming, but I'd rather not stick around for the after-party if this place decides to come down."

She nodded, allowing him to guide her toward the opening. Allowing him to help her. She was so weak. Outside, he could hear the sounds of emergency vehicles arriving, the organized chaos of a rescue operation forming.

"Can you make it through?" He eyed the tight passage dubiously.

"Watch me."

It would have made him feel a lot better if her voice hadn't come out so hoarsely, but he'd take the flash of her old spirit, even as she winced trying to squeeze through the narrow space.

He followed closely behind, ready to push her forward if she got stuck, hyperaware of every sound, every shift of rock above them. The opening seemed to have shrunk since he'd entered, making their exit even more perilous.

When Sabrina's boots finally emerged into sunlight, a cheer went up from the gathered rescue workers. Noah crawled out after her, blinking in the sudden brightness.

Sabrina swayed, paramedics already rushing forward. But her eyes stayed locked on Noah's face, something fierce and determined warring with weariness and other trauma in her gaze—the same look she'd had when they'd climbed in Moab, that blend of fearlessness and fire that had first drawn him to her like a moth to flame.

"Noah, I need to tell you—"

"Let them check you out first." He cut her off gently, unable to handle whatever she might say while adrenaline still coursed through his system, while his heart felt like it had been run through a meat grinder, tenderized to the point where the slightest touch might push it from its moorings completely. "We have time."

They had time. But that didn't mean he had the energy for anything else.

The relief of finding her alive warred with the memory of how she'd walked away, of how spilling his heart all over the place had sent her running for the exit like a building on fire. How she hadn't believed in what they could be together, what he knew soul deep—they were meant to be.

He'd pulled her from the cave, but the emotional chasm between them felt just as vast as before. This was a different kind of darkness, a different kind of trap. One he wasn't sure either of them knew how to escape.

She let the paramedics guide her to the ambulance, though her gaze kept finding his. He kept looking away, unable to let himself deconstruct what he saw in her depths.

When the medic insisted she ride with him to the hospital for observation, Noah stepped forward, his body moving on autopilot while everything beneath his skin remained caught in the undertow of emotion.

"I'll follow in my truck," he assured her and scrubbed at the back of his neck. "But I won't stay. Just long enough to make sure they take care of you."

Emotion flickered across her face—pain, understanding, resolve. "Noah, I was wrong. About everything. I need you to know—"

"Sabrina."

He stopped her with a gentle hand on her arm, the first deliberate touch since he'd helped her from the cave, and it burned like frostbite, that peculiar pain that feels like fire but comes from ice. His heart couldn't take confessions born of adrenaline and near-death experiences, couldn't weather the inevitable crash when reality returned and she remembered all the reasons she'd walked away.

"You're safe," he said. "That's all that matters now. Let the medic check you out, make sure you don't have anything we can't see going on."

She nodded. "And then we can talk later?"

His eyelids slammed closed, and he had to take a minute, aware that the ambulance was waiting. "I don't know what we'd talk about."

"Us, Noah." The catch in her voice nearly undid him. "I need to tell you some things—"

"I'm not at a place where I can hear them." It wasn't meant to be harsh, but neither could he lie. "After everything, I've become something I never thought I'd be. Cautious."

The irony was bitter on his tongue.

Here he was—the guy who jumped into everything at full speed, the one who never looked before he leaped—telling her he'd hit his own wall. That he needed space.

She didn't have to know it was because he wanted to gather her up and tell her he'd thought he'd lost her forever. That they'd wasted so much time already. Of course he forgave her and they should get married immediately.

The words would be easy. The recovery after she then crushed him *again*, not so much.

"Okay." She nodded, eyes bright with unshed tears that glittered in the sunlight. "But I'm not giving up on us. Just so you know."

"Let's get you to the hospital." He stepped back, trying to rebuild the professional distance that had crumbled the moment he'd heard her voice behind that wall of rock. But the wall between them now was his own construction—a hasty barricade of self-preservation built on his own shattered expectations. "I'll be right behind you."

She let the paramedics help her into the ambulance. The doors closed, and the ambulance pulled away, leaving Noah standing alone in the canyon that had brought them together. The same canyon that had claimed Annie Ross. The same canyon where he'd first recognized the echo of his own intensity in Sabrina's eyes.

He'd rescued Sabrina from the cave, but there was no one here to yank his heart from the labyrinth she'd left it in. He was stuck in the wilderness, with no clear path to follow. Just his own compass, spinning wildly, unable to find true north.

Chapter Twenty-Two

Hospitals had a way of stripping away pretense. Sabrina stared at the ceiling tiles above her bed, counting the tiny perforations in each square for the hundredth time. Twenty-four hours of observation, the doctor had ordered. For mild hypothermia, hypoxia, dehydration, and what he'd diplomatically called "environmental stress."

What he hadn't diagnosed was the hollow ache beneath her sternum that had nothing to do with being trapped in a cave and everything to do with the look on Noah's face when she'd tried to explain.

I'm not at a place where I can hear it.

His voice was on repeat in her head, drowning out the steady beep of monitors and the squeak of nurse's shoes in the corridor. The Noah who had rescued her was not the same one she'd last seen when he asked her to move in with him—this version had caution signs stamped all over him, his usual enthusiasm extinguished like embers in a downpour.

She'd done that to him.

The door to her room slid open, and Sabrina's heart leapt into her throat, only to crash back down when a petite nurse she hadn't seen before entered with a clipboard. Not Noah. Of course not. He'd followed the ambulance to the hospital as promised, spoken briefly with her doctor, and then disappeared with a painful formality that felt worse than if he'd yelled at her.

"How are we feeling?" The nurse checked her IV line with professional efficiency.

"Fine." Sabrina attempted a smile that felt like stretching plastic wrap over broken glass. "Any chance I can convince someone that I don't need to stay overnight?"

"Doctor's orders." The nurse's sympathetic look said she'd heard this plea a hundred times before. "Your body temperature is still lower than we'd like, and the doctor wants to monitor you for delayed symptoms of crush injuries."

"I wasn't crushed by anything." Just the weight of her own mistakes, but that wouldn't show up on any scan.

"Better safe than sorry." The nurse made a notation on her chart. "Besides, it's almost evening. Just one night, and you can go home tomorrow."

Home. The word felt hollow. Her place would be empty. Ripley wouldn't even be there unless someone had thought to take her dog home, but she didn't have a someone. She had herself only, exactly the way she'd thought she'd wanted it. Only she didn't.

"Do you know if my dog is okay?" The question scraped her throat raw.

The heroine of the hour deserved a T-bone steak and a nap on Sabrina's pillow, not an owner who'd messed up everything.

"Ripley?" The nurse smiled. "She's fine. Someone named Ryan Colton is taking care of her. He called to check on you earlier."

Relief took over her whole body. Ripley was safe with Noah's family. Which would make sense if she and Noah were still together. But Sabrina wasn't a Colton, even by association. Why was Ryan stepping up to help with her dog?

When the nurse left, Sabrina sank deeper into the sterile hospital pillow, replaying every moment in the cave. The cold. The darkness. The even darker realization that Noah didn't want to hear what she had to say.

She had been ready to die with regrets. Now she might have to live with them instead.

And live with the fact that she loved Noah Colton with every stubborn, terrified inch of her soul.

And she'd pushed him away before she could understand any of it.

A soft knock interrupted her spiraling thoughts. Expecting another nurse, Sabrina called a distracted "Come in."

The woman who entered wasn't wearing scrubs but rather dark slacks and a simple blouse beneath a white coat. Her ID badge read, "Ava Colton, PhD," and something in her warm brown eyes immediately identified her as Noah's family— the same directness, the same quiet confidence.

"Officer West." She approached the bed with a smile. "I'm Ava Colton, one of the hospital psychologists. I'm not officially on your case, but when I heard a Sabrina West had been admitted, I wanted to check on you myself."

"You're related to Noah," Sabrina stated, not needing the other woman's nod to know she was correct.

"His cousin." Ava's smile turned knowing. "Ryan is my brother. The Colton family network is efficient. News travels fast."

"Is he..." Sabrina hesitated, not sure what she was even asking. Is he okay? Is he coming back? Is he as miserable as I am?

"Noah's not very complicated." Ava pulled up a chair, settling into it with easy grace. "All the Colton men are easy to figure out, in their way. Though I suppose I should mention I have a bit of a professional advantage in reading people.

Occupational hazard. But Noah especially wears his heart on his sleeve." She smiled wryly.

"I know." The words came out choked.

"Do you?" Ava's tone wasn't accusatory, simply curious. "Noah cares, deeply, and isn't afraid of it. Never has been. When our aunt got cancer, he moved back from—where was it? Azerbaijan? Syria? Some war-torn place most people were trying to escape—to help care for her."

Sabrina's chest tightened. "He mentioned his mother was sick."

"She was like a second mother to all of us." Ava's expression softened with remembrance. "Sam and Kate Colton had the kind of marriage that made you believe in true love, you know? The real thing. When she got sick, Sam was devastated, but Noah—" Ava shook her head "—Noah became her rock. Rearranged his whole life to be there for her final months."

The picture Ava painted matched everything Sabrina had come to know about Noah. His fierce loyalty, his willingness to give everything to those he loved, his absolute commitment once he decided someone mattered.

"I hurt him." The admission burned her throat. "I didn't mean to, but I did."

"I gathered that." Ava's smile held no judgment. "For what it's worth, he's been less than subtle about his feelings for you. The whole family knows he's in love with you."

Heat crept up Sabrina's neck. "The whole family?"

"Noah doesn't do anything halfway," Ava said with a small laugh. "When he brought you by Uncle Richie's practice, Sassy texted everyone within minutes. The Colton grapevine rivals the hospital rumor mill."

"Great." Sabrina closed her eyes briefly. "So everyone knows I broke his heart."

"Relationships are never smooth sailing." Ava's voice gentled. "Noah tends to charge ahead like a bull in a China shop, so it's not surprising that he overwhelmed you."

"It wasn't that." Sabrina met Ava's gaze directly. "Well, not entirely."

How much was she supposed to divulge to Noah's cousin, who wasn't even here in a professional capacity? How much did she *want* to confess?

"He just brings everything to table, no holds barred." Her voice cracked slightly. "I've never met anyone like him. It's hard to believe he feels like that about *me*."

She trailed off, unable to find words big enough for what she meant.

Ava nodded, understanding in her eyes. "Noah's taught me a lot about love over the years. Not by talking about it, by living it. He shows up. Every time."

"He did." Tears pricked Sabrina's eyes. "I just don't know if he'll give me another chance."

"That's between you two," Ava said diplomatically. "But I will say the Noah I know doesn't give up easily on things that matter to him."

Before Sabrina could respond, the door opened again. This time, the man himself stood in the threshold, his broad shoulders filling the doorframe. His expression hadn't changed from earlier, outside the cave, and the lack of that spark she'd always associated with him—had come to love— hollowed out her chest.

"Sorry," he said, already backing away. "I didn't mean to interrupt."

"I was just leaving." Ava stood, shooting Sabrina a meaningful look. "Speaking both personally and professionally, sometimes near-death experiences provide clarity. I'll check on you tomorrow before discharge," she said before slipping past Noah.

Then they were alone, the silence stretching taut between

them like a rope bridge over a canyon—precarious, swaying and the only way across.

"Your cousin seems nice," Sabrina said, trying to break the ice, but it absolutely did not.

"She is." His voice was so stilted and formal it nearly made her cry. "When my mom was sick, Ava helped a lot. She's the type who isn't happy unless she's taking care of someone, whether it's a Colton or foster kids she considers family."

The Coltons closed ranks when it counted, a dynamic she knew nothing about. But wanted to, wanted to be worthy of being included in their tight circle. Noah came from a family unlike any she'd ever heard of. No wonder he did everything with zero fear—someone would always catch him.

Except her. She hadn't.

Noah still hadn't moved from the doorway. "I brought these." He held up a small duffel bag. "Some clothes from your place. Figured you'd want something other than a hospital gown to wear tomorrow."

"Thank you." The words felt woefully inadequate. "How's Ripley?"

"Good. Ryan's watching her. She's been hovering around my house like she expects you to materialize any second." A ghost of a smile touched his lips. "Smart dog."

"She saved my life." Sabrina swallowed hard. "You both did."

Noah stepped into the room finally, setting the bag on a chair. His movements were measured, deliberate—so unlike his usual fluid energy that it hurt to watch. He kept his distance, standing at the foot of the bed.

"There's something else." He pulled a folded paper from his jacket pocket. "Your SAR certification came through."

"What?" She stared at him. "How is that possible?"

"Emergency field certification." He set the paper on her

bedside table. "Based on demonstrated competence during an actual crisis situation. Ripley performed exactly as trained—located help, led rescuers back to you. It's a provisional certification pending formal evaluation, but it's valid. Congratulations."

The professional courtesy in his voice cut deeper than anger would have. "Noah—"

"I wrote the recommendation myself," he said, continuing as if she hadn't spoken. "You two make a good team."

"We do." She seized the opening. "Just like you and I make a good team."

His eyes finally met hers fully, and what she saw there—hurt and an utter lack of hope—nearly broke her.

"Sabrina." Her name sounded raw in his throat. "You don't have to do this."

"I love you." The words burst from her with the force of a flash flood, unstoppable and transformative. "I love you, and I was wrong, and I'm so sorry I hurt you."

Noah went completely still, wariness draped around him. "What happened in the cave—"

"Changed everything," she finished for him. "Not because I almost died, but because it forced me to see what I'd been running from. You were right, Noah. About all of it. About us."

He didn't move, but he felt farther away all at once. "I don't want you to say things you don't mean because you're grateful to be alive."

"This isn't gratitude." She pushed herself straighter in the bed, needing him to understand. "This is truth. The guy who chased me into that cave—he was there because of Annie Ross. Because we were getting too close to whatever happened to her."

Noah's focus sharpened instantly and he fairly bristled. "You were attacked? You didn't tell me—"

"Because the guy was already gone," she said softly. "But that's all I could think about while I was trapped. That you'd have protected me. And I've spent my whole life fighting against letting anyone get close enough to do that. Not because I like being alone. Because I was scared."

Noah crossed his arms. "What are you saying?"

"I'm saying I was afraid. Not of you, but of what you make me feel." The words tumbled out now, unstoppable. "My whole life, I've defined strength as not needing anyone. I thought being independent meant doing it alone. Not being part of a family. Not being part of a team. But that's not strength—it's isolation. And it's exhausting."

"Sabrina—"

"Let me finish. Please." She drew a shaky breath. "When you asked me to move in with you, I panicked. I thought you were trying to crowd me, to arrange my life to suit you, that you didn't know me at all. When, really, you knew exactly what I needed. You were offering to share your life, your family. I couldn't see the difference because I'd never had anyone offer me partnership before. Not real partnership."

Noah's jaw worked as he stared at a spot above her head. Not interrupting. But not flinging himself into her arms either.

But she couldn't stop confessing all of the things in her heart. Even if he turned his back on them.

"The cave showed me what real isolation feels like," she continued. "And it's not freedom. It's emptiness. I don't want to be alone anymore, Noah. I want to be part of Team Saboah Nobina forever. I want you."

"Sabrina." He ran a hand through his hair, that familiar gesture that made her heart ache. "I want to believe you mean these things. That this is real."

"It is real," she insisted, wishing he'd moved close enough for her to touch him. But she understood why he hadn't.

He made a noise in his throat. "You nearly died today.

That changes how people see things, feel things. I've watched it happen a dozen times in this work."

"This isn't about the cave," she said, though she could see he didn't believe her.

"Maybe not," he conceded. "But I need to know that when you're healed, when you're back to being you with both feet firmly on the ground, you'll still want the same things."

She nodded. That was fair.

But then the distance yawned again, opening up this fissure between them that she couldn't cross without different equipment, skills she didn't have at her disposal.

Bleakness pulled at his expression. "I can't do this again, Sabrina. I need more than words in a hospital room."

The truth in his statement stung, but she couldn't deny it. "What can I do, Noah?"

His eyes softened marginally. "I don't know. Focus on getting better. We can talk after you're discharged."

"Noah—"

"I'll keep Ripley," he said, pausing at the threshold. "Until you're back home."

And then he was gone, leaving Sabrina with the echo of all the things she hadn't managed to say. No, she'd said them. Noah hadn't wanted to hear them.

NOAH DUMPED HIS cold coffee into the kitchen sink and stepped back onto the porch, restlessness driving him to move, to do something other than replay the look on Sabrina's face in that hospital room on an endless loop. The evening light painted golden stripes across the training yard, burnishing the equipment to copper.

Dancer lay at his feet, but his usually steady partner kept glancing toward Ripley, who prowled the yard perimeter with the nervous energy of a dog who sensed something wrong in her world.

Smart dog. Everything *was* wrong.

Sabrina's voice echoed in his head, those three devastating words that should have been cause for celebration.

I love you.

Said in that clear, fierce voice that matched the fire in her eyes. The same fire that had drawn him that first day at the recovery site. The fire that had been missing when she'd walked away from him and his too-fast, too-much declaration.

Too much. That was the story of his life, wasn't it? All throttle, no brakes, Hurricane Noah roaring ashore and leaving people scattered in his wake.

Except Sabrina hadn't scattered. She'd been right there in front of him, saying the very words he'd been aching to hear.

And he'd walked away.

Because hearing those words now—after a near-death experience—triggered something in him. What had changed? Why was the offer of his entire soul good enough now, but it hadn't been a week ago?

Dancer's head came up sharply, ears perked toward the front of the property. A moment later, Ripley's stance mirrored his, both dogs alert and focused on the same thing.

Noah's heart rate spiked, his body instantly ahead of his brain. Because his body knew who was on his doorstep before conscious thought could form.

Sabrina.

Everything in him lurched toward her, even as caution kept his feet planted.

The sharp knock confirmed it. Noah inhaled deeply, pulling oxygen into lungs that suddenly felt starved, and headed for the door. He passed his reflection in the hall mirror, hair sticking up from where he'd raked his hands through it, jaw darkened with stubble, eyes hollow with a night's worth of replayed arguments with himself.

Perfect. Just how he wanted to look when facing the woman who held his heart in her hands.

When he opened the door, Ripley shot past him, nearly knocking Sabrina over in her enthusiasm. Her laugh, that rich, throaty sound he still heard in his sleep, curled around his heart like a fist. Like it always had. Like it always would.

"You should be resting," he said, fighting the urge to drag her into his arms and make sure she was real. That she was here. That she was okay.

"I'm fine." She knelt to greet Ripley, fingers finding the dog's sweet spots with the ease of true partnership. When she straightened, her eyes locked with his, steady and sure. "Noah, I need to talk to you."

He crossed his arms, a flimsy barrier against the hope threatening to crack him open. "I'm listening."

"Not here." She gestured toward his living room. "Can we sit?"

Every instinct screamed to protect himself this time, but when had he ever listened to caution where Sabrina was concerned? He led her to the couch where they'd spent so many evenings planning training sessions, tossing ideas back and forth about Annie Ross, trading stories that somehow never felt like enough. He could map every moment he'd fallen deeper in this room, on this couch, measuring the distance between them in heartbeats and half smiles.

"I submitted our registration as an official SAR team," she said without preamble, the declaration hitting him like a tree branch snapping in gale force winds.

"You what?"

She pulled out her phone, bringing up an email confirmation that she flashed in his direction.

"Team Colton-West, pending final approval." The determination in her eyes matched the set of her jaw. "I want us to work together, Noah. Professionally and in every other way."

Something cracked inside him, hairline fractures spiderwebbing through the walls he'd hastily erected. Professional partnership. A commitment in writing, a declaration of intent so Sabrina-esque that it almost made him smile. Almost.

"Sabrina—"

"I know what you're thinking." She leaned forward, all that wild energy he'd fallen for focused into laser intensity. "That I'm reacting to trauma. That I'll change my mind again." Her voice dropped, an intimacy that wrapped around him silkily. "This isn't impulse, Noah. This is choice. This is me, both feet on the ground, choosing us."

Her certainty pulled at him, tested boundaries he'd reinforced through a sleepless night. But he'd been burned before—not just by Sabrina but by everyone who'd ever found his hurricane-force enthusiasm too intense, his passion overwhelming, his tendency to go all in terrifying.

She was just the one who had hurt him the most.

"Partnership registration is a start," he said, "but—"

"I brought something else." The vulnerability in her expression nearly shattered his remaining defenses as she held up a toothbrush. "To prove I'm serious."

"A *toothbrush*?" The words escaped before he could stop them, defensive and edged. "What, so you spend the night occasionally and, oh yay, you have your own toothbrush. That's not what I want from you, Sabrina. It's not enough."

A smile ghosted across her lips. "Not just a toothbrush. Everything else, too."

"What do you mean, everything else?"

"Look out your window."

Confusion replaced wariness as he rose and crossed to the front window, pushing aside the curtain to reveal—

His pulse stuttered.

A moving truck. The words "Dark Canyon Rentals" emblazoned on its side, rear doors open to reveal furniture he recognized from Sabrina's place. Boxes labeled in her precise handwriting. A life packed up and delivered to his doorstep.

"Everything I own," Sabrina said, suddenly beside him. She was always in motion, his Sabrina, never still for long. "Everything that matters."

He couldn't tear his gaze from the truck and what it represented, the tangible, physical proof of what she was offering. What she was telling him without words.

"You asked me to move in with you, and I ran." Her voice held a thread of steel under the vulnerability. "Now I'm asking you. Can I come home, Noah? To you?"

Everything inside him unraveled, walls crumbling as if made of sand instead of the steel he'd thought he'd used. He turned to face her fully, searching her eyes for any trace of doubt or fear. "You're really doing this? No reservations, no panic, no running away when it gets too intense?"

"I can't promise I'll never be scared." The honesty in her admission reached places he'd thought untouchable. "But I can promise I won't run from us again. Not from you. Not from us." She reached for his hand, her fingers cool against his overheated skin. "I love you, Noah Colton. Not because I nearly died, but because living without you isn't really living at all."

Her words unlocked something in his chest, but caution, that unfamiliar emotion that had never been his companion until recently, still held him back. "This isn't too fast for you? You've made such a big deal about your space. About giving you time to figure things out."

"I was freaking out. I readily admit it." She stepped closer, her free hand rising to touch his face in a gesture so achingly tender it nearly undid him. "But I didn't really need space or time to know how I feel. What I needed was a kick in the pants to make me realize you were going to slip through my fingers if I didn't get my act together. I couldn't live with that. Or have any kind of life that you weren't in."

For a heartbeat, Noah stood frozen, searching her eyes as if he could read the future there.

Then he was in motion before he could think, pulling her against him with all the force of emotions he'd been damming up since finding her in that cave. Since before that— since the first moment he'd seen her staring down Bonner at the recovery site, fierce and unyielding.

"I love you," he murmured against her hair, the words inadequate for the torrent of feeling pouring through him. "I love you so much I can't find the words."

"There you are," she murmured, her arms crushing him in kind. "But why did you pull away at the canyon? The hospital? When I tried to tell you how I felt—you scared me."

"You scared *me*," he admitted, his voice rough with the confession. "I'm not scared of loving you. I was already there, no going back. But I couldn't watch you walk away again once the adrenaline wore off. Or hear you say things in the heat of the moment that you'd regret later."

"I won't regret it," she said, tightening her grip on his hand. "I love you, Noah. Cave or no cave, life-threatening situation or ordinary Tuesday. I love your intensity and your honesty and the way you dive into everything without looking for the landing pad first. I love that you push me to be better while accepting exactly who I am."

The last of his resistance melted as he hefted her deeper into his embrace. The scent of hospital antiseptic still clung to her, but beneath it was pure Sabrina—sunshine and adrenaline and the kind of trouble that had always been his weakness.

"I never thought I'd hear you say those words," he murmured against her temple.

"Get used to it." She leaned back to meet his gaze, her smile tremulous but real. "I plan to say them a lot."

His thumb traced the curve of her cheekbone, memorizing the feel of her skin. "I love you, Sabrina West. Every fierce, independent, terrifying inch of you."

"Even the parts that panic and run?" Her tone was light, teasing. But he heard the vulnerability beneath it.

"Especially those parts." His smile broke free, the first genuine one since finding her in that cave. "Besides, I'm pretty good at finding you when you run."

She smirked. "I'm counting on that. Though I don't plan on testing your skills again anytime soon."

"Good." He brushed his lips against hers, a promise. "Because I have plans for us, Sabrina West. Big ones."

"Like what?" The spark in her eyes had returned full force, challenging and irresistible.

"Like waking up together. Working cases together. Building a life where neither of us has to dial it back or pretend to be less than we are." His gaze held hers, utterly serious despite the smile he couldn't contain. "I want it all with you."

"I want that too," she whispered. "All of it."

When he kissed her, it wasn't gentle. This was his most authentic self—intense, passionate, holding nothing back. All the fear and longing of the past days poured into a connection that burned away any lingering doubts.

"I can't believe you rented a moving truck," he said when they finally broke apart, both breathless.

"I don't do anything halfway," she replied, throwing his own words back at him with a smile that lit up every dark corner inside him. "Not anymore. Not with you."

His answer was another kiss, fierce with promise and possibilities. "We should probably start unloading before it gets dark."

"Probably." But neither of them moved, too caught in the

miracle of reconnection. "We still have a case to solve," she added. "Annie Ross, the woman from the fire, the man who chased me. They're all connected."

"I know." He tucked a strand of hair behind her ear, marveling that he could touch her like this again. That she wanted him to. "But we'll figure it out. Together."

"Together." Her smile was like sunrise after the longest night. "My favorite word."

"Mine too." He kissed her again, briefly but with a promise that curled his toes. "Welcome home, Sabrina West."

As twilight transformed Dark Canyon into a landscape of shadows and possibility, they unloaded the truck box by box, piece by piece, their laughter echoing across the yard. The case wasn't over. Annie Ross's killer was still out there, the woman from the fire still unconscious, questions still unanswered.

But Noah had stopped looking for perfect landings. Sometimes you just had to jump and trust that the right person would be there to catch you.

Epilogue

Morning light streamed through the kitchen window, painting white gold-edged patterns across the dining table that Noah couldn't help but notice matched Sabrina's hair. She stood at the counter, her back to him, preparing coffee with the same laser focus she brought to everything. Dancer and Ripley were sprawled together on the oversized dog bed that now occupied the corner of his—their—living room, legs and tails intertwined in K-9 contentment.

Just like their owners.

Noah leaned against the doorframe, savoring the way Sabrina's presence filled spaces he'd never realized were waiting for her exact shape. It had been two weeks since she'd shown up with a moving truck and the most extraordinary declaration of love he'd ever witnessed. Two weeks of waking up beside her every morning, of shared training sessions, of building something real and lasting and more spectacular than anything he'd ever dared to imagine.

The woman who'd once run from the mere suggestion of commitment now moved through his space like she'd always belonged here—because she had. They'd just needed a little time to figure that out. Her hiking boots stood beside his at the door, her jacket hung on the peg next to his, her clutter mingled with his in the kind of perfect chaos that felt like home.

"Are you going to help with breakfast or just stand there staring?" Sabrina asked without turning around, that sixth sense of hers picking up on his presence.

"Definitely just staring." He grinned, pushing off from the doorframe to cross the kitchen. "The view's too good to miss."

She turned, coffee pot in hand, and the smile she gave him did that thing to his insides—a sensation that still caught him off guard. Every time.

"Smooth talker," she said, but the pink tinge climbing her neck told him she didn't mind. "Save it for after we finish the training report for Reynolds."

"You're the one who wanted to become an official SAR team," he reminded her, accepting the mug she handed him. Their fingers brushed, and even that small contact carried a current that he hoped lasted until they were both old and gray.

"Best decision I ever made." She leaned against the counter, studying him over the rim of her own mug. "Though I maintain that Reynolds's face when I told him will remain the highlight of my career. He actually looked impressed."

Noah laughed. "As he should be. Team Colton-West is already making waves. He mentioned that three other freelance agencies have called asking about our track record."

"Good. I can't wait to become known as the best team in Utah."

"Speaking of the job—" He paused, remembering she'd mentioned the selection committee would be contacting the district ranger applicants this morning. "Did they call you yet?"

Something flashed across Sabrina's face. "Oh, that. Yeah, they called."

"And?" He couldn't help the anticipation building in his chest. She'd worked so hard for this, competed ferociously against Bonner for months. The promotion had been her driving goal since before they'd met.

"I got it. And I turned it down."

None of those were words he'd prepared to hear. "You what?"

Sabrina shrugged, but the gesture wasn't casual. It carried the weight of careful consideration. "I declined the position. Informally. I have to go do some form to make it official."

Noah set his coffee down, trying to process what this meant. "Sabrina, you've been gunning for that promotion since day one. Beating Bonner was your whole mission."

"It was." She met his gaze steadily. "But missions change. Priorities shift."

"Was it because of us? Because if you think I wouldn't support—"

"It wasn't about us," she interrupted, though her expression softened. "Or not directly, anyway. It was about me. What I want now versus what I thought I needed then."

Noah studied her face, searching for any hint of regret or sacrifice. He found none. Just clear-eyed certainty.

"Tell me more," he said simply.

"The district ranger position—" she crossed her arms, leaning back against the counter "—I wanted it for all the wrong reasons. To prove I was better than Bonner. To validate myself to Reynolds, to my father, to everyone who ever doubted me. It was never about the actual job."

Noah nodded, understanding dawning. This was the Sabrina he'd fallen for at her brutally honest, fierce self.

"But SAR work, that's different." Her eyes lit up in that way that made his heart stutter. "It's not about being better than anyone else. It's about being the best version of myself, pushing my own limits, making a real difference. And doing it with the right partner."

Brightness bloomed in his chest, expanding with every

word. This wasn't Sabrina sacrificing her ambitions. This was Sabrina evolving, choosing her path not out of defiance or competition, but authentic desire.

He was so amazed by her.

"Besides," she added with a smirk, "Reynolds asked if I'd consider heading up the new K-9 division instead. Building it from the ground up, my way. I told him I'd think about it."

Noah couldn't help the grin spreading across his face. "Let me guess. You're thinking it might pair well with a certain SAR team's training schedule?"

"Convenient, isn't it?" She matched his grin. "Almost like I planned it."

"You're brilliant, no doubt," he agreed, pulling her against him. "I'm impressed."

"You should be. I'm very impressive." She looped her arms around his neck, the teasing light in her eyes warming to something deeper. "So, is this the part where you tell me you're proud of me for choosing what I really want instead of what I thought I should want?"

"Nope." He brushed his lips against her forehead. "This is the part where I say I've never been more certain that you're the most extraordinary woman I've ever met. And that I fall more in love with you every day."

Her expression turned serious. "Even when I'm not trying to be the best at everything?"

"Especially then." He tightened his arms around her. "Though I'll admit, watching you outperform everyone in the room does have its appeal."

"Good." She relaxed against him. "Because I plan to crush the K-9 division certification course next month."

"I'd expect nothing less."

Their comfortable moment was interrupted by Dancer's sharp bark. The lab had moved to the window, ears perked toward something outside. Ripley joined him, both dogs suddenly alert.

"Must be the delivery guy with our new training equipment," Noah said, reluctantly releasing Sabrina. "Though it's pretty early for deliveries."

She moved to the window, peering out. "It's Jacob," she reported, already heading for the door. "And he looks like he's got news."

Noah followed, doing his best to tamp back his excitement. Jacob rarely made house calls unless something significant had happened. The Annie Ross case had been proceeding slowly, hampered by dead ends and little information.

"Morning," Jacob greeted them as Sabrina opened the door. His brother looked tired but energized, the way he always did when a case started breaking. "Sorry to drop by unannounced, but I figured you'd want to hear this in person. The woman from the fire? She's awake."

Noah felt Sabrina tense beside him, her body practically vibrating with the same anticipation coursing through his veins.

"What did she say?" Noah asked. "Does she know Annie?"

"Don't know yet," Jacob replied, a rare smile crossing his features. "That's why we're having this conversation. If you want in on this, I'll give you a ride to the hospital."

Sabrina was already reaching for her jacket. "Give us five minutes."

As Jacob waited in his car, they moved through the familiar choreography of grabbing gear, securing the dogs, locking up. It struck Noah how seamlessly they operated now, anticipating each other's movements, sharing space like they'd always done it.

He'd even told Sabrina how weird everything felt knowing his dad was dating again, how it had colored his memories of his parents together. They'd talked long into the night about it a few days ago, and he finally felt okay about it. Okay about a lot of things, even the possibility of never traveling the world again as an investigative reporter.

Why would he want to leave when his whole entire world was right here?

"Ready to chase a lead, Officer West?" he asked as they stepped onto the porch.

"Always, Mr. Colton." She grinned, that competitive spark lighting her eyes. "Race you to the car."

"You know I'll let you win."

"And you know I don't need you to." She brushed a quick kiss across his lips. "That's why we work."

As they headed toward Jacob's waiting vehicle, the morning sun breaking through the clouds, Noah felt that bone-deep certainty again. They had a case to solve, a story to uncover, a life to build, and they were doing it all together, step for step, at full speed, no apologies.

Hurricane Noah had finally found his match, a force of nature just as wild, just as powerful and every bit as unstoppable. One day, he'd ask her to marry him, but on her schedule. When it felt right for both of them.

Meanwhile, the investigation wasn't over, the story wasn't finished, but they had all the time in the world to write the ending. Together.

* * * * *

COMING SOON!

We really hope you enjoyed reading this book.
If you're looking for more romance
be sure to head to the shops when
new books are available on

Thursday 26th February

To see which titles are coming soon, please visit
millsandboon.co.uk/nextmonth

MILLS & BOON

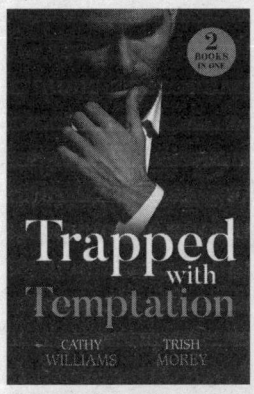

LET'S TALK

Romance

For exclusive extracts, competitions and special offers, find us online:

f MillsandBoon

X @MillsandBoon

⦿ @MillsandBoonUK

♪ @MillsandBoonUK

Get in touch on 01413 063 232